ADR
FROM MI

ADRIAN MOLE
from Minor to Major

The Mole Diaries: The First Ten Years

incorporating
The Secret Diary of Adrian Mole Aged 13¾
The Growing Pains of Adrian Mole
True Confessions of Adrian Albert Mole
and
Adrian Mole and the Small Amphibians

SUE TOWNSEND

Mandarin

*The line drawings in this volume
are by Caroline Holden*

A Mandarin Paperback
ADRIAN MOLE FROM MINOR TO MAJOR

First published in Great Britain 1991
by Methuen London
This edition published 1992
by Mandarin Paperbacks
an imprint of Reed Consumer Books Limited
Michelin House, 81 Fulham Road, London SW3 6RB
and Auckland, Melbourne, Singapore and Toronto

Reprinted 1992, 1993 (three times), 1994

The Secret Life of Adrian Mole Aged 13¾
was first published in 1982 by Methuen London
The Growing Pains of Adrian Mole
was first published in 1984 by Methuen London
The Confessions of Adrian Mole
was first published in 1989 by Methuen London

Copyright © 1982, 1984, 1989, 1991 by Sue Townsend
The author has asserted her moral rights
Drawings copyright © 1982, 1984, 1985, 1989, 1991
by Caroline Holden

A CIP catalogue record for this title
is available from the British Library
ISBN 0 7493 1120 7

Printed and bound in Great Britain
by Cox & Wyman Ltd, Reading, Berkshire

The Secret Diary of
Adrian Mole
Aged 13¾

For Colin
and also for Sean, Dan, Vicki and Elizabeth
with love and thanks

'Paul walked with something screwed up tight inside him ... yet he chatted away with his mother. He would never have confessed to her how he suffered over these things and she only partly guessed.'

D. H. Lawrence *Sons and Lovers*

Thursday January 1st
BANK HOLIDAY IN ENGLAND,
IRELAND, SCOTLAND AND WALES

These are my New Year's resolutions:

1. I will help the blind across the road.
2. I will hang my trousers up.
3. I will put the sleeves back on my records.
4. I will not start smoking.
5. I will stop squeezing my spots.
6. I will be kind to the dog.
7. I will help the poor and ignorant.
8. After hearing the disgusting noises from downstairs last night, I have also vowed never to drink alcohol.

My father got the dog drunk on cherry brandy at the party last night. If the RSPCA hear about it he could get done. Eight days have gone by since Christmas Day but my mother still hasn't worn the green lurex apron I bought her for Christmas! She will get bathcubes next year.

Just my luck, I've got a spot on my chin for the first day of the New Year!

Friday January 2nd
BANK HOLIDAY IN SCOTLAND. FULL MOON

I felt rotten today. It's my mother's fault for singing 'My Way' at two o'clock in the morning at the top of the stairs. Just my luck to have a mother like her. There is a chance my parents could be alcoholics. Next year I could be in a children's home.

The dog got its own back on my father. It jumped up and knocked down his model ship, then ran into the garden with the rigging tangled in its feet. My father kept saying, 'Three months' work down the drain', over and over again.

The spot on my chin is getting bigger. It's my mother's fault for not knowing about vitamins.

Saturday January 3rd

I shall go mad through lack of sleep! My father has banned the dog from the house so it barked outside my window all night. Just my luck! My father shouted a swear-word at it. If he's not careful he will get done by the police for obscene language.

I think the spot is a boil. Just my luck to have it where everybody can see it. I pointed out to my mother that I hadn't had any vitamin C today. She said, 'Go and buy an orange, then'. This is typical.

She still hasn't worn the lurex apron.

I will be glad to get back to school.

Sunday   January 4th
SECOND AFTER CHRISTMAS

My father has got the flu. I'm not surprised with the diet we get. My mother went out in the rain to get him a vitamin C drink, but as I told her, 'It's too late now'. It's a miracle we don't get scurvy. My mother says she can't see anything on my chin, but this is guilt because of the diet.

The dog has run off because my mother didn't close the gate. I have broken the arm on the stereo. Nobody knows yet, and with a bit of luck my father will be ill for a long time. He is the only one who uses it apart from me. No sign of the apron.

Monday   January 5th

The dog hasn't come back yet. It is peaceful without it. My mother rang the police and gave a description of the dog. She made it sound worse than it actually is: straggly hair over its eyes and all that. I really think the police have got better things to do than look for dogs, such as catching murderers. I told my mother this but she still rang them. Serve her right if she was murdered because of the dog.

My father is still lazing about in bed. He is supposed to be ill, but I noticed he is still smoking!

Nigel came round today. He has got a tan from his Christmas holiday. I think Nigel will be ill soon from the shock of the cold in England. I think Nigel's parents were wrong to take him abroad.

He hasn't got a single spot yet.

Tuesday   January 6th
EPIPHANY. NEW MOON

The dog is in trouble!

It knocked a meter-reader off his bike and messed all the cards up. So now we will all end up in court I expect. A policeman said we must keep the dog under control and asked how long it had been lame. My mother said it wasn't lame, and examined it. There was a tiny model pirate trapped in its left front paw.

The dog was pleased when my mother took the pirate out and it jumped up the policeman's tunic with its muddy paws. My mother fetched a cloth from the kitchen but it had strawberry jam on it where I had wiped the knife, so the tunic was worse than ever. The policeman went then. I'm sure he swore. I could report him for that.

I will look up 'Epiphany' in my new dictionary.

Wednesday   January 7th

Nigel came round on his new bike this morning. It has got a water bottle, a milometer, a speedometer, a yellow saddle, and very thin racing wheels. It's wasted on Nigel. He only goes to the shops and back on it. If I had it, I would go all over the country and have an experience.

My spot or boil has reached its peak. Surely it can't get any bigger!

I found a word in my dictionary that describes my father. It is *malingerer*. He is still in bed guzzling vitamin C.

The dog is locked in the coal shed.

Epiphany is something to do with the three wise men. Big deal!

Thursday   January 8th

Now my mother has got the flu. This means that I have to look after them both. Just my luck!

I have been up and down the stairs all day. I cooked a big dinner for them tonight: two poached eggs with beans, and tinned semolina pudding. (It's a good job I wore the green lurex apron because the poached eggs escaped out of the pan and got all over me.) I nearly said something when I saw they hadn't eaten *any* of it. They can't be that ill. I gave it to the dog in the coal shed. My grandmother is coming tomorrow morning, so I had to clean the burnt saucepans, then take the dog for a walk. It was half-past eleven before I got to bed. No wonder I am short for my age.

I have decided against medicine for a career.

Friday   January 9th

It was cough, cough, cough last night. If it wasn't one it was the other. You'd think they'd show some consideration after the hard day I'd had.

My grandma came and was disgusted with the state of the house. I showed her my room which is always neat and tidy and she gave me fifty pence. I showed her all the empty drink bottles in the dustbin and she was disgusted.

My grandma let the dog out of the coal shed. She said my mother was cruel to lock it up. The dog was sick on the kitchen floor. My grandma locked it up again.

She squeezed the spot on my chin. It has made it worse. I told grandma about the green apron and grandma said that she bought my mother a one hundred per cent acrylic cardigan every Christmas and my mother had *never ever* worn one of them!

Saturday   January 10th

a.m. Now the dog is ill! It keeps being sick so the vet has got to come. My father told me not to tell the vet that the dog had been locked in the coal shed for two days.

I have put a plaster over the spot to stop germs getting in it from the dog.

The vet has taken the dog away. He says he thinks it has got an obstruction and will need an emergency operation.

My grandma has had a row with my mother and gone home. My grandma found the Christmas cardigans all cut up in the duster bag. It is disgusting when people are starving.

Mr Lucas from next door has been in to see my mother and father who are still in bed. He brought a 'get well' card and some flowers for my mother. My mother sat up in bed in a nightie that showed a lot of her chest. She talked to Mr Lucas in a yukky voice. My father pretended to be asleep.

Nigel brought his records round. He is into punk, but I don't see the point if you can't hear the words. Anyway I think I'm turning into an intellectual. It must be all the worry.

p.m. I went to see how the dog is. It has had its operation. The vet showed me a plastic bag with lots of yukky things in it. There was a lump of coal, the fir tree from the Christmas cake, and the model pirates from my father's ship. One of the pirates was waving a cutlass which must have been very painful for the dog. The dog looks a lot better. It can come home in two days, worse luck.

My father was having a row with my grandma on the phone about the empty bottles in the dustbin when I got home.

Mr Lucas was upstairs talking to my mother. When Mr Lucas went, my father went upstairs and had an argument with my mother and made her cry. My father is in a bad mood. This means he is feeling better. I made my mother a cup of tea without her asking. This made her cry as well. You can't please some people!

The spot is still there.

Sunday   January 11th
FIRST AFTER EPIPHANY

Now I *know* I am an intellectual. I saw Malcolm Muggeridge on the television last night, and I understood nearly every word. It all adds up. A bad home, poor diet, not liking punk. I think I will join the library and see what happens.

It is a pity there aren't any more intellectuals living round here. Mr Lucas wears corduroy trousers, but he's an insurance man. Just my luck.

The first what after Epiphany?

Monday   January 12th

The dog is back. It keeps licking its stitches, so when I am eating I sit with my back to it.

My mother got up this morning to make the dog a bed to sleep in until it's better. It is made out of a cardboard box that used to contain packets of soap powder. My father said this would make the dog sneeze and burst its stitches, and the vet would charge even more to stitch it back up again. They had a row about the box, then my father went on about Mr Lucas. Though what Mr Lucas has to do with the dog's bed is a mystery to me.

Tuesday   January 13th

My father has gone back to work. Thank God! I don't know how my mother sticks him.

Mr Lucas came in this morning to see if my mother needed any help in the house. He is very kind. Mrs Lucas was next door cleaning the outside windows. The ladder didn't look very safe. I have written to Malcolm Muggeridge, c/o the BBC, asking him what to do about being an intellectual. I hope he writes back soon because I'm getting fed up being one on my own. I have written a poem, and it only took me two minutes. Even the famous poets take longer than that. It is called 'The Tap', but it isn't really about a tap, it's very deep, and about life and stuff like that.

> *The Tap, by Adrian Mole*
> The tap drips and keeps me awake,
> In the morning there will be a lake.
> For the want of a washer the carpet will spoil,
> Then for another my father will toil.
> My father could snuff it while he is at work.
> Dad, fit a washer don't be a burk!

I showed it to my mother, but she laughed. She isn't very bright. She still hasn't washed my PE shorts, and it is school tomorrow. She is not like the mothers on television.

Wednesday   January 14th

Joined the library. Got *Care of the Skin*, *Origin of Species*, and a book by a woman my mother is always going on about. It is called *Pride and Prejudice*, by a woman called Jane Austen. I could tell the librarian was impressed. Perhaps she is an intellectual like me. She didn't look at my spot, so perhaps it is getting smaller. About time!

Mr Lucas was in the kitchen drinking coffee with my mother. The room was full of smoke. They were laughing, but when I went in, they stopped.

Mrs Lucas was next door cleaning the drains. She looked as if she was in a bad mood. I think Mr and Mrs Lucas have got an unhappy marriage. Poor Mr Lucas!

None of the teachers at school have noticed that I am an intellectual. They will be sorry when I am famous. There is a new girl in our class. She sits next to me in Geography. She is all right. Her name is Pandora, but she likes being called 'Box'. Don't ask me why. I might fall in love with her. It's time I fell in love, after all I am $13\frac{3}{4}$ years old.

Thursday January 15th

Pandora has got hair the colour of treacle, and it's long like girls' hair should be. She has got quite a good figure. I saw her playing netball and her chest was wobbling. I felt a bit funny. I think this is it!

The dog has had its stitches out. It bit the vet, but I expect he's used to it. (The vet I mean; I know the dog is.)

My father found out about the arm on the stereo. I told a lie. I said the dog jumped up and broke it. My father said he will wait until the dog is completely cured of its operation then kick it. I hope this is a joke.

Mr Lucas was in the kitchen again when I got home from school. My mother is better now, so why he keeps coming round is a mystery to me. Mrs Lucas was planting trees in the dark. I read a bit of *Pride and Prejudice*, but it was very old-fashioned. I think Jane Austen should write something a bit more modern.

The dog has got the same colour eyes as Pandora. I only noticed because my mother cut the dog's hair. It looks worse than ever. Mr Lucas and my mother were laughing at the dog's new haircut which is not very nice, because dogs can't answer back, just like the Royal Family.

I am going to bed early to think about Pandora and do my backstretching exercises. I haven't grown for two weeks. If this carries on I will be a midget.

I will go to the doctor's on Saturday if the spot is still there. I can't live like this with everybody staring.

Friday January 16th

Mr Lucas came round and offered to take my mother shopping in the car. They dropped me off at school. I was glad to get out of the car what with all the laughing and cigarette smoke. We saw Mrs Lucas on the way. She was carrying big bags of shopping. My mother waved, but Mrs Lucas couldn't wave back.

It was Geography today so I sat next to Pandora for a whole hour. She looks better every day. I told her about her eyes being the same as the dog's. She asked what kind of dog it was. I told her it was a mongrel.

I lent Pandora my blue felt-tip pen to colour round the British Isles.

I think she appreciates these small attentions.

I started *Origin of Species* today, but it's not as good as the television series. *Care of the Skin* is dead good. I have left it open on the pages about vitamins. I hope my mother takes the hint. I have left it on the kitchen table near the ashtray, so she is bound to see it.

I have made an appointment about the spot. It has turned purple.

Saturday   January 17th

I was woken up early this morning. Mrs Lucas is concreting the front of their house, and the concrete lorry had to keep its engine running while she shovelled the concrete round before it set. Mr Lucas made her a cup of tea. He really is kind.

Nigel came round to see if I wanted to go to the pictures but I told him I couldn't, because I was going to the doctor's about the spot. He said he couldn't see a spot, but he was just being polite because the spot is massive today.

Dr Taylor must be one of those overworked GPs you are always reading about. He didn't examine the spot, he just said I mustn't worry and was everything all right at home. I told him about my bad home life and my poor diet, but he said I was well nourished and to go home and count my blessings. So much for the National Health Service.

I will get a paper-round and go private.

Sunday   January 18th
SECOND AFTER EPIPHANY. OXFORD HILARY TERM STARTS

Mrs Lucas and my mother have had a row over the dog. Somehow it escaped from the house and trampled on Mrs Lucas's wet concrete. My father offered to have the dog put down, but my mother started to cry so he said he wouldn't. All the neighbours were out in the street washing their cars and listening. Sometimes I really hate that dog!

I remembered my resolution about helping the poor and ignorant today, so I took some of my old *Beano* annuals to a quite poor family who have moved into the next street. I know they are poor because they have only got a black and white telly. A boy answered the door. I explained why I had come. He looked at the annuals and said, 'I've read 'em', and slammed the door in my face. So much for helping the poor!

Monday   January 19th

I have joined a group at school called the Good Samaritans. We go out into the community helping and stuff like that. We miss Maths on Monday afternoons.

Today we had a talk on the sort of things we will be doing. I have been put in the old age pensioners' group. Nigel has got a dead yukky job looking after kids in a playgroup. He is as sick as a parrot.

I can't wait for next Monday. I will get a cassette so I can tape all the old fogies' stories about the war and stuff. I hope I get one with a good memory.

The dog is back at the vet's. It has got concrete stuck on its paws. No wonder it was making such a row on the stairs last night. Pandora smiled at me in school dinner today, but I was choking on a piece of gristle so I couldn't smile back. Just my luck!

Tuesday   January 20th
FULL MOON

My mother is looking for a job!

Now I could end up a delinquent roaming the streets and all that. And what will I do during the holidays? I expect I will have to sit in a launderette all day to keep warm. I will be a latchkey kid, whatever that is. And who will look after the dog? And what will I have to eat all day? I will be forced to eat crisps and sweets until my skin is ruined and my teeth fall out. I think my mother is being very selfish. She won't be any good in a job anyway. She isn't very bright and she drinks too much at Christmas.

I rang my grandma up and told her, and she says I could stay at her house in the holidays, and go to the Evergreens' meetings in the afternoons and stuff like that. I wish I hadn't rung now. The Samaritans met today during break. The old people were shared out. I got an old man called Bert Baxter. He is eighty-nine so I don't suppose I'll have him for long. I'm going round to see him tomorrow. I hope he hasn't got a dog. I'm fed up with dogs. They are either at the vet's or standing in front of the television.

Wednesday   January 21st

Mr and Mrs Lucas are getting a divorce! They are the first down our road. My mother went next door to comfort Mr Lucas. He must have been very upset because she was still there when my father came home from work. Mrs Lucas has gone somewhere in a taxi. I think she has left for ever because she has taken her socket set with her. Poor Mr Lucas, now he will have to do his own washing and stuff.

My father cooked the tea tonight. We had boil-in-the-bag curry and rice, it was the only thing left in the freezer apart from a bag of green stuff which has lost its label. My father made a joke about sending it to the public health inspector. My mother didn't laugh. Perhaps she was thinking about poor Mr Lucas left on his own.

I went to see old Mr Baxter after tea. My father dropped me off on his way to play badminton. Mr Baxter's house is hard to see from the road. It has got a massive overgrown privet hedge all round it. When I knocked on the door a dog started barking and growling and jumping up at the letterbox. I heard the sound of bottles being knocked over and a man swearing before I ran off. I hope I have got the wrong number.

I saw Nigel on the way home. He told me Pandora's father is a milkman! I have gone off her a bit.

Nobody was in when I got home so I fed the dog, looked at my spots and went to bed.

Thursday   January 22nd

It is a dirty lie about Pandora's father being a milkman! He is an accountant at the dairy. Pandora says she will duff Nigel up if he goes round committing libel. I am in love with her again.

Nigel has asked me to go to a disco at the youth club tomorrow night; it is being held to raise funds for a new packet of ping-pong balls. I don't know if I will go because Nigel is a punk at weekends. His mother lets him be one providing he wears a string vest under his bondage T-shirt.

My mother has got an interview for a job. She is practising her typing and not doing any cooking. So what will it be like if she *gets* the job? My father should put his foot down before we are a broken home.

Friday   January 23rd

That is the last time I go to a disco. Everybody there was a punk except me and Rick Lemon, the youth leader. Nigel was showing off all night. He ended up putting a safety pin through his ear. My father had to take him to the hospital in our car. Nigel's parents haven't got a car because his father's got a steel plate in his head and his mother is only four feet eleven inches tall. It's not surprising Nigel has turned out bad really, with a maniac and a midget for parents.

I still haven't heard from Malcolm Muggeridge. Perhaps he is in a bad mood. Intellectuals like him and me often have bad moods. Ordinary people don't understand us and say we are sulking, but we're not.

Pandora has been to see Nigel in hospital. He has got a bit of blood poisoning from the safety pin. Pandora thinks Nigel is dead brave. I think he is dead stupid.

I have had a headache all day because of my mother's rotten typing, but I'm not complaining. I must go to sleep now. I've got to go and see Bert Baxter tomorrow at his house. It was the right number WORSE LUCK!

Saturday   January 24th

Today was the most terrible day of my life. My mother has got a job doing her rotten typing in an insurance office! She starts on Monday! Mr Lucas works at the same place. He is going to give her a lift every day.

And my father is in a bad mood – he thinks his big-end is going. But worst of all, Bert Baxter is not a nice old age pensioner! He drinks and smokes and has an alsatian dog called Sabre. Sabre was locked in the kitchen while I was cutting the massive hedge, but he didn't stop growling once.

But even worse than that! Pandora is going out with Nigel!!!!! I think I will never get over this shock.

Sunday   January 25th
THIRD AFTER EPIPHANY

10 a.m. I am ill with all the worry, too weak to write much. Nobody has noticed I haven't eaten any breakfast.

2 p.m. Had two junior aspirins at midday and rallied a bit. Perhaps when I am famous and my diary is discovered people will understand the torment of being a 13¾-year-old undiscovered intellectual.

6 p.m. Pandora! My lost love!

Now I will never stroke your treacle hair! (Although my blue felt-tip is still at your disposal.)

8 p.m. Pandora! Pandora! Pandora!

10 p.m. Why? Why? Why?

Midnight. Had a crab–paste sandwich and a satsuma (for the good of my skin). Feel a bit better. I hope Nigel falls off his bike and is squashed flat by a lorry. I will never speak to him again. He knew I was in love with Pandora! If I'd had a racing bike for Christmas instead of a lousy digital stereo alarm clock, none of this would have happened.

Monday   January 26th

I had to leave my sick-bed to visit Bert Baxter before school. It took me ages to get there, what with feeling weak and having to stop for a rest every now and again, but with the help of an old lady who had a long black moustache I made it to the front door. Bert Baxter was in bed but he threw the key down and I let myself in. Sabre was locked in the bathroom; he was growling and sounded as if he was ripping up towels or something.

Bert Baxter was lying in a filthy-looking bed smoking a cigarette, there was a horrible smell in the room, I think it came from Bert Baxter himself. The bed sheets looked as though they were covered in blood, but Bert said that was caused by the beetroot sandwiches he always eats last thing at night. It was the most disgusting room I have ever seen (and I'm no stranger to squalor). Bert Baxter gave me ten pence and asked me to get him the *Morning Star* from the newsagent's. So he is a communist as well as everything else! Sabre usually fetches the paper but he is being kept in as a punishment for chewing the sink.

The man in the newsagent's asked me to give Bert Baxter his bill (he owes for his papers, £31.97), but when I did Bert Baxter said, 'Smarmy four-eyed git', and laughed and ripped the bill up. I was late for school so I had to go to the school secretary's office and have my name put in the late book. That's the gratitude I get for being a Good Samaritan! I didn't miss Maths either! Saw Pandora and Nigel standing close together in the dinner queue but chose to ignore them.

Mr Lucas has taken to his bed because of being deserted so my mother is taking care of him when she finishes work. She is the only person he will see. So when will she find time to look after me and my father?

My father is sulking, I think he must be jealous because Mr Lucas doesn't want to see *him*.

Midnight. Goodnight Pandora my treacle-haired love.

XXXXXXXXX

Tuesday   January 27th

Art was dead good today. I painted a lonely boy standing on a bridge. The boy had just lost his first love to his ex-best friend. The ex-best friend was struggling in the torrential river. The boy was watching his ex-best friend drown. The ex-best friend looked a bit like Nigel. The boy looked a bit like me. Ms Fossington-Gore said my picture 'had depth', so did the river. Ha! Ha! Ha!

Wednesday   January 28th
LAST QUARTER

I woke up with a bit of a cold this morning. I asked my mother for a note to excuse me from games. She said she refused to namby-pamby me a day longer! How would she like to run about on a muddy field in the freezing drizzle, dressed only in PE shorts and a singlet? When I was in the school sports day three-legged race last year she came to watch me, *and* she had her fur coat on *and* she put a blanket round her legs, *and* it was only June! Anyway my mother is sorry now, we had rugger and my PE stuff was so full of mud that it has clogged up the drain hose on the washing machine.

The vet rang up to demand that we come and fetch the dog back from his surgery. It has been there nine days. My father says it will have to stay there until he gets paid tomorrow. The vet only takes cash and my father hasn't got any.

Pandora! Why?

Thursday   January 29th

The stupid dog is back. I am not taking it for a walk until its hair grows back on its shaved paws. My father looked pale when he came home from the vet's, he kept saying 'It's money down the drain', and he said that from now on the dog can only be fed on leftovers from his plate.

This means the dog will soon starve.

Friday   January 30th

That filthy commie Bert Baxter has phoned the school to complain that I left the hedge-clippers out in the rain! He claims that they have gone all rusty. He wants compensation. I told Mr Scruton, the headmaster, that they were already rusty but I could tell he didn't believe me. He gave me a lecture on how hard it was for old people to make ends meet. He has ordered me to go to Bert Baxter's and clean and sharpen the hedge-clippers. I wanted to tell the headmaster all about horrible Bert Baxter but there is something about Mr Scruton that makes my mind go blank. I think it's the way his eyes pop out when he is in a temper.

On the way to Bert Baxter's I saw my mother and Mr Lucas coming out of a betting shop together. I waved and shouted but I don't think they could have seen me. I'm glad Mr Lucas is feeling better. Bert Baxter didn't answer the door. Perhaps he is dead.

Pandora! You are still on my mind, baby.

Saturday   January 31st

It is nearly February and I have got nobody to send a Valentine's Day card to.

Sunday   February 1st
FOURTH AFTER EPIPHANY

There was a lot of shouting downstairs late last night. The kitchen waste-bin was knocked over and the back door kept being slammed. I wish my parents would be a bit more thoughtful, I have been through an emotional time and I need my sleep. Still I don't expect them to understand what it is like being in love. They have been married for fourteen-and-a-half years.

Went to Bert Baxter's this afternoon but thank God he has gone to Skegness with the Evergreens. Sabre looked out of the living-room window. I gave him the 'V' sign. I hope he doesn't remember.

Monday   February 2nd
PRESENTATION

Mrs Lucas is back! I saw her pulling trees and bushes out of the earth and putting them in the back of a van, then she put all the gardening tools in and drove off. The van had 'Women's Refuge' painted on the side. Mr Lucas came over to our house to talk to my mother, I went down to say 'hello' to him, but he was too upset to notice me. I asked my mother if she would get home early from work tonight, I'm fed up with waiting for my tea. She didn't.

Nigel got thrown out of school dinners today for swearing at the toad-in-the-hole, he said it was 'all bleeding hole and no toad'. I think Mrs Leech was quite right to throw him out, after all the first-years were present! We third-years must set an example. Pandora has got up a petition to protest about the toad-in-the-hole. I will not sign it.

It was Good Samaritans today. So I was forced to go round to Bert Baxter's. I have missed the Algebra test! Ha! Ha! Ha! Bert gave me a stick of broken Skegness rock and said he was sorry he rang the school to complain about the hedge-clippers. He said he was lonely and wanted to hear a human voice. If I was the loneliest person in the world I wouldn't phone up our school. I would ring the speaking clock; that talks to you every ten seconds.

Tuesday   February 3rd

My mother has not done any proper housework for days now. All she does is go to work, comfort Mr Lucas and read and smoke. The big-end has gone on my father's car. I had to show him where to catch a bus into town. A man of forty not knowing where the bus stop is! My father looked such a scruff-bag that I was ashamed to be seen with him. I was glad when the bus came. I shouted through the window that he couldn't sit downstairs and smoke but he just waved and lit up a cigarette. There is a fifty pounds' fine for doing that! If I was in charge of the buses I would fine smokers a thousand pounds *and* make them eat twenty Woodbines.

My mother is reading *The Female Eunuch*, by Germaine Greer. My mother says it is the sort of book that changes your life. It hasn't changed mine, but I only glanced through it. It is full of dirty words.

Wednesday   February 4th
NEW MOON

I had my first wet dream! So my mother was right about *The Female Eunuch*. It has changed my life.

The spot has got smaller.

Thursday   February 5th

My mother has bought some of those overalls that painters and decorators wear. You can see her knickers through them. I hope she doesn't wear them in the street.

She is having her ears pierced tomorrow. I think she is turning into a spendthrift. Nigel's mother is a spendthrift. They are always getting letters about having their electricity cut off and all because Nigel's mother buys a pair of high heels every week.

I would like to know where the Family Allowance goes, by rights it should be mine. I will ask my mother tomorrow.

Friday   February 6th
THE QUEEN'S ACCESSION, 1952

It is lousy having a working mother. She rushes in with big bags of shopping, cooks the tea then rushes around tarting herself up. But she is still not doing any tidying up before comforting Mr Lucas. There has been a slice of bacon between the cooker and the fridge for three days to my knowledge!

I asked her about my Family Allowance today, she laughed and said she used it for buying gin and cigarettes. If the Social Services hear about it she will get done!

Saturday   February 7th

My mother and father have been shouting at each other non-stop for hours. It started because of the bacon down the side of the fridge and carried on into how much my father's car is costing to repair. I went up to my room and put my Abba records on. My father had the nerve to crash my door open and ask me to turn the volume down. I did. When he got downstairs I turned it up again.

Nobody cooked any dinner so I went to the Chinese chip shop and bought a carton of chips and a sachet of soy sauce. I sat in the bus shelter and ate them, then walked about feeling sad. Came home. Fed dog. Read a bit of *Female Eunuch*. Felt a bit funny. Went to sleep.

Sunday   February 8th
FIFTH AFTER EPIPHANY

My father came into my bedroom this morning, he said he wanted a chat. He looked at my Kevin Keegan scrapbook, screwed the knob of my wardrobe door back on with his Swiss army knife and asked me about school. Then he said he was sorry about yesterday and the shouting, he said my mother and him are 'going through a bad patch'. He asked me if I had anything to say. I said he owed me thirty-two pence for the Chinese chips and soy sauce. He gave me a pound. So I made a profit of sixty-eight pence.

Monday   February 9th

There was a removal lorry outside Mr Lucas's house this morning. Mrs Lucas and some other women were carrying furniture from the house and stacking it on the pavement. Mr Lucas was looking out from his bedroom window. He looked a bit frightened. Mrs Lucas was laughing and pointing up to Mr Lucas and all the other women started laughing and singing 'Why was he born so beautiful?'

My mother phoned Mr Lucas up and asked him if he was all right. Mr Lucas said he wasn't going to work today because he had to guard the stereo and records from his wife. My father helped Mrs Lucas put the gas stove in the removal van, then he and my mother walked to the bus stop together. I walked behind them because my mother was wearing long dangly earrings and my father's trouser turn-ups had come down. They started to quarrel about something so I crossed over the road and went to school the long way round.

Bert Baxter was OK today. He told me about the First World War. He said his life was saved by a Bible he always carried in his breast pocket. He showed me the Bible, it was printed in 1956. I think Bert is going a bit senile.

Pandora! The memory of you is a constant torment!

Tuesday   February 10th

Mr Lucas is staying with us until he gets some new furniture.

My father has gone to Matlock to try to sell electric storage heaters to a big hotel.

Our gas boiler has packed in. It is freezing cold.

Wednesday   February 11th
FIRST QUARTER

My father rang up from Matlock to say he has lost his Barclaycard and can't get home tonight, so Mr Lucas and my mother were up all night trying to mend the boiler. I went down at ten o'clock to see if I could help but the kitchen door was jammed. Mr Lucas said he couldn't open it just at that moment because he was at a crucial stage with the boiler and my mother was helping him and she had her hands full.

Thursday   February 12th
LINCOLN'S BIRTHDAY

I found my mother dyeing her hair in the bathroom tonight. This
has come as a complete shock to me. For thirteen and three-quarter
years I have thought I had a mother with red hair, now I find out
that it is really light brown. My mother asked me not to tell my
father. What a state their marriage must be in! I wonder if my
father knows that she wears a padded bra? She doesn't hang them
on the line to dry, but I have seen them shoved down the side of
the airing cupboard. I wonder what other secrets my mother has
got?

Friday   February 13th

It was an unlucky day for me all right!

Pandora doesn't sit next to me in Geography any more. Barry
Kent does. He kept copying my work and blowing bubblegum in
my ears. I told Miss Elf but she is scared of Barry Kent as well,
so she didn't say anything to him.

Pandora looked luscious today, she was wearing a split skirt which
showed her legs. She has got a scab on one of her knees. She was
wearing Nigel's football scarf round her wrist, but Miss Elf saw
it and told her to take it off. Miss Elf is not scared of Pandora. I
have sent her a Valentine's Day card (Pandora, not Miss Elf).

Saturday   February 14th
ST VALENTINE'S DAY

I only got one Valentine's Day card. It was in my mother's handwriting so it doesn't count. My mother had a massive card delivered,
it was so big that a GPO van had to bring it to the door. She went
all red when she opened the envelope and saw the card. It was dead
good. There was a big satin elephant holding a bunch of plastic
flowers in its trunk and a bubble coming out of its mouth saying
'Hi, Honey Bun! I ain't never gonna forget you!'. There was no
name written inside, just drawings of hearts with 'Pauline' written
inside them. My father's card was very small and had a bunch of
purple flowers on the front. My father had written on the inside
'Let's try again'.

Here is the poem I wrote inside Pandora's card.

Pandora!
I adore ya.
I implore ye
Don't ignore me.

I wrote it left-handed so that she wouldn't know it was from me.

Sunday   February 15th
SEPTUAGESIMA

Mr Lucas moved back to his empty house last night. I expect he got fed up with all the rowing over the elephant Valentine's Day card. I told my father that my mother can't help it if a man secretly admires her. My father gave a nasty laugh and said 'You've got a lot to learn, son'.

I cleared off to my grandma's at dinner time. She cooked me a proper Sunday dinner with gravy and individual Yorkshire puddings. She is never too busy to make real custard either.

I took the dog with me and we all went for a walk in the afternoon to settle our dinners.

My grandma hasn't spoken to my mother since the row about the cardigans. Grandma says she 'won't set foot in that house again!' Grandma asked me if I believed in life after death. I said I didn't and grandma told me that she had joined the Spiritualist church and has heard my grandad talking about his rhubarb. My grandad has been dead for four years!!! She is going on Wednesday night to try to get in touch with him again and she wants me to go with her. She says I have got an aura around me.

The dog choked on a chicken bone but we held it upside down and banged it hard, and the bone fell out. I've left the dog at grandma's to recover from its ordeal.

Looked up 'Septuagesima' in my pocket dictionary. It didn't have it. Will look in the school dictionary, tomorrow.

Lay awake for ages thinking about God, Life and Death and Pandora.

Monday   February 16th
WASHINGTON'S BIRTHDAY OBSERVANCE

A letter from the BBC!!!!! A white oblong envelope with BBC in red fat letters. My name and address on the front! Could it be that they wanted my poems? Alas, no. But a letter from a bloke called John Tydeman, here is what he wrote:

> Dear Adrian Mole,
> Thank you for the poems which you sent to the BBC and which somehow landed up on my desk. I read them with interest and, taking into account your tender years, I must confess that they do show some promise. However they are not of sufficient quality for us to consider including them in any of our current poetry programmes. Have you thought of offering them to your School Magazine or to your local Parish Magazine? (If you have one.)
>
> If, in future, you wish to submit any of your work to the BBC may I suggest you get it typed out and retain, also, a copy for yourself. The BBC does not normally consider submissions in handwritten manuscript form and, despite the neatness of presentation, I did have some difficulty in making out *all* of the words – particularly at the end of one poem entitled 'The Tap' where there was a rather nasty blotch which had caused the ink to run. (A teastain or a tear-stain? A case of 'Your Tap runneth over'!)
>
> Since you wish to follow a literary career I suggest you will need to develop a thick skin in order to accept many of the inevitable future rejections you may receive with good grace and the minimum of personal pain.
>
> With my best wishes to you for future literary efforts – and, above all, Good Luck!
> Yours sincerely,
>   John Tydeman
>
> P.S. I enclose a poem by a certain John Mole which appeared in this week's *Times Literary Supplement*. Is he a relation? It is very good.

My mother and father were really impressed. I kept getting it out and reading it at school. I was hoping one of the teachers would ask to read it but none of them did.

Bert Baxter read it while I was doing his rotten washing up. He said they were 'all a load of drug addicts' in the BBC'! His brother-in-law's uncle once lived next door to a tea lady at Broadcasting House, so Bert knows all about the BBC.

Pandora got seventeen Valentine's Day cards. Nigel got seven. Even Barry Kent whom everybody hates got three! I just smiled when everybody asked me how many I got. Anyway I bet I am the only person in the school to get a letter from the BBC.

Tuesday   February 17th

Barry Kent said he would 'do me over' unless I gave him twenty-five pence every day. I told him that he was wasting his time demanding money with menaces from me. I never have any spare money. My mother puts my pocket money straight into my building-society account and gives me fifteen pence a day for a Mars bar. Barry Kent said I would have to give him my dinner money! I told him that my father pays it by cheque since it went up to sixty pence a day, but Barry Kent hit me in the goolies and walked off saying 'There's more where that came from'.

I have been to put my name down for a paper round.

Wednesday   February 18th
FULL MOON

Woke up with a pain in my goolies. Told my mother. She wanted to look but I didn't want her to so she said I would have to soldier on. She wouldn't give me a note excusing me from games, so I had to stumble around in the mud again. Barry Kent trod on my head in the scrum. Mr Jones saw him and sent him off for an early shower.

I wish I could have a non-painful illness so I could be excused games. Something like a weak heart would be all right.

Fetched the dog from grandma's, she has given it a shampoo and set. It smells like the perfume counter in Woolworth's.

I went to the Spiritualist meeting with my grandma, it was full of dead old people. One madman stood up and said he had a radio inside his head which told him what to do. Nobody took any notice of him, so he sat down again. A woman called Alice Tonks started grunting and rolling her eyes about and talking to somebody called Arthur Mayfield, but my grandad kept quiet. My grandma was a bit sad so when we got home I made her a cup of Horlicks. She gave me fifty pence and I walked home with the dog.

Started reading *Animal Farm*, by George Orwell. I think I might like to be a vet when I grow up.

Thursday   February 19th
PRINCE ANDREW BORN, 1960

It's all right for Prince Andrew, he is protected by bodyguards. He doesn't have Barry Kent nicking money off him. Fifty pence gone just like that! I wish I knew karate, I would chop Barry Kent in his windpipe.

It is quiet at home, my parents are not speaking to each other.

Friday   February 20th

Barry Kent told Miss Elf to 'get stuffed' in Geography today so she sent him to Mr Scruton to be punished. I hope he gets fifty lashes. I am going to make friends with Craig Thomas. He is one of the biggest third-years. I bought him a Mars bar in break today. I pretended I felt sick and didn't feel like eating it myself. He said, 'Ta Moley'. That is the first time he has spoken to me. If I play my cards right I could be in his gang. Then Barry Kent wouldn't dare touch me again.

My mother is reading another sex book, it is called *The Second Sex*, by a frog writer called Simone De Beauvoir. She left it on the coffee table in the living room where anybody could have seen it, even my grandma!

Saturday   February 21st

Had a dead good dream that Sabre was brutally savaging Barry Kent. Mr Scruton and Miss Elf were watching. Pandora was there, she was wearing her split skirt. She put her arms round me and said, 'I am of the second sex'. Then I woke up to find I had had my second W.D. I have to put my pyjamas in the washing machine so my mother doesn't find out.

Had a good look at my face in the bathroom mirror today. I have got five spots as well as the one on my chin. I have got a few hairs on my lip. It looks as if I shall have to start shaving soon.

Went to the garage with my father, he expected to get the car back today but it still isn't ready. All the bits are on the work-bench. My father's eyes filled up with tears. I was ashamed of him. We walked to Sainsbury's. My father bought tins of salmon, crab and shrimps and a black forest cake and some dead yukky white cheese covered in grape pips. My mother was dead mad at him when we got home because he had forgotten the bread, butter and toilet paper. She says he can't be trusted to go on his own again. My father cheered up a bit.

Sunday   February 22nd
SEXAGESIMA

My father has gone fishing with the dog. Mr Lucas came for dinner and stayed for tea. He ate three slices of the black forest cake. We played Monopoly. Mr Lucas was banker. My mother kept going into jail. I won because I was the only one concentrating properly. My father came in the front door and Mr Lucas went out of the back door. My father said he had been looking forward to the black forest cake all day. There was none left. My father said he had not had a bite to eat or a bite on his fishing line all day. My mother gave him grape-pip cheese on Ry-king for his supper. He threw it at the wall and said he wasn't a ******* mouse he was a ******* man and my mother said it was a long time since he had done any *******! I was sent out of the room then. It is a terrible thing to hear your own mother swearing. I blame it on all those books she has been reading. She hasn't ironed my school uniform yet, I hope she remembers.

I let the dog sleep in my room tonight, it doesn't like quarrelling.

Monday   February 23rd

Got a letter from Mr Cherry the newsagent to say I can start a paper round tomorrow. Worse luck!

Bert Baxter is worried about Sabre because he is off his food and not trying to bite anybody. He asked me to take him to the PDSA for a check-up. I said I would take him tomorrow if his condition hadn't improved.

I'm fed up with washing up for Bert. He seems to live off fried eggs, it is no joke trying to wash up in cold water without any

washing-up liquid. Also there is never a dry tea towel. In fact there
are never any tea towels and Sabre has ripped up all the bath towels
so I don't know how Bert can even have a wash! I think I'll see
if I can get Bert a home help.

I have got to concentrate on getting my GCEs if I want to be
a vet.

Tuesday   February 24th
ST MATTHIAS

Got up at six o'clock for my paper-round. I have got Elm Tree
Avenue. It is dead posh. All the papers they read are very heavy:
The Times, *The Daily Telegraph* and *The Guardian*. Just my luck!
Bert said Sabre is better, he tried to bite the milkman.

Wednesday   February 25th

Bed early tonight because of my paper round. Delivered twenty-five
*Punch*es as well as the papers.

Thursday   February 26th

The papers got mixed up today. Elm Tree Avenue got the *Sun* and
the *Mirror* and Corporation Row got the heavy papers.

I don't know why everybody went so mad. You'd think they
would enjoy reading a different paper for a change.

Friday   February 27th
LAST QUARTER

Early this morning I saw Pandora walking down the drive of 69
Elm Tree Avenue. She had a riding hat and jodphurs on so she
couldn't have been on her way to school. I didn't let her see me.
I don't want her to know that I am doing a menial job.

So now I know where Pandora lives! I had a good look at the
house. It is much bigger than ours. It has got rolled-up wooden
blinds at all the windows, and the rooms look like jungles because
of all the green plants. I looked through the letterbox and saw the
big ginger cat eating something on the kitchen table. They have
The Guardian, *Punch*, *Private Eye*, and *New Society*. Pandora reads

Jackie, the comic for girls; she is not an intellectual, like me. But I don't suppose Malcolm Muggeridge's wife is either.

Saturday   February 28th

Pandora has got a little fat horse called 'Blossom'. She feeds it and makes it jump over barrels every morning before school. I know because I hid behind her father's Volvo and then followed her to a field next to the disused railway line. I hid behind a scrap car in the corner of the field and watched her. She looked dead good in her riding stuff, her chest was wobbling like mad. She will need to wear a bra soon. My heart was beating so loudly in my throat that I felt like a stereo loudspeaker, so I left before she heard me.

   People complained because the papers were late. I had a *Guardian* left over in my paper bag so I took it home to read. It was full of spelling mistakes! It is disgusting when you think of how many people who can spell are out of work.

Sunday   March 1st
QUINQUAGESIMA. ST DAVID'S DAY

I took some sugar to Blossom before I did my paper-round. It brought me closer to Pandora somehow.

   Have strained my back because of carrying all the Sunday supplements. Took the leftover *Sunday People* home as a present to my mother but she said it was only fit for lining the dustbin. Got my two pounds and six pence for six mornings, it is slave labour! *And* I have to give Barry Kent half of it. Mr Cherry said he had a complaint from number 69 Elm Tree Avenue, that they didn't get a *Guardian* yesterday. Mr Cherry sent a *Daily Express* round with his apologies, but Pandora's father brought it back to the shop and said he 'would rather go without'.

   Didn't bother reading the papers today, I am fed up with papers. Had chow mien and beansprouts for Sunday dinner.

   Mr Lucas came round when my father had gone to visit grandma. He was wearing a plastic daffodil in his sports jacket.

   My spots have completely gone. It must be the early morning air.

Monday   March 2nd

My mother has just come into my room and said she had something awful to tell me. I sat up in bed and put a dead serious expression on my face just in case she'd got six months to live or she'd been caught shoplifting or something. She fiddled with the curtains, dropped cigarette ash all over my Concorde model and started mumbling on about 'adult relationships' and 'life being complicated' and how she must 'find herself'. She said she was fond of me. Fond!!! And would hate to hurt me. And then she said that for some women marriage was like being in prison. Then she went out.

Marriage is nothing like being in prison! Women are let out every day to go to the shops and stuff, and quite a lot go to work. I think my mother is being a bit melodramatic.

Finished *Animal Farm*. It is dead symbolic. I cried when Boxer was taken to the vet's. From now on I shall treat pigs with the contempt they deserve. I am boycotting pork of all kinds.

Tuesday   March 3rd
SHROVE TUESDAY

I gave Barry Kent his protection money today. I don't see how there can be a God. If there was surely he wouldn't let people like Barry Kent walk about menacing intellectuals? Why are bigger youths unpleasant to smaller youths? Perhaps their brains are easily worn out with all the extra work they have to do making bigger bones and stuff, or it could be that the big youths have got brain damage because of all the sport they play, or perhaps big youths just *like* menacing and fighting. When I go to university I may study the problem.

I will have my thesis published and I will send a copy to Barry Kent. Perhaps by then he will have learnt to read.

My mother had forgotten that today was pancake day. I reminded her at 11 p.m. I'm sure she burnt them deliberately. I will be fourteen in one month's time.

Wednesday   March 4th
ASH WEDNESDAY

Had a nasty shock this morning. Took my empty paper sack back to Mr Cherry's newsagent's and saw Mr Lucas looking at those magazines on the top shelf. I stood behind the Mills and Boon rack and distinctly saw him choose *Big and Bouncy*, pay for it and leave the shop with it hidden inside his coat. *Big and Bouncy* is extremely indecent. It is full of disgusting pictures. My mother should be informed.

Thursday   March 5th

My father got his car back from the garage today. He was cleaning it and gloating over it for a whole two hours. I noticed that the stick-on waving hand I bought him for Christmas was missing from the rear window. I told him he ought to complain to the garage but he said he didn't want to make a fuss. We went to my grandma's to test-drive the car. She gave us a cup of Bovril and a piece of yukky seedcake. She didn't ask how my mother was, she said my father was looking thin and pale and needed 'feeding up'.

She told me that Bert Baxter had been thrown out of the Evergreens because of his bad behaviour at Skegness. The coach was waiting for two hours for him at the coach station. A search party was sent out to look in the pubs, then Bert came back, drunk but alone and another search party was sent out to look for the first search party. In the end the police had to be sent for and they took hours to round up all the pensioners and get them in the coach.

My grandma said the journey back was a nightmare. All the pensioners kept falling out (with each other not out of the coach). Bert Baxter was reciting a dirty poem about an Eskimo and Mrs Harriman had a funny turn and had to have her corsets loosened.

Grandma said two pensioners had passed on since the outing, she blamed Bert Baxter and said 'He as good as murdered them', but I think it was more likely that the cold wind at Skegness killed them off. I said, 'Bert Baxter is not so bad when you get to know him'. She said she didn't understand why the Good Lord took my grandad and left scum like Baxter. Then she pulled her lips tight and dabbled her eyes with a handkerchief, so we left.

My mother was out when we got home, she has joined some woman's group.

Heard my father say 'goodnight' to the car. He must be cracking up!

Friday   March 6th
NEW MOON

Mr Cherry is very pleased with my work and he has raised my wages by two and a half pence an hour. He also offered me the Corporation Row evening round, but I declined his offer. Corporation Row is where the council put all the bad tenants. Barry Kent lives at number 13.

Mr Cherry gave me two back copies of *Big and Bouncy*. He told me not to tell my mother. As if I would! I have put them under my mattress. Intellectuals like me are allowed to be interested in sex. It is ordinary people like Mr Lucas who should be ashamed of themselves.

Phoned Social Services today and asked about a home help for Bert Baxter. I told a lie and said I was his grandson. They are sending a social worker to see him on Monday.

Used my father's library tickets to get *War and Peace* out. I have lost my own.

Took dog to meet Blossom. They got on well.

Saturday   March 7th

After paper round went back to bed and stayed there all morning reading *Big and Bouncy*. *Felt* like I have never *felt* before.

Went to Sainsbury's with my mother and father but the women in there reminded me of *Big and Bouncy*, even the ones over thirty! My mother said I looked hot and bothered and sent me back to the multi-storey car park to keep the dog company.

The dog already had company, it was barking and whining so loudly that a crowd of people were standing around saying 'the poor thing' and 'how cruel to leave it tied up in such a fashion'. The dog had twisted its collar on the gear lever and its eyes were bulging out of its head. When it saw me it tried to jump up and nearly killed itself.

I tried to explain to the people that I was going to be a vet when

I grew up, but they wouldn't listen and started to say things about the RSPCA. The car was locked so I was forced to break the little window open and unlock the door by putting my hand through. The dog went mad with joy when I untangled him, so the people went away. But my father didn't go mad with joy when he saw the damage, he went mad with rage. He threw the Sainsbury's bags down, broke the eggs, squashed the cakes and drove home too fast. Nobody said anything on the way home, and only the dog was smiling.

Finished *War and Peace*. It was quite good.

Sunday   March 8th
FIRST IN LENT

My mother has gone to a woman's workshop on assertiveness training. Men aren't allowed. I asked my father what 'assertiveness training' is. He said 'God knows, but whatever it is, it's bad news for me'.

We had boil-in-the-bag cod in butter sauce and oven-cooked chips for Sunday dinner, followed by tinned peaches and Dreamtopping. My father opened a bottle of white wine and let me have some. I don't know much about wine but it seemed a pleasant enough vintage. We watched a film on television, then my mother came home and started bossing us around. She said, 'The worm has turned', and 'Things are going to be different around here', and things like that. Then she went into the kitchen and started making a chart dividing all the housework into three. I pointed out to her that I already had a paper round to do, an old age pensioner to look after and a dog to feed, as well as my school work, but she didn't listen, she put the chart on the wall and said 'We start tomorrow'.

Monday   March 9th
COMMONWEALTH DAY

Cleaned toilet, washed basin and bath before doing my paper round. Came home, made breakfast, put washing in machine, went to school. Gave Barry Kent his menaces money, went to Bert Baxter's, waited for social worker who didn't come, had school dinner. Had Domestic-Science – made apple crumble. Came home. Vacuumed hall, lounge, and breakfast room. Peeled potatoes, chopped up cabbage, cut finger, rinsed blood off cabbage. Put chops under grill, looked in cookery book for a recipe for gravy. Made gravy. Strained lumps out with a colander. Set table, served dinner, washed up. Put burnt saucepans in to soak. Got washing out of machine; everything blue, including white underwear and handkerchiefs. Hung washing on clothes-horse. Fed dog. Ironed PE kit, cleaned shoes. Did homework. Took dog for a walk, had bath. Cleaned bath. Made three cups of tea. Washed cups up. Went to bed. Just my luck to have an assertive mother!

Tuesday   March 10th
PRINCE EDWARD BORN, 1964

Why couldn't I have been born Prince Edward and Prince Edward been born Adrian Mole? I am treated like a serf.

Wednesday   March 11th

Dragged myself to school after doing paper round and housework. My mother wouldn't give me a note excusing me from games so I left my PE kit at home. I just couldn't face running about in the cold wind.

That sadist Mr Jones made me run all the way home to fetch my PE kit. The dog must have followed me out of the house because when I got to the school gate it was there before me. I tried to shut the dog out but it squeezed through the railings and followed me into the playground. I ran into the changing rooms and left the dog outside but I could hear its loud bark echoing around the school. I tried to sneak into the playing fields but the dog saw me and followed behind, then it saw the football and joined in the lesson! The dog is dead good at football, even Mr Jones was laughing until the dog punctured the ball.

Mr Scruton, the pop-eyed headmaster, saw everything from his window. He ordered me to take the dog home. I told him I would miss my sitting for school dinners but he said it would teach me not to bring pets to school.

Mrs Leech, the kitchen supervisor, did a very kind thing. She put my curry and rice, spotted dick and custard into the oven to keep warm. Mrs Leech doesn't like Mr Scruton so she gave me a large marrow-bone to take home for the dog.

Thursday   March 12th

Woke up this morning to find my face covered in huge red spots. My mother said they were caused by nerves but I am still convinced that my diet is inadequate. We had been eating a lot of boil-in-the-bag stuff lately. Perhaps I am allergic to plastic. My mother rang Dr Gray's receptionist to make an appointment, but the earliest he can see me is next Monday! For all he knows I could have lassa fever and be spreading it all around the district! I told my mother to say that I was an emergency case but she said I was 'over-reacting as usual'. She said a few spots didn't mean I was dying. I couldn't believe it when she said she was going to work as usual. Surely her child should come before her job?

I rang my grandma and she came round in a taxi and took me to her house and put me to bed. I am there now. It is very clean and peaceful. I am wearing my dead grandad's pyjamas. I have just had a bowl of barley and beef soup. It is my first proper nourishment for weeks.

I expect there will be a row when my mother comes home and finds that I have gone. But frankly, my dear diary, I don't give a damn.

Friday   March 13th
MOON'S FIRST QUARTER

The emergency doctor came to my grandma's last night at 11.30 p.m. He diagnosed that I am suffering from *acne vulgaris*. He said it was so common that it is regarded as a normal state of adolescence. He thought it was highly unlikely that I have got lassa fever because I have not been to Africa this year. He told grandma to take the disinfected sheets off the doors and windows. Grandma said she would like a second opinion. That was when the doctor lost his temper. He shouted in a very loud voice, 'The lad has only got a few teenage spots, for Christ's sake!'

Grandma said she would complain to the Medical Council but the doctor just laughed and went downstairs and slammed the door. My father came round before he went to work and brought my

Social Studies homework and the dog. He said that if I was not out of bed when he got home at lunchtime he would thrash me to within an inch of my life.

He took my grandma into the kitchen and had a loud talk with her. I heard him saying, 'Things are very bad between me and Pauline, and all we are arguing over now is who *doesn't* get custody of Adrian'. Surely my father made a mistake. He must have meant who *did* get custody of me.

So the worst has happened, my skin has gone to pot and my parents are splitting up.

Saturday   March 14th

It is official. They are getting a divorce! Neither of them wants to leave the house so the spare room is being turned into a bedsitter for my father. This could have a very bad effect on me. It could prevent me from being a vet.

My mother gave me five pounds this morning and told me not to tell my father. I brought some bio-spot cream for my skin and the new Abba LP.

I rang Mr Cherry and said I had personal problems and would be unable to work for a few weeks. Mr Cherry said that he knew that my parents were divorcing because my father had cancelled my mother's *Cosmopolitan*.

My father gave me five pounds and told me not to tell my mother. I spent some of it on buying some purple paper and envelopes so that the BBC will be impressed and read my poems. The rest of it will have to go on Barry Kent and his menaces money. I don't think anybody in the world can be as unhappy as me. If I didn't have my poetry I would be a raving loonie by now.

Went out for a sad walk and took Pandora's horse two pounds of cooking apples. Thought of a poem about Blossom. Wrote it down when I got back to the house where I live.

> *Blossom, by Adrian Mole, aged nearly fourteen*
>
> Little Brown Horse
> Eating apples in a field,
> Perhaps one day
> My heart will be healed.

I stroke the places Pandora has sat
Wearing her jodphurs and riding hat.
Goodbye, brown horse.
I turn and retreat,
The rain and mud are wetting my feet.

I have sent it to the BBC. I marked the envelope 'Urgent'.

Sunday   March 15th
SECOND IN LENT

The house is very quiet. My father sits in the spare room smoking and my mother sits in the bedroom smoking. They are not eating much.

Mr Lucas has phoned my mother three times. All she says to him is 'not yet, it's too early'. Perhaps he has asked her to go to the pub for a drink and take her mind off her troubles.

My father has put the stereo in his bedroom. He is playing his Jim Reeves records and staring out of the window. I took him a cup of tea and he said 'Thanks, son' in a choked-up voice.

My mother was looking at old letters in my father's handwriting when I took her tea in; she said, 'Adrian, what must you think of us?' I said that Rick Lemon, the youth leader, thinks divorce is society's fault. My mother said, 'Bugger society'.

I washed and ironed my school uniform ready for school tomorrow. I am getting quite good at housework.

My spots are so horrific that I can't bear to write about them. I will be the laughing stock at school.

I am reading *The Man in the Iron Mask*. I know exactly how he feels.

Monday   March 16th

Went to school. Found it closed. In my anguish I had forgotten that I am on holiday. Didn't want to go home, so went to see Bert Baxter instead. He said the social worker had been to see him and had promised to get Sabre a new kennel but he can't have a home help. (Bert, not Sabre.)

There must have been a full week's washing-up in the sink again. Bert says he saves it for me because I make a good job of it. While I washed up I told Bert about my parents getting a divorce. He said he didn't hold with divorce. He said he was married for thirty-five miserable years so why should anybody else get away with it? He told me that he has got four children and that none of them come to see him. Two of them are in Australia so they can't be blamed, but I think the other two should be ashamed of themselves. Bert showed me a photograph of his dead wife, it was taken in the days before they had plastic surgery. Bert told me that he was a hostler when he got married (a hostler is somebody doing things with horses) and didn't really notice that his wife looked like a horse until he left to work on the railways. I asked him if he would like to see a horse again. He said he would, so I took him to see Blossom.

It took us ages to get there. Bert walks dead slow and he kept having to sit down on garden walls, but we got there eventually. Bert said that Blossom was not a horse, she was a girl pony. He kept patting her and saying 'who's a beauty then, eh?' Then Blossom went for a run about so we sat down on the scrap car, and Bert had a Woodbine and I had a Mars bar. Then we walked back to Bert's house. I went to the shops and bought a packet of Vesta chow mein and a butterscotch Instant Whip for our dinner, so Bert ate a decent meal for once. We watched *Pebble Mill at One*, then Bert showed me his old horse brushes and photographs of the big house where he worked when he was a boy. He said he was made into a communist when he was there, but he fell asleep before he could tell me why.

Came home, nobody was in so I played my Abba records at the highest volume until the deaf woman next door banged on the wall.

Tuesday   March 17th
ST PATRICK'S DAY. BANK HOLIDAY IN N. IRELAND AND REP. OF IRELAND

Looked at *Big and Bouncy*. Measured my 'thing'. It was eleven centimetres.

Mr O'Leary who lives across the road from us was drunk at ten o'clock in the morning! He got thrown out of the butcher's for singing.

Wednesday   March 18th

My mother and father are both speaking to solicitors. I expect they are fighting over who gets custody of me. I will be a tug-of-love child, and my picture will be in the newspapers. I hope my spots clear up before then.

Thursday   March 19th

Mr Lucas has put his house up for sale. My mother says the asking price is thirty thousand pounds!!

What will he do with all that money?

My mother says he will buy another bigger house. How stupid can you get?

If I had thirty thousand pounds I would wander the world having experiences.

I wouldn't take any real money with me because I have read that most foreigners are thieves. Instead I would have three thousand pounds' worth of traveller's cheques sewn into my trousers. Before I set off, I would:

- a) Send Pandora three dozen red roses.
- b) Pay a mercenary fifty pounds to duff Barry Kent up.
- c) Buy the best racing bike in the world and ride it past Nigel's house.
- d) Order a massive crate of expensive dog food so that the dog is properly fed while I'm away.
- e) Buy a housekeeper for Bert Baxter.
- f) Offer my mother and father a thousand pounds (*each*) to stay together.

When I came back from the world I would be tall, brown and full of ironical experiences and Pandora would cry into her pillow at night because of the chance she missed to be Mrs Pandora Mole. I would qualify to be a vet in record time then I would buy a farmhouse. I would convert one room into a study so that I could have somewhere quiet to be intellectual in.

I wouldn't waste thirty thousand pounds on buying a semi-detached house!

Friday   March 20th
FIRST DAY OF SPRING. FULL MOON

It is the first day of spring. The council have chopped all the elms
down in Elm Tree Avenue.

Saturday   March 21st

My parents are eating different things at different times, so I usually
have six meals a day because I don't want to hurt anyone's feelings.

The television is in my room now because they couldn't decide
who it belongs to. I can lie in bed and watch the late-night horror.

I am starting to get a bit suspicious about my mother's feelings
towards Mr Lucas. I found a note she had from him; it says: 'Pauline
how much longer? For God's sake come away with me. Yours forever, Bimbo.'

Although it was signed 'Bimbo' I know it was from Mr Lucas
because it was written on the back of his red electricity bill.

My father should be informed. I have put the note under my
mattress next to the *Big and Bouncy* magazines.

Sunday   March 22nd
THIRD IN LENT. BRITISH SUMMER TIME BEGINS

It is my grandma's birthday today; she is seventy-six and looks it.
I took her a card and a pot plant; it is called Leopard Lily, its foreign
name is *Dieffenbachia*. It had a plastic label stuck in the soil which
said, 'The sap in this plant is poisonous so take care'. My grandma
asked me who chose the plant. I told her my mother did.

My grandma is quite pleased that my parents are getting a
divorce! She said that she always thought that my mother had a
wanton streak in her and that now she had been proved right.

I didn't like to hear my mother being spoken of in such a way
so I came home. I pretended to grandma that I had promised to
meet a friend. But I haven't really got a friend any more, it must
be because I'm an intellectual. I expect people are in awe of me.
Looked in my dictionary to find out what 'wanton' means. It is not
very nice!

Monday   March 23rd

Back to school, worse luck! We had Domestic Science today. We did baked potatoes in the oven with cheese filling. My potatoes were bigger than anyone else's so they weren't properly cooked by the time the lesson ended, so I finished them off at Bert Baxter's. He wanted to see Blossom again which was a bit of a drag because he takes so long to walk anywhere. But we went, anything is better than doing Maths at school.

Bert took his horse brushes with him and gave Blossom a good clean, she was shining like a conker by the time he'd finished. Bert got out of breath so he sat on the scrap car and had a Woodbine, then we walked back to Bert's house.

Sabre is in a better temper since he got his new kennel and Bert's house is in a better condition as a result of Sabre being outside. Bert told me that the social worker thought he ought to go into an old people's home where he can be properly looked after. Bert doesn't want to. He told a lie to the social worker, he said his grandson came in every day and looked after him. The social worker is going to check up so I could be in trouble for impersonation!!! I don't know how much more worry I can take.

Tuesday   March 24th

Late last night I saw my mother and Mr Lucas going out in Mr Lucas's car. They went somewhere special because my mother was wearing a boiler suit with sequins. She did look a bit wanton. Mr Lucas was wearing his best suit and he had a lot of gold jewellery on. For an old person he certainly knows how to dress.

If my father took more care of his appearance, none of this would have happened. It stands to reason that any woman would prefer a man to wear a suit and a lot of gold jewellery to one like my father who hardly ever shaves and wears old clothes and no jewellery.

I am going to stay awake and find out what time my mother comes home.

Midnight. Mother still not home.

2 a.m. No sign of my mother.

Wednesday   March 25th
ANNUNCIATION OF B.V. MARY

Fell asleep, so don't know what time my mother got home. My father said she had gone to the insurance firm's Christmas dinner and dance. In March! Come off it dad! I was not born yesterday! We had swimming in Games today. The water was freezing cold and so were the changing cubicles. I will try to get athlete's foot so that I don't have to go next week.

Thursday   March 26th

Barry Kent has been done by the police for riding a bike without a rear light. I hope he gets sent to a Detention Centre. A short sharp shock will do him good.

Friday   March 27th

Pandora and Nigel have split up! It is all round the school. This is the best news I have had for ages.

I am reading *Madame Bovary*, by another frog writer.

Saturday   March 28th
LAST QUARTER

Nigel has just left, he is heartbroken. I tried to comfort him. I said that there are plenty more pebbles on the beach and fish in the sea. But he was much too upset to listen.

I told him about my suspicions about my mother and Mr Lucas and he said that it had been going on for a long while. Everybody knew except me and my father!!

We had a long talk about racing bikes, then Nigel went home to think about Pandora.

It is Mother's Day tomorrow. I am in two minds about whether to buy her something or not. I have only got sixty-eight pence.

Sunday   March 29th
FOURTH IN LENT. MOTHERING SUNDAY

My father gave me three pounds last night. He said, 'Get your mother something decent, son, it could be the last time'. I certainly wasn't going all the way into town for her, so I went to Mr Cherry's and bought a box of Black Magic, and a card saying 'To a wonderful mother'.

Card manufacturers must think that all mothers are wonderful because every single card has 'wonderful' written on it somewhere. I felt like crossing 'wonderful' out and putting 'wanton' in its place, but I didn't. I signed it 'from your son, Adrian'. I gave it to her this morning. She said, 'Adrian, you shouldn't have'. She was right, I shouldn't have.

Must stop now. My mother has arranged what she called 'a civilized meeting'. Mr Lucas is going to be there. Naturally *I* am not invited! I am going to listen at the door.

Monday   March 30th

A terrible thing happened last night. My father and Mr Lucas had a fight in the *front* garden, the whole street came outside to watch! My mother tried to separate them but they both told her to 'keep out of it'. Mr O'Leary tried to help my father, he kept shouting 'Give the smarmy bugger one for me, George'. Mrs O'Leary was shouting horrible things at my mother. By the sounds of things she had been watching my mother's movements since Christmas. The civilized meeting broke up at about five o'clock when my father found out how long my mother and Mr Lucas had been in love.

They had another civilized meeting at about seven o'clock, but when my mother disclosed that she was leaving for Sheffield with Mr Lucas my father became uncivilized and started fighting. Mr Lucas ran into the garden but my father rugby-tackled him by the laurel bush and the fight broke out again. It was quite exciting really. I had a good view from my bedroom window. Mrs O'Leary said, ' 'Tis the child I feel sorry for', and all the people looked up and saw me, so I looked especially sad. I expect the experience will give me a trauma at some stage in the future. I'm all right at the moment, but you never know.

Tuesday   March 31st

My mother has gone to Sheffield with Mr Lucas. She had to drive because Mr Lucas couldn't see out of his black eyes. I have informed the school secretary of my mother's desertion. She was very kind and gave me a form to give to my father; it is for free school dinners. We are now a single-parent family.

Nigel has asked Barry Kent to stop menacing me for a few weeks. Barry Kent said he would think about it.

Wednesday April 1st

Nigel rang up this morning and pretended he was an undertaker and asked when he was to pick up the body. My father answered the phone. Honestly! He has got no sense of humour.

I had a good laugh telling girls that their petticoats were showing when they weren't. Barry Kent brought a packet of itching powder into the Art lesson, he put some down Ms Fossington-Gore's flying boots. She is another one without any sense of humour. Barry Kent put some down my back. It wasn't funny. I had to go to the matron and have it removed.

The house is looking extremely squalid because my father is not doing any housework. The dog is pining for my mother.

I was born exactly thirteen years and three hundred and sixty-four days ago.

Thursday April 2nd

I am fourteen today! Got a track suit and a football from my father. (He is completely insensitive to my needs.) *A Boy's Book of Carpentry* from my grandma Mole. (No comment.) One pound inside a card from my grandad Sugden. (Last of the big spenders.) Best of all was ten pounds from my mother and five pounds from Mr Lucas. (Conscience money.)

Nigel sent a joke card; it said on the front, 'Who's sexy, charming intelligent and handsome?'. Inside it said, 'Well it certainly ain't you buddy!!!'. Nigel wrote 'No offence mate'. He put ten pence inside the envelope.

Bert Baxter sent a card to the school because he doesn't know where I live. His handwriting is dead good, I think it is called 'brass plate'. His card had a picture of an alsatian on the front. Inside Bert had written, 'Best wishes from Bert and Sabre. P.S. Drain blocked up'. Inside the card there was a book token for ten shillings. It expired in December 1958, but it was a kind thought.

So at last I am fourteen! Had a good look at myself in the mirror tonight and I think I can detect a certain maturity. (Apart from the rotten spots.)

Friday   April 3rd

Got full marks in the Geography test today. Yes! I am proud to report that I got twenty out of twenty! I was also complimented on the neat presentation of my work. There is nothing I don't know about the Norwegian leather industry. Barry Kent seems to take delight in being ignorant. When Miss Elf asked him where Norway was in relation to Britain he said, 'First cousin twice removed'. It hurts me to relate that even Pandora laughed with the rest of the class. Only Miss Elf and I remained composed. Unblocked Bert Baxter's drain, it was full of old bones and tea leaves. I told Bert that he really ought to use tea-bags. After all this is the twentieth century! Bert said that he would give them a try. I told him that my mother has run away with an insurance man, he said 'Was it an Act of God?' Then he laughed until his eyes watered.

Saturday   April 4th
NEW MOON

Me and my father cleaned the house up today. We had no choice: my grandma is coming for tea tomorrow. We went to Sainsbury's in the afternoon. My father chose a trolley that was impossible to steer. It also squeaked as if somebody was torturing mice. I was ashamed to be heard with it. My father chose food that is bad for you. I had to put my foot down and insist that he brought some fresh fruit and salad. When we got to the check-out he couldn't find his banker's card, the cashier wouldn't take a cheque without it, so the supervisor had to come and stop the argument. I had to lend my father some of my birthday money. So he owes me eight pounds thirty-eight and a half pence. I made him write an IOU on the back of the till roll.

But I must say that I take my hat off to Sainsbury's, they seem to attract a better class of person. I saw a vicar choosing toilet paper; he chose a four-roll pack of purple three-ply. He must have money to burn! He could have bought some shiny white and given the difference to the poor. What a hypocrite!

Sunday   April 5th
PASSION SUNDAY

Nigel came round this morning. He is still mad about Pandora. I
tried to take his mind off her by talking about the Norwegian
leather industry but he couldn't get interested somehow.

I made my father get up at 1 p.m. I don't see why he should
lie stinking in bed all day when I am up and about. He got up and
went outside to clean the car. He found one of my mother's earrings down the side of the back seat and he just sat there staring
at it. He said, 'Adrian, do you miss your mother?' I replied, 'Of
course I do, but life must go on.' He then said, 'I don't see why'.
I took this to mean that he was suicidal, so I immediately went upstairs and removed anything harmful from the bathroom.

After we had eaten our frozen roast-beef dinner and I was washing up, he shouted from the bathroom for his razor. I lied and
shouted back that I didn't know where it was. I then removed every
knife and sharp instrument from the kitchen drawer. He tried to
get his battery razor to work but the batteries had leaked and gone
all green.

I like to think I am broad-minded but the language my father
used was beyond the pale, and all because he couldn't have a shave!
Tea was a bit of a drag. My grandma kept saying horrible things
about my mother and my father kept rambling on about how much
he missed her. Nobody even noticed I was in the room! The dog
got more attention than me!

My grandma told my father off for growing a beard. She said,
'You may think it amusing to look like a communist, George, but
I don't'. She said that even in the trenches at Ypres my
grandad had shaved every day. Sometimes he had to stop rats from
eating his shaving soap. She said that my grandad was even shaved
by the undertaker when lying in his coffin, so if the dead could
shave there was no excuse for the living. My father tried to explain,
but grandma didn't stop talking once so it was a bit difficult.

We were both glad when she went home.

Looked at *Big and Bouncy*. It is Passion Sunday after all!

Monday   April 6th

Had a postcard from my mother. It said 'they' were staying with friends until they found a flat. She said I could go and stay for a weekend when they were fixed up.

I didn't show it to my father.

Tuesday   April 7th

My precious Pandora is going out with Craig Thomas. That's the last time you get a Mars bar from me, Thomas!

Barry Kent is in trouble for drawing a nude woman in Art. Ms Fossington-Gore said that it wasn't so much the subject matter but his ignorance of basic biological facts that was so upsetting. I did a good drawing of the Incredible Hulk smashing Craig Thomas to bits. Ms Fossington-Gore said it was a 'powerful statement of monolithic oppression'.

Phone call from my mother. Her voice sounded funny as if she had a cold. She kept saying, 'You'll understand one day, Adrian'. There was a slurping sound in the background. I expect it was that Lucas creep kissing her neck. I have seen them do it on the films.

Wednesday   April 8th

My father wouldn't give me a note excusing me from Games so I spent nearly all morning dressed in pyjamas diving into a swimming pool and picking up a brick from the bottom. I had a bath when I came home but I still smell of chlorine. I just don't see the point of the above lesson. When I am grown up I am hardly going to walk along a river bank in my pyjamas am I? And who would be stupid enough to dive into a river for a boring old brick? Bricks are lying around all over the place!

Thursday   April 9th

My father and me had a good talk last night. He asked me who I would prefer to live with, him or my mother? I said both. He told me he has made friends with a woman at work, she is called Doreen Slater. He said he would like me to meet her one day. Here we go again; so much for the suicidal, heartbroken, deserted husband!

Friday   April 10th

Rang my grandmother to tell her about Doreen Slater. My grandma didn't sound too pleased, she said it was a common-sounding name and I am inclined to agree with her.

Got *Waiting for Godot* out of the library. Disappointed to find that it was a play. Still, I will give it a go. I have been neglecting my brain lately.

Nigel asked me if I wanted to stay the weekend. His parents are going to a wedding in Croydon. My father said I could. He looked quite pleased. I am going round to Nigel's in the morning.

I broke up for the Easter holidays today. Must make sure my brain keeps active.

Saturday   April 11th
FIRST QUARTER

Nigel is dead lucky. His house is absolutely fantastic! Everything is modern. I don't know what he must think of our house, some of our furniture is over a hundred years old!

His bedroom is massive and he has got a stereo, a *colour* television, a tapedeck, a Scalextric track, an electric guitar and amplifier. Spotlights over his bed. Black walls and a white carpet and a racing car continental quilt. He has got loads of back issues of *Big and Bouncy*, so we looked through them, then Nigel had a cold shower while I cooked the soup and cut the french loaf. We had a good laugh at *Waiting for Godot*. Nigel had hysterics when I said that Vladimir and Estragon sounded like contraception pills.

I had a go on Nigel's racing bike. I now want one more than anything in the world. If I had to choose between Pandora and a racing bike, I would choose the bike. Sorry, Pandora, but that's how things are.

We went to the chip shop and had the works. Fish, chips, pickled onions, gherkins, sloppy peas. Nothing was too expensive for Nigel, he gets loads of pocket money. We walked round for a bit then we came back and watched *The Bug Eyed Monster Strikes Back* on the television. I said the bug-eyed monster reminded me of Mr Scruton the headmaster. Nigel had hysterics again. I think I have got quite a talent to amuse people. I might change my mind about becoming a vet and try writing situation comedy for television.

When the film finished Nigel said, 'How about a nightcap?'. He went to the bar in the corner of the lounge and he poured us both a stiff whisky and soda. I hadn't actually tasted whisky before and I never will again. How people can drink if for pleasure I don't know. If it was in a medicine bottle they would pour it down the sink!

Don't remember going to bed, but I must have done because I am sitting up in Nigel's parents' bed writing my diary.

Sunday   April 12th
PALM SUNDAY

This weekend with Nigel has really opened my eyes! Without knowing it I have been living in poverty for the past fourteen years. I have had to put up with inferior accommodation, lousy food and paltry pocket money. If my father can't provide a decent standard of living for me on his present salary, then he will just have to start looking for another job. He is always complaining about having to flog electric storage heaters anyway. Nigel's father has worked like a slave to create a modern environment for *his* family. Perhaps if *my* father had built a formica cocktail bar in the corner of *our* lounge my mother would still be living with us. But oh no. My father actually boasts about our hundred-year-old furniture.

Yes! Instead of being ashamed of our antiques, he is proud of the clapped-out old rubbish.

My father should take lessons from Great Literature. Madame Bovary ran away from that idiot Doctor Bovary because he couldn't supply her needs.

Monday   April 13th

Had a note from Mr Cherry asking me when I can resume my paper round. I sent a note back to say that due to my mother's desertion I am still in a mental state. This is true. I wore odd socks yesterday without knowing it. One was red and one was green. I must pull myself together. I could end up in a lunatic asylum.

Tuesday   April 14th

Had a postcard from my mother. She has found a flat and she wants me to visit her and Lucas as soon as possible.

Why can't my mother write a letter like any normal person? Why should the postman be able to read my confidential business? Her new address is 79A, President Carter Walk, Sheffield.

I asked my father if I could go; he said, 'Yes, providing she sends the train fare'. So I have written a letter asking her to send eleven pounds eighty.

Wednesday   April 15th

Went to the youth club with Nigel. It was dead good. We played ping-pong until the balls cracked. Then we had a go on the football table. I beat Nigel fifty goals to thirteen. Nigel went into a sulk and said that he only lost because his goalkeeper's legs were stuck on with Sellotape but he was wrong. It was my superior skill that did it.

A gang of punks passed unkind comments about my flared trousers but Rick Lemon, the youth leader, stepped in and led a discussion on personal taste. We all agreed it should be up to the individual to dress how he or she likes. All the same I think I will ask my father if I can have a new pair of trousers. Not many fourteen years olds wear flared trousers today, and I don't wish to be conspicuous.

Barry Kent tried to get in the fire-doors to avoid paying his five-pence subs. But Rick Lemon pushed him back outside into the rain. I was very pleased. I owe Barry Kent two pounds' menaces money.

Thursday   April 16th

Got a birthday card from my Auntie Susan, two weeks late! She always forgets the right day. My father said that she's under a lot of pressure because of her job, but I can't see it myself. I'd have thought that being a prison wardress was dead cushy, it is only locking and unlocking doors after all. She has sent a present via the GPO so with luck I should get it by Christmas. Ha! Ha!

Friday   April 17th
GOOD FRIDAY

Poor Jesus, it must have been dead awful for him. I wouldn't have had the guts to do it myself.

The dog has mauled the hot-cross buns; it doesn't respect any traditions.

Saturday   April 18th

Got parcel from Auntie Susan. It is an embroidered toothbrush holder and it was made by one of the prisoners! She is called Grace Pool. Auntie Susan said that I should write and thank her! It is bad enough that my father's sister works in Holloway Prison. But now I am expected to start writing to the prisoners! Grace Pool could be a murderess or anything!

Still waiting for the eleven pounds eighty pence. It doesn't seem as if my mother is desperate to see me.

Sunday   April 19th
EASTER SUNDAY

Today is the day that Jesus escaped from the cave. I expect that Houdini got the idea from him.

My father forgot to go to the bank on Friday so we are penniless. I had to take the pop bottles back to the shop to buy myself an Easter egg. Watched film, then had a fantastic tea at grandma's. She made a cake covered in little fluffy chicks. Some of the fluff got into my father's mouth, he had to have his back thumped hard. He always manages to spoil things. He has got no Social Decorum at all. Went to see Bert Baxter after tea. He was pleased to see me and I felt a bit rotten because I have neglected him lately. He gave me a pile of comics. They are called the *Eagle* and they have got great pictures. I read them until 3 a.m. this morning. Us intellectuals keep anti-social hours. It does us good.

Monday   April 20th
BANK HOLIDAY IN UK (EXCEPT SCOTLAND)

My father is in a rage because the bank is still shut. He has run out of cigarettes. It will do him good. No sign of the eleven pounds eighty pence.

Wrote to Grace Pool. She is in 'D' Wing. I put:

Dear Miss Pool,
Thank you for making the toothbrush holder. It is charming.
    Yours, with kind regards, Adrian

Tuesday   April 21st

My father was first in the queue at the bank this morning. When
he got inside the cashier said he couldn't have any money because
he hadn't got any left. My father demanded to see the manager.
I was dead ashamed so I sat behind a plastic plant and waited until
the shouting had stopped. Mr Niggard, the head bloke, came out
and calmed my father down. He said he would arrange a temporary
overdraft. My father looked dead pathetic, he kept saying, 'It was
that bloody vet's bill'. Mr Niggard looked as if he understood. Perhaps he has got a mad dog as well. We can't be the only ones, can
we?

The eleven pounds, etc., came by second post so I am going to
Sheffield tomorrow morning. I've never been on a train on my own
before. I am certainly stretching my wings lately.

Wednesday   April 22nd

My father gave me a lift to the station. He also gave me a bit of
advice about the journey; he said I was not to buy a pork pie from
the buffet car.

I stood in the train with my head out of the window and my father
stood on the platform. He kept looking at his watch. I couldn't think
of anything to say and neither could he. In the end I said, 'Don't
forget to feed the dog, will you?' My father gave a nasty laugh, then
the train started to move so I waved and went to look for a non-
smoking seat. All the filthy smokers were crammed together
choking and coughing. They were a rough-looking, noisy lot so I
hurried through their small carriage holding my breath. The non-
smoking carriages seemed to have a quieter type of person in them.
I found a window seat opposite an old lady. I had wanted to look
at the landscape or read my book but the old bat started on about
her daughter's hysterectomy and telling me things I didn't want
to hear. She just about sent me barmy! It was nag, nag, nag. But
thank God she got off at Chesterfield. She left her *Woman's Own*
behind so I had a good laugh at the Problem Page, read the story,

and then the train slowed down for Sheffield. My mother started crying when she saw me. It was a bit embarrassing but quite nice at the same time. We got a taxi from the station, Sheffield looks OK, just like home really. I didn't see any knife and fork factories. I expect Margaret Thatcher has closed them all down.

Lucas was out flogging insurance so I had my mother all to myself until eight o'clock. The flat is dead grotty, it is modern but small. You can hear the neighbours coughing. My mother is used to better things. I am dead tired, so will stop.

I hope my father is being kind to the dog. I wish my mother would come home, I had forgotten how nice she is.

Thursday   April 23rd
ST GEORGE'S DAY

Me and mum went shopping today. We bought a Habitat lampshade for her bedroom and a new pair of trousers for me. They are dead good, really tight.

We had a Chinese Businessman's Lunch and then went to see a Monty Python film all about the life of Jesus. It was dead daring, I felt guilty laughing.

Lucas was at the flat when we got back. He had got the dinner ready but I said I wasn't hungry and I went to my room. It would choke me to eat anything that creep had touched! Later on I phoned my father from a call-box; I just had time to shout, 'Don't forget to feed the dog', before the pips went.

Retired to bed early because of all the slopping Lucas was doing. He calls my mother 'Paulie' when he knows very well that her name is Pauline.

Friday   April 24th

Helped my mother to paint her kitchen. She is doing it brown and cream, it looks awful, just like the toilets at school. Lucas bought me a penknife. He is trying to bribe me into liking him again. Hard luck, Lucas! Us Moles never forget. We are just like the Mafia, once you cross us we bear a grudge all our lives. He has stolen a wife and mother so he will have to pay the price! It is a shame because the penknife is full of gadgets that would be useful to me in my everyday life.

Saturday   April 25th

Lucas doesn't work on Saturdays so I had to put up with his lechery all day. He is constantly touching my mother's hand or kissing her or putting his arm round her shoulders, I don't know how she stands it, it would drive me mad.

Lucas drove us out into the countryside this afternoon, it was hilly and high up. I got cold so I sat in the car and watched my mother and Lucas making an exhibition of themselves. Thank God, no members of the public were around. It is not a pretty sight to see old people running up hills laughing.

Came back, had a bath, thought about the dog, went to sleep.

Home tomorrow.

3 a.m. Just had a dream about stabbing Lucas with the toothpick on my penknife. Best dream I've had for ages.

Sunday   April 26th

2.10 p.m. So my little sojourn in Sheffield is drawing to a close. I am catching the 7.10 p.m. train which only leaves five hours to do my packing. My father was right. I didn't need two suitcases of clothes. Still it is better to be safe than sorry, I always say. I shan't be sorry to leave this sordid flat with the coughing neighbours, though naturally I have some regrets about my mother's stubborness in refusing to come home with me.

I told her that the dog was pining to death for her but she rang my father up and like a fool he told her that the dog had just eaten a whole tin of Pedigree Chum and a bowl of Winalot.

I told her about my father and Doreen Slater, hoping to send her mad with jealousy, but she just laughed and said, 'Oh is Doreen still making the rounds?' I have done my best to get her back, but must admit defeat.

11 p.m. Journey back a nightmare, non-smoking compartments all full, forced to share carriage with pipes, cigars and cigarettes. Queued for twenty minutes for a cup of coffee in the buffet. Just got to the counter when the grill came down and the man put up a sign saying: 'Closed due to signal failure'! Got back to seat, found a soldier in my place. Found another seat, but had to endure maniac sitting opposite telling me he had a radio inside his head controlled by Fidel Castro.

My father met me at the station, the dog jumped up to meet me, missed, and nearly fell in front of the 9.23 p.m. Birmingham express.

My father said he had had Doreen Slater for tea. By the state of the house I should think he'd had her for breakfast, dinner and tea! I have never seen the woman, but from the evidence she left behind I know she has got bright red hair, wears orange lipstick and sleeps on the left side of the bed.

What a homecoming!

My father said Doreen had ironed my school clothes ready for the morning. What did he expect? Thanks?

Monday   April 27th

Mrs Bull taught us to wash up in Domestic Science. Talk about teaching your grandmother to suck eggs! I must be one of the best washer-uppers in the world! Barry Kent broke an unbreakable plate so Mrs Bull sent him out of the room. I saw him smoking quite openly in the corridor. He has certainly got a nerve! I felt it was my duty to report him to Mrs Bull. I did this purely out of concern for Barry Kent's health. He was taken to pop-eye Scruton and his Benson and Hedges were confiscated. Nigel said he saw Mr Scruton smoking them in the staff room at dinner-time, but surely this can't be true?

Pandora and Craig Thomas are creating a scandal by flaunting their sexuality in the playground. Miss Elf had to knock on the staff-room window and ask them to stop kissing.

Tuesday   April 28th

Mr Scruton made a speech in assembly this morning. It was about the country's lack of morals, but really he was talking about Pandora and Craig Thomas. The speech didn't do any good because while we were singing 'There is a Green Hill Far Away', I distinctly saw glances of a passionate nature pass between them.

Wednesday   April 29th

My father is worried, electric storage heaters are not selling well. My father says this proves that consumers are not as stupid as everyone thinks. I'm fed up with him mooning about the house at night. I have advised him to join a club or get a hobby but he is determined to feel sorry for himself. The only time he laughs is when those advertisements for electric storage heaters are shown on television. Then he laughs himself silly.

Thursday   April 30th

I was seriously menaced at school today. Barry Kent threw my snap-lock executive brief-case on to the rugby pitch. I have got to find two pounds quickly before he starts throwing *me* on to the rugby pitch. It's no good asking my father for money, he is in despair because of all the red bills.

Friday   May 1st

Grandma rang early this morning to say 'Cast ne'er a clout till May be out'. I haven't got the faintest idea what she was going on about. All I know is that it has something to do with vests.

I am pleased to report that Barry Kent and his gang have been banned from the 'Off The Streets' youth club. (But this means that they are now *on* the streets, worse luck.) They filled a French letter with water and threw it at a bunch of girls and made them scream. Pandora burst the thing with a badge pin and Rick Lemon came out of his office and slipped in the water. Rick was dead mad, he got dirty marks all over his yellow trousers. Pandora helped Rick to throw the gang out, she looked dead fierce. I expect she will win the medal for 'Most helpful member of the year'.

Saturday   May 2nd

Had a letter from Grace Pool! This is what it said:

> Dear Adrian,
> Thank you for your charming letter of thanks. It fair bright-ened up my day. The girls are all joshing me about my suitor.

I am due for parole on June 15th, would it be possible to come and see you? Your Auntie Susan is one of the best screws in here, that's why I obliged and made the toothbrush holder. See you on the fifteenth then.

> Yours with fond regards,
> Grace Pool

P.S. I was falsely convicted of arson but that is all in the past now.

My God! What shall I do?

Sunday   May 3rd
SECOND AFTER EASTER

There is nothing left in the freezer, nothing in the pantry and only slimming bread in the bread bin. I don't know what my father does with all the money. I was forced to go round to grandma's before I died from malnutrition. At four o'clock I had one of those rare moments of happiness that I will remember all my life. I was sitting in front of grandma's electric coal fire eating dripping toast and reading the *News of the World*. There was a good play on Radio Four about torturing in concentration camps. Grandma was asleep and the dog was being quiet. All at once I felt this dead good feeling. Perhaps I am turning religious.

I think I have got it in me to be a Saint of some kind.

Phoned Auntie Susan but she is on duty in Holloway. Left a message with her friend Gloria, asking Auntie Susan to ring me urgently.

Monday   May 4th
BANK HOLIDAY IN UK. NEW MOON

Auntie Susan rang to say that Grace Pool has had her parole cancelled because she set fire to the embroidery workshop and destroyed a gross of toothbrush holders.

Their loss is my gain!

Tuesday   May 5th

Saw our postman on the way to school, he said that my mother is coming to visit me on Saturday. I've a good mind to report him to the Postmaster General for reading a person's private postcard!

My father had also read my postcard by the time I got home from school. He looked pleased and started cleaning rubbish out of the lounge, then he rang Doreen Slater and said he would have to 'take a rain check on Saturday's flick'. Grown ups are always telling adolescents to speak clearly then they go and talk a lot of gibberish themselves. Doreen Slater shouted down the phone. My father shouted back that he 'didn't want a long-term relationship', he had 'made that clear from the start', and that 'nobody could replace his Pauline'. Doreen Slater went shrieking on and on until my father slammed the phone down. The phone kept ringing until my father took the phone off the hook. He went mad doing housework until 2 a.m. this morning, and it's only Tuesday! What will he be like on Saturday morning? The poor fool is convinced that my mother is coming back for good.

Wednesday   May 6th

I am proud to report that I have been made a school-dinner monitor. My duties are to stand at the side of the pig bin and make sure that my fellow pupils scrape their plates properly.

Thursday   May 7th

Bert Baxter rang the school to ask me to call round urgently. Mr Scruton told me off, he said the school telephone was not for the convenience of the pupils. Get stuffed, Scruton, you pop-eyed git!!! Bert was in a terrible state. He has lost his false teeth. He has had them since 1946, they have got sentimental value for him because they used to belong to his father. I looked everywhere for them, but couldn't find them.

I went to the shops and brought him a tin of soup and a butterscotch Instant Whip. It was all he could manage at the moment. I have promised to go round tomorrow and look again. Sabre was happy for once; he was chewing something in his kennel.

My father is still cleaning the house up. Even Nigel commented on how clean the kitchen floor looked. I wish my father wouldn't wear the apron though, he looks like a poofter in it.

Friday   May 8th

Found Bert's teeth in Sabre's kennel. Bert rinsed them under the tap and put them back in his mouth! This is the most revolting thing I have ever seen.

My father has got bunches of flowers to welcome my mother home. They are all over the house stinking the place out.

Mr Lucas's house has been sold at last. I saw the estate agent's minion putting the board up. I hope the new people are respectable. I am reading the *Mill on the Floss*, by a bloke called George Eliot.

Saturday   May 9th

I was woken up at 8.30 by a loud banging on the front door. It was an Electricity Board official. I was amazed to hear that he had come to turn off our electricity! My father owes £95.79p. I told the official that we need electricity for life's essentials like the television and stereo, but he said that people like us are sapping the country's strength. He went to the meter cupboard, did something with tools, and the second hand on the kitchen clock stopped. It was dead symbolic. My father came in from fetching the *Daily Express*. He was whistling and looking dead cheerful. He even asked the official if he would like a cup of tea! The official said, 'No thank you', and hurried up the path and got into his little blue van. My father switched the electric kettle on. I was forced to tell him.

Naturally I got the blame! My father said I should have refused entry. I told him that he should have put all the bill money away each week like grandma does. But he just went berserk. My mother turned up with Lucas! It was just like old times with everybody shouting at once. I took the dog to the shops and bought five boxes of candles. Mr Lucas lent me the money.

When I got back I stood in the hall and heard my mother say, 'No wonder you can't pay the bills, George; just look at all these flowers. They must have cost a fortune'. She said it very kindly. Mr Lucas said he would lend my father a 'ton' but my father was very dignified and said, 'All I want from you, Lucas, is my wife'. My mother complimented my father on how nicely he was keeping the house. My father just looked sad and old. I felt dead sorry for him.

I was sent outside while they talked about who was getting custody of me, the arguing went on for ages. In fact until it was time to light the candles.

Lucas spilt candle-wax over his new suede shoes. It was the only cheerful incident in a tragic day.

When my mother and Lucas had gone off in a taxi I went to bed with the dog. I heard my father talking to Doreen Slater on the phone, then the front door slammed and I looked out of my window to see him driving off in the car. The back seat was full of flowers.

Sunday   May 10th
THIRD AFTER EASTER. MOTHER'S DAY, USA AND CANADA. MOON'S FIRST QUARTER

Didn't get up until half-past four this afternoon. I think I am suffering from depression. Nothing happened at all today, apart from a hail storm around six o'clock.

Monday   May 11th

Bert Baxter offered to lend us a paraffin heater. Our gas central heating won't work without electricity. I thanked him but refused his kind offer. I have read that they are easily knocked over and our dog would no doubt cause a towering inferno.

If it gets out that our electricity has been cut off, I will cut my throat. The shame would be too much to bear.

Tuesday   May 12th

Had a long talk with Mr Vann the Careers teacher today. He said that if I want to be a vet I will have to do Physics, Chemistry and Biology for O level. He said that Art, Woodwork and Domestic Science won't do much good.

I am at the Crossroads in my life. The wrong decision now could result in a tragic loss to the veterinary world. I am hopeless at science. I asked Mr Vann which O levels you need to write situation comedy for television. Mr Vann said that you don't need qualifications at all, you just need to be a moron.

Wednesday   May 13th

Had an in-depth talk about O levels with my father, he advised me to only do the subjects that I am good at. He said that vets spend half their working life with their hands up cows' bums, and the other half injecting spoiled fat dogs. So I am rethinking my future career prospects.

I wouldn't mind being a sponge-diver, but I don't think there is much call for them in England.

Thursday   May 14th

Miss Sproxton told me off because my English essay was covered in drops of candle-wax. I explained that I had caught my overcoat sleeve on the candle whilst doing my homework. Her eyes filled with tears and she said I was 'a dear brave lad', and she gave me a merit mark.

After supper of cream crackers and tuna fish, played cards in the candlelight. It was dead good. My father cut the ends off our gloves, we looked like two criminals on the run.

I am reading *Hard Times*, by Charles Dickens.

Friday   May 15th

My grandma has just made a surprise visit. She caught us huddled round our new Camping-gaz stove eating cold beans out of a tin. My father was reading *Playboy* under cover of the candlelight and I was reading *Hard Times* by my key-ring torch. We were quite contented. My father had just said that it was a 'good training for when civilization collapses' when grandma burst in and started having hysterics. She has forced us to go to her house so I am there now sleeping in my dead grandad's bed. My father is sleeping downstairs on two armchairs pushed together. Grandma has written a Giro cheque for the electricity money, she is furious because she wanted the money for restocking her freezer. She buys two dead cows a year.

Saturday   May 16th

Helped grandma with the weekend shopping. She was dead fierce in the grocer's; she watched the scales like a hawk watching a field-mouse. Then she pounced and accused the shop assistant of giving her underweight bacon. The shop assistant was dead scared of her and put another slice on.

Our arms were dead tired by the time we'd staggered up the hill carrying big bags of shopping. I don't know how my grandma does it when she's alone. I think the council ought to put escalators on hills; they would save money in the long run, old people wouldn't go about collapsing all over the place. My father paid the electricity bill at the post office today, but it will be at least a week before the computer gives permission for our electricity to be reconnected.

Sunday   May 17th

My grandma made us get up early and go to church with her. My father was made to comb his hair and wear one of his dead father's ties. Grandma held both our arms and looked proud to be with us. The church service was dead boring. The vicar looked like the oldest man alive and spoke in a feeble sort of voice. My father kept standing up when we were supposed to sit down and vice versa. I copied what grandma did, she is always right. My father sang too loudly, everyone looked at him. I shook the vicar's hand when we were allowed outside. It was like touching dead leaves.

After dinner we listened to my grandma's records of Al Jolson, then grandma went upstairs for a sleep and my father and me washed up. My father broke a forty-one-year-old milk jug! He had to go out for a drink to recover from the shock. I went to see Bert Baxter but he wasn't in, so I went to see Blossom instead. She was very pleased to see me. It must be dead boring standing in a field all day long. No wonder she welcomes visitors.

Monday   May 18th

Grandma is not speaking to my father because of the milk jug. Can't wait to get home where things like milk jugs don't matter.

Tuesday   May 19th
FULL MOON

My father is in trouble for staying out late last night. Honestly! He is the same age as the milk jug so surely he can come in what time he likes!

Told my father about being menaced today. I was forced to because Barry Kent seriously damaged my school blazer and tore the school badge off. My father is going to speak to Barry Kent tomorrow *and* he is going to get all the menaces money back off him, so it looks like I could be rich!

Wednesday May 20th

Barry Kent denied all knowledge of menacing me and laughed when my father asked him to repay the money. My father went to see his father and had a serious argument and threatened to call the police. I think my father is dead brave. Barry Kent's father looks like a big ape and has got more hair on the back of his hands than my father has got on his entire head.

The police have said that they can't do anything without proof so I am going to ask Nigel to give them a sworn statement that he has seen me handing menaces money over.

Thursday May 21st

Barry Kent duffed me up in the cloakroom today. He hung me on one of the coathooks. He called me a 'coppers' nark' and other things too bad to write down. My grandma found out about the menacing (my father didn't want her to know on account of her diabetes). She listened to it all then she put her hat on, thinned her lips and went out. She was gone one hour and seven minutes, she came in, took her coat off, fluffed her hair out, took £27.18 from the anti-mugger belt round her waist. She said, 'He won't bother you again, Adrian, but if he does, let me know'. Then she got the tea ready. Pilchards, tomatoes and ginger cake. I bought her a box of diabetic chocolates from the chemist's as a token of my esteem.

Friday May 22nd

It is all round the school that an old lady of seventy-six frightened Barry Kent and his dad into returning my menaces money. Barry Kent daren't show his face. His gang are electing a new leader.

Saturday   May 23rd

Home again, the electricity has been reconnected. All the plants are dead. Red bills on the doormat.

Sunday   May 24th
ROGATION SUNDAY

I have decided to paint my room black; it is a colour I like. I can't live a moment longer with Noddy wallpaper. At my age it is positively indecent to wake up to Big Ears and all the rest of the Toyland idiots running around the walls. My father says I can use any colour I like so long as I buy the paint and do it myself.

Monday   May 25th

I have decided to be a poet. My father said that there isn't a suitable career structure for poets and no pensions and other boring things, but I am quite decided. He tried to interest me in becoming a computer operator, but I said, 'I need to put my soul into my work and it is well known that computers haven't got a soul.' My father said, 'The Americans are working on it.' But I can't wait that long.

Bought two tins of black vinyl silk-finish paint and a half-inch brush. Started painting as soon as I got home from the DIY centre. Noddy keeps showing through the black paint. Looks like it'll need two coats. Just my luck!

Tuesday   May 26th
MOON'S LAST QUARTER

Now put on two coats of black paint! Noddy still showing through! Black paw-marks over landing and stairs. Can't get paint off hands. Hairs falling out of brush. Fed up with whole thing. Room looks dark and gloomy. Father hasn't lifted a finger to help. Black paint everywhere.

Wednesday   May 27th

Third coat. Slight improvement, only Noddy's hat showing through now.

Thursday   May 28th
ASCENSION DAY

Went over Noddy's hat with kid's paintbrush and last of black paint, but bloody hat bells are still showing through!

Friday   May 29th

Went over hat bells with black felt-tip pen, did sixty-nine tonight, only a hundred and twenty-four to go.

Saturday   May 30th

Finished last bell at 11.25 p.m. Know just how Rembrandt must have felt after painting the Sistine Chapel in Venice.
2 a.m. The paint is dry but it must have been faulty because it is all streaky, and here and there you can see Gollywog's striped trousers and Mr Plod's nose. Thank God the bloody bells don't show through! My father has just been in to tell me to go to sleep, he said my room reminded him of a Salvador Dali painting. He said it was a surrealist nightmare, but he is only jealous because he has got yukky roses on his bedroom walls.

Sunday   May 31st
SUNDAY AFTER ASCENSION

I bought a joss stick from Mr Singh's shop. I lit it in my room to try and get rid of the paint smell. My father came into my room and threw the joss stick out of the window, he said he 'wouldn't have me messing with drugs'! I tried to explain but my father was too angry to listen. I stayed in my room for a few hours but the black walls seemed to be closing in on me so I went to see Bert Baxter. Couldn't make him hear, so I came home and watched religion on the television. Had tea, did Geography homework, went to bed. Dog won't stay in room any more; it whimpers to be let out.

Monday June 1st
BANK HOLIDAY IN THE REP. OF IRELAND

My father had a letter that made his face go white: he has been made redundant from his job! He will be on the dole! How can we live on the pittance that the government will give us? The dog will have to go! It costs thirty-five pence a day for dog food, not counting Winalot. I am now a single-parent child whose father is on the dole! Social Security will be buying my shoes!

I didn't go to school today, I rang the school secretary and told her that my father is mentally ill and needs looking after. She sounded dead worried and asked if he was violent. I said that he hadn't shown any signs of being violent, but if he started I would call the doctor. I made my father lots of hot, sweet drinks for shock, he kept going on about electric storage heaters and saying that he would spill the beans to the media.

He rang Doreen Slater up and she came round straightaway, she had a horrible little kid called Maxwell with her. It was quite a shock to see Doreen Slater for the first time. Why my father wanted to have carnal knowledge of her I can't imagine. She is as thin as a stick insect. She has got no bust and no bum.

She is just straight all the way up and down, including her nose and mouth and hair. She put her arms round my father as soon as she came into the house. Maxwell started to cry, the dog started to bark, so I went back to my black room and counted how many things were now showing through the paint: a hundred and seventeen!

Doreen left at 1.30 p.m. to take Maxwell to play-school. She did some shopping for us then cooked a sloppy sort of meal made of spaghetti and cheese. She is a one-parent family; Maxwell was born out of wedlock. She told me about herself when we were washing up. She would be quite nice if she were a bit fatter.

Tuesday June 2nd
NEW MOON

Doreen and Maxwell stayed the night. Maxwell was supposed to sleep on the sofa, but he cried so much that he ended up sleeping in the double bed between my father and Doreen, so my father was unable to extend his carnal knowledge of Doreen. He was as sick as a pig, but not as sick as Maxwell was. Ha! Ha! Ha!

Wednesday   June 3rd

Went to school today, couldn't concentrate, kept thinking about the stick insect. She has got lovely white teeth (straight of course). She made some jam tarts for when I came home from school. She is not stingy with the jam like some women are.

My father is smoking and drinking heavily, but he has been made temporarily impotent according to Doreen. This is something I do not wish to know! Doreen talks to me as if I were another adult instead of her lover's son aged fourteen and two months and one day.

Thursday   June 4th

Doreen answered the phone to my mother first thing this morning. My mother asked to speak to me. She demanded to know what Doreen was doing in the house. I told her that my father was having a breakdown and that Doreen Slater was looking after him. I told her about his redundancy. I said he was drinking heavily, smoking too much and generally letting himself go. Then I went to school. I was feeling rebellious, so I wore red socks. It is strictly forbidden but I don't care any more.

Friday   June 5th

Miss Sproxton spotted my red socks in assembly! The old bag reported me to pop-eyed Scruton. He had me in his office and gave me a lecture on the dangers of being a nonconformist. Then he sent me home to change into regulation black socks. My father was in bed when I got home; he was having his impotence cured. I watched *Play School* with Maxwell until he came downstairs. I told him about the sock saga.

He instantly turned into a raving loonie! He phoned the school and dragged Scruton out of a caretakers' strike-meeting. He kept shouting down the phone; he said, 'My wife's left me, I've been made redundant, I'm in charge of an idiot boy,' – Maxwell, I presume – 'and you're victimizing my son because of the colour of his socks!' Scruton said if I came to school in black socks everything would be forgotten but my father said I would wear whatever colour socks I liked. Scruton said he was anxious to maintain standards. My father said that the England World Cup team in 1966 did not wear black socks, nor did Sir Edmund Hillary in 1953. Scruton seemed to go quiet then. My father put the phone down. He said, 'Round one to me'.

This could well get into the papers: 'Black socks row at school.' My mother might read about it and come home.

Saturday   June 6th

Oh Joy! Oh Rapture! Pandora is organizing a sock protest! She came round to my house today! Yes! She actually stood on our front porch and told me that she admired the stand I was taking! I would have asked her in, but the house is in a squalid state so I didn't. She is going round the school with a petition on Monday morning. She said I was a freedom fighter for the rights of the individual. She wants me to go round her house tomorrow morning. A committee is being set up, and I am the principal speaker! She wanted to see the red socks but I told her they were in the wash.

Doreen Slater and Maxwell went home today. My grandma is coming round tonight, so all traces of them have got to be wiped out.

Sunday   June 7th
WHIT SUNDAY

Grandma found Maxwell's dummy in my father's bed. I lied and said that the dog must have brought it in off the street. It was a nasty moment. I am not a good liar, my face goes bright red and my grandma has got eyes like Superman's, they seem to bore right through you. To divert her I told her about the red-sock row, but she said rules were made to be kept.

Pandora and the committee were waiting for me in the big lounge of her house. Pandora is Chairperson, Nigel is Secretary and Pandora's friend Claire Neilson is Treasurer. Craig Thomas and his brother Brett are just ordinary supporters. I am not allowed to hold high office because I am the victim.

Pandora's parents were in the wooden kitchen doing *The Sunday Times* crossword. They seem to get on quite well together.

They brought a tray of coffee and health biscuits into the lounge for us. Pandora introduced me to her parents. They said they

admired the stand that I was taking. They are both members of the
Labour Party and they went on about the Tolpuddle Martyrs.
They asked me if the fact that I had chosen to protest in *red*
socks had any significance. I lied and said that I had chosen red
because it was a symbol of revolution, then I blushed revolutionary
red. I am turning into quite a liar recently.

Pandora's mother said I could call her Tania. Surely that is a
Russian name? Her father said I could call him Ivan. He is very
nice, he gave me a book to read; it is called *The Ragged Trousered
Philanthropists*. I haven't looked through it yet but I'm quite
interested in stamp collecting so I will read it tonight.

Washed red socks, put them on radiator to dry ready for the
morning.

Monday   June 8th

Woke up, dressed, put red socks on before underpants or vest.
Father stood at the door and wished me luck. Felt like a hero.
Met Pandora and rest of committee at corner of our road; all of
us were wearing red socks. Pandora's were lurex. She has certainly
got guts! We sang 'We shall not be moved' all the way to school.
I felt a bit scared when we went through the gates but Pandora
rallied us with shouts of encouragement.

Pop-eyed Scruton must have been tipped off because he was
waiting in the fourth-year cloakroom. He was standing very still
with his arms folded, staring with poached egg eyes. He didn't
speak, he just nodded us upstairs. All the red socks trooped
upstairs. My heart was beating dead loud. He went silently into
his office and sat at his desk and started tapping his teeth with a
school pen. We just stood there.

He smiled in a horrible way then rang the bell on his desk. His
secretary came in, he said, 'Sit down and take a letter, Mrs Claricoates'. The letter was to our parents, it said:

> Dear Mr and Mrs . . . .,
> It is my sad duty to inform you that your son/daughter has
> deliberately flaunted one of the rules of this school.
> I take an extremely serious view of this contravention. I am
> therefore suspending your son/daughter for a period of one
> week. Young people today often lack sufficient moral guidance

in the home, therefore I feel that it is my duty to take a firm stand in my school. If you wish to discuss the matter further with me do not hesitate to ring my secretary for an appointment.

> Yours faithfully,
> R. G. Scruton
> Headmaster

Pandora started to say something about her O levels suffering but Scruton roared at her to shut up! Even Mrs Claricoates jumped. Scruton said that we could wait until the letters had been typed, duplicated and signed and then we had better 'hot foot it out of school'. We waited outside Scruton's office. Pandora was crying (because she was angry and frustrated, she said). I put my arm round her a bit. Mrs Claricoates gave us our letters. She smiled very kindly, it can't be very easy working for a despot.

We went round to Pandora's house but it was locked, so I said everyone could come round to my house. It was quite tidy for once, apart from the dog hairs. My father raged about the letter. He is supposed to be a Conservative but he is not being very conservative at the moment.

I can't help wishing that I had worn black socks on Friday.

Tuesday   June 9th
MOON'S FIRST QUARTER

My father saw Scruton today and told him that if he didn't allow me back to school in whatever colour socks I liked he would protest to his MP. Mr Scruton asked my father who his MP was. My father didn't know.

Wednesday   June 10th

Pandora and I are in love! It is official! She told Claire Neilson, who told Nigel, who told me.

I told Nigel to tell Claire to tell Pandora that I return her love. I am over the moon with joy and rapture. I can overlook the fact that Pandora smokes five Benson and Hedges a day and has her own lighter. When you are in love such things cease to matter.

Thursday   June 11th

Spent all day with my love. Can't write much, my hands are still trembling.

Friday   June 12th

Had a message from the school to say that Bert Baxter wanted to see me urgently. Went round with Pandora (we are inseparable). Bert is ill. He looked awful. Pandora made his bed up with clean sheets (she didn't seem to mind the smell) and I phoned the doctor. I described Bert's symptoms. Funny breathing, white face, sweating.

We tried to clean the bedroom up a bit, Bert kept saying stupid things that didn't make sense. Pandora said that he was delirious. She held his hand until the doctor came. Dr Patel was quite kind, he said that Bert needed oxygen. He gave me a number to ring for an ambulance, it seemed to take ages to come. I thought about how I had neglected Bert lately and I felt a real rat fink. The ambulancemen took Bert downstairs on a stretcher. They got stuck on the corner of the stairs and knocked a lot of empty beetroot jars over. Pandora and me cleared a path through the rubbish in the downstairs hall and they steered him through. He was wrapped in a big, fluffy red blanket before he went outside. Then they shut him up in the ambulance and he was sirened away. I had a big lump in my throat and my eyes were watering. It must have been caused by the dust.

Bert's house is very dusty.

Saturday   June 13th

Bert is in intensive care, he can't have visitors. I ring up every four hours to find out how he is. I pretend to be a relative. The nurses say things like 'He is stable'.

Sabre is staying with us. Our dog is staying at grandma's because it is scared of alsatians.

I hope Bert doesn't die. Apart from liking him, I have got nothing to wear to a funeral.

Still madly in love with P.

Sunday   June 14th

Went to see Bert, he has got tubes all over him. I took him a jar of beetroot for when he is better. The nurse put it in his locker. I took some 'get well' cards, one from Pandora and me, one from my grandma, one from my father and one from Sabre.

Bert was asleep so I didn't stay long.

Monday   June 15th

The Red Sock Committee has voted to give way to Scruton for the time being. We wear red socks underneath our black socks. This makes our shoes tight but we don't mind because a principle is involved.

Bert has made a slight improvement. He is awake more. I'll go round and see him tomorrow.

Tuesday   June 16th

Bert has only got a few tubes left inside him now. He was awake when I went into his room. He didn't recognize me at first because I was wearing a mask and gown. He thought I was a doctor. He said, 'Get these bleedin' tubes out of my private parts, I ain't an underground system'. Then he saw it was me and asked how Sabre was. We had a long talk about Sabre's behaviour problems, then the nurse came in and told me I had to go. Bert aked me to tell his daughters that he is on his death bed; he gave me half-a-crown for the phone calls! Two of them live in Australia! He said the numbers are written down in the back of his old army pay-book.

My father says that half-a-crown is roughly worth twelve and a half pence. I am keeping the half-a-crown. It has got a nice chunky feel about it and it will no doubt be a collector's item one day.

Wednesday   June 17th

Pandora and me searched Bert's house looking for his army pay-book. Pandora found a pile of brown and cream postcards that were very indecent. They were signed '*avec tout mon amour chéri, Lola*'. I felt a bit funny after looking through them, so did Pandora. We exchanged our first really passionate kiss. I felt like doing a French kiss but I don't know how it's done so I had to settle for an ordinary English one.

No sign of the pay-book.

Thursday   June 18th

Bert is now tubeless. He is being moved into an ordinary ward tomorrow. I told him about not finding the army pay-book, he said it doesn't matter now he knows he's not dying.

Pandora came with me tonight. She got on well with Bert; they talked about Blossom. Bert passed on a few tips about grooming ponies. Then Pandora went out to arrange the flowers she'd bought and Bert asked me if I'd had my 'leg over' yet. Sometimes he is just a dirty old man who doesn't deserve visitors.

Friday   June 19th

Bert is on a big ward full of men with broken legs and bandaged chests. He looks a lot better now that he has got his teeth in. Some of the men whistled at Pandora when she walked down the ward. I wish she wasn't taller than me. Bert is in trouble with the ward sister for getting beetroot juice on the hospital sheets. He is supposed to be on a fluid diet.

Saturday   June 20th

I hope Bert can come home soon. My father is fed up with Sabre and my grandma is sick to death of our dog.

Bert's consultant has told him to give up smoking but Bert says at eighty-nine years old it is hardly worth it. He has asked me to buy him twenty Woodbines and a box of matches. What shall I do?

Sunday   June 21st
FIRST AFTER TRINITY. FATHER'S DAY

Couldn't sleep last night for worrying about the Woodbines. After much heart-searching decided not to grant Bert's wish. Then went to the hospital to find that Bert had bought his stinking fags from the hospital trolley!

Just measured my thing. It has grown one centimetre. I might be needing it soon.

Monday   June 22nd

Woke up with sore throat, couldn't swallow, tried to shout downstairs but could only manage a croak. Tried to attract my father's attention by banging on my bedroom floor with school shoe but my father shouted, 'Stop that bloody banging'. Eventually I sent the dog downstairs with a message tucked inside its collar. I waited for ages, then I heard the dog barking in the street. It hadn't delivered the message! I was close to despair. I had to get up to go to the toilet but how I got there I don't know; it is all a hazy blur. I stood at the top of the stairs and croaked as loud as I could but my father had his Alma Cogan records on so I was forced to go downstairs and tell him I was ill. My father looked in my mouth and said, 'Christ Almighty, Adrian, your tonsils look like Polaris missiles! What are you doing down here? Get back into bed at once, you fool'. He took my temperature: it was 112° Fahrenheit. By rights I should be dead.

It is now five minutes to midnight, the doctor is coming in the morning. I just pray that I can last out until then. Should the worst happen, I hereby leave all my worldly goods to Pandora Braithwaite of 69 Elm Tree Drive. I think I am of sound mind. It is very hard to tell when you've got a temperature of 112° Fahrenheit.

Tuesday   June 23rd

I have got tonsillitis. It is official. I am on antibiotics. Pandora sits by my bed reading aloud to me. I wish she wouldn't, every word is like a rock dropping on my head.

Wednesday   June 24th

A 'get well' card from my mother. Inside a five-pound note. I asked my father to spend it on five bottles of Lucozade.

Thursday   June 25th
MOON'S LAST QUARTER

I have delirious dreams about Lady Diana Spencer; I hope I am
better in time for the wedding. Temperature is still 112° Fahrenheit.

My father can't cope with Sabre, so Pandora has taken him home
with her. (Sabre, not my father).

Friday   June 26th

Doctor said our thermometer is faulty. I feel slightly better.

Got up for twenty minutes today. Watched *Play School*; it was
Carol Leader's turn, she is my favourite presenter.

Pandora brought me a 'get well' card. She made it herself with
felt-tip pens. She signed it: 'Forever yours, Pan.'

I wanted to kiss her but my lips are still cracked.

Saturday   June 27th

Why hasn't my mother been to see me?

Sunday   June 28th
SECOND AFTER TRINITY

My mother has just left to catch the train for Sheffield. I am worn
out with all the emotion. I am having a relapse.

Monday   June 29th

Pandora went to see Bert Baxter. She said the nurses are getting
fed up with him because he won't stay in bed or do anything he
is told to do. He is being discharged on Thursday.

I long for the peace and quiet of a hospital ward. I would be
a perfect patient.

Pandora's father has put Sabre into kennels, it is costing him three
pounds a day, but Pandora's father says that it is worth every penny.

Tuesday   June 30th

I am entering a period of convalescence. I will have to take things
very easily if I am to regain my former vigour.

Wednesday July 1st

The truant officer came round this afternoon; he caught me sitting in a deckchair in the front garden. He didn't believe I was ill! He is reporting me to the school! The fact that I was sipping Lucozade whilst wearing pyjamas, dressing gown and slippers seemed to have escaped him. I offered to show him my yukky tonsils but he backed away and trod on the dog's paw. The dog has got a low pain threshold so it went a bit berserk. My father came out and separated them but things could get nasty for us.

Thursday July 2nd

The doctor said I can go back to school tomorrow, depending on how I feel. You can depend that I won't feel up to it.

Friday July 3rd

A brown-skinned family are moving into Mr Lucas's old house! I sat in my deckchair and had a good view of their furniture being carried out of the removal van. The brown-skinned ladies kept taking massive cooking pots into the house so it looks as if they are a large family. My father said that it was 'the beginning of the end of our street'. Pandora is in the Anti-Nazi League. She said she thinks that my father is a possible racist.

I am reading *Uncle Tom's Cabin*.

Saturday July 4th

The street is full of brown-skinned people arriving or departing in cars, vans and mini-buses. They keep trooping in and out of Mr Lucas's old house. My father says they have probably got three families to each room.

Pandora and I are going round to welcome them to our district. We are determined to show that not all white people are racist fanatics.

Bert Baxter is still in hospital.

Sunday   July 5th
THIRD AFTER TRINITY

Stayed in bed until 6 p.m. There was no point in getting up. Pandora has gone to a gymkhana.

Monday   July 6th

Mrs O'Leary is trying to organize a street party for the Royal Wedding. The only people to put their names down so far are the Singh family.

Tuesday   July 7th

Bert Baxter has escaped from hospital. He telephoned the National Council for Civil Liberties and they told him he could sign himself out, so he did. He is in our spare room. My father is going up the wall.

Pandora, Bert and I have put our names down for the street party. Bert is looking much better now that he can smoke as many Woodbines as he likes.

Pandora's father has been round to talk to my father about what to do about Bert and Sabre. They both got drunk and started arguing about politics. Bert banged on the floor and asked them to keep their voices down.

Wednesday   July 8th

My father is near to despair because of Bert's snoring. It doesn't bother me, I put Blu-tack in my ears.

Went to school today. I have decided to take Domestic Science, Art, Woodwork and English O levels. I am doing Geography, Maths and History for CSE.

Pandora is taking nine O levels. But she has had more advantages than me. She has been a member of the library since she was three.

Thursday   July 9th

School breaks up for eight weeks tomorrow. Pandora is going to Tunisia soon. How I will survive without my love is anybody's guess. We have tried French kissing but neither of us liked it, so we have gone back to the English.

My skin is dead good. I think it must be a combination of being in love and Lucozade.

Friday   July 10th

It was magic at school today. All the teachers were in good moods. A rumour went round that pop-eyed Scruton was seen laughing but I didn't believe it myself.

Barry Kent climbed up the flagpole and flew a pair of his mother's knickers in the breeze. Pandora said it was probably the first airing they had had for years.

Sean O'Leary is nineteen today. He has invited me to his birthday party. It is only over the road so I won't have far to go.

I am writing up my diary now just in case I have one too many. People seem to get drunk just stepping over the O'Leary's threshold.

Saturday   July 11th

First proper hangover. Aged fourteen years, five months and nine days. Pandora put me to bed. She gave me a fireman's lift up the stairs.

Sunday   July 12th
FOURTH AFTER TRINITY

My father took me, Pandora and Bert to the Wagtails boarding kennels this morning. Mrs Kane, the proprietor, has refused to keep Sabre any longer. It was very touching to see Bert and Sabre reunited. Mrs Kane is a hard woman, she got very nasty when my father refused to pay Sabre's boarding fees, she kept smoothing her black moustache with her horny fingers and using unladylike language.

Bert said he won't be parted from Sabre again. He said that Sabre is his only friend in the world! After all *I* have done for him!! If it wasn't for me he would be a corpse by now, and Sabre would be an orphan living with the RSPCA.

Monday   July 13th

Bert has been talking to Mrs Singh! He speaks fluent Hindi! He says she has found some indecent magazines under the lino in the bathroom. An heirloom from that creep Lucas!

Mr Singh is outraged. He has written to the estate agents to complain that his house has been defiled.

Bert showed me one of the magazines. They are not indecent in my opinion, but then I am a man of the world. I have put it under my mattress with the *Big and Bouncy*s. It is called *Amateur Photographer*.

Tuesday   July 14th

Bert's social worker came round tonight. She is called Katie Bell. She talked to Bert in a stupid way. She said that Bert had been offered a place in the Alderman Cooper Sunshine Home. Bert told her that he didn't want to go. Katie Bell said that he has got to go. Even my father said that he felt sorry for Bert. But not sorry enough to invite Bert to live with us permanently I noticed!

Poor Bert, what will happen to him?

Wednesday   July 15th

Bert has moved in with the Singhs. Mr Singh fetched Sabre's kennel so it is official. Bert looks dead happy. His favourite food is curry.

Pandora has allowed me to touch her bust. I promised not to tell anyone, but there was nothing to tell really. I couldn't tell where her bust began through all the layers of underclothes, dress, cardigan and anorak.

I am reading *Sex, The Facts*, by Dr A. P. G. Haig.

Thursday   July 16th

11 a.m. My father got his redundancy cheque today. He did cowboy whoops up and down the hall. He has asked Doreen Slater to go out with him to celebrate. Guess who Maxwell's baby sitter is going to be? Yes, dear diary, you guessed right! It is I!

11 p.m. Maxwell has only just gone to sleep, Pandora rang up at nine-thirty and asked how I was doing. I couldn't hear her properly because Maxwell was screaming so loudly. Pandora said I should try putting vodka in some hot milk and forcing it down his vile throat. I have just done it. And it worked.

He is not a bad kid when he is asleep.

Friday   July 17th
FULL MOON

My precious love leaves these shores tomorrow. I am going to the airport to see her off. I hope her plane won't suffer from metal fatigue. I have just checked the world map to see where Tunisia is, and I am most relieved to see that Pandora won't have to fly through the Bermuda triangle.

If anything happened to my love I would never smile again.

I have brought her a book to read during the flight. It is called *Crash!*, by a bloke called William Goldenstein, III. It is very good on what to do if the worst happens.

Saturday   July 18th

Pandora read the *Crash!* book in the coach on the way to the airport. When her flight was called she had slight hysterics and her father had to carry her up the steps. I waved to the plane until it had retreated into a large cloud, then I sadly got on a coach and came back home. How I will get through the next fortnight I don't know. Good-night, my Tunisian beauty.

Sunday   July 19th
FIFTH AFTER TRINITY

Stayed in bed and looked at Tunisia on the map.

Monday   July 20th

Not had a postcard from my love yet.

Tuesday   July 21st

Bert came round this morning. He said that Tunisia is full of hazards.

Wednesday   July 22nd

Why haven't I had a postcard yet? What can have happened?

Thursday   July 23rd

Asked our postman about communications between Tunisia and England. He said that they were 'diabolical'; he said that the Tunisian GPO depends on camels.

Friday   July 24th
MOON'S LAST QUARTER

Went to see Mr Singh. He said that Tunisia is very unhygenic. Everybody but me seems to be familiar with Tunisia!

Saturday   July 25th

PANDORA! PANDORA! PANDORA!

> Oh! my love,
> My heart is yearning,
> My mouth is dry,
> My soul is burning.
> You're in Tunisia,
> I am here.
> Remember me and shed a tear.
> Come back tanned and brown and healthy.
> You're lucky that your dad is wealthy.

She will be back in six days.

Sunday   July 26th
SIXTH AFTER TRINITY

Went for tea at grandma's. I was sad and withdrawn because of
Pandora's sojourn in Tunisia. Grandma asked if I was constipated.
I nearly said something, but what's the use of trying to explain
love to a woman of seventy-six who thinks the word is obscene?

Monday   July 27th

A camel postcard! It said:

> Dearest,
> Economic conditions here are quite dreadful. I was going to
> buy you a present but instead I gave all my money to a beggar.
> You have such a generous heart Adrian that I feel sure you
> will understand.
> All my love into infinity.
>> For ever,
>> Pandora   X

Fancy giving my present money to a filthy, idle beggar! Even
our postman was disgusted.

Tuesday   July 28th

It's a wonder I have the strength to hold my pen! I have been
on the go all day with preparations for the Royal Wedding street
party. Mrs O'Leary came over and asked if I would help with the
bunting. I said 'I feel it is my patriotic duty'. Mrs O'Leary said
that if I climbed the ladder she would pass the bunting up to me.
I was all right for the first four or five rungs but then I made
the mistake of looking down and I had a vertigo attack, so Mrs
O'Leary did all the climbing. I couldn't help noticing Mrs
O'Leary's knickers. They are surprisingly sexy for someone who
goes to church every day and twice on Sundays. Black lace! With
red-satin ribbons! I got the feeling that Mrs O'Leary knew that
I was looking at her knickers because she asked me to call her
Caitlin. I was glad when Mr O'Leary came to take over from me.
Mr and Mrs Singh have hung a huge Union Jack out of their front
bedroom window. Bert told me that it was one he stole when he
was in the army.

Our house is letting the street down. All my father has done is pin a Charles and Diana tea towel to the front door.

My father and I watched the Royal Wedding firework display on television. All I can say is that I tried to enjoy it but failed. My father said it was one way of burning money. He is still bitter about being out of work.

I hope the Prince remembers to remove the price ticket off the bottom of his shoes; my father didn't at his wedding. Everyone in the church read the ticket. It said: '9½ reject, 10 shillings'.

Wednesday   July 29th

ROYAL WEDDING DAY!!!!!

How proud I am to be English!

Foreigners must be as sick as pigs!

We truly lead the world when it comes to pageantry! I must admit to having tears in my eyes when I saw all the cockneys who had stood since dawn, cheering heartily all the rich, well-dressed, famous people going by in carriages and Rolls-Royces.

Grandma and Bert Baxter came to our house to watch the wedding because we have got a twenty-four-inch colour. They got on all right at first but then Bert remembered he was a communist and started saying anti-royalist things like 'the idle rich' and 'parasites', so grandma sent him back to the Singhs' colour portable.

Prince Charles looked quite handsome in spite of his ears. His brother is dead good-looking; it's a shame they couldn't have swapped heads just for the day. Lady Diana melted my heartstrings in her dirty white dress. She even helped an old man up the aisle. I thought it was very kind of her considering it was her wedding day. Loads of dead famous people were there. Nancy Reagan, Spike Milligan, Mark Phillips, etc., etc. The Queen looked a bit jealous. I expect it was because people weren't looking at *her* for a change.

The Prince had remembered to take the price ticket off his shoes. So that was one worry off my mind.

When the Prince and Di exchanged rings my grandma started to cry. She hadn't brought her handkerchief so I went upstairs to get the spare toilet roll. When I came downstairs they were married. So I missed the Historic moment of their marriage!

I made a cup of tea during all the boring musical interval, but

I was back in time to see that Kiwi woman singing. She has certainly got a good pair of lungs on her.

Grandma and I were just settling down to watch the happy couple's triumphant ride back to the palace when there was a loud banging on the front door. We ignored it so my father was forced to get out of bed and open the door. Bert and Mr and Mrs Singh and all the little Singhs came in asking for sanctuary. Their telly had broken down! My grandma tightened her lips, she is not keen on black, brown, yellow, Irish, Jewish or foreign people. My father let them all in, then took grandma home in the car. The Singhs and Bert gathered round the television talking in Hindi.

Mrs Singh handed round some little cornish pasties. I ate one of them and had to drink a gallon of water. I thought my mouth had caught fire! They were not cornish pasties.

We watched television until the happy couple left Victoria station on a very strange-looking train. Bert said it was only strange-looking because it was clean.

Mrs O'Leary came in and asked if she could borrow our old chairs for the street party. In my father's absence I agreed and helped to carry them out on to the pavement. Our street looked dead weird without cars and with flags and bunting flapping about.

Mrs O'Leary and Mrs Singh swept the street clean. Then we all helped to put the tables and chairs out into the middle of the road. The women did all the work, the men stood around on the pavement drinking too much and making jokes about Royal Nuptials.

Mr Singh put his stereo speakers out of his lounge windows and we listened to a Des O'Connor LP whilst we set the tables with sandwiches, jam tarts, sausage rolls and sausages on sticks. Then everyone in our street was given a funny hat by Mrs O'Leary and we sat down to eat. At the end of the tea Mr Singh made a speech about how great it was to be British. Everyone cheered and sang 'Land of Hope and Glory'. But only Mr Singh knew all the words. Then my father came back with four party packs of light ale and two dozen paper cups, and soon everyone was acting in an undignified manner.

Mr O'Leary tried to teach Mrs Singh an Irish jig but he kept getting tangled up in her sari. I put my Abba LP on and turned the volume up high and soon even the old people of forty and over were dancing! When the street lamps came on Sean O'Leary climbed up and put red, white and blue crepe paper over the bulbs to help the atmosphere and I fetched our remaining candles and put them on the tables. Our street looked quite Bohemian.

Bert told some lies about the war, my father told jokes. The party went on until one o'clock in the morning!

Normally they get a petition up if you clear your throat after eleven o'clock at night!

I didn't dance, I was an amused, cynical observer. Besides my feet were aching.

Thursday   July 30th

I have seen the Royal Wedding repeats seven times on television.

Friday   July 31st
NEW MOON

Sick to death of Royal Wedding.

Pandora, the beggar's friend, is coming home tomorrow.

Saturday   August 1st

Postcard from my mother, she wants me to go on holiday with her and creep Lucas. They are going to Scotland. I hope they enjoy themselves.

Pandora's flight has been delayed because of a baggage-handlers' strike in Tunis.

Sunday   August 2nd
SEVENTH AFTER TRINITY

The baggage-handlers are still on strike and Pandora's father has had his American Express card stolen by a beggar!

Pandora said that her mother has been bitten by a camel but is recovering in the Ladies' toilet at Tunis airport. It was wonderful to hear Pandora's voice on the telephone, we talked to each other for over half an hour. How clever it was of her to arrange a reverse-charge call from Tunisia!

Monday   August 3rd
BANK HOLIDAY IN SCOTLAND AND REP. OF IRELAND

The Tunisian baggage-handlers have agreed to go to arbitration.
Pandora says that with luck she'll be home by Thursday.

Tuesday   August 4th

The Tunisian baggage-handlers can see light at the end of the
tunnel.
   Pandora is surviving on packets of dates and Polo mints.

Wednesday   August 5th

The Tunisian baggage-handlers are now handling baggage. *Pandora
home FRIDAY EVENING!*

Thursday   August 6th

My father refused a reverse-charges call from Tunisia. Our lines
of communication have been cut.

Friday   August 7th
MOON'S FIRST QUARTER

I rang Tunisia whilst my father was in the bath. He shouted down
to ask whom I was phoning. I told a lie. I said I was phoning
the speaking clock.
   Pandora's flight left safely. She should be home around midnight.

Saturday   August 8th

At 7 a.m. Pandora rang from St Pancras station. She said that due
to electrification of the track at Flitwick she would be delayed.
   I got dressed and went down to the station, got a platform ticket,
waited on platform two for six cold, lonely hours. Went home to
find a note from Pandora. This is what is said:

> Adrian,
> I confess to feeling hearbroken at your apparent coldness
> concerning my arrival. I felt sure that we would have an

emotional reunion on platform three. But it was not to be.
Adieu,
Pandora

Went to Pandora's house. Explained. Had an emotional reunion behind her father's tool shed.

Sunday   August 9th
EIGHTH AFTER TRINITY

Touched Pandora's bust again. This time I think I felt something soft. My thing keeps growing and shrinking, it seems to have a life of its own. I can't control it.

Monday   August 10th

Pandora and I went to the swimming baths this morning. Pandora looked superb in her white string bikini. She has gone the same colour as Mrs Singh. I didn't trust my thing to behave so I sat in the spectators' gallery and watched Pandora diving off the highest diving board. Got back to my house. Showed her my black room. Lit a joss stick. Put Abba LP on, sneaked a bottle of Sanatogen upstairs. We indulged in a bit of light petting but then Pandora developed a headache and went home to rest.

I was racked with sexuality but it wore off when I helped my father put manure on our rose bed.

Tuesday   August 11th

Got another postcard from my mother.

Dear Aidy,
You've no idea how much I long to see you. The mothering bond is as strong as ever. I know you feel threatened by my involvement with Bimbo, but really Aidy there is no need. Bimbo fulfils my sexual needs. No more, no less. So, Aidy, grow up and come to Scotland.
Lots of love,
Pauline (mother)

P.S. We leave on the fifteenth. Catch 8.22 train to Sheffield.

The postman said that if my mother was his wife he would give her a good thrashing. He doesn't know my mother. If anybody laid a finger on *her* she would beat them to pulp.

Wednesday   August 12th

Pandora thinks a trial separation will do us good. She says our light to medium petting will turn quite heavy soon. I must admit that the strain is having a detrimental affect on my health. I have got no energy and my sleep is constantly interrupted with dreams about Pandora's white bikini and Mrs O'Leary's knickers.

I might go to Scotland after all.

Thursday   August 13th

My father has decided to go to Skegness on the fifteenth. He has booked a four-berth caravan. He is taking Doreen and Maxwell with him! He expects me to go!

If I go people will automatically assume that Doreen is my mother and Maxwell is my brother!

I am going to Scotland.

Friday August 14th

Had tragic last night with Pandora. We have both sworn to be true. I have done all my packing. The dog has been taken round to grandma's with fourteen tins of Pedigree Chum and a giant sack of Winalot.

I am taking *Escape from Childhood*, by John Holt, to read on the train.

Saturday   August 15th
FULL MOON

My father, Stick Insect and Maxwell House saw me off at the station. My father didn't mind a bit that I chose to go to Scotland instead of Skegness. In fact he looked dead cheerful. The train journey was terrible. I had to stand all the way to Sheffield. I spoke to a lady in a wheelchair who was in the guard's van. She was very nice, she said that the only good thing about being handicapped was that you always got a seat in trains. Even if it *was* in the guard's van.

My mother and creep Lucas met me at Sheffield. My mother looked dead thin and has started dressing in clothes that are too young for her. Lucas creep was wearing jeans! His belly was hanging over his belt. I pretended to be asleep until we got to Scotland.

Lucas mauled my mother about even whilst he was driving.

We are at a place called Loch Lubnaig. I am in bed in a log cabin. My mother and Lucas have gone to the village to try to buy cigarettes. At least that is their story.

Sunday   August 16th
NINTH AFTER TRINITY

There is a loch in front of the cabin and a pine forest and a mountain behind the cabin. There is nothing to do. It is dead boring.

Monday   August 17th

Did some washing in a log cabin launderette. Spoke to an American tourist called Hamish Mancini; he is the same age as me. His mother is on her honeymoon for the fourth time.

Tuesday   August 18th

Rained all day.

Wednesday   August 19th

Sent postcards. Phoned Pandora, reversed charges. Her father refused to accept them.

Thursday   August 20th

Played cards with Hamish Mancini. His mother and stepfather and my mother and her lover have gone to see a waterfall in the car. Big deal!

Friday   August 21st

Walked two and a half miles into Callander to buy Mars bar. Played on Space Invaders. Came back, had tea. Phoned Pandora from log cabin phone box. Reversed charges. She still loves me. I still love her. Went to bed.

Saturday   August 22nd
MOON'S LAST QUARTER

Went to see Rob Roy's grave. Saw it, came back.

Sunday   August 23rd
TENTH AFTER TRINITY

My mother has made friends with a couple called Mr and Mrs Ball. They have gone off to Stirling Castle. Mrs Ball has got a daughter who is a writer. I asked her how her daughter qualified to be one. Mrs Ball said that her daughter was dropped on her head as a child and has been 'a bit queer' ever since.

It is Mrs Ball's birthday so they all came back to our log cabin to celebrate. I complained about the noise at 1 a.m., 2 a.m., 3 a.m. and 4 a.m. At 5 a.m. they decided to climb the mountain! I pointed out to them that they were blind drunk, too old, unqualified, unfit and lacking in any survival techniques, had no first-aid kit, weren't wearing stout boots, and had no compass, map or sustaining hot drinks.

My protests fell on deaf ears. They all climbed the mountain, came down and were cooking eggs and bacon by 11.30 a.m.

As I write, Mr and Mrs Ball are canoeing on the loch. They must be on drugs.

Monday   August 24th

Went to Edinburgh. Saw the castle, the toy museum, the art gallery. Bought a haggis. Came back to log cabin, read *Glencoe*, by John Prebble. We are going there tomorrow.

Tuesday   August 25th

The massacre of Glencoe took place on February 13 1692. On February 14, John Hill wrote to the Earl of Tweeddale, 'I have ruined Glencoe'.

He was dead right, there is nothing there. Glasgow tomorrow.

Wednesday   August 26th

We drove through Glasgow at 11 a.m. in the morning yet I counted twenty-seven drunks in one mile! All the shops except the DIY shops had grilles at the windows. Off-licences had rolls of barbed wire and broken glass on their roofs. We had a walk round for a bit, then my mother nagged Lucas creep into taking her to the Glasgow art gallery. I intended to sit in the car and read *Glencoe*, but because of all the drunks staggering around I reluctantly followed them inside.

How glad I am that I did! I might have gone through life without having an important cultural experience!

Today I saw Salvador Dali's painting of the Crucifixion !!! *The real one!* Not a reproduction!

They have hung it at the end of a corridor so that it changes as you get nearer to it. When you are finally standing up close to it you feel like a midget. It is absolutely fantastic!

Huge! With dead good colours and Jesus looks like a real bloke. I bought six postcards of it from the museum but of course it is not the same as the real thing.

One day I will take Pandora to see it. Perhaps on our honeymoon.

Thursday   August 27th

Oban today. Bumped into Mr and Mrs Swallow who live in the next street to me. Everyone kept saying, 'It's a small world isn't it?' Mrs Swallow asked creep Lucas how his wife was. Lucas told her that his wife had left him for another woman. Then everyone blushed and said 'what a small world it was' and parted company. My mother went mad at Lucas. She said 'Do you have to tell everyone?' and 'How do you think I feel living with a lesbian's estranged husband?'. Lucas whined on for a bit but then my mother started looking like my grandma. So he kept quiet.

Friday   August 28th

Fort William today. Ben Nevis was another disappointment. I couldn't tell where it began or stopped. The other mountains and hills clutter it up. Lucas fell in the burn (Scottish for 'little river') but unfortunately it was too shallow to drown in.

Saturday   August 29th
FULL MOON

Went for a walk around the loch with Hamish Mancini. He told me that he thinks his mother is heading for her fifth divorce. He is going home tonight; he has got an appointment with his analyst in New York on Monday morning.

I have finished my packing and I am waiting for my mother and creep Lucas to come back from their furtive love-making somewhere in the pine forest.

We leave at dawn.

Sunday   August 30th
ELEVENTH AFTER TRINITY

I made Lucas stop for souvenirs at Gretna Green. I bought Pandora a pebble shaped like an otter, Bert a tam-o'-shanter, the dog a tartan bow for its neck, grandma a box of tartan fudge, Stick Insect Tartan biscuits, Maxwell a tartan sweet dummy. I bought my father a tartan tea towel.

I bought myself a tartan scribbling pad. I am determined to become a writer.

Here is an extract from 'My thoughts on Scotland' written on the M6 at 120 mph:

> The hallowed mist rolls away leaving Scotland's majestic peaks revealed in all their majesty. A shape in the translucent sky reveals itself to be an eagle, that majestic bird of prey. Talons clawing, it lands on a loch, rippling the quiet majesty of the turbulent waters. The eagle pauses only to dip its majestic beak into the aqua before spreading its majestic wings and flying away to its magisterial nest high in the barren, arid, grassless hills.

The Highland cattle. Majestic horned beast of the glens lowers its brown eyed shaggy haired majestic head as it ruminates on the mysteries of Glencoe.

There are a couple too many 'majestics'. But I think it reads rather well. I will send it to the BBC when it's finished. Got home at 6 p.m. Too tired to write more.

Monday   August 31st
BANK HOLIDAY IN UK (EXCEPT SCOTLAND)

Everyone is broke. The banks are closed and my father can't remember the secret code on his plastic moneycard. He had the nerve to borrow five pounds from Bert Baxter. Fancy asking an old age pensioner for money! It lacks dignity.

Pandora and I are now insanely in love! The separation only served to fuel our passion. Our hormones are stirred every time we meet. Pandora slept with the otter pebble in her hand last night. How I wish the otter pebble could have been me.

Tuesday   September 1st

Mr Singh has had to return to India to look after his aged parents, so Bert has been told that he will have to move back into his dirty old house! Mr Singh says that he cannot trust his womenfolk to be alone in the house with Bert. How stupid can you get? Bert doesn't mind too much; he said that it is 'quite a compliment'.

Pandora and I are going to clean Bert's house and help him move back. He owes the council two hundred and ninety-four pounds in rent arrears. He has got to pay the arrears off at fifty pence a week, so it is a certainty that Bert will die in debt.

Wednesday   September 2nd

Pandora and I went to look at Bert's house today. It is a truly awesome sight. If Bert took all his empty beer bottles back to the off-licence he might get enough money on the empties to pay off his rent arrears.

Thursday September 3rd

My father helped us to move all of the furniture out of the ground floor of Bert's house, the woodworms came out to sunbathe. When we lifted the carpets we discovered that Bert had been walking about on a layer of dirt, old newspapers, hairpins, marbles and decomposed mice for years. We hung the carpets on the washing line and beat them all afternoon, but the dust billowed out non-stop. Pandora got excited at about 5 p.m., she claimed she could see a pattern emerging on one carpet, but closer examination showed it to be squashed fairy cake. We are going back tomorrow with Pandora's mother's carpet-shampooer. Pandora said it has been tested by *Which?*, but I bet it has never had to clean a filthy hovel like Bert Baxter's before.

Friday September 4th

I have just witnessed a miracle! This morning Bert's carpets were dark grey in colour. Now one is a red Axminster and the other is a blue Wilton. The carpets are hanging on the clothes line to dry. We have scraped all the floors clean and washed the furniture down with a fungicide disinfectant. Pandora took the curtains down but they fell to pieces before she could get them to the sink. Bert has been sitting in a deckchair criticizing and complaining. He can't see what's wrong with living in a dirty house.

What *is* wrong with living in a dirty house?

Saturday September 5th

My father took Bert's bottles to the off-licence this morning. The boot, back seat and floor of the car were filled with them. The car stank of brown ale. He ran out of petrol on the way and called the AA. The AA man was most uncivil, he said it wasn't the Automobile Association my father needed, it was Alchoholics Anonymous!

Sunday September 6th
TWELFTH AFTER TRINITY. MOON'S FIRST QUARTER

Bert's house looks great. Everything is dead clean and shiny. We have moved his bed into the lounge so that he can watch television in bed. Pandora's mother has done very artistic arrangements with flowers, and Pandora's father has made an alsatian flap in the back door so that Bert doesn't keep having to get up to answer the door to Sabre.

Bert is moving back in tomorrow.

Monday   September 7th
LABOR DAY, USA AND CANADA

An airmail letter from Hamish Mancini.

> Hi Aid!
> Howya doin'? I hope the situation Pandora-wise is ongoing! She sounds kinda zappy! Scotland blew my mind! It was so far out as to be nuked! You're a great human being, Aid. I guess I was kinda traumatized when we rapped but Dr Eagelburger (my shrink) is doing great things with my libido. Mom's really wiped out right now, turns out number four is a TV and has a better collection of Calvin Kleins than she do! Don't you think the fall is a drag? Son-of-a-bitch leaves everywhere!
> > See you, Buddy!!!
> > Hamish

I showed it to Pandora, my father and Bert but nobody understands it. Bert doesn't like Americans because it took them too long to come into the war or something.

Bert now in his clean house. He hasn't said thank-you, but he seems happy.

Tuesday   September 8th

Lousy stinking school on Thursday. I tried my old uniform on but I have outgrown it so badly that my father is being forced to buy me a new one tomorrow.

He is going up the wall but I can't help it if my body is in a growth period can I? I am only five centimetres shorter than Pandora now. My thing remains static at twelve centimetres.

Wednesday   September 9th

Grandma phoned, she has found out about Doreen and Maxwell going to Skegness. She is never speaking to my father again.

Here is my shopping list:

Blazer	£29.99
2 pairs grey trousers	£23.98
2 white shirts	£11.98
2 grey pullovers	£7.98
3 pairs black socks	£2.37
1 pair PE shorts	£4.99
1 PE vest	£3.99
1 track suit	£11.99
1 pair training shoes	£7.99
1 pair football boots and studs	£11.99
1 pair football socks	£2.99
Football shorts	£4.99
Football shirt	£7.99
Adidas sports bag	£4.99
1 pair black shoes	£15.99
1 calculator	£6.99
Pen and pencil set	£3.99
Geometry set	£2.99

My father can easily spare a hundred pounds. His redundancy payment must have been huge, so why he is lying on his bed moaning I don't know. He is just a mean skinflint! He hasn't paid with *real* money anyway! He used his American Express card.

Pandora admired me in my new uniform. She says she thinks I stand a good chance of being made a prefect.

Thursday   September 10th

A proud start to the new term. I am a prefect! My first duty is as late duty prefect. I have to wait by the gap in the railings and take the name of anyone sneaking late into school. Pandora is also a prefect. She is in charge of silence in the dinner queue.

My new timetable was given to me today by my new form tutor, Mr Dock. It includes my O level and CSE lessons, and it is compulsary to do Maths, English, PE and Comparative Religion. But they do give you a choice of Cultural and Creative subjects. So I have chosen Media Studies (dead easy, just reading newspapers and watching telly) and Parentcraft (just learning about sex, I hope). Mr Dock also teaches English Literature, so we are bound to get on, by now I am surely the best-read kid in the school. I will be able to help him out if he gets stuck.

Asked my father for five pounds fifty for school trip to the British Museum. He went beserk and said, 'What happened to free education?' I told him that I didn't know.

Friday   September 11th

Had a long talk with Mr Dock. I explained that I was a one-parent-family child with an unemployed, bad-tempered father. Mr Dock said he wouldn't care if I was the offspring of a black, lesbian, one-legged mother and an Arab, leprous, humpbacked-dwarf father so long as my essays were lucid, intelligent and unpretentious. So much for pastoral care!

Saturday   September 12th

Wrote lucid, intelligent and unpretentious essay about Scottish wild life in the morning. In afternoon did shopping in Sainsbury's with my father. Saw Rick Lemon dithering at the fruit counter; he said selecting fruit was an 'overtly political act'. He rejected South African apples, French golden delicious apples, Israeli oranges, Tunisian dates, and American grapefruits. In the end he selected English rhubarb, 'Although,' he said, 'the shape was phallic, possibly sexist'. His girlfriend, Tit (short for Titia), was cramming the trolley with pulses and rice. She had a long skirt on but now and again I caught a glimpse of her hairy ankles. My father said he preferred a nice shaven leg any day. My father likes stockings, suspenders, mini-skirts and low necklines! He is dead old-fashioned.

Sunday   September 13th
THIRTEENTH AFTER TRINITY

Went to see Blossom. Pandora doesn't ride her now because her feet drag on the ground. Pandora is having a proper horse delivered

next week. It is called Ian Smith. The people who are selling it
used to live in Africa, in Zimbabwe.

Tomorrow is my mother's birthday. She is thirty-seven.

Monday   September 14th
FULL MOON

Phoned my mother before school. There was no answer. I expect
she was lying in bed with that stinking rat Lucas.

School dinners are complete crap now. Gravy seems to have
been phased out along with custard and hot puddings. A typical
menu is: hamburger, baked beans, chips, carton of yoghurt or a
doughnut. It's not enough to build healthy bone and sinew. I am
considering making a protest to Mrs Thatcher. It won't be our
fault if we grow up apathetic and lacking in moral fibre. Perhaps
Mrs Thatcher wants us to be too weak to demonstrate in years
to come.

Tuesday   September 15th

Barry Kent has been late three times in one week. So it is my
unfortunate duty to report him to Mr Scruton.

Unpunctuality is the sign of a disordered brain. So he cannot
go unpunished.

Wednesday   September 16th

Our form is going to the British Museum on Friday. Pandora and
I are going to sit together on the coach. She is bringing her *Guardian*
from home so that we can have some privacy.

Thursday   September 17th

Had a lecture on the British Museum from Ms Fossington-Gore.
She said it was a 'fascinating treasure house of personkind's achieve-
ments'. Nobody listened to the lecture. Everyone was watching
the way she felt her left breast whenever she got excited.

Friday   September 18th

2 a.m. Just got back from London. Coach driver suffered from motorway madness on the motorway. I am too shaken by the experience to be able to give a lucid or intelligent account of the day.

Saturday   September 19th

The school may well want a clear account by an unprejudiced observer of what happened on the way to, during, and coming back from our trip to London. I am the only person qualified. Pandora, for all her qualities, does not possess my nerves of steel.

Class Four-D's Trip to the British Museum
7 a.m.   Boarded coach.
7.05   Ate packed lunch, drank low-calorie drink.
7.10   Coach stopped for Barry Kent to be sick.
7.20   Coach stopped for Claire Neilson to go to the Ladies.
7.30   Coach left school drive.
7.35   Coach returned to school for Ms Fossington-Gore's handbag.
7.40   Coach driver observed to be behaving oddly.
7.45   Coach stopped for Barry Kent to be sick again.
7.55   Approached motorway.
8 a.m.   Coach driver stopped coach and asked everyone to stop giving 'V' signs to lorry drivers.
8.10   Coach driver loses temper, refuses to drive on motorway until 'bloody teachers control kids'.
8.20   Ms Fossington-Gore gets everyone sitting down.
8.25   Drive on to motorway.
8.30   Everyone singing 'Ten Green Bottles'.
8.35   Everyone singing 'Ten Green Snotrags'.
8.45   Coach driver stops singing by shouting very loudly.
9.15   Coach driver pulls in at service station and is observed to drink heavily from hip-flask.
9.30   Barry Kent hands round bars of chocolate stolen from self-service shop at service station. Ms Fossington-Gore chooses Bounty bar.
9.40   Barry Kent sick in coach.
9.50   Two girls sitting near Barry Kent are sick.

9.51 Coach driver refuses to stop on motorway.

9.55 Ms Fossington-Gore covers sick in sand.

9.56 Ms Fossington-Gore sick as a dog.

10.30 Coach crawls along on hard shoulder, all other lanes closed for repairs.

11.30 Fight breaks out on back seat as coach approaches end of motorway.

11.45 Fight ends. Ms Fossington-Gore finds first-aid kit and sees to wounds. Barry Kent is punished by sitting next to driver.

11.50 Coach breaks down at Swiss Cottage.

11.55 Coach driver breaks down in front of A A man.

12.30 Class Four-D catch London bus to St Pancras.

1 p.m. Class Four-D walk from St Pancras through Bloomsbury.

1.15 Ms Fossington-Gore knocks on door of Tavistock House, asks if Dr Laing will give Barry Kent a quick going-over. Dr Laing in America on lecture tour.

1.30 Enter British Museum. Adrian Mole and Pandora Braithwaite awestruck by evidence of heritage of World Culture. Rest of class Four-D run beserk, laughing at nude statues and dodging curators.

2.15 Ms Fossington-Gore in state of collapse. Adrian Mole makes reverse-charge phone call to headmaster. Headmaster in dinner lady strike-meeting, can't be disturbed.

3 p.m. Curators round up class Four-D and make them sit on steps of museum.

3.05 American tourists photograph Adrian Mole saying he is a 'cute English schoolboy'.

3.15 Ms Fossington-Gore recovers and leads class Four-D on sightseeing tour of London.

4 p.m. Barry Kent jumps in fountain at Trafalgar Square, as predicted by Adrian Mole.

4.30 Barry Kent disappears, last seen heading towards Soho.

4.35 Police arrive, take Four-D to mobile police unit, arrange coach back. Phone parents about new arrival time. Phone headmaster at home. Claire Neilson has hysterical fit. Pandora Braithwaite tells Ms Fossington-Gore she is a disgrace to teaching profession. Ms Fossington-Gore agrees to resign.

6 p.m.   Barry Kent found in sex shop. Charged with theft of 'grow-it-big' cream and two 'ticklers'.

7 p.m.   Coach leaves police station with police escort.

7.30   Police escort waves goodbye.

7.35   Coach driver begs Pandora Braithwaite to keep order.

7.36   Pandora Braithwaite keeps order.

8 p.m.   Ms Fossington-Gore drafts resignation.

8.30   Coach driver afflicted by motorway madness.

8.40   Arrive back. Tyres burning. Class Four-D struck dumb with terror. Ms Fossington-Gore led off by Mr Scruton. Parents up in arms. Coach driver charged by police.

Sunday   September 20th
FOURTEENTH AFTER TRINITY. MOON'S LAST QUARTER

Keep having anxiety attacks every time I think about London, culture or the M1. Pandora's parents are lodging an official complaint to everyone they can think of.

Monday   September 21st

Mr Scruton complimented Pandora and I on our leadership qualities. Ms Fossington-Gore is on sick leave. All future school trips have been cancelled.

Tuesday   September 22nd

The police have dropped charges against coach driver because there is 'evidence of severe provocation'. The sex shop are not pressing charges either because officially Barry Kent is a child. A child! Barry Kent has never been a child.

Wednesday   September 23rd

Mr Scruton has now read my report on the trip to London. He gave me two merit marks for it!

It was on the news today that the British Museum is thinking of banning school parties.

Thursday   September 24th

Pandora and I are enjoying the last of the autumn together by walking through leaves and sniffing bonfires. This is the first year I have been able to pass a horse-chestnut tree without throwing a stick at it.

Pandora says I am maturing very quickly.

Friday   September 25th

Went out conkering with Nigel tonight. I found five big beauties and smashed Nigel's into pulp. Ha! Ha! Ha!

Saturday   September 26th

Took Blossom to see Bert. He can't walk far these days.

Blossom is being sold to a rich family, a girl called Camilla is going to learn to ride on her. Pandora says Camilla is so posh as to be unintelligible. Bert was dead sad, he said, 'You and me will both end up in the knacker's yard, gel'.

Sunday   September 27th
FIFTEENTH AFTER TRINITY

Blossom went off at 10.30 a.m. I gave her a sixteen-pence apple to take her mind off the heartbreak. Pandora ran after the little horse-box shouting, 'I've changed my mind', but it carried on.

Pandora has also changed her mind about Ian Smith. She never wants to see another pony or horse again. She is guilt-ridden about selling Blossom.

Ian Smith turned up at 2.30 p.m. and was turned away. There was an evil look on his black face as he stood in his horse-box and was driven away. Pandora's father is going to his bank early tomorrow to cancel the cheque he wrote out last Thrusday. There was an evil look on his face as well.

Monday   September 28th
NEW MOON

Bert has got something wrong with his legs. The doctor says he needs daily nursing. I went in today but he is too heavy for me to lug about. The district nurse thinks that Bert will be better off in the Alderman Cooper Sunshine Home. But I don't think he will. I pass by it on my way to school. It looks like a museum. The old people look like the exhibits.

> Bert, you are dead old.
> Fond of Sabre, beetroot and Woodbines.
> We have nothing in common,
> I am fourteen and a half,
> You are eighty-nine.
> You smell, I don't.
> Why we are friends
> Is a mystery to me.

Tuesday   September 29th

Bert doesn't get on with his district nurse. He says he doesn't like having his privates mauled about by a woman. Personally, I wouldn't mind it.

Wednesday   September 30th

I am glad September is nearly over, it has been nothing but trouble. Blossom gone. Pandora sad. Bert on his last legs. My father still out of work. My mother still besotted with creep Lucas.

Thursday   October 1st

7.30 a.m. Just woke up to find chin covered in spots! How can I face Pandora?

10 p.m. Avoided Pandora all day but she caught up with me in school dinners. I tried to eat with my hand over my chin but it proved very difficult. I confessed to her during the yoghurt. She accepted my disability very calmly. She said it made no difference to our love but I couldn't help thinking that her kisses lacked their usual passion as we were saying good-night after youth club.

Friday   October 2nd

6 p.m. I am very unhappy and have once again turned to great literature for solace. It's no surprise to me that intellectuals commit suicide, go mad or die from drink. We feel things more than other people. We know the world is rotten and that chins are ruined by spots. I am reading *Progress, Coexistence and Intellectual Freedom*, by Andrei D. Sakharov.

It is 'an inestimably important document' according to the cover.

11.30 p.m. Progress, Coexistence and Intellectual Freedom is inestimably *boring*, according to me, Adrian Mole.

I disagree with Sakharov's analysis of the causes of the revivalism of Stalinism. We are doing Russia at school so I speak from knowledge.

Saturday   October 3rd

Pandora is cooling off. She didn't turn up at Bert's today. I had to do his cleaning on my own.

Went to Sainsbury's as usual in the afternoon; they are selling Christmas cakes. I feel that my life is slipping away.

I am reading *Wuthering Heights*. It is brilliant. If I could get Pandora up somewhere high, I'm sure we could regain our old passion.

Sunday   October 4th
SIXTEENTH AFTER TRINITY

Persuaded Pandora to put her name down for the youth club's mountain survival course in Derbyshire. Rick Lemon is sending an equipment list and permission form to our parents. Or in my case to my parent. I have only got two weeks to reach peak condition. I try to do fifty press-ups a night. I try to do them but fail. Seventeen is my best so far.

Monday   October 5th

Bert has been kidnapped by Social Services! They are keeping him at the Alderman Cooper Sunshine Home. I have been to see him. He shares a room with an old man called Thomas Bell. They have both got their names on their ashtrays. Sabre has got a place in the RSPCA hostel.

Our dog has gone missing. It is a portent of doom.

Tuesday   October 6th
MOON'S FIRST QUARTER

Pandora and I went to visit Bert, but it was a waste of time really.

His room had a strange effect on us, it made us not want to talk about anything. Bert says he is going to sue Social Services, for depriving him of his rights. He says he has to go to bed at nine-thirty! It is not fair because he is used to staying up until after *The Epilogue*. We passed the lounge on our way out. The old people sat around the walls in high chairs. The television was on but nobody was watching it, the old people looked as though they were thinking.

Social Services have painted the walls orange to try to cheer the old people up. It doesn't seem to have worked.

Wednesday   October 7th

Thomas Bell died in the night. Bert says that nobody leaves the home alive. Bert is the oldest inmate. He is dead worried about dying. He is now the only man in the entire home. Pandora says that women outlive men. She says it is a sort of bonus because women have to suffer more earlier on.

Our dog is still missing. I have put an advert in Mr Cherry's shop.

Thursday   October 8th

Bert is still alive so I took Sabre to visit him today. We propped
Bert up at the window of his room and he waved to Sabre who
was on the lawn outside. Dogs are not allowed inside the home.
It is another of their poxy rules.

Our dog is still missing, now presumed dead.

Friday   October 9th

The matron of the home says that if Bert is dead good he can
come out for the day on Sunday. He is coming to our house for
Sunday dinner and tea. The phone bill has come. I have hidden
it under my mattress. It is for £289.19p.

Saturday   October 10th

I am really worried about our dog. It has vanished off the face
of our suburb. Nigel, Pandora and I have walked the cul-de-sacs
looking for it.

Another worry is my father. He lies in bed until noon, then
fries a mess in a pan, eats it, opens a can or bottle, then sits
and watches *After Noon Plus*. He is making no attempt to find
another job. He needs a bath, a haircut and a shave. It is Parents'
Night at school next Tuesday. I have taken his best suit to the
cleaner's.

I bought a book from W. H. Smith's, it was only five pence.
It was written by an unsuccessful writer called Drake Fairclough;
it is called *Cordon Bleu for the Elderly*. Bert is coming tomorrow.
Pandora's father has ordered their phone to be taken out. He has
found out about the reverse-charge calls.

Sunday   October 11th
SEVENTEENTH AFTER TRINITY

BERT'S VISIT
I got up early this morning and cleared the furniture out of the
hall so that Bert's wheelchair had room for manoeuvre. I made
my father a cup of coffee and took it up to him in bed, then I
started cooking geriatric *coq au vin*. I left it on to boil whilst I

went back upstairs to reawaken my father. When I got downstairs I knew that I'd made a mess of the *coq au vin*. All the vinegar had boiled away and left burnt chicken. I was most disappointed because I was thinking of making my debut as a cook today. I wanted to impress Pandora with my multi talents, I think she is getting a bit bored with my conversation about great literature and the Norwegian leather industry.

Bert insisted on bringing a big trunk with him when Pandora's father picked him up at the home. So what with that and his wheelchair and Bert sprawling all over the back seat I was forced to crouch in the hatch of the hatchback car. It took ages to get Bert out of the car and into his wheelchair. Almost as long as it took me to get my father out of bed.

Pandora's father stayed for a quick drink, then a pre-lunch one, then a chaser, then one for the road. Then he had one to prove that he never got drunk during the day. Pandora's lips started to go thin (women must teach young girls to do this). Then she confiscated her father's car keys and phoned her mother to come and collect the car. I had to endure watching my father do his imitation of some bloke called Frank Sinatra singing 'One for my baby and one more for the road'. Pandora's father pretended to be the bartender with our Tupperware custard jug. They were both drunkenly singing when Pandora's mother came in. Her lips were so thin they had practically disappeared. She ordered Pandora and Pandora's father out into the car, then she said that it was about time my father pulled himself together. She said she knew my father felt humiliated, alienated and bitter because he was unemployed, but that he was setting a bad example to an impressionable adolescent. Then she drove off at 10 mph. Pandora blew me a kiss through the rear windscreen.

I object strongly! Nothing my father does impresses me any more. Had Vesta curry and rice for dinner, during which Mrs Singh came round and talked Hindi to Bert. She seemed to find our curry very funny, she kept pointing to it and laughing. Sometimes I think I am the only person in the world who still has manners.

Bert told my father that he is convinced the matron is trying to poison him (Bert, not my father), but my father said that all institutional food is the same. When it was time to go home, Bert started crying. He said, 'Don't make me go back there', and other sad things. My father explained that we didn't have the skill to look after him at our house, so Bert was wheeled to the car (although he kept putting the brake of the wheelchair on). He asked us to keep his trunk at our house. He said it was to be opened on his death. The key is round his neck on a bit of string.

Dog is still AWOL.

Monday   October 12th
COLUMBUS DAY, USA. THANKSGIVING DAY, CANADA

Went to the 'off-the-streets' youth club tonight. Rick Lemon gave us a lecture on survival techniques. He said that the best thing to do if you are suffering from hypothermia is to climb into a plastic bag with a naked woman. Pandora made a formal objection, and Rick Lemon's girlfriend, Tit, got up and walked away. It is just my luck to be on the mountain with a frigid woman!

RIP Dog.

Tuesday   October 13th
FULL MOON

Had an angry phone call from my grandma to ask when we were coming round to collect the dog! The stupid dog turned up at her house on the 6th October. I went round immediately and was shocked at the dog's condition: it looks old and grey. In human years it is eleven years old. In dog years it should be drawing a pension. I have never seen a dog age so quickly. Those eight days with grandma must have been hell. My grandma is very strict.

Wednesday   October 14th

I have nearly got used to the old ladies in the home now. I call in every afternoon on my way home from school. They seem pleased to see me. One of them is knitting me a balaclava for my survival weekend. She is called Queenie.

Did thirty-six and a half press-ups tonight.

Thursday   October 15th

Went to the youth club to try yukky, lousy old walking boots for size. Rick Lemon has hired them from a mountaineering shop. To make mine fit I have to wear three pairs of socks. Six of us are going. Rick is leading us.

He is unqualified but experienced in surviving bad conditions. He was born and brought up in Kirkby New Town. I went to Sainsbury's and bought my survival food. We have got to carry our food and equipment in our rucksacks, so weight is an important factor. I bought:

> 1 box cornflakes
> 2 pints milk
> box tea-bags
> tin rhubarb
> 5 lb spuds
> ½ lb lard
> ½ lb butter
> 2 loaves bread
> 1 lb cheese
> 2 packets biscuits
> 2 lb sugar
> toilet roll
> washing-up liquid
> 2 tins tuna
> 1 tin stewed steak
> 1 tin carrots

I could hardly carry my survival food home from Sainsbury's, so how I will manage it on a march across the hills I don't know! My father suggested leaving something out. So I have not packed the toilet roll or cornflakes.

Friday   October 16th

Have decided not to take my diary to Derbyshire. I cannot guarantee that it will not be read by hostile eyes. Besides it won't fit into my rucksack.

Must finish now, the mini-bus is outside papping its hooter.

Saturday   October 17th

Sunday   October 18th
EIGHTEENTH AFTER TRINITY

8 p.m. It is wonderful to be back in civilization!

I have lived like an ignoble savage for the past two days! Sleeping on rough ground with only a sleeping-bag between me and the elements! Trying to cook chips over a tiny primus stove! Trudging through streams in my torturous boots! Having to perform my natural functions out in the open! Wiping my bum on leaves! Not being able to have a bath or clean my teeth! No television or radio or anything! Rick Lemon wouldn't even let us sit in the mini-bus when it started to rain! He said we ought to make a shelter out of nature's bounty! Pandora found a plastic animal-food sack so we took it in turns sitting under it.

How I survived I don't know. My eggs broke, my bread got saturated, my biscuits got crushed and nobody had a tin-opener. I nearly starved. Thank God cheese doesn't leak, break, soak up water or come in a tin. I was glad when we were found and taken to the Mountain Rescue headquarters. Rick Lemon was told off for not having a map or compass. Rick said he knew the hills like the back of his hand. The chief mountain rescuer said that Rick must have been wearing gloves because we were seven miles from our mini-bus and heading in the wrong direction!

I shall now sleep in a bed for the first time in two days. No school tomorrow because of blisters.

Monday   October 19th

I have got to rest my feet for two days. Doctor Gray was very unpleasant: he said that he resented being called out for a few foot blisters.

I was very surprised at his attitude. It is a well-known fact that mountaineers get gangrene of the toes.

Tuesday October 20th
MOON'S LAST QUARTER

Here I am lying in bed unable to walk because of excruciating pain and my father carries out his parental responsibilities by throwing a few bacon sandwiches at me three times a day!

If my mother doesn't come home soon I will end up deprived and maladjusted. I am already neglected.

Wednesday October 21st

Hobbled to school. All the teachers were wearing their best clothes because it is Parents' Evening tonight. My father got cleaned up and put his best suit on. He looked OK, Thank God! Nobody could tell he was unemployed. My teachers all told him that I was a credit to the school.

Barry Kent's father was looking as sick as a pig. Ha! Ha! Ha!

Thursday October 22nd

Limped half-way to school. Dog followed me. Limped back home. Shut dog in coal shed. Limped all the way to school. Fifteen minutes late. Mr Scruton said it was not setting a good example for the late prefect to be late. It is all right for him to talk! He can ride to school in a Ford Cortina and then all he has to do is be in charge of a school. I have got a lot of problems and no car.

Friday October 23rd

I have had a letter from the hospital to say that I have got to have my tonsils out on Tuesday the twenty-seventh. This has come as a complete shock to me! My father says I have been on the waiting list since I was five years old! So I have had to endure an annual bout of tonsillitis for nine years just because the National Health Service is starved of finance!

Why can't midwives remove babies' tonsils at birth? It would save a lot of trouble, pain and money.

Saturday October 24th
UNITED NATIONS' DAY

Went shopping for new dressing gown, slippers, pyjamas, and toiletries. My father was moaning as usual. He said he didn't see why I couldn't just wear my old night-clothes in hospital. I told him that I would look ridiculous in my Peter Pan dressing gown and Winnie the Pooh pyjamas. Apart from the yukky design they are too small and covered in patches. He said that when he was a lad he slept in a nightshirt made out of two coal sacks stitched together. I phoned my grandma to check this suspicious statement and my father was forced to repeat it down the phone. My grandma said that they were not coal sacks but flour sacks, so I now know that my father is a pathological liar!

My hospital rig came to fifty-four pounds nineteen; this is before fruit, chocolates and Lucozade. Pandora said I looked like Noël Coward in my new bri-nylon dressing gown. I said, 'Thanks, Pandora', although to be honest I don't know who Noël Coward is or was. I hope he's not a mass murderer or anything.

Sunday October 25th
NINETEENTH AFTER TRINITY. BRITISH SUMMER TIME ENDS

Phoned my mother to tell her about my coming surgical ordeal. No reply. This is typical. She would sooner be out having fun with creep Lucas than comforting her only child!

Grandma rang and said that she knew somebody who knew somebody who knew somebody who had their tonsils out and bled to death on the operating theatre table. She ended up by saying, 'Don't worry Adrian, I'm sure everything will be all right for you.'

Thanks a million, grandma!

Monday October 26th
BANK HOLIDAY IN THE REP. OF IRELAND

11 a.m. I did my packing, then went to see Bert. He is sinking fast so it could be the last time we see each other. Bert also knows somebody who bled to death after a tonsils' extraction. I hope it's the same person.

Said goodbye to Pandora: she wept very touchingly. She brought me one of Blossom's old horseshoes to take into hospital. She said a friend of her father had a cyst removed and didn't come out of the anaesthetic. I'm being admitted to Ivy Swallow Ward at 2 p.m. Greenwich Mean Time.

6 p.m. My father has just left my bedside after four hours of waiting around for permission to leave. I have had every part of my body examined. Liquid substances have been taken from me, I have been weighed and bathed, measured and prodded and poked, but nobody has looked in my throat!

I have put our family medical dictionary on my bedside table so that the doctors see it and are impressed. I can't tell what the rest of the ward is like yet because the nurses have forgotten to remove the screens. A notice has been hung over my bed; it says 'Liquids Only'. I am dead scared.

10 p.m. I am starving! A black nurse has taken all my food and drink away. I am supposed to go to sleep but it is like bedlam in here. Old men keep falling out of bed.

Midnight. There is a new notice over my bed; it says 'Nil by Mouth'. I am dying of thirst! I would give my right arm for a can of Low Cal.

Tuesday   October 27th
NEW MOON

4 a.m. I am dehydrated!

6 a.m. Just been woken up! Operation is not until 10 a.m. So why couldn't they let me sleep? I have got to have another bath. I told them that it is the *inside* of my body that is being operated on, but they don't listen.

7 a.m. A Chinese nurse stayed in the bathroom to make sure I didn't drink any water. She kept staring so I had to put a hospital sponge over my thing.

7.30 a.m. I am dressed like a lunatic, ready for the operation. I have had an injection, it is supposed to make you sleepy but I'm wide awake listening to a row about a patient's lost notes.

8 a.m. My mouth is completely dry, I shall go mad from thirst, I haven't had a drink since nine forty-five last night, I feel very floaty, the cracks in the ceiling are very interesting. I have got to find somewhere to hide my diary. I don't want prying Nosy Parkers reading it.

8.30 a.m. My mother is at my bedside! She is going to put my diary in her organizer-handbag. She has promised (on the dog's life) not to read it.

8.45 a.m. My mother is in the hospital grounds smoking a cigarette. She is looking old and haggard. All the debauchery is catching up with her.

9 a.m. The operating trolley keeps coming into the ward and dumping unconscious men into beds. The trolley-pushers are wearing green overalls and wellingtons. There must be loads of blood on the floor of the theatre!

9.15 a.m. The trolley is coming in my direction!

Midnight. I am devoid of tonsils. I am in a torrent of pain. It took my mother thirteen minutes to find my diary. She doesn't know her way round her organizer-handbag yet. It has got seventeen compartments.

Wednesday   October 28th

I am unable to speak. Even groaning causes agony.

Thursday   October 29th

I have been moved to a side ward. My suffering is too much for the other patients to bear.

Had a 'get well' card from Bert and Sabre.

Friday   October 30th

I was able to sip a little of grandma's broth today. She brought it in her Thermos flask. My father brought me a family pack of crisps; he might just as well have brought me razor blades!

Pandora came at visiting time, I had little to whisper to her. Conversation palls when one is hovering between life and death.

Saturday   October 31st
HALLOWE'EN

3 a.m. I have been forced to complain about the noise coming from the nurses' home. I am sick of listening to (and watching) drunken nurses and off-duty policemen cavorting around the grounds dressed as witches and wizards. Nurse Boldry was doing something particularly unpleasant with a pumpkin.

I am joining BUPA as soon as they'll have me.

Sunday November 1st
TWENTIETH AFTER TRINITY

The nurses have been very cold towards me. They say that I am taking up a bed that could be used by an ill person! I have got to eat a bowl of cornflakes before they let me out. So far I have refused; I cannot bear the pain.

Monday November 2nd

Nurse Boldry forced a spoon of cornflakes down my damaged throat, then, before I could digest it, she started stripping my bed. She offered to pay for a taxi, but I told her that I would wait for my father to come and carry me out to the car.

Tuesday November 3rd
ELECTION DAY, USA

I am in my own bed. Pandora is a tower of strength. She and I communicate without words. My voice has been damaged by the operation.

Wednesday November 4th

Today I croaked my first words for a week. I said, 'Dad, phone mum and tell her that I am over the worst'. My father was overcome with relief and emotion. His laughter was close to hysteria.

Thursday November 5th
MOON'S FIRST QUARTER

Dr Gray says my malfunctioning voice is 'only adolescent wobble'. He is always in a bad mood!

He expected me to stagger to his surgery and queue in a germ-filled waiting room! He said I ought to be outside with other lads of my age building a bonfire. I told him that I was too old for such paganistic rituals. He said he was forty-seven and he still enjoyed a good burn-up.

Forty-seven! It explains a lot, he should be pensioned off.

Friday   November 6th

My father is taking me to an organized bonfire party tomorrow (providing I am up to it, of course). It is being held to raise funds for Marriage Guidance Councillors' expenses.

Pandora's mother is cooking the food and Pandora's father is in charge of the fireworks. My father is going to be in charge of lighting the bonfire so I'm going to stand at least a hundred metres away. I have seen him singe his eyebrows many times.

Last night some irresponsible people down our street had bonfire parties in their own back gardens!

Yes!

In spite of being warned of all the dangers by the radio, television, *Blue Peter* and the media they went selfishly ahead. There were no accidents, but surely this was only luck.

Saturday   November 7th

The Marriage Guidance Council bonfire was massive. It was a good community effort. Mr Cherry donated hundreds of copies of a magazine called *Now*! He said they had been cluttering up the back room of his shop for over a year.

Pandora burnt her collection of *Jackie* comics, she said that they 'don't bear feminist analysis' and she 'wouldn't like them to get into young girls' hands'.

Mrs Singh and all the little Singhs brought along Indian firecrackers. They are much louder than English ones. I was glad our dog was locked in the coal shed with cotton wool in its ears.

Nobody was seriously burnt, but I think it was a mistake to hand out fireworks at the same time the food was being served.

I burnt the red phone bill that came this morning.

Sunday   November 8th
TWENTY-FIRST AFTER TRINITY. REMEMBRANCE SUNDAY

Our street is full of acrid smoke. I went to see the bonfire, the *Now* magazines are still in the hot ashes, they are refusing to burn properly. (Our red phone bill has disappeared, thank God!)

Mr Cherry is going to have to dig a big pit and pour quick-lime over the *Now* magazines before they choke the whole suburb.

Went to see Bert. He was out with Queenie.

Monday   November 9th

Back to school. The dog is at the vet's having the cotton wool surgically removed.

Tuesday   November 10th

My nipples have swollen! I am turning into a girl!!!

Wednesday   November 11th

VETERANS' DAY, USA. REMEMBRANCE DAY, CANADA. FULL MOON

Dr Gray has struck me off his list! He said nipple-swelling is common in boys. Usually they get it when they are twelve and a half. Dr Gray said I was emotionally and physically immature! How can I be immature? I have had a rejection letter from the BBC! And how could I have walked to the surgery with swollen nipples?

I don't know why he calls it a surgery anyway; he never does any surgery in it.

Thursday   November 12th

Told Mr Jones I couldn't do PE because of swollen nipples. He was extremely crude in his attitude. I don't know what they teach them at teacher-training college.

Friday   November 13th

Pandora and I had a frank talk about our relationship tonight. She doesn't want to marry me in two years' time!

She wants to have a career instead!

Naturally I am devastated by this blow. I told her I wouldn't mind her having a little job in a cake shop or something after our wedding, but she said she intended to go to university and that the only time she would enter a cake shop would be to buy a large crusty.

Harsh words were exchanged between us. (Hers were harsher than mine.)

Saturday   November 14th

Charred *Now!* magazines are blowing all over our cul-de-sac. They seem to have special powers of survival. The council have sent a special cleaning squad to try and trap them all.

The dog's ears are now clear of cotton wool. It only pretends not to hear.

Went to see B.B. but he is out with Queenie. She is pushing him around the leisure centre.

Sunday   November 15th
TWENTY-SECOND AFTER TRINITY

Read *A Town Like Alice*, by Nevil Shute, it is dead brill. I wish I had an intellectual friend whom I could discuss great literature with. My father thinks *A Town Like Alice* was written by Lewis Carroll.

Monday   November 16th

I came home from school with a headache. All the noise and shouting and bullying is getting me down! Surely teachers should be better behaved!

Tuesday   November 17th

My father is a serious worry to me. Even the continuing news of Princess Diana's conception does not cheer him up.

Grandma has already knitted three pairs of bootees and sent them off care of Buckingham Palace. She is a true patriot.

Wednesday   November 18th
MOON'S LAST QUARTER

The trees are stark naked.
Their autumnal clothes

Litter the pavements.
Council sweepers apply fire
Thus creating municipal pyres.
I, Adrian Mole,
Kick them
And burn my Hush Puppies.

I have copied it out carefully and sent it to John Tydeman at the BBC. He strikes me as a man who might like poems about autumn leaves.

I have got to get something broadcast or printed soon else Pandora will lose all respect for me.

Thursday November 19th

Pandora has suggested I start a literary magazine using the school duplicator. I wrote the first edition during dinner time. It is called *The Voice of Youth*.

Friday November 20th

Pandora looked at *The Voice of Youth*. She suggested that instead of writing the whole magazine myself, I invite contributions from other talented scribblers.

She said she would do a piece about window-box gardening. Claire Neilson has submitted a punk poem, it is very avant garde, but I am not afraid to break new ground.

Punk Poem
Society is puke,
Soiled vomit.
On the Union Jack
Sid was vicious
Johnnie's rotten,
Dead, dead, dead.
Killed by greyness.
England stinks.
Sewer of the world.
Cess-pit of Europe.
Hail punks,
Kings and Queens
Of the street.

She wants it put in under an assumed name, her father is a Conservative councillor.

Nigel has written a short piece about racing-bike maintenance. It is very boring but I can't tell him because he is my best friend.

We go to press on Wednesday.

Pandora is typing the stencils over the weekend.

Here is my first editorial:

> Hi Kids,
> Well here's your very own school magazine. Yes! Written and produced entirely using child labour. I have tried to break new ground in our first edition. Many of you will be unaware of the miracles of window-box gardening and the joys of racing-bike maintenance. If so, hang on to your hats, you're in for a magic surprise!
> ADRIAN MOLE, EDITOR

We are going to charge twenty-five pence a copy.

Saturday November 21st

Pandora's father has stolen a box of stencils from his office. As I write, Pandora is typing the first pages of *The Voice of Youth*. I am half-way through writing an exposé about Barry Kent. It is called 'Barry Kent: The Truth!' He hasn't dared to lay a finger on me since grandma's dramatic intervention, so I know I shall be safe.

Too busy to go and see Bert, I will go tomorrow.

Sunday November 22nd
LAST AFTER TRINITY

Finished the exposé on Barry Kent. It will rock the school to its foundations. I have mentioned Barry Kent's sexual perversions – all about his disgusting practice of showing his thing for five pence a look.

Monday November 23rd

Had a Christmas card from grandma, and a letter from the post office to say that they are cutting the phone off!

Forgot to call round and see Bert. Pandora and I were too busy putting the paper to bed. How I wish I was putting Pandora to bed.

2 a.m. What am I going to do about the phone bill?

Tuesday   November 24th

Nigel has just gone off in a sulk. He objected to the editing I did on his article. I tried to point out to him that one thousand five hundred words on bicycle spokes was pure self-indulgence, but he wouldn't listen. He has withdrawn his article. Thank God! Two pages less to fold.

The Voice of Youth hits the classrooms tomorrow.

Must go and see Bert tomorrow.

Wednesday   November 25th

We have been hit by a wildcat strike! Mrs Claricoates, the school secretary, has refused to handle *The Voice of Youth*. She says there is nothing in her job description to say she has to mess about with school magazines.

The editorial team offered to duplicate copies ourselves, but Mrs Claricoates says that she alone knows how to 'work the wretched thing'. I am in despair. A whole six hours' work wasted!

Thursday   November 26th
THANKSGIVING DAY, USA. NEW MOON

Pandora's father is photocopying *The Voice of Youth* on his office machine. He didn't want to, but Pandora sulked in her room and refused to eat until he agreed.

Friday   November 27th

Five hundred copies of *The Voice of Youth* were on sale in the dinner hall today.

Five hundred copies were locked in the games cupboard by the end of the afternoon. Not one copy was sold! Not one! My fellow pupils are nothing but Philistines and Morons!

We are dropping the price to twenty pence on Monday.

My mother phoned and wanted to speak to my father. I told her that he is on a fishing weekend with the Society of Redundant Electric Storage Heater Salesmen.

A postcard from the post office to say that unless my father phones the post office before five-thirty our phone will be disconnected.

Saturday   November 28th

A telegram! Addressed to me! The BBC? No, from my mother:
    ADRIAN STOP COMING HOME STOP
    What does she mean 'Stop coming home'? How can I 'stop coming home'? I live here.
    The phone has been cut off! I am considering running away from home.

Sunday   November 29th
ADVENT SUNDAY

My mother has just turned up with no warning! She had all her suitcases with her. She has thrown herself on the mercy of my father. My father has just thrown himself on the body of my mother. I tactfully withdrew to my bedroom where I am now trying to work out how I feel about my mother's return. On the whole I am over the moon, but I'm dreading her looking around our squalid house. She will go mad when she finds out that I have lent Pandora her fox-fur coat.

Monday   November 30th
ST ANDREW'S DAY

My mother and father were still in bed when I left for school.
    Sold one copy of *The Voice of Youth*, to Barry Kent. He wanted to discover the truth about himself. He is a slow reader so it will probably take him until Friday to find out. We are going to try dropping the price to fifteen pence to try to stimulate demand. There are now four hundred and ninety-nine copies to be sold!
    My mother and father are in bed again and its only 9 p.m.!
    The dog is very pleased my mother is back. It has been going about smiling all day.

Tuesday   December 1st

I called the post office and pretended to be my father. I spoke in a very deep voice and told a lot of lies. I said that I, George Mole, had been in a lunatic asylum for three months and I needed the phone to ring up the Samaritans, etc. The woman sounded dead horrible, she said she was fed up with hearing lame excuses from irresponsible non-payers. She said that the phone would only be reconnected when £289.19 had been paid, plus £40 reconnection fee, plus a deposit of £40!

Three hundred and sixty-nine pounds! When my parents get out of bed and discover the lack of dialling tone, I will be done for!

Wednesday   December 2nd

My father tried to phone up after a job today! He has gone beserk.

My mother cleaned my bedroom, she turned up my mattress and found the *Big and Bouncy*s and the blue phone bill.

I sat on the kitchen stool while they interrogated me and shouted abuse. My father wanted to give me a 'to-within-an-inch-of-his-life thrashing', but my mother stopped him. She said, 'It would be more of a punishment to make the tight-fisted sod cough up some of his building-society savings'. So that is what I'm being forced to do.

Now I will never be an owner-occupier.

Thursday   December 3rd

Drew out two hundred pounds from my building-society account. I don't mind admitting that there were tears in my eyes. It will take another fourteen years before I can replace it.

Friday   December 4th
MOON'S FIRST QUARTER

I am suffering from severe depression. It is all Pandora's father's fault. He should have had a holiday in England.

Saturday   December 5th

Had a letter from grandma to ask why I hadn't sent her a Christmas card yet.

Sunday   December 6th
SECOND IN ADVENT

I am still being treated like a criminal. My mother and father are not speaking to me, and I'm not allowed out. I might just as well turn to delinquency.

Monday   December 7th

Stole a Kevin Keegan key ring from Mr Cherry's shop. It will do for Nigel's Christmas present.

Tuesday   December 8th

I am dead worried about the key ring; we did Morals and Ethics at school today.

Wednesday   December 9th

Can't sleep for worrying about the key ring. The papers are full of stories about old ladies getting done for shoplifting. I tried to over-pay Mr Cherry for my Mars bar, but he called me back and gave me my change.

Thursday   December 10th

Had a dream about a jailer locking me in a prison cell. The big iron key was attached to the Kevin Keegan key ring.

The lousy, stinking, sodding phone is reconnected!

Friday   December 11th
FULL MOON

Phoned the Samaritans and confessed my crime. The man said, 'Put it back then, lad'. I will do it tomorrow.

Saturday   December 12th

Mr Cherry caught me in the act of replacing the key ring. He has written a letter to my parents. I might as well do myself in.

Sunday   December 13th
THIRD IN ADVENT

Thank God there is no post on Sundays.

My mother and father had a festive time decorating the Christmas tree. I watched them hanging the baubles with a heavy heart.

I am reading *Crime and Punishment*. It is the most true book I have ever read.

Monday   December 14th

Got up at 5 a.m. to intercept the postman. Took the dog for a walk in the drizzle. (It wanted to stay asleep, but I wouldn't let it.) The dog moaned and complained all the way round the block so in the end I let it climb back into it's cardboard box. I wish I was a dog; they haven't got any ethics or morals.

The postman delivered the letters at seven-thirty when I was sitting on the toilet. This is just my luck!

My father collected the letters and put them behind the clock. I had a quick look through them while he was coughing on his first cigarette of the day. Sure enough there was one addressed to my parents in Mr Cherry's uneducated handwriting!

My mother and father slopped over each other for a few minutes and then opened the letters whilst their Rice Krispies were going soggy. There were seven lousy Christmas cards, which they put up on a string over the fireplace. My eyes were focused on Mr Cherry's letter. My mother opened it, read it and said, 'George, that old git Cherry's sent his bloody paper bill in'. Then 'hey ate their Rice Krispies and that was that. I wasted a lot of adrenalin worrying. I won't have enough left if I'm not careful.

Tuesday   December 15th

My mother has told me why she left creep Lucas and returned to my father. She said, 'Bimbo treated me like a sex object, Adrian, and he expected his evening meal cooked for him, and he cut his toe-nails in the living room, and besides I'm very fond of your father'. She didn't mention me.

Wednesday   December 16th

I am in an experimental Nativity play at school. It is called *Manger to Star*. I am playing Joseph. Pandora is playing Mary. Jesus is played by the smallest first-year. He is called Peter Brown. He is on drugs to make him taller.

Thursday   December 17th

Another letter from the BBC!

> Dear Adrian Mole,
> Thank you for submitting your latest poem. I understood it perfectly well once it had been typed. However, Adrian, understanding is not all. Our Poetry Department is inundated with Autumnal poems. The smell of bonfires and the crackling of leaves pervade the very corridors. Good try, but try again, eh?
> Yours with Best Wishes,
> John Tydeman

'Try again'! He is almost giving me a commission. I have written back to him:

> Dear Mr Tydeman,
> How much will I get if you broadcast one of my poems on the radio? When do you want me to send it? What do you want it to be about? Can I read it out myself? Will you pay my train fare in advance? What time will it go out on the airways? I have to be in bed by ten.
> Yours faithfully,
> A. Mole

> P.S. I hope you have a dead good Christmas.

Friday   December 18th
MOON'S LAST QUARTER

Today's rehearsal of *Manger to Star* was a fiasco. Peter Brown has grown too big for the crib, so Mr Animba, the Woodwork teacher, has got to make another one.

Mr Scruton sat at the back of the gym and watched rehearsals. He had a face like the north face of the Eiger by the time we'd got to the bit where the three wise men were reviled as capitalist pigs.

He took Miss Elf into the showers and had a 'Quiet Word'. We all heard every word he shouted. He said he wanted to see a traditional Nativity play, with a Tiny Tears doll playing Jesus and three wise men dressed in dressing gowns and tea towels. He threatened to cancel the play if Mary, alias Pandora, continued to go into simulated labour in the manger. This is typical of Scruton, he is nothing but a small-minded, provincial, sexually-inhibited fascist pig. How he rose to become a headmaster I do not know. He has been wearing the same hairy green suit for three years. How can we change it all now? The play is being performed on Tuesday afternoon.

My mother has had a Christmas card from creep Lucas! Inside he had written, 'Paulie, Have you got the dry-cleaning ticket for my best white suit? Sketchley's are being very difficult'. My mother was very upset. My father rang Sheffield and ordered Lucas to cease communications, or risk getting a bit of Sheffield steel in between his porky shoulder blades. My father looked dead good on the telephone. He had a cigarette stuck between his lips. My mother was leaning on the corner of the fridge. She had a cigarette in her hand. They looked a bit like the Humphrey Bogart and Lauren Bacall postcard on my wall. I wish I was a *real* gangster's son, at least you would see a bit of life.

Saturday   December 19th

I've got no money for Christmas presents. But I have made my Christmas list in case I find ten pounds in the street.

> Pandora – Big bottle of Chanel No. 5 (£1.50)
> Mother – Egg-timer (75p)
> Father – Bookmark (38p)

Grandma – Packet of J cloths (45p)
Dog – Dog chocolates (45p)
Bert – 20 Woodbines (95p)
Auntie Susan – Tin of Nivea (60p)
Sabre – Box of Bob Martins, small (39p)
Nigel – Family box of Maltesers (34p)
Miss Elf – Oven-glove (home-made)

Sunday   December 20th
FOURTH IN ADVENT

Pandora and I had a private Mary and Joseph rehearsal in my
bedroom. We improvised a great scene where Mary gets back from
the Family Planning Clinic and tells Joseph she's pregnant. I played
Joseph like Marlon Brando in *A Streetcar Named Desire*. Pandora
played Mary a bit like Blanche Dubois; it was dead good until my
father complained about the shouting. The dog was supposed to be
the lowly cattle, but it wouldn't keep still long enough to make a
tableau.

After tea my mother casually mentioned that she was going to
wear her fox-fur coat to the school concert tomorrow. Shock!
Horror! I immediately went round to Pandora's house to get the
mangy coat, only to find that Pandora's mother has borrowed it to
go to the Marriage Guidance Christmas dinner and dance! Pandora
said that she hadn't realized that the coat was only on loan; she
thought it was a lover's gift! How can a $14\frac{1}{2}$-year-old schoolboy
afford to give a fox-fur coat as a gift? Who does Pandora think
I am, a millionaire like Freddie Laker?

Pandora's mother won't be back until the early hours so I will
have to go round before school and sneak the coat into its plastic
cover. It's going to be difficult, but then nothing in my life is simple
or straightforward any more. I feel like a character in a Russian
novel half the time.

Monday   December 21st

Woke up with a panic attack to see that it was eight-fifty by my
bedside digital! My black walls looked unusually light and sparkly;
one glance outside confirmed my suspicions that indeed the snow
lay outside like a white carpet.

I stumbled through the snow to Pandora's house in my father's fishing boots but found that the house was devoid of humans. I looked through the letterbox and saw my mother's fur coat being mauled about by Pandora's ginger cat. I shouted swear-words at it but the lousy stinking cat just looked sarcastic and carried on dragging the coat around the hall. I had no choice but to shoulder-charge the laundry room door and rush into the hall and rescue my mother's coat. I left quickly (as quickly as anyone can wearing thigh-length fishing boots, four sizes too big). I put the fur coat on to keep me warm on my hazardous journey home. I nearly lost my bearings at the corner of Ploughman's Avenue and Shepherd's Crook Drive, but I fought my way through the blizzard until I saw the familiar sight of the prefabricated garages on the corner of our cul-de-sac.

I fell into our kitchen in a state of hypothermia and severe exhaustion; my mother was smoking a cigarette and making mince pies. She screamed, 'What the bloody hell are you doing wearing my fox-fur coat?' She was not kind or concerned or anything that mothers are supposed to be. She fussed about, wiping snow off the coat and drying the fur with a hair dryer. She didn't even offer to make me a hot drink or anything. She said, 'It's been on the radio that the school is closed because of the snow, so you can make yourself useful and check the camp beds for rust. The Sugdens are staying over Christmas.' The Sugdens! My mother's relations from Norfolk! Yuk, Yuk. They are all inbred and can't speak properly!

Phoned Pandora to explain about the fox fur and the damage, etc., but she had gone skiing on the slope behind the Co-op bakery. Pandora's father asked me to get off the line, he had to make an urgent phone call to the police station. He said he had just come home and discovered a break-in! He said the place was a shambles (the cat must have done it, I was very careful), but fortunately the only thing that was missing was an old fox-fur coat that Pandora had lined the cat's basket with.

Sorry Pandora, but this is the final straw that broke the donkey's back! You can find yourself another Joseph, I refuse to share the stage with a girl who puts her cat's comfort before her boyfriend's dilemma.

Tuesday   December 22nd

School was closed this morning because the teachers couldn't manage to get in on time because of the snow. That will teach them to live in old mill houses and windmills out in the country! Miss Elf lives with a West Indian in a terraced house in the town, so she bravely turned out to prepare for the school concert in the afternoon. I decided to forgive Pandora for the fox fur in the cat's basket incident after she had pointed out that the cat was an expectant mother.

The school concert was not a success. The bell ringing from class One-G went on too long, my father said 'The Bells! The Bells!', and my mother laughed too loudly and made Mr Scruton look at her.

The school orchestra was a disaster! My mother said, 'When are they going to stop tuning-up and start playing?' I told her that they had just played a Mozart horn concerto. That made my mother and father and Pandora's mother and father start laughing in a very unmannerly fashion. When ten-stone Alice Bernard from Three-C come on stage in a tutu and did the dying swan I thought my mother would explode. Alice Bernard's mother led the applause, but not many people followed.

The Dumbo class got up and sang a few boring old carols. Barry Kent sang all the vulgar versions (I know because I was watching his lips) then they sat down cross-legged, and brain-box Henderson from Five-K played a trumpet, Jew's harp, piano and guitar. The smarmy git looked dead superior when he was bowing during his applause. Then it was the interval and time for me to change into my white T-shirt-and-Wranglers Joseph costume. The tension backstage was electric. I stood in the wings (a theatrical term — it means the side of the stage) and watched the audience filing back into their places. Then the music from *Close Encounters* boomed out over the stereo speakers, and the curtains opened on an abstract manger and I just had time to whisper to Pandora 'Break a leg, darling', before Miss Elf pushed us out into the lights. My performance was brilliant! I really got under the skin of Joseph but Pandora was less good, she forgot to look tenderly at Jesus/Peter Brown.

The three punks/wise men made too much noise with their chains and spoiled my speech about the Middle East situation, and the angels representing Mrs Thatcher got hissed by the audience so loudly that their spoken chorus about unemployment was wasted.

Still, all in all, it was well received by the audience. Mr Scruton got up and made a hypocritical speech about 'a brave experiment' and 'Miss Elf's tireless work behind the scenes', and then we all sang 'We wish you a Merry Christmas'!

Driving home in the car my father said, 'That was the funniest Nativity play I have ever seen. Whose idea was it to turn it into a comedy?' I didn't reply. It wasn't a comedy.

Wednesday   December 23rd

9 a.m. Only two shopping days left for Christmas and I am still penniless. I have made a Blue Peter oven-glove for Miss Elf, but in order to give it to her in time for Christmas I will have to go into the ghetto and risk getting mugged.

I will have to go out carol singing, there is nothing else I can do to raise finance.

10 p.m. Just got back from carol singing. The suburban houses were a dead loss. People shouted, 'Come back at Christmas', without even opening the door. My most appreciative audience were the drunks staggering in and out of the Black Bull. Some of them wept openly at the beauty of my solo rendition of 'Silent Night'. I must say that I presented a touching picture as I stood in the snow with my young face lifted to the heavens ignoring the scenes of drunken revelry around me.

I made £3.13½ plus an Irish tenpence and a Guinness bottle-top. I'm going out again tomorrow. I will wear my school uniform, it should be worth a few extra quid.

Thursday   December 24th

Took Bert's Woodbines round to the home. Bert is hurt because I haven't been to see him. He said he didn't want to spend Christmas with a lot of malicious old women. Him and Queenie are causing a scandal. They are unofficially engaged. They have got their names on the same ashtray. I have invited Bert and Queenie for Christmas Day. My mother doesn't know yet but I'm sure she won't mind, we have got a big turkey. I sang a few carols for the old ladies. I made two pounds eleven pence out of them so I went to Woolworth's to buy Pandora's Chanel No. 5. They hadn't got any so I bought her an underarm deodorant instead.

The house looks dead clean and sparkling, there is a magic smell of cooking and satsumas in the air. I have searched around for my presents but they are not in the usual places. I want a racing bike, nothing else will please me. It's time I was independently mobile.

11 p.m. Just got back from the Black Bull. Pandora came with me, we wore our school uniforms and reminded all the drunks of their own children. They coughed up conscience money to the tune of twelve pounds fifty-seven! So we are going to see a pantomime on Boxing Day and we will have a family bar of Cadbury's Dairy Milk each!

Friday   December 25th
CHRISTMAS DAY

Got up at 5 a.m. to have a ride on my racing bike. My father paid for it with American Express. I couldn't ride it far because of the snow, but it didn't matter. I just like looking at it. My father had written on the gift tag attached to the handlebars, 'Don't leave it out in the rain this time' – as if I would!

My parents had severe hangovers, so I took them breakfast in bed and gave them my presents at the same time. My mother was overjoyed with her egg-timer and my father was equally delighted with his bookmark, in fact everthing was going OK until I casually mentioned that Bert and Queenie were my guests for the day, and would my father mind getting out of bed and picking them up in his car.

The row went on until the lousy Sugdens arrived. My grandma and grandad Sugden and Uncle Dennis and his wife Marcia and their son Maurice all look the same, as if they went to funerals every day of their lives. I can hardly believe that my mother is related to them. The Sugdens refused a drink and had a cup of tea whilst my mother defrosted the turkey in the bath. I helped my father carry Queenie (fifteen stone) and Bert (fourteen stone) out of our car. Queenie is one of those loud types of old ladies who dye their hair and try to look young. Bert is in love with her. He told me when I was helping him into the toilet.

Grandma Mole and Auntie Susan came at twelve-thirty and

pretended to like the Sugdens. Auntie Susan told some amusing stories about life in prison but nobody but me and my father and Bert and Queenie laughed.

I went up to the bathroom and found my mother crying and running the turkey under the hot tap. She said, 'The bloody thing won't thaw out, Adrian. What am I going to do?' I said, 'Just bung it in the oven'. So she did.

We sat down to eat Christmas dinner four hours late. By then my father was too drunk to eat anything. The Sugdens enjoyed the Queen's Speech but nothing else seemed to please them. Grandma Sugden gave me a book called *Bible Stories for Boys*. I could hardly tell her that I had lost my faith, so I said thank-you and wore a false smile for so long that it hurt.

The Sugdens went to their camp beds at ten o'clock. Bert, Queenie and my mother and father played cards while I polished my bike. We all had a good time making jokes about the Sugdens. Then my father drove Bert and Queenie back to the home and I phoned Pandora up and told her that I loved her more than life itself.

I am going round to her house tomorrow to give her the deodorant and escort her to the pantomime.

Saturday   December 26th

BANK HOLIDAY IN UK AND REP. OF IRELAND (a day may be given in lieu). NEW MOON

The Sugdens got up at 7 a.m. and sat around in their best clothes looking respectable. I went out on my bike. When I got back my mother was still in bed, and my father was arguing with Grandad Sugden about our dog's behaviour, so I went for another ride.

I called in on Grandma Mole, ate four mince pies, then rode back home. I got up to 30 mph on the dual carriageway, it was dead good. I put my new suede jacket and corduroy trousers on (courtesy of my father's Barclaycard) and called for Pandora; she gave me a bottle of after-shave for my Christmas present. It was a proud moment, it signified the *End of Childhood*.

We quite enjoyed the pantomime but it was rather childish for our taste. Bill Ash and Carole Hayman were good as Aladdin and the Princess, but the robbers played by Jeff Teare and Ian Giles were best. Sue Pomeroy gave a hilarious performance as Widow

Twankey. In this she was greatly helped by her cow, played by Chris Martin and Lou Wakefield.

Sunday December 27th
1ST AFTER CHRISTMAS

The Sugdens have gone back to Norfolk, thank God!

The house is back to its usual mess. My parents took a bottle of vodka and two glasses to bed with them last night. I haven't seen them since.

Went to Melton Mowbray on my bike, did it in five hours.

Monday December 28th

I am in trouble for leaving my bike outside last night. My parents are not speaking to me. I don't care, I have just had a shave and I feel magic.

Tuesday December 29th

My father is in a bad mood because there is only a bottle of V.P. sherry left to drink. He has gone round Pandora's house to borrow a bottle of spirits.

The dog has pulled the Christmas tree down and made all the pine needles stick in the shag-pile.

I have finished all my Christmas books and the library is still shut. I am reduced to reading my fathers *Reader's Digest*s and testing my word power.

Wednesday December 30th

All the balloons have shrivelled up. They look like old women's breasts shown on television documentaries about the Third World.

Thursday December 31st

The last day of the year! A lot has happened. I have fallen in love. Been a one-parent child. Gone Intellectual. And had two letters from the BBC. Not bad going for a $14\frac{3}{4}$ year old!

My mother and father have been to a New Year's Eve dance at

the Grand Hotel. My mother actually wore a dress! It is over a year since she showed her legs in public.

Pandora and I saw the New Year in together, we had a dead passionate session accompanied by Andy Stewart and a bagpiper.

My father came crashing through the front door at 1 a.m. carrying a lump of coal in his hand. Drunk as usual.

My mother started going on about what a wonderful son I was and how much she loved me. It's a pity she never says anything like that when she is sober.

Friday   January 1st
BANK HOLIDAY IN UK, REP. OF IRELAND, USA AND CANADA

These are my New Year's resolutions:

1. I will be true to Pandora.
2. I will bring my bike in at night.
3. I will not read unworthy books.
4. I will study hard for my O levels, and get Grade 'A's.
5. I will try to be more kind to the dog.
6. I will try to find it in my heart to forgive Barry Kent his multiple sins.
7. I will clean the bath after use.
8. I will stop worrying about the size of my thing.
9. I will do my back-stretching excercises every night without fail.
10. I will learn a new word and use it every day.

Saturday   January 2nd
BANK HOLIDAY IN SCOTLAND (a day may be given in lieu)

How interesting it is that Aabec should be an Australian bark used for making sweat.

Sunday   January 3rd
SECOND AFTER CHRISTMAS. MOON'S FIRST QUARTER

I wouldn't mind going to Africa and hunting an Aardvark.

Monday   January 4th

Whilst in Africa I would go South and look out for an Aardwolf.

Tuesday   January 5th

And I would avoid tangling with an Aasvogel.

Wednesday　January 6th
EPIPHANY

I keep having nightmares about the bomb. I hope it isn't dropped before I get my GCE results in August 1982. I wouldn't like to die an unqualified virgin.

Thursday　January 7th

Nigel came round to look at my racing bike. He said that it was mass produced, unlike his bike that was 'made by a craftsman in Nottingham'. I have gone off Nigel, and I have also gone off my bike a bit.

Friday　January 8th

Got a wedding invitation from Bert and Queenie, they are getting married on January 16th at Pocklington Street Register Office.

In my opinion it is a waste of time. Bert is nearly ninety and Queenie is nearly eighty. I will leave it until the last minute before I buy a wedding present.

It has started snowing again. I asked my mother to buy me some green wellingtons like the Queen's but she came back with dead common black ones. I only need them to walk Pandora to our gate. I am staying in until the snow melts. Unlike most youths of my age, I dislike frolicking in the snow.

Saturday　January 9th
FULL MOON

Nigel said the end of the world is coming tonight. He said the moon is having a total collapse. (Nigel should read *Reader's Digest* and increase his word power.) True enough it did go dark, I held my breath and feared the worst but then the moon recovered and life went on as usual, except in York where fate has flooded the town centre.

Sunday   January 10th
FIRST AFTER EPIPHANY

I can't understand why my father looks so old at forty-one compared to President Reagan at seventy. My father has got no work or worries yet he looks dead haggard. Poor President Reagan has to carry the world's safety on his shoulders yet he is always smiling and looking cheerful. It doesn't make sense.

Monday   January 11th

I've been looking through last year's diary and have been reminded that Malcolm Muggeridge never did reply to my letter about what to do if you are an intellectual. That is a first-class stamp wasted! I should have written to the British Museum, that's where all the intellectuals hang out.

Tuesday   January 12th

Pandora and I went to the youth club tonight. It was quite good. Rick Lemon led a discussion on sex. Nobody said anything, but he showed some interesting slides of wombs cut in half.

Wednesday   January 13th

Pandora's parents have had a massive row. They are sleeping in separate bedrooms. Pandora's mother has joined the SDP and Pandora's father is staying loyal to the Labour Party.
    Pandora is a Liberal, so she gets on all right with them both.

Thursday   January 14th

Pandora's father has come out of the closet and admitted that he is a Bennite. Pandora is staying loyal to him, but if the Co-op Dairy find out he will be finished.

Friday   January 15th

Thank God the snow is melting! At last I can walk the streets in safety, secure in the knowledge that no one is going to ram a snowball down the back of my anorak.

Saturday   January 16th
MOON'S LAST QUARTER

Bert got married today.

The Alderman Cooper Sunshine Home hired a coach and took the old ladies to form a guard of honour with their walking-frames.

Bert looked dead good. He cashed his life insurance in and spent the money on a new suit. Queenie was wearing a hat made of flowers and fruit. She had a lot of orange make-up on her face to try and cover the wrinkles. Even Sabre had a red bow round his neck. I think it was kind of the RSPCA to let Sabre out for his master's wedding. My father and Pandora's father carried Bert's wheelchair up the steps with Bert a single man and then down again with Bert a married man. The old ladies threw rice and confetti and my mother and Pandora's mother gave Queenie a kiss and a lucky horseshoe.

A newspaper reporter and photographer made everyone pose for photographs. I was asked my name, but I said I didn't want publicity for my acts of charity to Bert.

The reception took place back at the home. Matron made a cake with 'B' and 'Q' written in Jellytots.

Bert and Queenie are moving into a bungalow on Monday, after they have had their honeymoon in the home.

Honeymoon! Ha! Ha! Ha!

Sunday   January 17th

SECOND AFTER EPIPHANY

Last night I dreamed about a boy like me collecting pebbles in the rain. It was a dead strange dream.

I am reading *The Black Prince*, by Iris Murdoch. I can only understand one word in ten. It is now my ambition to actually enjoy one of her books. Then I will know I am above the common herd.

Monday   January 18th

School. First day of term. Loads of GCE homework. I will never cope. I am an intellectual but at the same time I am not very clever.

Tuesday   January 19th

Brought four hundred and eighty three copies of *The Voice of Youth* home in my satchel and Adidas bag. Mr Jones needs the games cupboard.

Wednesday   January 20th

Two-and-a-half hours of homework! I will crack under the strain.

Thursday   January 21st

My brain is hurting. I have just had two pages of *Macbeth* to translate into English.

Friday   January 22nd

I am destined to become a manual worker. I can't keep working under this pressure. Miss Elf said my work is perfectly satisfactory, but that isn't good enough when Pandora keeps getting 'Excellent' in red pen on everything she does.

Saturday   January 23rd

Stayed in bed until five-thirty to make sure I missed Sainsburys.' Listened to Radio Four play about domestic unhappiness. Phoned Pandora. Did Geography homework. Teased dog. Went to sleep. Woke up. Worried for ten minutes. Got up. Made cocoa.

I am a nervous wreck.

Sunday   January 24th
THIRD AFTER EPIPHANY

My mother blames my bad nerves on Iris Murdoch. She says painful adolescence shouldn't be read about when one is studying for O levels.

Monday   January 25th
NEW MOON

Couldn't do my Maths homework. Phoned the Samaritans. The
nice man on the end of the phone told me the answer was nine-
eighths. He was dead kind to someone in despair.

Tuesday   January 26th

The stupid Samaritan got the answer wrong! It's only seven-fifths.
I only got six out of twenty. Pandora got them all right. In fact
she got a hundred per cent.

Wednesday   January 27th

My mother is holding her woman's rights meetings in our lounge.
I can't concentrate on my homework properly with women laughing
and shouting and stamping up the stairs. They are not a bit ladylike.

Thursday   January 28th

Got fifteen out of twenty for History. Pandora got twenty-one out
of twenty. She got an extra mark for knowing Hitler's father's name.

Friday   January 29th

Came home from school early with a severe migraine (missed the
Comparative Religion test). Found my father watching *Play School*
and pretending to be an acorn growing into an oak.
   Went to bed too shocked to speak.

Saturday   January 30th

Migraine. Too ill to write.

Sunday   January 31st
FOURTH AFTER EPIPHANY

Pandora came round. I copied her homework. Feel better.

Monday   February 1st
MOON'S FIRST QUARTER

My mother has given my father an ultimatum: either he finds a job, or starts doing housework, or leaves.

He is looking for a job.

Tuesday   February 2nd
CANDLEMAS (SCOTTISH QUARTER-DAY)

Grandma Mole came round to tell me that the end of the world was announced at her Spiritualist church last week. She said it should have all ended yesterday.

She would have come round sooner only she was washing her curtains.

Wednesday   February 3rd

My father has had his credit cards taken off him! Barclays, Nat West and American Express have got fed up with his reckless spending. Time is running out for us. He has only got a few quids' redundancy money left in his sock drawer.

My mother is looking for a job.

I have got a sense of *déjà vu*.

Thursday   February 4th

Went round to see Bert and Queenie. Their bungalow is so full of knick-knacks that there is hardly room for a person to move. Sabre knocks at least ten things over every time he wags his tail. They both seem happy enough, though their sex life can't be up to much.

Friday   February 5th

I've got to write an essay on the causes of the Second World War. What a waste of time! Everyone knows the causes. You can't go anywhere without seeing Hitler's photo.

Saturday   February 6th

Finished essay; copied it out of *Pear's Encyclopedia*.

My mother has gone to a woman's workshop on self-defence. So if my father moans at her for burning the toast she will be able to karate-chop him in the windpipe.

Sunday   February 7th
SEPTUAGESIMA

Bored stiff all day. My parents never do anything on Sundays but read the Sunday papers. Other families go out to safari parks, etc. But we never do.

When I am a parent I will fill my children with stimulation at weekends.

Monday   February 8th
FULL MOON

My mother has found a job. She collects money from Space Invader machines. She started today in response to an urgent phone call from the job agency that she is registered with.

She said that the fullest machines are those in unrespectable cafés and university common rooms.

I think my mother is betraying her principles. She is pandering to an obsession of weak minds.

Tuesday   February 9th

My mother has given up her job. She said she is sexually harassed during her work and she is also allergic to ten-pence pieces.

Wednesday   February 10th

My father is going to start his own business making spice-racks. He has spent the last of his redundancy money on buying pine and glue. Our spare bedroom has been turned into a workshop. Sawdust is all over the house.

I am very proud of my father. He is now a company director, and I am a company director's son!

Thursday   February 11th

Delivered Mrs Singh's massive spice-rack after school. It took two of us to carry it round and install it on her kitchen wall. We had a cup of sickly Indian tea and Mrs Singh paid my father and then started to fill up her shelves with exotic Indian spices. They looked a lot more interesting than my mother's boring parsley and thyme.

My father bought a bottle of champagne to celebrate his first sale! He has got no respect for capital investment.

Friday   February 12th

Pandora has gone to London with her father to hear Tony Benn speak. Pandora's mother has gone to a SDP rally in Loughborough. It is a sad day when families are split asunder by politics.

I'm not sure how I will vote. Sometimes I think Mrs Thatcher is a nice kind sort of woman. Then the next day I see her on television and she frightens me rigid. She has got eyes like a psychotic killer, but a voice like a gentle person. It is a bit confusing.

Saturday   February 13th

Pandora has got a crush on Tony Benn, just like the one she had on Adam Ant. She says that older men are exciting.

I am trying to grow my moustache. Valentine's Day tomorrow. A big card came today, it had a Sheffield postmark.

Sunday   February 14th
SEXAGESIMA. ST VALENTINE'S DAY

At last I have had a valentine from somebody who is not a blood relation! Pandora's card was charming, she had written a simple message of love:

Adrian, it is you alone.

I gave Pandora a false Victorian card, inside I wrote:

> My young love,
> Treacle hair and knee-socks
> Give my system deep shocks.
> You've got a magic figure:
> I'm Roy Rogers, you are Trigger.

It doesn't scan very well, but I was in a hurry. Pandora didn't get the literary reference to Roy Rogers, so I have lent her my father's old Roy Rogers annuals.

My father threw the Sheffield card in the waste bin. My mother took it out when my father had gone to the pub. Inside it said:

Pauline, I am in anguish.

My mother smiled and ripped it up.

Monday   February 15th
WASHINGTON'S BIRTHDAY, USA. MOON'S LAST QUARTER

Came home from school to hear my mother talking to creep Lucas on the phone. She was using a yukky voice and saying things like: 'Don't ask me to do it, Bimbo', and 'It's all over between us now, darling. We must try to forget'.

I can't stand much more emotional stress. I am up to my ears in it already what with studying hard and vying with Tony Benn for Pandora's attention.

Tuesday   February 16th

Pandora's mother came round last night to complain about her spice-rack. It fell off the wall and spilt rosemary and tumeric all over her cork tiles. My mother apologized on behalf of my father who was hiding in the coal shed.

I am seriously thinking of giving everything up and running away to be a tramp. I would quite enjoy the life, providing I could have a daily bath.

Wednesday   February 17th

Miss Elf told us about her boyfriend today. He is called Winston Johnson. He is a Master of Arts and can't get a job! So what chance do I stand?

Miss Elf said that school-leavers are despairing all over the country. She said that Mr Scruton should be ashamed to have a portrait of Mrs Thatcher over his desk.

I think I am turning radical.

Thursday February 18th

This morning the whole school was ordered to go to the assembly hall. Mr Scruton got up on the stage and acted like the films of Hitler. He said in all his long years of teaching he had never come across an act of such serious vandalism. Everybody went dead quiet and wondered what had happened. Scruton said that somebody had entered his office and drawn a moustache on Margaret Thatcher and written 'Three million unemployed' in her cleavage.

He said that defiling the greatest leader this country has ever known was a crime against humanity. It was tantamount to treason and that when the culprit was found they would be immediately expelled. Scruton's eyes bulged out so far that a few of the first-years started to cry. Miss Elf led them outside to safety.

The whole school has got to have handwriting tests.

Friday February 19th

Miss Elf has resigned. I will miss her, she was responsible for my political development. I am a committed radical. I am against nearly everything.

Saturday February 20th

Pandora, Nigel, Claire Neilson and myself have formed a radical group. We are the 'Pink Brigade'. We discuss things like war (we are against it); peace (we are for it); and the ultimate destruction of capitalist society.

Claire Neilson's father is a capitalist: he owns a greengrocer's shop. Claire is trying to get her father to give cheap food to the unwaged but he refuses. He waxes fat on their starvation!

Sunday February 21st
QUINQUAGESIMA

Had an argument with my father over the *Sunday Express*. He can't see that he is a willing tool of the reactionary right. He refuses to change to the *Morning Star*. My mother reads anything; she is prostituting her literacy.

Monday February 22nd

Once again I am spotty. I am also extremely sexually frustrated. I'm sure a session of passionate lovemaking would improve my skin.

Pandora says she is not going to risk being a single parent just for the sake of a few spots. So I will have to fall back on self-indulgence.

Tuesday February 23rd
SHROVE TUESDAY. NEW MOON

Ate nine pancakes at home, three at Pandora's and four at Bert and Queenie's. Grandma was very hurt when I refused her kind offer to whip me a batter, but I was full up.

It is disgusting when the Third World is living on a few grains of rice.

I feel dead guilty.

Wednesday February 24th
ASH WEDNESDAY

Our school dinner-ladies have got the sack! The dinners now come in hot boxes from a central kitchen. I would have staged a protest but I have got a Geography test tomorrow.

Mrs Leech was presented with a microwave oven for her thirty years of toil over the custard jug.

Thursday February 25th

Got fifteen out of twenty for Geography. I lost points for saying that the Falkland Islands belonged to Argentina.

Friday February 26th

My thing is now thirteen centimetres long when it is extended. When it is contracted it is hardly worth measuring. My general physique is improving. I think the back-stretching exercises are paying off. I used to be the sort of boy who had sand kicked in his face, now I'm the sort of boy who watches somebody else have it kicked in their face.

Saturday   February 27th

My father hasn't made or sold a single spice-rack all week. We are now living on Social Security and dole money.

My mother has stopped smoking. The dog is down to half a tin of Chum a day.

Sunday   February 28th
QUADRAGESIMA (FIRST IN LENT)

Had egg and chips and peas for Sunday dinner! No pudding! Not even a proper serviette.

My mother says we are the *nouveau poor*.

Monday   March 1st
ST DAVID'S DAY (WALES)

My father has stopped smoking. He is going around with a white face finding fault with everything I do.

My mother and him had their first row since she came back. The dog caused it by eating the Spam for tea. It couldn't help it, the poor thing was half crazed with hunger. It is back on a full tin of Chum a day.

Tuesday   March 2nd
MOON'S FIRST QUARTER

My parents are suffering severe nicotine withdrawal symptoms. It is quite amusing to a non-smoker like me.

Wednesday   March 3rd

I had to lend my father enough money for a gallon of petrol, he had an interview for a job. My mother cut his hair and gave him a shave and told him what to say and how to behave. It is pathetic to see how unemployment has reduced my father to childish dependence on others.

He is waiting to hear from Manpower Services.

He is still ill from not smoking. His temper has reached new peaks of explosion.

Thursday   March 4th

No news yet about the job. I spend as much time as I can out of the house. My parents are unbearable. I almost wish they would start smoking again.

Friday   March 5th

He got it!!!

He starts on Monday as a Canal Bank Renovation Supervisor. He is in charge of a gang of school-leavers. To celebrate he bought my mother sixty Benson and Hedges and himself sixty Players. I got a family pack of Mars bars.

Everybody is dead happy for once. Even the dog has cheered up a bit. Grandma is knitting my father a woolly hat for work.

Saturday   March 6th

Pandora and I went to see the bit of canal bank that my father is now in charge of. If he worked for a thousand years he will never get it cleaned of all the old bikes and prams and weeds and Coca-Cola tins! I told my father that he was in a no-win situation, but he said, 'On the contrary, in one year's time it will be a beauty spot'. Yes! And I am Nancy Reagan, Dad!

Sunday   March 7th
SECOND IN LENT

My father went to see his canal bank this morning. He came home and shut himself in his bedroom. He is still there, I can hear my mother saying encouraging words to him.

It is uncertain whether or not he will turn up for work tomorrow. On the whole I think not.

Monday   March 8th

He went to work.

After school I walked home along the canal bank. I found him bossing a gang of skinheads and punks about. They were looking surly and unco-operative. None of them wanted to get their clothes dirty. My father seemed to be the only one doing any work. He was covered in mud. I attempted to exchange a few civilities with the lads, but they spurned my overtures. I pointed out that the lads are alienated by a cruel, uncaring society, but my father said, 'Bugger off home, Adrian. You're talking a load of lefty crap'. He will have a mutiny on his hands soon if he's not careful.

Tuesday March 9th
FULL MOON

My schoolwork is plummeting down to new depths. I only got five out of twenty for spelling. I think I might be anorexic.

Wednesday March 10th

My father has asked me not to bring Pandora to the canal after school. He says he can't do anything with the lads after she has gone. It's true that she is stunningly beautiful, but the lads will just have to learn self-control. I have had to learn it. She has refused to consummate our relationship. Sometimes I wonder what she sees in me.

I live in daily terror of our relationship ending.

Thursday March 11th

Pandora and Pandora's mother have joined my mother's woman's group. No men or boys are allowed in our front room. My father had to be in charge of the crêche in our dining room.

Rick Lemon's baby daughter Herod was crawling under the table shouting: 'Tit! Tit!' My father kept telling Herod to shut up until I explained that Tit was Herod's mother's name. Herod is a very radical baby who never eats sweets and stays up until 2 a.m.

My father says that women ought to be at home cooking. He said it in a whisper so that he wouldn't be karate-chopped to death.

Friday March 12th

My father had a good day on the canal bank. He is almost through to the grass now. To celebrate he brought the skinheads and punks round to our house for a glass of home-made beer. Mrs Singh and my mother looked shocked when the lads trooped into our kitchen, but my father introduced Baz, Daz, Maz, Kev, Melv and Boz and my mother and Mrs Singh relaxed a bit.

Boz is going to help me fix the brakes on my bike, he is an expert bike-fixer. He has been stealing them since he was six.

Saturday   March 13th

Boz offered me a sniff of his glue today, but I declined it with thanks.

Sunday   March 14th
THIRD IN LENT

All the women I know have gone to rally to protest about a woman's right to work. Mrs Singh has gone wearing a disguise.

Saw Rick Lemon on the park, he was pushing Herod too high on a swing. Herod was shouting: 'Tit! Tit!'

Monday   March 15th

I am loved by two women! Elizabeth Sally Broadway gave Victoria Louise Thomson a note in Science. It said: 'Ask Adrian Mole if he wants to go out with me.'

Victoria Louise Thomson (hereafter known as V.L.T.) passed on the message. I replied to V.L.T. in the negative.

Elizabeth Sally Broadway (hereafter known as E.S.B.) looked dead sad and started to cry into her bunsen burner.

It is really wonderful to know that Pandora and Elizabeth are both in love with me.

Perhaps I am not so ugly after all.

Tuesday   March 16th

Pandora and E.S.B. have had a fight in the playground. I am disgusted with Pandora. At the last meeting of the Pink Brigade she swore to be a pacifist all her life.

Pandora won! Ha! Ha! Ha!

Wednesday March 17th
ST PATRICK'S DAY. BANK HOLIDAY (IRELAND). MOON'S
LAST QUARTER

Mr O'Leary was brought home by a police car at 10.30 p.m. Mrs
O'Leary came over to ask my father if he would help her to get
Mr O'Leary upstairs to bed. My father is still over there. I can
hear the music and singing through my double-glazing.

It is no joke when you need your sleep for school.

Thursday March 18th

I am reading *How Children Fail*, by John Holt. It is dead good. If
I fail my O levels it will be all my parents' fault.

Friday March 19th

My creative English essay:

> *Spring*, by A Mole
> The trees explode into bud, indeed some of them are in leaf.
> Their branches thrust to the sky like drunken scarecrows.
> Their trunks writhe and twist into the earth and form a pleth-
> ora of roots. The brilliant sky hovers uncertainly like a shy
> bride at the door of her nuptial chamber. Birds wing and
> scrape their erratic way into the cotton-wool clouds like
> drunken scarecrows. The translucent brook gurgles majesti-
> cally towards its journey's end. 'To the sea!' it cries, 'to the
> sea!' it endlessly repeats.
>
> A lonely boy, his loins afire, sits and watches his calm
> reflection in the torrential brook. His heart is indeed heavy.
> His eyes fall on to the ground and rest on a wondrous majestic
> many-hued butterfly. The winged insect takes flight and the
> boy's eyes are carried far away until they are but a speck on
> the red-hued sunset. He senses on the zephyr a hope for
> mankind.

Pandora thinks this is the best thing I have ever written, but I know
I have got a long way to go until I have learned my craft.

Saturday   March 20th
VERNAL EQUINOX

My mother has had all her hair cut off. She looks like one of Auntie
Susan's inmates. She doesn't look a bit maternal any more. I don't
know whether to get her anything for Mother's Day or not. She was
going on about it last night, saying it was a commercial racket fed
by gullible fools.

Sunday   March 21st
FOURTH IN LENT. MOTHERING SUNDAY

11.30 a.m.   Didn't get my mother anything so she has been in a bad
mood all morning.
1 p.m.   My father said, 'If I were you, lad, I'd nip round Cherry's
and get your mother a card and present'. He gave me two pounds
so I got a card saying 'Mummy I love you' (it was the only one left,
just my luck), and five boxes of liquorice allsorts (going cheap
because the boxes were squashed). She cheered up and didn't even
mind when my father took a bunch of tulips round to grandma's
and came back five hours later smelling of drink.
   Pandora's mother was taken out and spoilt in a restaurant. I will
do the same for my mother when I am famous.

Monday   March 22nd

I have catalogued my bedroom library. I have got a hundred and
fifty-one books, not counting the Enid Blytons.

Tuesday   March 23rd

I will be fifteen in eleven days. So I have only got to wait one year
and eleven days to get married, should I want to.

Wednesday   March 24th

The only thing that really worries me about my appearance now is
my ears. They stick out at an angle of ninety degrees. I have checked
them with my geometry set so I know it is a scientific fact.

Thursday   March 25th
LADY DAY (QUARTER DAY). NEW MOON

I have had a spiritual awakening. Two nice men representing a religious group called the Sunshine People called at the house. They talked about how they alone could bring peace to the world. It is twenty pounds to join. I will get the money somehow. Nothing is too expensive where peace is concerned.

Friday   March 26th

Tried to persuade Pandora to join the Sunshine People. She was not swayed by my arguments. They are calling round tomorrow to meet my parents and sign the agreement.

Saturday   March 27th

The Sunshine People came at six o'clock. My father made them stand on the doorstep in the rain. Their robes got wet through. My father said they were trying to brainwash a simple child. When they left my mother watched them walk up the cul-de-sac. She said, 'They don't look very charismatic now, they just look bloody wet'. I wept a few tears. I think I was weeping out of relief – twenty quid is a lot of money.

Sunday   March 28th
PASSION SUNDAY. BRITISH SUMMER TIME BEGINS

My father forgot to change the clocks last night so I was late for the Pink Brigade's meeting in Pandora's lounge. We voted to exclude Pandora's father from the meeting on the grounds of his extreme left-wing views. We have decided to back Roy Hattersley in the expected fight for the leadership.

Pandora has gone off Tony Benn since she found out that he is a lapsed aristocrat.

Claire Neilson introduced a new member, her name is Barbara Boyer. She is dead good-looking and also dead intelligent. She disagreed with Pandora over NATO's nuclear arms policy. Pandora had to concede that China was an unknown factor. Pandora asked Claire Neilson not to bring Barbara again.

Monday   March 29th

I ate my school dinner sitting next to Barbara Boyer. She is a truly wonderful girl. She pointed out that Pandora has got a lot of faults. I was forced to agree with her.

Tuesday   March 30th

I am committing non-sexual adultery with Barbara. I am at the centre of an eternal triangle. Nigel is the only one to know: he has been sworn to secrecy.

Wednesday   March 31st

Nigel has blabbed it all over the school. Pandora spent the afternoon in matron's office.

Thursday   April 1st
ALL FOOLS' DAY. MOON'S FIRST QUARTER

Barbara Boyer has ended our brief *affaire*. I rang her up at the pet shop where she works part time cleaning the cages out. She said she couldn't bear to see the pain in Pandora's eyes. I asked her if it was an April Fools' joke, she said no and pointed out that it was after 12 a.m.

I have learnt an important lesson, because of lust I am without love.

I am fifteen tomorrow.

Had a shave to cheer myself up.

Friday   April 2nd

I am fifteen, but legally I am still a child. There is nothing I can do today that I couldn't do yesterday. Worse luck!

Had seven cards from relations and three from friends. My presents were the usual load of Japanese rubbish, though I did get a model aeroplane from Bert that was made in West Germany.

Pandora has ignored my birthday. I don't blame her. I betrayed her trust.

Boz, Baz, Daz, Maz, Kev and Melv came back from the canal and gave me the bumps. Boz gave me a tube of glue for my model aeroplane.

Saturday   April 3rd

8 a.m.   Britain is at war with Argentina!!! Radio Four has just announced it. I am overcome with excitement. Half of me thinks it is tragic and the other half of me thinks it is dead exciting.

10 a.m.   Woke my father up to tell him Argentina has invaded the Falklands. He shot out of bed because he thought the Falklands lay off the coast of Scotland. When I pointed out that they were eight thousand miles away he got back into bed and pulled the covers over his head.

4 p.m.   I have just had the most humiliating experience of my life. It started when I began to assemble my model aeroplane. I had nearly finished it when I thought I would try an experimental sniff of glue. I put my nose to the undercarriage and sniffed for five seconds, nothing spiritual happened but my nose stuck to the plane! My father took me to Casualty to have it removed, how I endured the laughing and sniggering I don't know.

The Casualty doctor wrote 'Glue Sniffer' on my outpatient's card.

I rang Pandora; she is coming round after her viola lesson. Love is the only thing that keeps me sane...

*The Growing Pains
of Adrian Mole*

To Mum, Dad and the whole family,
with love and thanks

'The aristocratic rebel, since he has enough to eat, must have other causes of discontent.'

Bertrand Russell *The History of Western Philosphy*

ADRIAN MOLE:

His basic table of interpersonal relationships at this moment in time.

(April 4th)

MRS TANIA BRAITHWAITE + MR IVAN BRAITHWAI[TE]

↑
DAUGHTER OF

PANDORA BRAITHWAITE (FUTURE WIFE)

DOG (UNKNOWN PARENTAGE) ←

ADRIA[N]

So[N]

MAXWELL HOUSE
↑
SON OF
↑
STICK INSECT ← LOVER
(DOREEN SLATER)
UNMARRIED

GEORGE MO[LE]

SUSAN MOLE
(PRISON WARDER)
↑
DAUGHTER OF

SON

MAY MOLE
+
GRANDAD MOLE
(DECEASED)

ENEMIES OF FAMILY

BARRY KENT - (BULLY)
POPEYE SCRUTON. (HEADMASTER)
MANPOWER SERVICES COMMISSION (FATHER'S BOSS)
MARGARET THATCHER (PRIME MINISTER)

SABRE
(ALSATIAN)

BERT'S CHILDREN
IN AUSTRALIA

GOOD SAMARITAN
TO

BERT BAXTER
MARRIED TO
QUEENIE BAXTER
(2nd WIFE)

NEIGHBOUR →
NEXT DOOR
MR SINGH
MRS SINGH
ALL THE LITTLE SINGHS

OVER THE ROAD
O'LEARYS

MOLE

F

LOVER OF MR (CREEP) LUCAS
MARRIED AND SEPARATED
FROM

MRS LUCAS

AULINE MOLE

DAUGHTER OF

MR AND MRS
SUGDEN

FRIENDS OF FAMILY

NIGEL (BEST FRIEND)
RICK LEMON (YOUTH LEADER)
COURTNEY ELLIOT (POSTMAN)
MR TYDEMAN (OF THE B.B.C.)
HAMISH MANCINI (AMERICAN PEN-PAL)

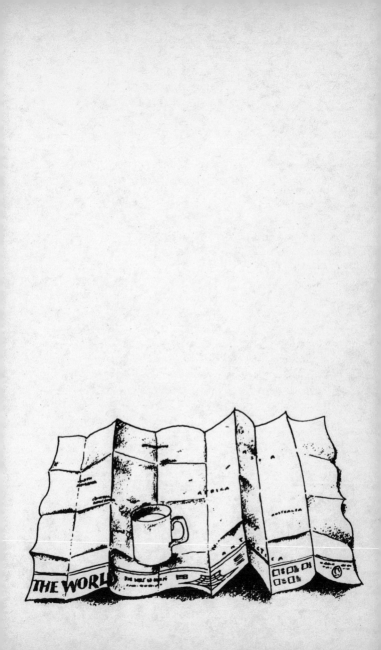

Sunday   April 4th

My father has sent a telegram to the War Office. He wants to take part in the war with Argentina. His telegram read:

QUALIFIED HEATING ENGINEER STOP A1 FITNESS STOP OFFERS HIMSELF IN THE SERVICE OF HIS COUNTRY STOP READY FOR IMMEDIATE MOBILIZATION

My mother says that my father will do anything to avoid working for Manpower Services as a canal bank renovator.

At tea-time I was looking at our world map, but I couldn't see the Falkland Islands anywhere. My mother found them; they were hidden under a crumb of fruitcake.

I feel guilty about mentioning a personal anguish at this time of national crisis, but ever since last night when a model aeroplane became stuck fast to my nose with glue, I have suffered torment. My nose has swollen up so much that I am frantic with worry that it might burst and take my brain with it.

I rang the Casualty Department and, after a lot of laughing, the nurse who removed the plane came on the line. She said that I was 'probably allergic to the glue', and that the swelling would go down in a few days. She added, 'Perhaps it will teach you not to sniff glue again.' I tried to explain but she put the phone down.

Pandora has been round but I declined to see her. She would go straight off me if she saw my repulsive nose.

Monday   April 5th

Just my luck! It is the first day of the school holidays and I can't go out because of my gigantic swollen nose. Even my mother is a bit worried about it now. She wanted to prick it with a sterilized needle, but I wouldn't let her. She can't sew an accurate patch on a pair of jeans with a needle, let alone do delicate medical procedures with one. I've begged her to take me to a private nose specialist, but she has refused. She says she needs the money for her 'Well Woman' test. She is having her primary and secondary sexual organs checked. Yuk!

The dog is in love with a cocker spaniel called Mitzi. The dog stands no chance, though: (a) it isn't a pedigree, and (b) it doesn't keep itself looking smart like most dogs. I tried to explain these things to the dog, but it just looked sad and mournful and went back to lying outside Mitzi's gate. Being in love is no joke. I have the same problem with Pandora that the dog has with Mitzi. We are both in a lower social class than our loved ones.

Tuesday   April 6th

The nation has been told that Britain and Argentina are not at war, we are at conflict.

I am reading *Scoop* by a woman called Evelyn Waugh.

Wednesday   April 7th

Wrote and sent Pandora a love letter and a poem. The letter said:

> Pandora my love,
> Due to an unfortunate physical disability I am unable to see you in person, but every fibre of my being cries out for your immediate physical proximity. Be patient, my love, soon we will laugh again.
>
> Yours with undying love,
> Adrian
>
> PS. What are your views on the Argentinian conflict, with particular reference to Lord Carrington's resignation?

> *The Discontented Tuna*
> I am a Tuna fish,
> Swimming in the sea of discontent.
> Oh, when, when,
> Will I find the spawning ground?

I hope Pandora sees through my poem and realizes the symbolism of 'spawning ground'. I am sick of being the only virgin in our class. Everybody but me is sexually experienced. Barry Kent boasts about how many housewives he makes love to on his father's milkround. He says they are the reason why he is always late for school.

Thursday April 8th
MAUNDY THURSDAY. FULL MOON

Nose has gone down a bit.

My mother came home from her 'Well Woman' check in a bad mood.

I allowed Pandora to visit me in my darkened bedroom. We had a brilliant kissing session. Pandora was wearing her mother's Janet Reger full-length silk slip under her dress and she allowed me to touch the lace on the hem. I was more interested in the lace near the shoulder straps but Pandora said, 'No darling, we must wait until we've got our "O" levels.'

I pointed out to Pandora that all this sexual frustration is playing havoc with my skin. But she said, 'If you really love me you will wait.'

I said, 'If you really love me you *wouldn't* wait.'

She went then: she had to replace the Janet Reger slip before her mother got back from work.

I have got thirty-eight spots: twenty-eight on my face and the rest on my shoulders.

Friday April 9th
GOOD FRIDAY

Barry Kent has been spreading malicious rumours that I am addicted to Bostik. His Auntie is a cleaner in the hospital and heard about the nose-stuck-to-model-aeroplane incident. I think it is disgusting that cleaners are allowed to talk about patients' private medical secrets. They should be made to take the Hippocratic oath, like doctors and nurses.

My mother is fed up. She is just sitting around the house smoking and sighing. There was a programme on BBC 2 about French babies being born into swimming pools; it was most interesting (and erotic) but my mother quickly switched over to ITV and watched BERNIE WINTERS!!! When I protested she screamed, 'Why don't you clear off and sulk in your room like other teenagers?'

My father is as baffled as I am as to why my mother is depressed. She's been like it since she came back from the 'Well Woman' clinic.

Perhaps she's not well.

The *Canberra* has gone to the Falklands and taken Barry Kent's older brother, Clive, with it.

Saturday   April 10th

Bert has been thrown out of the British Legion club for saying that the Falklands belong to Argentina. Bert doesn't mind, he only used to go to take advantage of their OAP cheap beer offer.

Grandma came round to check our pantry for Argentinian corned beef. We passed the test because our corned beef was made by Brazilian cows.

Grandma has got a funny look in her eyes. My mother says it is called Jingoism, but I think it is more likely to be cataracts forming. We did them in human biology last term, so I speak from knowledge.

Sunday   April 11th
EASTER DAY

The working classes are toiling round the clock to mend Britain's old battleships. Britain is planning to spring a surprise attack on Argentina in six weeks' time.

Grandma made me go to church. The vicar forced us to pray for the Falkland Islanders. He said that they were 'under the tyranny of the jackboot of facism'. He got dead mad talking about world peace. His sermon went on far too long in my opinion; even Grandma started fidgeting and whispering about getting back to switch her sprouts on.

I have made my mind up to confess to Grandma that I am no longer a Christian believer. She'll just have to find somebody else to help her up the hill to the church. Didn't get an Easter egg: my mother and father said I am too old. Anybody would think there is a law against people of fifteen eating Easter eggs!

Monday   April 12th
EASTER MONDAY

I think mother is cracking up; she is behaving even more

strangely than usual. She came into my bedroom to change my sheets and when I objected to her dropping cigarette ash on my Falklands Campaign map she said, 'For God's sake, Adrian, this room is like a bloody shrine! Why don't you leave your clothes on the floor like *normal* teenagers?'

I said that I like things to be neat and tidy but she said, 'You're a bloody obsessive,' and went out.

My mother and father are always arguing about their bedroom. My father's side of the room is dead neat, but my mother's side is disgusting: overflowing ashtrays, old yellow *Observer*'s, books, magazines and puddles of nylon knickers on the floor. *Her* bedside shelves are full of the yukky junk she buys from second-hand shops, one-armed statues, broken vases and stinking old books etc. I pity my father having to share a room with her. All *he's* got on his shelves are his AA book and a photograph of my mother in a wedding dress. She's the only bride I've seen who's got cigarette smoke coming out of her nostrils.

I just can't understand why my father married her.

Tuesday April 13th

After *Crossroads* had finished I asked my father why he had married my mother. Talk about opening the floodgates! Fifteen years of bitterness and resentment spilled out. He said, 'Never make the mistake I made, Adrian. Don't let a woman's body blind you to her character and habits.'

He explained that he met my mother when miniskirts were in fashion. He said that in those days my mother had superb legs and thighs. He said, 'You must realize that most women looked bloody awful in miniskirts, so your mother had a certain rarity value.'

I was shocked at his sexist attitude and told him that I was in love with Pandora because of her brains and compassion for lesser mortals. My father gave a nasty laugh and said, 'Oh yeah! And if Pandora was as ugly as sin you wouldn't have noticed her bloody IQ and bleeding heart in the first place.'

He ended our first man-to-man talk by saying, 'Look, kiddo, don't even think about getting married until you've spent a few months sharing a bedroom with a bird. If she leaves her knickers on the floor for more than three days running forget it!'

Wednesday April 14th

Mitzi's owner came round to ask my mother to keep our dog away from Mitzi. My mother said that the dog lived in a liberal household and was allowed to go where it pleased.

Mitzi's owner, a Mrs Carmichael, said that if our dog 'continued harassing Mitzi' she would be forced to report our dog to the police. My mother laughed and said, 'Why don't you go the whole hog and take a High Court injunction out?'

Mr Carmichael came round half an hour later. He said that Mitzi was being prepared for Crufts and mustn't suffer any stress. My mother said, 'I've got better things to do than to stand here talking about a romance between a bloody cocker spaniel and a mongrel.' I hoped this would mean she would cook some dinner but no, she went into the kitchen and read *The Guardian* from cover to cover, so I opened a tin of tuna again.

Thursday April 15th

Woke up at 4 a.m. with a toothache. Took six junior aspirins for the pain. At 5 a.m. I woke my mother and father and told them that I was in torment.

My father said, 'It's your own bloody fault for missing your last three dentist's appointments.'

At 5.30 a.m. I asked my father to drive me to the hospital Casualty Department, but he refused and turned over in bed. It's all right for him: he hasn't got any real teeth. I sat up, racked with agony, and watched the sky get light. The lucky toothless birds started their horrible squawking and I swore that from this day forward I would go to the dentist's four times a year, whether I was in pain or not.

At nine o'clock my mother woke me up to tell me that she'd made me an appointment at the dentist's emergency clinic. I told her that the pain had stopped and instructed her to cancel the appointment.

Friday April 16th
MOON'S LAST QUARTER

Woke up at 3 a.m. in agony with toothache. I tried to suffer in silence but my pain-racked sobs must have filtered through to my parents' bedroom because my father crashed into my room and asked me to be quiet. He showed no sympathy, just moaned on about how he had to work on the canal tomorrow and he needed his sleep. On his way back to bed he slipped on one of my mother's *Cosmopolitan*s that she'd left on her side of the bedroom floor. His swearing woke the dog up. Then my mother woke up. Then the lousy birds started. So once again I watched dawn's grey fingers infiltrate the night.

Saturday   April 17th

Still in bed with toothache.

My parents are showing me no sympathy, they keep saying, 'You should have gone to the dentist's.'

I have phoned Pandora: she is coming round tomorrow. She asked me if I needed anything; I said a Mars bar would be nice. She said (quite irritably I thought), 'Heavens above, Adrian, aren't your teeth rotten enough?'

The dog has been howling outside Mitzi's gate all day. It is also off its Pedigree Chum and Winalot.

Sunday   April 18th
LOW SUNDAY

Pandora has just left my bedroom. I am just about devastated with frustration. I can't go on like this. I have written to Auntie Clara, the Agony Aunt.

> Dear Aunt Clara,
> I am a fifteen-year-old schoolboy. My grandma tells me that I am attractive and many people have commented on how mature I am for my years. I am the only child of a bad marriage (apart from the dog). My problem is this: I am deeply in love with an older girl (by three months). She is in a class above me (I don't mean in school: we are in the same class at school. I mean that she is a social class above me.) but she claims that this doesn't matter to our relationship. We have been very happy until recently when I have started to be obsessed by sex. I have fallen to

self-manipulation quite a lot lately, and it is OK for a bit but it soon wears off. I know that a proper bout of lovemaking would do me good. It would improve my skin and help my mind to concentrate on my 'O' level studies.

I have tried all sorts of erotic things, but my girl-friend refuses to go the whole hog. She says we are not ready.

I am quite aware of the awesome things about bringing an unwanted baby into the world and I would wear a protective dildo.

> Yours in desperation,
> Poet of the Midlands

Monday   April 19th

We had a dead good debate in Social Studies this morning. It was about the Falklands.

Pandora put the proposition 'That this class is against the use of force to regain the Falkland Islands'.

The standard of debate was quite good for a change. I made a brilliant speech in favour of the motion. I quoted from *Animal Farm* and *The Grapes of Wrath*. I got quite a good round of applause when I sat down.

Barry Kent spoke *against* the proposition. He said, 'Er, I er, fink we should er, you know, like, bomb the coast of Argentina.' He was quoting from his father, yet *he* sat down to a standing ovation!

Dentist's at 2.30, worse luck!

4 p.m. I am now minus a front tooth! The stupid Australian dentist took it *out* instead of repairing it. He even had the nerve to wrap it in a bit of tissue paper and give it to me to take home!

I said, 'But I've got a gap!' He said, 'So has Watford, and if Watford can get used to it so can you.'

I asked him if another tooth would grow in its place. He said, 'Bloody ignorant Poms,' under his breath, but he didn't answer my question.

As I was stumbling out of his surgery clutching my frozen-up jaw he said that he had often seen me walking home from school eating a Mars bar, and it would be entirely my own fault if I was toothless at thirty.

I will walk home another way in future.

Tuesday   April 20th

I have now got the kind of face that you see on 'Wanted' posters.
I look like a mass murderer. My mother is dead mad with the
dentist; she has written him a letter demanding that he makes a
false tooth free of charge.

School was terrible; Barry Kent started calling me 'Gappy
Mole' and soon everyone was at it; even Pandora was a bit
distant. I sent her a note in Physics asking her if she still loved
me. She sent a note back saying, 'I will love you for as long
as Britain has Gibraltar.'

Wednesday   April 21st

It has just been on the news that Spain wants Gibraltar back.

Thursday   April 22nd

I couldn't face taking my gap to school this morning so I stayed
in bed until 12.45 p.m. I asked my mother for an excuse note. I
gave it to Ms Fossington-Gore during afternoon registration.
She read it angrily then said, 'At least your mother is honest. It
makes a change from the usual lies one has come to expect from
most parents.'

She showed me the letter. It said:

> Dear Ms Fossington-Gore,
> Adrian did not come to school this morning because he
> didn't get out of bed until 12.45.
>> Yours faithfully,
>> Ms Pauline Mole

I will get my father to write my excuse notes in future; he is a
born liar.

Friday   April 23rd
ST GEORGE'S DAY (ENGLAND). NEW MOON

Barry Kent came to school in a Union Jack tee-shirt today. Ms
Fossington-Gore sent him home to change. Barry Kent shouted,
'I'm celebratin' our patron saint's birthday ain't I?'

Ms Fossington-Gore shouted back, 'You're wearing a symbol of fascism, you nasty NF lout.'

Today is also Shakespeare's birthday. One day I will be a great writer like him. I am well on the way: I have already had two rejection letters from the BBC.

Saturday   April 24th

Barry Kent's father is on the front of the local paper tonight. He is pictured holding Barry Kent's Union Jack tee-shirt. The caption underneath his picture says: 'A Patriot mourns loss of National Pride.'

The article said:

> Burly World War Two veteran Frederick Kent (45) spoke to our reporter in his homely Council house lounge about his profound feelings of regret that his son Barry (15) was ridiculed and humiliated because he wore a Union Jack tee-shirt to school. Barry is a pupil at Neil Armstrong Comprehensive School. Mrs Kent (35) said, 'My son Barry is a sensitive boy who worships his country and is very fond of St George, so he wore a tee-shirt what had a picture of our great English flag.' Mr Frederick Kent interjected, 'On account of how it was St George's birthday yesterday.'
>
> Mr Kent is refusing to let his son attend school until the teacher concerned, Ms Fossington-Gore (31), makes a public apology.
>
> Mr Reginald Scruton (57), headmaster of the school, said on the telephone today: 'I know the wretched Kent family only too well and I'm sure that we can work something out so that it doesn't make the local rag.' When it was pointed out to Mr Scruton that he was in fact talking to Roger Greenhill, our Education correspondent, Mr Scruton apologized and made the following statement: 'No comment.'

Sunday   April 25th
SECOND AFTER EASTER.
DAYLIGHT SAVING TIME BEGINS (USA AND CANADA)

British troops have recaptured South Georgia. I have adjusted my campaign map accordingly.

Found a strange device in the bathroom this morning. It looked like an egg timer. It said 'Predictor' on the side of the box. I hope my mother is not dabbling with the occult.

Monday   April 26th

A mysterious conversation! My mother said, 'George it's positive.' My father said, 'Christ, I can't go through all that three o'clock in the morning stuff again, not at my age.'

It sounds as if my mother is making unreasonable sexual demands on my father.

Tuesday   April 27th

Got a letter from Aunt Clara! I read it on the way to school.

> Dear Poet of the Midlands,
> Well, well, well, you are in a lather aren't you, lovey! Look, you're fifteen, your body's in a whirl, your hormones are in a maelstrom. Your emotions are up and down like a yo-yo.
> And of course you want sex. Every lad of your age does. But, my dear, there are people who crave penthouse apartments and exotic holidays. We can't have what we want all the time.
> You sound as if you've got a nice sensible lassie; enjoy each other's company. Take up a hobby, keep physically and mentally alert and learn to control your breathing.
> Sex is only a small part of life, my dear lad. Enjoy your precious teenage years.
> Sincerely,
> Aunt Clara

Enjoy my precious teenage years! They are nothing but trouble and misery. I can't wait until I am fully mature and can make urban conversation with intellectuals.

Wednesday   April 28th

Stick Insect (alias Doreen Slater) called round to our house today. I haven't seen her since my father and her broke it off.

She was breathing dead quickly and she had a funny look in

her eyes. When my father came to the door she didn't say anything, she just opened her coat (she's put a bit of weight on) and said, 'I thought you ought to know, George,' and turned and went down the garden path.

My father didn't say anything. He just leaned against the bannisters sort of weakly.

I said, 'She's looking well isn't she?'

My father muttered, 'Blooming', then he put his coat on and went to catch her up.

Five minutes later my mother came back from her Jane Fonda's robot class at the neighbourhood centre, she was dead pleased because she had broken the pain barrier.

She shouted, 'George,' looked in all the rooms, then asked, 'When did you last see your father?'

I kept quiet, like the kid in the painting. My mother goes berserk if anyone mentions Stick Insect's name.

Thursday   April 29th

School is dead brilliant now that Barry Kent's shaved head and ferocious boots are but a bad memory.

Went to the dentist's for an impression. He called me 'Matilda'. I was unable to object because my mouth was full of putty.

Friday   April 30th
MOON'S FIRST QUARTER

My mother and father are getting through a bottle of Vodka a week. Not a minute goes by without one or the other of them bashing the ice tray or slicing a lemon or running to the off-licence for Schweppes.

This is a bad sign. It means something is going to happen.

Saturday   May 1st

Grandma rang with her annual gibberish about 'Cast ne'er a clout'. I know it's got something to do with keeping your vest on. But so what? I keep my vest on all the year round anyway.

Britain has bombed Port Stanley airport and put it out of action.

Sunday May 2nd
THIRD AFTER EASTER

Went round to Nigel's and was astounded to hear that his parents are trying to emigrate to Australia! How could any English person want to live abroad? Foreigners can't help living abroad because they were born there, but for an English person to go is ridiculous, especially now that sun-tan lamps are so readily available.

Nigel agrees with me. He asked me if he could stay behind and live at our house. I warned him about the poor standard of living but he said he would bring all his consumer durables with him.

Monday May 3rd
MAY DAY HOLIDAY (UK EXCEPT SCOTLAND)
BANK HOLIDAY (SCOTLAND)

This morning I spent half an hour in the bathroom studying my nose, after my so-called best friend Nigel asked me last night if I realized I was a Dustin Hoffman look-alike.

I hadn't realized that my nose had grown to such an abnormal size. But the more I looked at it the more I could see that it *is* huge.

My mother bashed on the door and shouted, 'Whatever you're doing in there, stop it at once and come down and eat your breakfast. Your cornflakes are getting soggy!'

When I got downstairs I asked my mother if I reminded her of Dustin Hoffman. She said, 'You should be so lucky, dearie.'

Tuesday May 4th

My mother has stopped wearing a bra. Her bust looks like two poached eggs that have been cooked for too long. I wish she wouldn't wear such tight tee-shirts. It's not dignified in somebody her age (37).

Wednesday May 5th

A strange phone call. The phone rang and I picked it up but before I could say our number a posh woman said: 'Clinic here.

You have an appointment with us on Friday at 2 p.m. Will you be able to keep the appointment, Mrs Mole?'

I said, 'Yes,' in a falsetto voice.

'You will be with us for two hours, during that time you will see two doctors and a counsellor who is very experienced in your particular problem,' she said mechanically.

I said, 'Thank you,' in a high-pitched squeak.

She went on, 'Please bring a sample of urine with you, a *small* sample, no full-to-the-brim pickle jars, please.'

'All right,' I croaked.

'Don't upset yourself, Mrs Mole,' the woman said slushily. 'We are here to help, you know.' Then she said, 'Please don't forget our fee. It will be forty-two pounds for your initial consultation.'

'No,' I whispered.

'So Friday at 2 o'clock. Please be punctual'. Then she put the phone down.

What does it all mean? My mother has not said anything about being ill. What is her particular problem? Which 'clinic?'

Thursday   May 6th

I heard some very yukky woman talking on Radio Four tonight about how she became a millionairess from writing romantic fiction books. She said that women readers like books about doctors and electronics wizards and people like that. I am going to have a go myself. I could do with a million pounds. The woman said it is important for an author of romantic fiction to have an evocative name, so, after much thought, I have decided to call myself Adrienne Storme. I have already written half the first page:

Longing for Wolverhampton by Adrienne Storme
Jason Westmoreland's copper-flecked eyes glanced cynically around the terrace. He was sick of Capri and longed
for Wolverhampton.

   He flexed his remaining fingers and examined them
critically. The accident with the chain saw had ended his
brilliant career in electronics. His days were now devoid of

microchips. There was a yawning chasm in his life. He had tried to fill it with travel and self-gratification but nothing could blot out the memories he had of Gardenia Fetherington, the virginal plastic surgeon at St Bupa's in Wolverhampton.

Jason brooded, blindly blinking back big blurry tears . . . .

Friday   May 7th

My mother and father were having a discussion about feminism in the car on the way to Sainsbury's this evening. My father said that since my mother's consciousness had been raised he had noticed that she had lost two inches round her bust.

My mother said angrily, 'What have my breasts got to do with anything?' There was a silence then she said, 'But don't you think I have grown as a person, George?'

My father said, 'On the contrary, Pauline, you are much smaller since you stopped wearing high heels.'

Me and my father laughed quite a lot but not for long because my mother gave us one of her powerful glances, then she looked out of the car window. She had a few tears in her eyes.

She looked at me and said, 'If only I had a daughter to talk to.'

My father said, 'We can't take the risk of having another baby like Adrian, Pauline.' Then they began to talk about my babyhood. They made me sound like Damian in the film of *The Omen*.

My mother said, 'It's that bloody Dr Spock's fault that Adrian has turned out like he has.'

I said, 'What *have* I turned out like?'

My mother said, 'You're an anal retentive, aren't you?' and my father said, 'You're tight-fisted, and you've always got your perfectly groomed head in a book.'

I was so shocked I couldn't speak for a bit but, trying to keep my voice light and melodious (not easy when your heart is pierced with the arrows of criticism), I said, 'What sort of son did you want then?'

Their answer took us all around Sainsbury's, through the queue at the checkout, and back to the multi-storey car park.

My father's ideal son was a natural athlete, he was cheerful and outgoing, he was a fluent linguist, he was tall with ruddy unblemished cheeks, he took his hat off to ladies. He went fishing with his father and swapped jokes. He was good with his hands and had a hobby making grandfather clocks. He was good officer material. He would vote Conservative and would marry into a good family. He would set up his own computer business in Guildford.

However, my mother's ideal son would be intense and saturnine. He would go to a school for the Intellectually Precocious. He would fascinate girls and women at an early age, he would enthral visitors with his witty conversation. He would wear his clothes with panache, he would be completely non-sexist, non-agist, non-racist. (His best friend would be an old African woman.) He would win a scholarship to Oxford, he would take the place by storm and be written about in future biographies. He would turn down offers of safe parliamentary seats in Britain. Instead, he would go to South Africa and lead the blacks into a successful revolution. He would return to England where he would be the first man deemed fit to edit *Spare Rib*. He would move in sparkling social circles. He would take his mother everywhere he went.

When they'd both finished spouting on I said, 'Well I'm sorry if I'm a disappointment to you.'

My mother said, 'It's not your fault, Adrian, it's ours, we should have called you BRETT!!!'

Saturday May 8th
FULL MOON

I needed to talk to somebody about my sense of inferiority (which grew even bigger in the night as I lay awake and thought about Brett Mole, the phantom son). So I went to Grandma's. She showed me my baby photos. I must admit that I *was* a bit grotesque: I was completely bald until I was two and I always had a dead fierce expression on my face. Now I know why my mother hasn't got a Technicolor gilt-framed photograph of me on top of our television like other mothers.

But I'm glad I went to Grandma's; she thinks everything about me is brilliant. I told her about Brett Mole, the boy that never was. She said, 'He sounds a right nasty piece of work to me. I'm glad you didn't turn out like *him*.'

Grandma had a bit of arthritis in her shoulder so she took her dress off and I sprayed Ralgex on the pain. Grandma's corset looks like a parachute harness. I asked her how she gets in and out of it. She told me it was all down to self-discipline. She has got a theory that since corsets went out of fashion England has lost its backbone.

Sunday   May 9th
4TH AFTER EASTER. MOTHER'S DAY (USA AND CANADA)

I have just realized that I have never seen a dead body or a real female nipple. This is what comes of living in a cul-de-sac.

Monday   May 10th

I asked Pandora to show me one of her nipples but she refused. I tried to explain that it was in the interests of widening my life experience, but she buttoned her cardigan up to the neck and went home.

Tuesday   May 11th

We did diabetes in human biology today. Mr Dooher taught us to measure our blood sugar level by testing our wee. This reminded me that I forgot to tell my mother about her appointment at the clinic. Still, I don't suppose it was important.

Wednesday   May 12th

I received the following letter from Pandora this morning:

> Adrian,
> I am writing to terminate our relationship. Our love was once a spiritual thing. We were united in our appreciation of art and literature, but Adrian you have changed. You have become morbidly fixated with my body. Your request to look at my left nipple last night finally convinced me that we must part.

Do not contact me,
Pandora Braithwaite

P.S. If I were you I would seek professional psychiatric help for your hypochondria and your sex mania. Anthony Perkins, who played the maniac in *Psycho* was in analysis for ten years, so there is no need to be ashamed.

Thursday   May 13th

Yesterday before I opened *that* letter I was a normal type of intellectual teenager. Today I know what it is to suffer. I am now an adult. I am no longer young. In fact I have noticed wrinkles forming on my forehead. I wouldn't be surprised if my hair doesn't turn white overnight.

I am in total anguish!
I love her!
I love her!
I love her!
Oh God!
Oh Pandora!

3 a.m. I have used a whole Andrex toilet roll to mop up my tears. I haven't cried so much since the wind blew my candy floss away at Cleethorpes.

5 a.m. I slept fitfully, then got out of bed to watch the dawn break. The world is no longer exciting and colourful. It is grey and full of heartbreak. I thought of doing myself in, but it's not really fair on the people you leave behind. It would upset my mother to come into my room and find my corpse. I shan't bother doing my 'O' levels. I'll be an intellectual road sweeper. I will surprise litter louts by quoting Kafka as they pass me by.

Friday   May 14th

Why oh why did I ask Pandora to show me *her* nipple? Anybody's nipple would have done. Nigel says that Sharon Botts will show *everything* for 50p and a pound of grapes.

I have written Pandora a short note.

Pandora Darling,
What can I say? I was crude and clumsy and should have

known you would run from me like a startled faun.

Please, at least grant me an audience and let me apologize in person.

Yours with unvanquished love,

Adrian

I think it hits the right note. I got the 'startled faun' bit from one of Grandma's yucky romantic novels. I have sprayed a bit of my mother's 'Tramp' perfume onto the envelope and I will deliver it by hand after dark tonight.

Tramp! Fancy calling a perfume *Tramp*! Ha! Ha! Ha!

Saturday   May 15th
SCOTTISH QUARTER DAY

There were a lot of visitors at Pandora's house. I could hardly get up the drive for Jaguars and Rovers and Volvos. At first I thought there had been a death in the family because I could see two nuns and a priest eating sausage rolls in the kitchen. Then a gorilla walked in and took a bottle of wine out of the fridge so I realized it must be a fancy dress party. I hid behind the summer house so that I could get a better view: there was a cowboy and a devil talking in one bedroom and a frogman and three gipsies laughing in another. A knight in armour was clanking about in the garden. He was being followed by a cavewoman who was shouting, 'Stand still, Damian. I've found a tin opener!'

Assorted fairies and Kermits and clowns were dancing downstairs, then the gorilla burst in and started dancing with a belly dancer who was wearing a most disgusting flimsy costume which showed her navel and most of her nipples. The belly dancer kept her yashmak on which I thought was hypocritical—as if anybody was interested in looking at her face!

I couldn't see Pandora anywhere, so after about half an hour I ran up to the door and put my letter through the letterbox. As I turned to run back down the drive Toulouse Lautrec shuffled out and was sick in one of the bay tree tubs.

I got home to find Queen Victoria and Prince Albert in our kitchen. Queen Victoria said, 'We're going to the Braithwaites.' Prince Albert said, 'The dog needs feeding.' Then they swept regally out of the kitchen and up the road to Pandora's. Nobody tells me anything in this house.

Sunday   May 16th
ROGATION SUNDAY. MOON'S LAST QUARTER

3 p.m. My mother keeps being sick. It serves her right for staying out until 4 a.m. drinking. My father is still in bed, but he will have to get up soon. He has promised to take Grandma to the garden centre after tea.

7 p.m. Garden centres must be the most boring places on earth, yet adults walk around them with expressions of ecstasy on their faces!

My grandma bought a dozen rose sticks and a bag of fertilizer and a plastic Cupid urn.

My father bought a rose stick called 'Pauline'. He and my mother looked at each other in a sloppy sort of way and held hands over the stick. I left them to it and went and looked at the poisons on the bottom shelves.

I was toying with the idea of buying a bottle when Grandma shouted and asked me to come and carry the fertilizer to the car. Thus my mind was torn from thoughts of death.

Monday   May 17th

I was doing my maths homework in the fourth years' cloakroom when I overheard Pandora's confident voice ringing out.

'Yes it *was* a brillo party. But, my dear, I'm rather worried.'

Claire Neilson said, 'Why's that, Pan?'

Pandora said seriously, 'I so *enjoyed* dressing up as a belly dancer, even though it's quite against my feminist principles to exhibit my body.'

Then they moved away down the corridor gassing about Claire Neilson's cat who is expecting kittens.

So, Pandora, who refused to show me *one* of her nipples in the privacy of my bedroom is quite prepared to flaunt *both* nipples at a mixed gathering!!!

Tuesday   May 18th

Bumped into Stick Insect in the library. She had her son, Maxwell House, with her. For a thin woman she certainly looked fat.

Maxwell chucked books off the shelves while Stick Insect and I talked about the days when she had been my father's girl-friend. I told her that she had had a lucky escape from my father, but she defended him, saying, 'He is another person when he is on his own with me. He is so sweet and kind.' Yes, and so was Dr Jekyll.

Got *The Condition of the Working Class in England* by Frederick Engels out of the library.

10.30 p.m. I have just realized that Stick Insect used the present tense when she was referring to her relationship with my father. It is absolutely disgraceful. A woman of thirty not knowing the fundamentals of grammar!

Wednesday   May 19th

No word from Pandora. When we meet at school she looks through me as if I were the Invisible Man. I have asked Nigel where I can find Sharon Botts. I also went to the greengrocer's to find out how much grapes cost per pound.

Thursday   May 20th
ASCENSION DAY

Started reading Fred Engels' book tonight. My father saw me reading it and said, 'I don't want that Commie rubbish in my house.'

I said, 'It's about the class you came from yourself.'

My father said, 'I have worked and slaved and fought to join the middle classes, Adrian, and now I'm here I don't want my son admiring proles and revolutionaries.'

He is deluding himself if he thinks he has joined the middle classes. He still puts HP sauce on his toast.

Friday   May 21st

While I was listening to *The Archers* my mother asked me if I minded being an only child. I said on the contrary, I preferred it.

Saturday   May 22nd

My father has just asked me if I would like a sister or a brother. I said neither. Why do they keep drivelling on about kids? I hope they aren't thinking about adopting one. They are terrible parents. Look at me, I'm a complete neurotic.

Sunday   May 23rd
SUNDAY AFTER ASCENSION. NEW MOON

I couldn't sleep so I got up very early and went for a walk past Pandora's house. I thought about her lying in her Habitat bed wearing her Laura Ashley nightgown and I don't mind admitting that tears sprang to my eyes. However I dashed them away and went to call on old Bert and Queenie.

A wild old woman answered the door, she said, 'What have you got me out of bed for?' It was Queenie with her hair on end and no make-up on.

I apologized and went home to wake my parents up with a cup of tea. Were they grateful? No! My mother said, 'For God's sake, Adrian, it's cockcrow on Sunday morning. Push off and buy the papers or something.'

I bought the papers, read them, then took them up to my parents. I think the central heating must need turning down because my parents were both very red in the face. As I went out I heard my mother say, 'George, we will have to get a lock on that door.'

Monday   May 24th
VICTORIA DAY (CANADA)

Went to the youth club tonight. Barry Kent was there with his gang worse luck! Rick Lemon was showing a film about potholing in Derbyshire. I was very interested but I found it hard to concentrate on it because Barry Kent kept putting his fingers in front of the projector and making rabbits and giraffes and other animal shapes.

When Barry Kent had gone to the coffee bar to harass the Youth Work student behind the counter I told Rick Lemon about my problems. He said, 'Hey that's bad news, Adrian, but

I'm busy tonight. Come and see me at 6 p.m. tomorrow night and we'll have a good rap.'

I think this means that he wants to talk to me at 6 p.m. tomorrow.

Tuesday   May 25th

Went to Rick's office in the Youth Club. We had a long talk about my problems. Rick said I was a 'typical product of the petty-bourgeoisie'. He said my problems were the result of my generation's 'alienation from an increasingly urbanized society'. He said my parents were 'morally bankrupt and spiritually dead'. He lit a long, loose herbal cigarette and said, 'Adrian, loosen up. Don't run with the herd. Try and live your life unfettered by convention.' Then he looked at his watch and said, 'Christ I told her I'd be home by seven.'

We walked outside and he got into his wobbly Citroën and said, 'You must come round for supper one night.'

I asked if he was still squatting in the old tyre factory. He said, 'No we've moved into Badger's Copse, the new Barratt housing estate.'

I can't decide if I feel better or worse after talking to Rick. On the whole I think I feel worse.

John Nott has announced on the news that 'one of our ships has been badly damaged.' I hope it is not the *Canberra*. Barry Kent's brother is on it.

Wednesday   May 26th

My mother is pregnant! My mother!!!!!!!!!!!!!!!!!

I will be the laughing stock at school. How could she do this to me? She is three months pregnant already, so in November a baby will be living in this house. I hope they don't expect me to share my room with it. There's no way I'm getting up in the night to give it its bottle.

My parents didn't prepare me or anything. We were all eating spaghetti on toast when my father said casually, 'Oh, by the way, Adrian, congratulations are in order, your mother's three months pregnant.'

Congratulations! What about my 'A' levels in two years' time?

How can I study with a toddler smashing the place up around me?

10 p.m. Kissed my poor mother goodnight. She said, 'Are you pleased about the baby, Adrian?' I lied and said 'Yes'.

The ship that went down was the *Coventry*. It is very sad. I am glad that my dad got turned down by the War Office.

Thursday   May 27th

Got an airmail letter from Hamish Mancini, the American we met on holiday last year.

> 1889 West 33rd Street,
> New York

> Hi there Aid!
> Fazed huh! Yeah well, thought I'd communicate. Been feelin kinda unzapped lately, guess mom's divorce to number four kinda unhinged me some. But! Hamish Mancini aint gonna stick around and take no more adult crap, no sir Aid. I'm comin over to visit you some. I got finance. I got documentation, I got nothin keepin me here. Tomorrow I get a flight and wowee I get to see your olde British cottage in the ancient Midlands region.
> We'll promenade around ancient ruins. We'll explore Shakesphere land. Huh? I got me some good Lebanon.
> See you Saturday buddy,
> Hamish Mancini

After reading it and rereading it I think it means that Hamish Mancini is coming to stay with us on Saturday! I wish I hadn't told him that I lived in a thatched cottage.

I haven't told my parents yet. My mother said he ruined her adulterous holiday *avec* Lucas with his constant yapping.

Friday   May 28th

Dentist's after school for a false tooth fitting. He took advantage of my weak position in the dentist's chair to make disparaging remarks about British teeth. His assistant is from Malaya so they are both bitter about having lived under the Colonial jungleboot.

I walked home slowly, I was dreading breaking the news about Hamish Mancini's arrival. The dog met me halfway up the cul-de-sac. It was nice to see its happy face.

When I got in I made a big fuss over my poor pregnant mother, I made her a cup of coffee and insisted she put her feet up on the sofa. I put a cushion behind her head and gave her the *Radio Times* to read. I've seen it done in old films (Cary Grant did it to Doris Day).

My mother said, 'It's very kind of you, Adrian, but I can only sit down for a few minutes; I'm playing squash in half an hour.'

But she was in a good mood so I told her about Hamish. She rolled her eyes a bit and pulled her lips tight, but she didn't go mad. So perhaps being with child has improved her temper.

Saturday May 29th
MOON'S FIRST QUARTER

11.30 p.m. The spare room is prepared, the pantry is full of tinned pumpkin pie, the freezer is bursting with pork grits and corn on the cob and pot roasts. The bathroom has been cleaned to American hygiene standards, the dog has been brushed but Hamish Mancini is not here.

We watched the nine o'clock news but no airliners had crashed into the Atlantic today or any other day this week.

At 11 p.m. my father said, 'Well, I'm not sitting around in my best clothes a minute longer.' So we all took our best clothes off and went to bed.

5 a.m. Hamish Mancini is in the spare room. He is playing Appalachian mountain songs on his steel guitar. He got a taxi from Heathrow airport (130 miles!); the taxi driver found our house all right, but Hamish refused to believe that it was the right address and made the poor bloke drive round our suburb, looking for a thatched cottage. Eventually the taxi driver drove back to our house and got my father out of bed. Hamish paid the worn-out taxi driver with dollar bills.

Sunday   May 30th
WHIT SUNDAY

Hamish made a terrible *faux pas* at breakfast. He asked my mother, 'Hey, Pauline, where's that guy, Lucas?'

There was an awful silence, then my father said coldly, 'My wife and Mr Lucas are no longer friends.'

But Hamish went on! 'Gee that's too bad, Mr Lucas was cool y'know? What happened?'

My mother said, 'We don't usually talk about personal matters at breakfast, not in England,' she added.

He said, 'Wow, that great British reserve I've heard about.' He seemed really happy, as if he'd found a whole village full of thatched cottages.

In the afternoon we took him to see Bert and Queenie, he was beside himself with joy. On the way back in the car he kept saying, 'Jee-sus! A genuine Derby [he pronounced it to rhyme with Herbie] and Joan!'

I went to bed at 10 p.m. worn out with his constant enthusiastic exclamations.

Monday   May 31st
SPRING HOLIDAY (EXCEPT SCOTLAND)
BANK HOLIDAY (SCOTLAND) MEMORIAL DAY (USA)

We took Hamish to the fun fair on our recreation ground. For once Hamish looked a bit subdued. He said, 'I guess Disneyland has kinda given me a false expectation-of-enjoyment level.'

He took my mother on the dodgems and I went on the Flying Whiplash with my father. I was dumbstruck with terror, so was my father; I was OK until I looked down and saw the moron working the machinery. He looked like a Neanderthal man in denims and I had put my life in his clumsy paws!

My father had aged ten years by the time he got off the Flying Whiplash. But when my mother asked him if he had enjoyed himself he said, 'It was grand.'

Our dog has become Hamish's devoted companion; it follows him wherever he goes. Hamish calls our dog 'ol' Blue' and sings it sickly songs about American dogs who sit on their dead masters' graves.

It makes me sick to see how easily the dog's affections are bought.

Tuesday   June 1st

Hamish wants to meet Pandora. I told him how things stand between Pandora and me, but Hamish wouldn't listen. He just said, 'But that doesn't stop *me* from meeting her, for Christ's sake.'

Grandma rang up at tea-time and asked if my father would come and collect her but I told her that we'd got an American in the house, so she said she wouldn't bother. She said, 'I'm just too old to cope with Americans, Adrian.' I know how she feels.

Hamish got Pandora's number from our pop-up phone index on the hall table, then he rang her up and invited himself round for supper!

Still, at least the house is peaceful. I am reading *The Quiet American* by Graham Greene, Hughie Greene's brother.

Wednesday   June 2nd

Hamish has gone skiing on a dry ski slope with Pandora. I hope they both break something, preferably their necks.

Thursday   June 3rd

I took Hamish to see how an English comprehensive school works today. The only previous knowledge he had of English schools was taken from reading *Tom Brown's Schooldays*, so Hamish was a bit disappointed to find that ritual floggings and roastings had been done away with.

Mr Dock, my English teacher, asked Hamish to give our class a short talk on 'His impressions of England.' Hamish wasn't a bit shy. He went to the front of the class, spat his chewing gum into Mr Dock's wicker basket and said, 'Well, England's great, cute, real fine. Jee-sus it's green! I mean like real green! And I just love your flues [chimneys, translated by Mr Dock]. In the Apple [New York] we don't have flues [chimneys]. I guess the coolest thing, though, is your girls. [Here his eyes met Pandora's.] They may look like icebergs on the surface, but Jee-sus the seven-eighths that's under the surface sure gets a guy warmed up.' He drivelled on for another ten minutes! I was glad when the bell rang.

It is twenty-four days since Pandora spoke to me.

Friday   June 4th

Hamish is spending every waking moment at Pandora's house. It is an abuse of our hospitality. A telegram came from America. It was addressed to MANCINI but I opened it, in case his mother had dropped dead or something.

> BABY STOP COME HOME TO MOM STOP WE MUST TRY TO INTERACT POSITIVELY STOP HOW THE BRITS TREATING YOU STOP WIRE ME AND GIVE ME YOUR ARRIVAL AT KENNEDY STOP I GOT A NEW SHRINK STOP HE IS PORTUGUESE STOP ETHEL GLITTENSTEINER SWEARS HE CURED HER KLEPTOMANIA STOP HOW'S THE WEATHER STOP IT'S AWFUL HOT HERE STOP BUT IT IS NOT SO MUCH THE HEAT AS THE HUMIDITY STOP SAY HELLO TO ADRIAN PAULINE AND MISTER LUCAS FOR ME STOP I LOVE YOU BABY

I delivered the telegram to Pandora's house. Pandora took it from me without a word. I turned away without a word.

Saturday   June 5th

Hamish has gone home to Mom. The next time he runs away from home I hope he goes to Cape Horn or the Arctic Circle or anywhere I'm not likely to be.

Sunday   June 6th
TRINITY SUNDAY. FULL MOON

Stayed in my room all day bringing my Falklands campaign map up to date. I am very aware that I am living through a historical period and I, Adrian Mole, predict that the British People will force the government to resign.

Monday June 7th
HOLIDAY (REPUBLIC OF IRELAND)

> My mother
> Claire Neilson's cat
> Mitzi

What have the above all got in common?

The fact that they are all expecting babies, kittens or puppies. The fecundity on this suburb is just amazing. You can't walk down the street without bumping into pregnant women and it has all happened since the council put fluoride in the water.

Tuesday June 8th

Saw Bert Baxter outside the newsagent's. He was sitting in his wheelchair reading the *Morning Star*. We had a long talk about working-class culture. Bert said that if he were a younger man he would infiltrate into the *Sun* newspaper and smash the presses up!

He tried to get me to join the Young Communists. I said I would think about it. I thought about it for five minutes then decided not to. The GCE examiners might get to hear about it.

Wednesday June 9th

It is time I was done with childish things so I have taken all my Enid Blyton books off my bookshelves. I have packed them into an Anchor butter box and put them outside my door. I hope my parents take the hint and stop talking to me as if I were a moron. Anyone who can understand how the International Monetary Fund works (I did it in Maths last week) deserves more respect.

Thursday June 10th

Stick Insect is pregnant!

I saw her in the Co-op this afternoon. Maxwell House was having a tantrum at the checkout so I was spared from speaking to her. The poor woman looked dead miserable. Still it serves her right for being promiscuous. I wonder who the father is?

Friday   June 11th

My father is getting fed up with his job as a canal bank renovation supervisor. He says that no sooner do Boz, Baz, Maz, Daz and Gaz, his gang, clear a section of canal than some slob comes along in the night and tips a month's household rubbish on the virgin bank.

The gang are getting a bit disheartened and morale is low. I offered to set up a vigilante group but my father said that anyone who has carried an old mattress 300 yards in the dark is not going to be put off dumping it by a gaggle of spotty schoolboys.

Saturday   June 12th

I have written to Mr Tydeman at the BBC and sent him another poem. I chose Norway as my theme, as I am quite an expert on the Norwegian Leather Industry.

> Dear Mr Tydeman,
> I had a few moments to spare so I thought I would pen you a letter and also send you my new poem 'Norway'. It (the poem) is in the modernist school of poetry, in other words it isn't about flowers and stuff and it doesn't rhyme. If you can't understand it, could you pass it on to someone who will explain it for you? Any modern poet will do.
> Yours faithfully,
> Adrian Mole (Aged 15¼)
> P.S. If you bump into Terry Wogan in the corridor could you ask him to mention my grandma on the air? Her name is May Mole and she is a seventy-six-year-old diabetic.

Norway
Norway! Land of difficult spelling.
Hiding your beauty behind strange vowels.
Land of long nights, short days and dots over 'O's.
Ruminating majestic reindeers
Tread warily on ice floes
Ever aware of what happened to the
Titanic.
One day I will sojourn to your shores
I live in the middle of England
But!

Norway! My soul resides in your watery ~~fiords fyords fiiords~~
Inlets.

Sunday June 13th
FIRST AFTER TRINITY

Spent the day at Grandma's reading the *News of the World* and
eating proper food for a change. We had roast lamb and mint
sauce made from the window box. Grandma is hoping that her
next grandchild is a girl. She said, 'You can dress girls nicely.'
She has already knitted a purple matinée jacket and half a pair of
bootees.

She is using neutral colours 'just in case'. I am dreading the
day when there are feet inside the bootees.

Monday June 14th
MOON'S LAST QUARTER

Our usual postman has been replaced by another one called
Courtney Elliot. We know his name because he knocked on the
door and introduced himself. He is certainly no run-of-the-mill
postman, he wears a ruffled shirt and a red-spotted bow tie with
his grey uniform.

He invited himself into the kitchen and asked to be introduced
to the dog. When the dog had been brought in from the back
garden Courtney looked it in the eye and said, 'Hail fellow, well
met.' Don't ask me what it means; all I know is that our dog
rolled over and let Courtney tickle its belly. Courtney refused a
cup of instant coffee, saying that he only drank fresh-ground
Brazilian, then he gave my father the letters saying, 'One from
the Inland Revenue I fear, Mr Mole,' tipped his hat to my
mother and left. The letter was from the tax office. It was to tell
my father that they had 'received information' that during the
previous tax year he had been running a spice rack construction
company business from his premises, but that they had no record
of such a business and so could he fill in the enclosed form? My
father said, 'Some rotten sod's shopped me to the tax!' I went off
to school. On the way I saw Courtney coming out of the Singhs'
eating a chapati.

Tuesday   June 15th

Today Courtney brought a letter from the Customs and Excise Department. It asked my father (in very curt terms) why he hadn't registered his spice rack business for VAT.

My father shouted at the letter and said, 'Somebody's got it in for me!' My mother and father counted how many enemies they had made in their lives. It came to twenty-seven, not counting relations.

Wednesday   June 16th

My father is getting to dread Courtney Elliot's cheerful knock on our door in the morning. This morning it was a letter from Access threatening to cut my father's card in half.

I was hit on the head by a cricket ball today. It was my own fault. When I saw it coming towards me I shut my eyes and ran in the opposite direction. I am at home in bed waiting to see if concussion sets in.

Stick Insect has walked past our house six times.

Thursday   June 17th

I have just found a list at the bottom of my mother's shopping bag.

FOR IT	AGAINST IT
Might be a girl	Loss of Independence
More family allowance	George doesn't want it
	Months of looking like the side of a house
	Pain during labour
	Adrian bound to be jealous
	Dog might not take to it
	Am I too old at 37?
	Varicose veins
	PAS

Friday   June 18th

I pretended to be enthusiastic about the baby at breakfast today. I asked my mother if she had thought of any names yet. My mother said, 'Yes. I'm going to call her Christabel.'

Christabel! It sounds like somebody out of *Peter Pan*. Nobody is called Christabel. The poor kid.

Saturday June 19th

Nigel and I went for a bike ride today. We set out to look for a wild piece of countryside so that we could get back to nature and stuff. We pedalled for miles but all the woods and fields were guarded by barbed wire and 'KEEP OUT' notices, so we could only get near to nature.

On the way back we had a philosophical discussion about war. Nigel is dead keen on it. It is his ambition to join the army. He said, 'It's a good life, and when I come back to civvy street I'll have a trade.'

I thought, 'What, as a contract killer?' But I didn't say anything. Most of the army cadets I know forget that real soldiers have to kill people.

Sunday June 20th
SECOND AFTER TRINITY. FATHERS' DAY

My father has hogged the television for over a week, watching the lousy, stinking World Cup. This afternoon when I asked if I could watch a BBC 2 documentary about rare Norwegian plants he refused to let me switch over, and he sat in the dark watching France versus Kuwait. He was sulking because I forgot it was Fathers' Day. I made an official protest to my mother but she refused to arbitrate, so I went up to my room and brought my Falklands campaign map up to date. I also checked my Building Society account to see if I can afford a black-and-white portable. I am sick of being dependent on my parents' television set.

I went downstairs just in time to see a dead good pitch invasion led by an Arab bloke in a head-dress. I don't mind watching an interesting pitch invasion, it's the football I can't stand.

Monday June 21st
LONGEST DAY. NEW MOON

Mr Scruton summoned the whole school into the assembly hall this morning. Even the teachers who are atheists were forced to attend.

I was dead nervous. It's ages since I broke a school rule but Scruton makes you feel dead guilty somehow. When the doors were closed and the whole school was lined up in rows Scruton nodded to Mrs Figges, who was sitting at the piano, and she started playing 'Hallelujah!'

Some of the fifth years (including Pandora) sang along using different words: 'Hallelujah!/What's it to you?' etc. It was quite impressive. Though I thought it was time that the blind piano tuner called again.

When the singing stopped and Mrs Figges was still, Mr Scruton walked up to his lectern, paused, and then said, 'Today is a day that will go down in history.' He paused long enough for a rumour to travel along the rows that he was resigning, then he shouted, 'Quiet!' and continued, 'Today at three minutes to nine a future King of England was born.' All the girls, apart from Pandora, (she is a republican) said, 'Ooh! Lady Di's 'ad it!'

Claire Neilson shouted: 'How much did he weigh?'

Mr Scruton smiled his horrible smile and ignored her.

Pandora shouted, 'How much will he *cost?*' and Mr Scruton suddenly developed good hearing and ordered her out of the assembly hall.

Poor Pandora, her face was as red as the Russian flag as she walked along the rows to the exit door, when she passed me I tried to give her a supportive smile, but it must have come out wrong because she whispered, 'Still leering at me, Adrian?'

Mr Scruton dismissed the school after giving us a talk on what a good job the Royal Family do for British exports.

Went to bed early; it had been a long day.

Tuesday June 22nd

The new prince left the hospital today. My father is hoping that he will be called George, after him. My mother said that it's time the Royal Family came up to date and called the Prince Brett or Jason.

Scotland are out of the World Cup. They drew 2–2 with Russia. My father called the Russian team 'those Commie bastards'. He was not a bit gracious in defeat.

Wednesday   June 23rd

Pandora has been put into isolation at school. She is working at a desk outside Scruton's office. I left the following note on her peg in the cloakroom:

> Pandora,
> A short note to say that I admired your spirited stand on Monday.
>> From Adrian Mole, your ex-lover
> P.S. My mother is with child.

Thursday   June 24th
MIDSUMMER DAY (QUARTER DAY)

Found a note on my peg at break this morning.

> Adrian,
> We were never lovers so it was inaccurate, indeed libellous, of you to sign your note 'ex-lover'. However, I thank you for your note of support.
>> Pandora
> P.S. I am shocked to learn that your mother is *enceinte*. Tell her to ring the Clinic.

Friday   June 25th

My thing is 14cm extended and about 3cm in its unwoken state. I am dead worried. Donkey Dawkins of 5P says his thing comes off the end of a ruler, yet he is only a week older than me.

Saturday   June 26th

It was with great pleasure that I saw Mr Roy Hattersley on television tonight. Once again I was struck by his obvious sincerity and good vocabulary. Mr Hattersley was predicting that there will be an early election. He denied that Mr Michael Foot is too scruffy to be the next Prime Minister.

Sunday June 27th
THIRD AFTER TRINITY

I can't go on with this charade of churchgoing every Sunday. I will have to tell Grandma that I have become an agnostic atheist. If there *is* a God then He/She must know that I am a hypocrite. If there isn't a God then, of course, it doesn't matter.

Monday June 28th
MOON'S FIRST QUARTER

Bert rang me when I got home from school to bellow that Social Services had paid for him to have a phone installed in his pensioner's bungalow. Bert told me that he had already phoned one of his daughters in Melbourne, Australia, and Queenie had phoned her eldest son in Ontario, Canada. They had listened to Dial-a-Disc, the Recipe for the Day, the Weather Forecast, the Cricket News, and they were both looking forward to listening to the GPO's Bedtime Story. I pointed out to Bert that he would have to pay for each phone call he made, but he laughed his wheezy laugh and said, 'I shall probably be a gonner before the bill comes in.' (Bert is nearly ninety.)

Tuesday June 29th

Usual last-minute discussion about where we are going for our summer holiday. My father said, 'It'll probably be our last. This time next year we'll have the nipper.' My mother got dead mad, she said that having a baby was not going to restrict her. She said that if she felt like walking in the Hindu Kush next year, then she would strap the baby on her back and go.

The Hindu Kush! She moans if she has to walk to the bus stop.

I suggested the Lake District. I wanted to see if living there for a bit would help my poetry.

My father suggested Skegness. My mother suggested Greece. Nobody could agree, so we each wrote our choice on a scrap of old till roll and put them into a tupperware gravy maker. We didn't trust each other to make the draw so my mother went and fetched Mrs Singh.

Mrs Singh and all the little Singhs came and stood in our kitchen. Mrs Singh asked, 'Why are you having this procedure, Mrs Mole? Can't your husband decide?' My mother explained that Mr Mole had no superior status in our house. Mrs Singh looked shocked, but she drew a piece of paper out of the hat. It said 'Skegness'. Worse luck!

Mrs Singh excused herself, saying that she must get back to prepare her husband's meal. As she left I noticed my father glance wistfully at her in her pretty sari and jewelled sandals.

I also noticed him looking sadly at my mother in her overalls and ankle boots. My mother said, 'That poor downtrodden woman.'

My father sighed and said, 'Yes.'

Wednesday   June 30th

My mother wants to move. She wants to sell the house that I have lived in all my life. She said that we will need more room 'for the baby'. How stupid can you get? Babies hardly take any space at all. They are only about twenty-one inches long.

Thursday July 1st
DOMINION DAY (CANADA)

Nigel has arranged for me to have a blind date with Sharon
Botts. I am meeting her at the roller-skating rink on Saturday. I
am dead nervous. I don't know how to roller-skate – let alone
make love.

Friday July 2nd

Borrowed Nigel's disco-skates and practised skating on the
pavement in our cul-de-sac. I was OK so long as I had a privet
hedge to grab at, but I dreaded skating past the open-plan
gardens where there is nothing to hold on to.

I wanted to wear my skates in the house so that I would
develop confidence, but my father moaned about the marks the
wheels made on the cushion floor in the kitchen.

Saturday July 3rd

12.15 p.m. Got up at 6 a.m. for more roller-skating practice. Mr
O'Leary shouted abuse because of the early morning noise, so I
went to the little kids' play park and practised there, but I had to
give up. There was so much broken glass and dog muck lying
about that I feared for the ballbearings in the skates. I waited for
the greengrocer's to open, bought a pound of grapes, went home,
had a bath, washed my hair and cut my toenails etc. Then I put
my entire wardrobe of clothes out onto the bed and tried to
decide what to wear.

It was a pitiful collection. By the time I had eliminated my
school uniform I was left with: three pairs of flared jeans
(FLARES! Yuk! Yuk! Nobody wears flares except the worst kind
of moron), two shirts, both with long pointed collars (LONG
POINTS! Yuk!), four of Grandma's handknitted jumpers
(HANDKNITTED! Ugh!). The only possible clothes were my
bottle-green elephant cords and my khaki army sweater. But which

shoes? I had left my trainers at school and I can't wear my formal wedding shoes to a roller-skating rink, can I?

At 10.30 I rang Nigel and asked him what youths wore at roller-skating rinks. He said, 'They wear red satin side vent running shorts, sleeveless satin vests, white knee socks, Sony Walkman earphones and one gold earring.' I thanked him, put the phone down and went and had another look at my clothes.

The nearest I could get were my black PE shorts, my white string vest and my grey knee socks. I am the only person in the world not to have a Sony Walkman and I haven't had my ears pierced so I couldn't manage those two items, but I hope that Sharon Bott won't mind too much.

Do I go in my shorts etc or do I change when I get to the rink? And how will I know which girl is Sharon Bott? I've only seen her in school uniform and in my experience girls are unrecognizable when they are in civilian clothes.

Must stop, it's time to go.

6 p.m. That's the first and last time I go roller-skating. Sharon Bott is an expert. She went whizzing off at 40 mph, only stopping now and again to do the splits in mid-air.

She sometimes slowed down to say, 'Let go of the barrier, Dumbo,' but she didn't stay long enough for me to divert her into having a longer conversation. When it was time for the under-twelves to monopolise the rink, she sped to the barrier and helped me into the coffee bar. We had a Coke then I clumped off to the cloakroom to get the grapes. When I gave her them she said, 'Why have you bought me grapes? I'm not poorly.' I dropped a hint by looking knowingly at her figure in its lycra body stocking and miniskirt but then the roller disco started and she sped off to do wild disco dancing on her skates. She was soon surrounded by tall skated youths in satin shorts so I staggered off to get changed.

I rang Nigel when I got home. I complained that Sharon Bott was a dead loss. He said that Sharon Bott had already rung him to complain that I had showed her up by dressing in my school PE kit.

Nigel said that he is giving up matchmaking.

Sunday   July 4th
FOURTH AFTER TRINITY. AMERICAN INDEPENDENCE DAY

I was just starting to eat my Sunday dinner when Bert Baxter rang and asked me to go round urgently. I bolted my spaghetti Bolognese down as quickly as I could and ran round to Bert's.

Sabre, the vicious Alsatian, was standing at the door looking worried. As a precaution I gave him a dog choc and hurried into the bungalow. Bert was sitting in the living room in his wheelchair, the television was switched off so I knew something serious had happened. He said, 'Queenie's had a bad turn.' I went into the tiny bedroom. Queenie was lying in the big saggy bed looking gruesome (she hadn't put her artificial cheeks or lips on). She said, 'You're a good lad to come round, Adrian.' I asked her what was wrong. She said, 'I've been having pains like red hot needles in my chest.'

Bert interrupted, 'You said the pains were like red-hot knives five minutes ago!'

'Needles, knives, who cares?' she said.

I asked Bert if he had called the doctor. He said he hadn't because Queenie was frightened of doctors. I rang my mother and asked for her advice. She said she'd come round.

While we waited for her I made a cup of tea and fed Sabre and made Bert a beetroot sandwich.

My mother and father came and took over. My mother phoned for an ambulance. It was a good job they did because while it was coming Queenie went a bit strange and started talking about ration books and stuff.

Bert held her hand and called her a 'daft old bat.'

The ambulance men were just shutting the doors when Queenie shouted out, 'Fetch me pot of rouge. I'm not going until I've got me rouge.' I ran into the bedroom and looked on the dressing table. The top was covered in pots and hair nets and hairpins and china dishes and lace mats and photos of babies and weddings. I found the rouge in a little drawer and took it to Queenie. My mother went off in the ambulance and me and my father stayed behind to comfort Bert. Two hours later my mother rang from the hospital to say that Queenie had had a stroke and would be in hospital for ages.

Bert said, 'What am I going to do without my girl to help me?'

Girl! Queenie is seventy-eight.

Bert wouldn't come home with us. He is scared that the council will take his bungalow away from him.

Monday July 5th
INDEPENDENCE DAY HOLIDAY (USA)

Queenie can't speak. She is sort of awake but she can't move her mouth muscles. My mother has been round at Bert's all day cleaning and cooking. My father is going to call in every day on his way home from the canal. I have promised to take horrible Sabre for his morning and evening walks.

Tuesday July 6th
FULL MOON

Bert's social worker, Katie Bell, has been to see Bert. She wants Bert to go back into the Alderman Cooper Sunshine Home temporarily. Bert said he 'would prefer death to that morgue.'

Katie Bell is coming round to see us tomorrow. She is checking Bert's lie that my mother and father and me are providing twenty-four-hour care for him. Queenie is still very poorly.

Wednesday July 7th

Katie Bell is a strange woman. She talks (and looks) a bit like Rick Lemon. She was wearing a donkey jacket and denim jeans and she had long greasy hair parted down the middle. Her nose is long and pointed (from poking into other people's business my father said). She sat in our lounge rolling a cigarette in one hand and taking notes with the other.

She said Bert was stubborn and suffering from slight senile dementia and that what he needed was to see a consultant psychogeriatrician. My mother got dead mad and shouted, 'What he needs is a day- and a night-nurse.' Katie Bell went red and said, 'Day and night care is prohibitively expensive.'

My father asked how much it would cost to put an old person in an old people's home. Katie Bell said, 'It costs about two hundred pounds a week.'

My father shouted, 'Give me two hundred pounds a week and

I'll move in and look after the old bugger.'

Katie Bell said, 'I can't relocate funds, Mr Mole.' As she was going she said, 'Look, I don't like the system any more than you do. I know it stinks, but what can I do?'

My mother said, 'You could wash your hair, dear; you'd feel much better without it straggling around your face.'

Thursday   July 8th

I left a note on Pandora's peg today. It said:

> Pandora,
> Queenie Baxter is in hospital after a stroke. Bert is on his own in the bungalow. I am going round and doing what I can, but it would be nice if you could visit him for a bit. He is dead sad. Have you got any photos of Blossom?
>
> > Yours, as ever,
> > Adrian

Friday   July 9th

A brilliant day today. School broke up for eight fabbo weeks. Then something *even better* happened tonight.

I was in tne middle of ironing Bert's giant underpants when Pandora walked into the living room. She was carrying a jar of home-pickled beetroot. I was transfixed. She gets more beautiful every day. Bert cheered up no end. He sent me off to make some tea. I could hardly keep my hands still. I felt as if I'd had an electric shock. I looked yearningly at Pandora as I handed her her tea. And she looked yearningly back at me!!!!!!!!

We sat around looking at photos of Blossom, Pandora's ex-pony. Bert droned on about ponies and horses he had known when he was an ostler.

At 9.30 I washed Bert, sat him on the commode and then put him to bed. We sat by the electric coal fire until he started snoring, then we fell into each other's arms with little sighs and moans. We stayed like that until Bert's clock struck 10 p.m. Sex didn't cross my mind once. I just felt dead calm and comfortable.

On the way home I asked Pandora when she realized that she still loved me. She said, 'When I saw you ironing those horrible underpants. Only a superior type of youth could have done it.'

It has just been on the news that a man has been found in the Queen's bedroom. Radio Four said that the man was an intruder and was previously unknown to the Queen. My father said: 'That's her story.'

Saturday   July 10th

My father took Bert to visit Queenie, so I went to Sainsbury's on the bus. My mother gave me thirty pounds and asked me to buy enough food for five days. I remembered our last Domestic Science lesson, in which Mrs Appleyard taught us how to make cheap meals with maximum nourishment, so I bought:

> 2 lb Lentils
> 1 lb Dried peas
> 3 lb Wholemeal flour
> 1 pkt Yeast
> 1 lb Caster sugar
> 2 pints Plain yogurt
> 20 lb King Edward's
> 2 lb Brown rice
> 1 lb Dried apricots
> 1 Tub cream cheese
> ½ lb Krona margarine
> A large cabbage
> 2 lb Breast of lamb
> A huge Swede
> 4 lb Parsnips
> 2 lb Carrots
> 2 lb Onions

How I dragged it all to the bus stop I'll never know. The bus conductor was no help. He didn't assist me to pick a single potato from off the floor of the bus.

I am going to write and complain to Sainsbury's about their lousy brown carrier bags. They ought to stand up to being dragged half a mile without splitting. My mother didn't thank me when I handed her fifteen pounds change! She whined on and on about forgetting the frozen black forest gâteaux and tinned peas etc.

She went mad when she saw that I had not bought a white thick-sliced loaf. I pointed out that she had all the ingredients with which to make her own bread. She said, 'Correction. *You* have the ingredients!'

Spent all evening bashing dough about, then chucking it into tins. I don't know what went wrong. I opened the oven door and checked it every five minutes but it just wouldn't rise.

Sunday   July 11th
FIFTH AFTER TRINITY

Pandora says I should have kept the oven door shut.

My father refused to eat his breast of lamb stew. He went to the pub and had a microwave mince and onion pie and crinkle-cut chips.

He is asking for a coronary.

Monday   July 12th
HOLIDAY (NORTHERN IRELAND)

Brainbox Henderson has started a youth club poetry magazine. I have submitted some of my Juvenilia plus a more recent mature poem called:

> *Ode to Engels*
> *or*
> *Hymn to the Modern Poor*
> Engels, you catalogued the misfortunes of the poor in days
>   of yore,
> Little thinking that the poor would still be with us in nearly
>   1984.
> Yet stay! What is this I see in 1983?
> 'Tis a queue of hungry persons outside the Job Centre.
> Though rats and TB be but sad memories
> The pushchairs of the modern poor contain pasty babies
>   with hacking coughs
> Young mothers draw on number six
> Young fathers queue to pay fines
> Old people watch life pass by the plate-glass windows of
>   council homes

Oh Engels that you were still amongst us pen in hand
Your indignation a-quiver
Your fine nose tuned to the bad smells of 1983.

Pandora read it at Bert's. She says that it is a work of genius.

I have sent a copy to Bert Baxter. He is always going on about Engels.

Tuesday   July 13th

Brainbox Henderson showed me Barry Kent's pathetic entry for the poetry competition. Kent is convinced he is going to win the first prize of £5. It is called 'Tulips'.

Nice, red, tall, stiff,
In a vase,
On a table,
In a room,
In our house.

According to Henderson, Kent's poem shows Japanese cultural influences! How stupid can you get?

The nearest Barry Kent has been to Japanese culture is sitting on the pillion of a stolen Honda.

Wednesday   July 14th
MOON'S LAST QUARTER

Every night this week I have been round to Bert's and taken vile Sabre for one of his four-mile walks, but I couldn't face it tonight. I hate the way people cross the road to avoid us. Sabre hasn't bitten anybody for ages, but he always *looks as if he's about to*. Even other Alsatians flatten themselves against walls when they see Sabre approaching. I wish that Queenie would hurry up and get better; she is proud to be seen out with Sabre. She says, 'An Alsatian a day keeps the muggers at bay.'

Thursday   July 15th
ST SWITHIN'S DAY

Pandora's parents took Bert to the hospital to visit Queenie this evening, so Pandora and I spent two brillo hours lying on her parents' bed watching the video of *Rocky 1*. I kept my hands strictly away from Pandora's erotic zones. When the film finished we talked about our futures. Pandora said that after University she would like to dig water holes in the Third World countries. She demonstrated how an artesian well is sunk by using her lit cigarette. Unfortunately the cigarette fell out of her hand and burnt a hole in the duvet. Pandora is dead worried; her parents are fanatical non-smokers.

I am reading *Lucky Jim* by a bloke called Kingsley Amis. My father says that Kingsley Amis used to be the editor of the *New Statesman*. It is surprising how much my father knows about literary matters. He never reads books but he is forced to listen to Radio Four on his car radio because the dial has jammed and he can't get Terry Wogan.

Friday   July 16th

5.30 p.m. Stick Insect has just rung to ask if my father is back from work yet. I told her that he calls in on Bert Baxter on his way home every night. She said, 'Thank you, I'll ring back later,' in a sad sort of voice. I expect she is regretting her promiscuous behaviour now that her baby is imminent.

I told my mother it was a wrong number; pregnant women should not be upset.

Saturday   July 17th

I have just seen my father and Stick Insect walking along the canal towpath arm in arm. I know the path is a bit cobbly but surely Stick Insect could have walked without assistance. It's kind of my father to support Stick Insect in her hour of need but he should be more careful of public opinion. If people see an old-looking man arm in arm with a pregnant woman they are bound to assume that he is the father of the foetus. I hid behind the old bridge until they'd passed out of sight, then went to call for Pandora.

Sunday July 18th
SIXTH AFTER TRINITY

My father announced at breakfast that he is going to have a vasectomy. I pushed my sausages away untouched.

Monday July 19th

Went to see Grandma after Bert's. She was making her Christmas cake. She let me drop the twenty pence pieces in the mixture and stir it around a bit while I made a wish. I was dead selfish really; I could have wished for world peace or Queenie's quick recovery or for a safe confinement for my mother, but instead I wished that the spots on my shoulders would clear up before my summer holiday. I am dreading baring my back to gawping holiday-makers on Skegness beach.

The Queen's personal detective, Commander Trestrail, has had to resign because the papers have found out that he is a homosexual. I think this is dead unfair. It's not against the law and I bet the Queen doesn't mind. Barry Kent calls *ME* a poofter because I like reading and hate sport. So I understand what it is like to be victimized.

Tuesday July 20th
NEW MOON

Got a foreign letter, it is addressed to me but it must be a mistake. I don't know any foreigners.

> Norsk rikskringkasting, BERGEN, Norway.
> Kjaere Adrian Mole,
> John Tydeman viste meg ditt dikt 'Norge' og jeg var dypt rørt av de følelser de uttrykte. Jeg håper du en dag vil besøke vårt land. Det er vakkert og du vil kunne oppleve fjordene og se hvor Ibsen og Grieg levde. Som en intellektuell person burde det interessere deg. Når du besøker oss og snakker med oss vil du oppdage at våre vokaler ikke er så eiendommelige. Husk at vi bare har lange netter og korte dager om vinteren. I juni er det helt motsatt. Så kom om sommeren — vi skal ta imot deg på beste måte.

Til lykke med dine studier av norsk laerindustri.
Hjertelig hilsen
Din,
Knut Johansen

Wednesday   July 21st

Only eight days to go before my holiday in Skegness begins. I
have asked my father if Pandora can come with us. I can't bear
the thought of being alone with my parents for a fortnight. My
father said, 'She's welcome to come along providing she stumps
up a hundred and twenty quid.'

Thursday   July 22nd

When we were round at Bert's doing his cleaning I asked
Pandora if she would like to come to Skegness. She said,
'Darling, I would follow you into Hell, but I draw the line at
Skegness.'

Bert said, 'Pandora, you're nought but a stuck-up little
Madam. It'll do you good to mingle with the proletariat. Life
ain't all dry ski slopes and viola lessons you know.' He gave a big
sigh and said, 'Personally I'd give me right ball for a week in
Skeggy.'

Pandora blushed a lovely pink colour and said, 'I'm awfully
sorry, Bert. One tends to forget that one's privileged.'

Bert lit a Woodbine, sighed again and said: 'I shan't 'ave
another holiday now, not at my age. No: *death*'s the only rest I've
got to look forward to.'

To create a diversion Pandora phoned the hospital and asked
how Queenie was. The nurse said, 'Mrs Baxter asked for her pot
of rouge today.' Bert cheered up when he heard this news; he
said: 'That means the old gel's on the mend.' We put Bert to
bed, then I walked Pandora home.

We had a dead good half-French, half-English kiss, then
Pandora whispered, 'Adrian, take me to Skegness.' It was the
most romantic sentence I have ever heard.

Friday   July 23rd

11 a.m. A dirty white cat turned up on our doorstep this

morning. It had a tag round its neck which said, 'My name is Roy' but there was no address. It ignored me when I got the milk in so I ignored it back.

6 p.m. My mother and father have had a big row about Roy. My father accused my mother of encouraging Roy to stay by giving him (the cat) a saucer of milk. My mother accused my father of being an animal hater.

The dog looks a bit worried; I expect it feels insecure. Roy spent the day asleep on the toolshed roof, unaware of the trouble it was causing.

Saturday July 24th

Went shopping for holiday clothes today. My mother came with me. I wanted to buy a grey zip-up cardigan from Marks and Spencer (there is a cold wind at Skegness). I tried it on but my mother said it made me look like Frank Bough and refused to pay for it. We had a bit of an argument about my taste in clothes versus her taste in clothes. In fact, looking around, I could see quite a few teenagers were having arguments with their parents.

We walked around the rest of the shops without speaking for a bit until my mother dragged me into a punk shop and tried to interest me in a lime-green leopard-skin-print tee-shirt. I refused to try the tasteless thing on, so she bought it for herself!

The sadistic-looking shop assistant said, 'That's a cool mother you got.' I pretended not to hear him. It wasn't difficult: Sid Vicious was singing a filthy version of 'My Way' on the shop's stereo system. It was so loud that the chain jackets and studded belts were reverberating.

Our next stop was at Mothercare, where my mother went mad buying miniature clothes and stretch-mark cream. I was hoping that she would buy a nice respectable maternity dress for the dreaded day when her lump starts to show, but she informed me that she was intending to carry on wearing her dungarees. I will be a laughing-stock at school.

Sunday July 25th
SEVENTH AFTER TRINITY

Did a bit of 'O' level revising. I've got the lousy stinking mocks to do when I get back to school. I am doing English, Geography and History at 'O' level and Woodwork and Domestic Science and Biology at CSE.

It's all a big waste of time, though, because intellectuals like me don't need qualifications to get jobs or worldly success: it just comes automatically to us. It is because of our rarity value. The only problem is getting influential people to *recognize* that you are an intellectual. So far nobody has recognized it in me, yet I have been using long words like 'multi-structured' in my daily intercourse for ages.

Monday July 26th

Courtney Elliot brought bad news this morning. It was a letter from the Manpower Services Commission telling my father that his canal bank clearance project was 'seriously behind schedule'. My father stormed on and on about, 'What do they expect if they pay slave wages?'

My mother said (quite mildly for her), 'Well you've hardly *worked* like a slave, George. You're always home by four-thirty.'

My father went out and slammed the kitchen door. I ran after him and offered to help him on the canal bank, but he said, 'No, stay at home and help your mother with the holiday packing.'

My mother and Courtney Elliot were doing the *Guardian* crossword together, and the holiday clothes were still in the Ali Baba basket waiting to be washed so I took the dog round to Bert's and watched the Falklands Memorial Service on television.

St Paul's Cathedral was full of widows and bereaved people. I went home and chucked my Falklands campaign map in the bin.

Tuesday July 27th
MOON'S FIRST QUARTER

My mother had a pompous note from Pandora's father today. He is refusing to give Pandora £120 for Skegness!

The mean git says that he has already forked out four hundred quid for a canoeing holiday down the Wye for his family in September, and Pandora's made-to-measure wet suit was costing forty quid so he was 'unable to stretch his finances further.' So, a fortnight without Pandora looms ahead, unless I can think of a way to make £120 in a hurry. Pandora hasn't got any money of her own; she spends all her pocket money on viola strings.

Wednesday   July 28th

My mother's lump started showing today, but she is doing nothing to disguise it. In fact she seems quite *proud* of it. She is showing it to everybody who comes to the house.

I have to go out of the room.

Thursday   July 29th

My father has been working flat out on the canal bank for the past three days. He hasn't been getting home until 10 p.m. at night. He is getting dead neurotic about leaving it and going on holiday.

Went to see Queenie in hospital. She is on a ward full of old ladies with sunken-in white faces. It's a good job that Queenie was wearing her rouge, I wouldn't have recognized her without it.

Queenie can't speak properly so it was dead embarrassing trying to work out what she was saying. I left after twenty minutes, worn out with smiling. I tried not to look at the old ladies as I walked back down the ward, but it didn't stop them shouting out to me and waving. One of them asked me to fetch a nice piece of cod for her husband's tea. The tired-looking nurse said that a lot of the old ladies were living in the past. I can't say I really blame them; their present is dead horrible.

Friday   July 30th

Our family went to Pandora's house to discuss what was involved in looking after Bert while we are on holiday.

Bert grumbled all the way through the meeting. He's never a

bit grateful for anything you do for him. Sometimes I wish he *would* go and live in the Alderman Cooper Sunshine Home.

My mother gave this list to Pandora's mother:

1. He will only drink out of the George V Coronation cup.
2. He takes three heaped spoons of sugar in tea.
3. Don't let him watch *Top of the Pops*; it over-excites him.
4. District Nurse comes on Tuesdays to check for pressure sores.
5. He'll *only* eat beetroot sandwiches, scrambled eggs, Vesta curries and various Dream Toppings. Don't waste your energy in trying to extend his range. I've tried and failed.
6. He moves his bowels at 9.05 a.m. precisely. So please make sure you arrive at his bungalow in plenty of time to arrange the commode.
7. Sabre needs *at least* a four-mile walk *every day*. Any less and he becomes quite impossible.
8. Don't talk to Bert during *Crossroads*.
9. Mrs Singh will cover for you in an emergency, but she *must* be chaperoned.
10. He's OK to be left at night providing he's had his quota of brown ales (THREE BOTTLES).
11. He'll accuse you of fiddling him out of his pension. Ignore him.
12. *The Best of British Luck!*

Saturday   July 31st

Rio Grande Boarding House, Skegness

Pandora came round early this morning to say goodbye; normally I would have been in anguish at the prospect of being without her for two weeks, but I was too busy packing my cases and looking for my swimming trunks to break down. Pandora helped me by packing my medical supplies for me. We finally left our cul-de-sac at 6 p.m.

The car broke down at Grantham so we didn't arrive at the Rio Grande until 12.30. The boarding house was locked and in complete darkness. We stood on the steps ringing the bell for ages, eventually a miserable-looking bloke unlocked the door. He said 'Mole Family? Yer late. These doors are locked at 11 p.m. an' there's a 50p fine for latecomers.'

My mother said, 'And whom might you be?'

The man said, 'I'm Bernard Porke, that's whom I am – Proprietor of the Rio Grande.'

My mother said, 'Well, thank you for your effusive welcome, Mr Porke.' She signed the register while I went and helped my father get the cases off the roof rack.

The tarpaulin had disappeared somewhere *en route*, so everything was wet through. I am writing this in my basement room. It overlooks the dustbins. I can hear Mr and Mrs Porke quarrelling in the kitchen next door.

I wish I was back in the Midlands.

Sunday   August 1st
EIGHTH AFTER TRINITY. LAMMAS (SCOTTISH QUARTER DAY)

I was woken up by Mr Porke shouting, 'Only one piece of bacon per plate, Beryl. Are you trying to ruin me?'

I got dressed quickly and ran up six flights of stairs to my parents' attic room. Woke them up and told them that breakfast was nearly ready. My father told me to run down to the dining room and bag a decent table. (He is experienced in seaside boarding houses.)

I sat at a table next to the massive picture window and watched my fellow boarders take their places at the tables. For some reason everyone was whispering. Mothers kept telling their children to sit still, sit up straight, etc. Fathers stared at the cruet.

My parents' arrival caused a bit of a stir. My mother never keeps her voice down, so everyone heard her complaining about the nylon sheets, including Mr Porke. I'm sure that's why our table only got two pieces of fried bread.

Monday   August 2nd
BANK HOLIDAY (SCOTLAND). HOLIDAY (REPUBLIC OF IRELAND)

My father has gone back to his proletarian roots. He bought a

'Kiss me Quick, Squeeze me Slowly' hat and walked along the promenade swigging out of a can of lager.

I wore my dark glasses and kept well behind him.

Tuesday   August 3rd

Eleven days to go and I have already spent all my money on the slot machines.

Wednesday   August 4th
FULL MOON

The sun came out today!

Also Prince William was christened. The Rio Grande celebrated by giving everyone an extra boiled egg at tea time.

Thursday   August 5th

A man called Ray Peabody has joined our table. He is a divorcee from Corby. He spent his *honeymoon* at the Rio Grande. (No wonder he is divorced.) He comes to Skegness to take part in the talent contests. He is a singer and juggler. He showed us a bit of juggling with the cruet until Mr Porke told him to 'stop abusing the facilities.'

Friday   August 6th

Sent Pandora a donkey postcard.

> Dear Pan,
> The sun came out on Wednesday, but it didn't reach into the black despair caused by our separation. It is a cultural desert here.
> Thank God I have brought my Nevil Shute books.
> Yours unto infinity,
> Adrian X

Saturday   August 7th

Went to Gibraltar Point in the car to see the wild-life sanctuary. Saw the sanctuary but no wild life. I expect they were all sheltering from the wind.

Read *The Cruel Sea* by a bloke called Nicholas something.

Sunday   August 8th
NINTH AFTER TRINITY

My father went on a sea fishing trip today with the Society of Redundant Electric Storage Heater Salesmen.

My mother and I spent the day on the beach reading the Sunday papers. She is quite nice when you get her on your own. The sun was dead hot but I've got eighteen spots on my shoulders so I couldn't take my shirt off.

Monday   August 9th

We bought day tickets and went to a holiday camp today.

The sight of all the barbed wire and the pale listless people walking aimlessly around inside gave me a weird feeling.

My father started whistling 'The Bridge on the River Kwai' and it *was* like being in a prisoner of war camp. Nobody was actually tortured or starved, but you got the feeling that the attendants could turn quite nasty. My parents went straight to a bar, so I went on all the pathetic free rides, watched a knobbly knees competition, then a tug of war, then I stood outside the bar waiting for my parents.

They had selfishly chosen a 'No under-eighteens' bar.

At 1.30 my father came out with a bottle of Vimto and a packet of crisps for me.

At 2.30 I put my head round the door and asked how long they would be. My father snarled, 'Stop whining. Go and find something to do.' I watched the Donkey Derby for a bit then got fed up and went and sat in the car.

At 4 p.m. a loudspeaker shouted, 'Would Adrian Mole aged fifteen please go to the lost children's centre where his mummy and daddy are waiting for him.'

The humiliation!

The torment of being given a lollipop by a morose attendant!

My parents thought it was dead funny; they laughed all the way back to the ranch.

Tuesday   August 10th

During the evening meal Mr Porke brought my father a message to say that a close friend had been taken into the Royal Hospital and would he please ring ward twelve immediately. It was a mystery to all of us. My father hasn't got any close friends.

My father left the table in a panic. My mother got up to follow him but he said, 'No Pauline, it's got nothing to do with you.'

He was gone for about fifteen minutes, when he came back he said, 'I've got something to tell you both, let's go somewhere private.'

We sat in a wind shelter on the promenade and he informed me and my mother that he was the father of Stick Insect's one-day-old baby boy.

About sixty hours passed, then my mother said, 'What's he called?'

My father said, '*Brett*. Sorry.'

I couldn't think of anything to say so I kept quiet. I still can't think of anything to say so I am going to sleep.

Wednesday   August 11th

12.30 p.m. My father has gone to see Brett and Stick Insect. My mother made him go.

I can't think of anything to say to my mother. I always knew I had no small talk, and now I know I've got no big talk either.

8 p.m. She just sits in her attic room with her hands over her lump. She hasn't cried once, I am dead worried.

9 p.m. I phoned Pandora's mother and told her everything. She was very sympathetic. She said she would get Bert settled for the night and then drive to Skegness and pick us up.

I packed all the suitcases and made my mother wash her face and do her hair, then we sat and waited for Mrs Braithwaite.

Thursday August 12th
MOON'S LAST QUARTER

Home.

11 p.m. As soon as she saw Mrs Braithwaite my mother started to cry. Mrs Braithwaite said, 'They're *all* bastards, Pauline,' and gave ME a filthy look! It's just not fair! I intend to stay completely and totally true to Pandora. All else is chaos.

We got home at 4.30 a.m. this morning. Mrs Braithwaite doesn't like driving over 30 mph.

I went straight to bed. I didn't dare check to see if my father was in his room.

Friday August 13th

The day augured ill.

My father's razor had gone from out of the bathroom so I was forced to use my mother's pink underarm one. It cut my face to ribbons (but there was a very satisfactory amount of bristle around the side of the washbasin).

I had to have a shave because Grandma came round to be told the awful news that her son had fathered an illegitimate child, whilst his wife of fourteen years was expecting a legitimate one.

Grandma took it quite well. She said, 'Which hospital is this woman in?' My mother told her and she straightened her hat and left in a taxi.

Pandora told me that her mother is close to having a nervous breakdown because Bert Baxter has been playing her up all week.

Personally, myself, I think the world has gone mad. Barry Kent won the 'Off the Street' Youth Club poetry competition. His grinning moronic face was in the evening paper. I can't take much more.

Saturday August 14th

Grandma has gone over to the other side!

She has given some of *our* baby's clothes to Brett Slater, Stick Insect's son. I know Grandma doesn't like my mother, but at least my mother is my father's legal wife.

I am just about sick and tired of adults! They have the nerve to tell kids what to do and then they go ahead and break all their own rules.

Pandora's father came round this morning to ask my mother if she wanted any help. My mother said, 'Bugger off home and help your own wife.' At this rate she'll have no men friends left.

Barclays Bank was open this morning. I bet my father was first in the queue. He always forgets to go on Fridays.

Sunday   August 15th
TENTH AFTER TRINITY

My father came round and asked if he could come home. I wanted my mother to say yes, but she said no. So my father has gone to live with Grandma.

The rat fink has taken the stereo with him. My mother says she doesn't care, she says that after her baby is born she is going to get a highly paid job and buy the best stereo system in the world.

Monday   August 16th

Pandora shocked me today by asking if I was curious about my '*brother Brett*.' It's dead strange to think I've got a brother. I hope the poor kid has better luck with his skin than me.

Tuesday   August 17th

A cheque for fifty pounds arrived today from my father. My mother ripped it up and posted the pieces back. How stupid can you get?

Even my mother regretted it later on.

Stick Insect, Maxwell House and Brett have moved into Grandma's house.

Wednesday   August 18th

Took the dog for a walk and called casually round to Grandma's and casually looked into Brett Slater's cot. The kid's skin is covered in white flaky stuff. He's got loads of wrinkles as well.

I didn't see Stick Insect or my father. Grandma was teaching Maxwell manners at the tea table.

I didn't stay long. I didn't tell my mother I had been, either. It was only a casual visit.

Thursday   August 19th
NEW MOON

Mrs Braithwaite is on Librium because of Bert Baxter, so Mrs Singh has taken over her duties. I haven't seen Bert for ages. I know he will make crude comments about my father's virility, so I am keeping away.

I have gone right off sex. It seems to cause nothing but trouble, especially to women.

Friday   August 20th

My mother is too depressed to do any cooking so I am having to do it. So far we have had salad with either corned beef or tuna, but I think I will try something different tomorrow – ham perhaps.

My father keeps ringing up to see how my mother is. Today he asked me if she had mentioned divorce. I said no, she hadn't mentioned it but she certainly looked as if she was thinking about it.

Saturday   August 21st

Casually called in at Grandma's again. Brett has got my father's big nose. Grandma was changing his yukky nappy. I was amazed at how big his thing is.

Stick Insect is *breast feeding* Brett. (The poor kid must be hungry because the last time I had a close look she hadn't got any breasts.)

My father and Stick Insect were out, buying baby equipment between feeds.

Sunday   August 22nd
ELEVENTH AFTER TRINITY

Went out and bought the Sunday papers, but didn't bother sneaking a look at the *News of the World* behind the greetings card rack like I usually do. I've got enough sex scandals in my own family without reading about anyone else's.

Mr Cherry, the newsagent, asked if he was to cancel my father's fishing and DIY magazines. I told him to go ahead.

The papers weighed 3lbs, but there was nothing in them apart from the PLO fleeing from Beirut again.

Monday   August 23rd

Barry Kent's mother has had another baby; Pandora passed by the church just as the Kents were emerging from the Christening service. She said the baby looked just like all the other Kents – fierce eyes and massive fists.

They have called the baby Clarke, after Superman. Yuk! Yuk! Yuk!

Tuesday   August 24th

Mrs Singh has arranged for Bert to go on holiday with some charity for elderly Hindus. I asked how long Bert had been a Hindu. Mrs Singh said, 'I don't care if he's not a Hindu. I don't care if he's a Moonie or a Divine Light Missionary so long as he is far away from me.'

Sabre is staying at the RSPCA hostel. I hope he is in isolation for the sake of the other dogs.

Wednesday   August 25th

Courtney Elliot was sipping Brazilian coffee in the kitchen when I came downstairs. He said, 'I bear an important missive for Master Mole.' It was a letter from the BBC!

I took the letter up to my room and stared at it, willing it to say, 'Yes we are giving you an hour-long poetry programme; it will be called "Adrian Mole, a Youth and his Poetry".'

I wanted it to say that, but of course it didn't. It said:

British Broadcasting Corporation
19th July

Dear Adrian Mole,

Thank you for your very neat letter and for the new poem entitled 'Norway'. It is a considerable development on your previous work and indicates that you are maturing as a poet. If your School Magazine rejected 'Norway' then the Editor of the magazine probably needs his (or her) head seeing to. Unless, of course, you have a lot of very good poets at your school. I agree with you about those boring rhyming poems about flowers and stuff but you must remember that before you can break the rules of rhyme and rhythm you do have to know what those rules are about. It is like a painter who wishes to do abstract paintings – he has to know how to draw precisely from life before he jumbles things up. Picasso is a very good case in point to cite.

I hope you were successful in your test on the Norwegian Leather Industry. The Norwegian colleague (he is a Radio Producer in Bergen, Norway) to whom I showed your poem was very impressed that you were studying his country so diligently. I attach a translation of a letter he sent you which must have been rather difficult to understand since it was in Norwegian. Incidentally, I think 'Fjords' is a better word than 'Inlets'. Don't worry about the spelling, a good editor will always correct details like that. I like your use of the explosive 'But!' in the penultimate line. There isn't anything practical I can do with this particular work but I will put it on the file as an *aide memoire* to your progress as a poet (remember there is not much money in poetry . . .).

I seldom get to see Terry Wogan in the corridors as he works in Radio Two and I work for Radios Three and Four. Also his show goes on the air very early and he has usually left the building by the time I get to my desk.

With my best wishes and again my thanks for having let me see your latest work.

Yours sincerely,
John Tydeman (Radio Four)

Dear Adrian

John Tydeman showed me your poem 'Norway' and I was
very moved by its sentiments. I hope you will be able to
visit our country one day. It is very beautiful and you will be
able to visit the Fjords and see where Ibsen and Grieg
lived. As an intellectual, this should be of interest to you.
Perhaps when you visit us and speak with us you will not
find our vowels so strange. Remember we only have long
nights and short days in winter. In June it is the opposite.
So come in summer and we will make you very welcome.

Good luck with your study of the Norwegian Leather
industry.

Yours sincerely,
Knut Johansen

What a brilliant letter! 'Considerable Development', 'Maturing as a Poet'! The translation was even better; it was an
invitation to go to Norway! Well, almost. There was no actual
mention of paying my fare, but, 'Come in summer, we will make
you very welcome!'

My mother and Courtney Elliot read the letters. Courtney
said, 'You have a very singular son, Mrs Mole.'

My mother's reply was brief yet touching. 'I know,' she said.

Thursday   August 26th
MOON'S FIRST QUARTER

I tackled Courtney Elliot about the late delivery of my BBC
letter, which was dated July 19th so had taken over a month to
travel 104 miles. Courtney said, 'I believe that there was a
derailment of the Mail Train at Kettering in July. It is possible
that your letter was in one of those unfortunate mail bags that lay
at the bottom of the embankment until being discovered by a
homeward-bound ploughman.'

The Post Office have always got an excuse!

Friday   August 27th

The bank rate has been reduced to 10½% so my mother has
made an appointment to see Mr Niggard, the Bank Manager.

She wants to borrow some money because she hasn't got any left.

I hope she gets a loan; I haven't had any pocket money for two weeks.

Saturday   August 28th

Pandora is taking canoeing lessons in preparation for her River Wye holiday. She had her first lesson today and she invited me to watch and, if necessary, give her the kiss of life in case she fell out and nearly drowned.

She looked dead erotic in her black wetsuit and crash helmet. And for the first time in yonks I felt my thing moving on its own.

I can't remember anything more about the lesson, so was unable to join in Pandora's enthusiastic conversation on the way home in her dad's car.

Sunday   August 29th
TWELFTH AFTER TRINITY

Stayed in bed all day. My mother went to a picnic with some women at a place called Greenham Common. It was dark when she got back. I was dead worried.

Monday   August 30th
LATE SUMMER HOLIDAY (UK EXCEPT SCOTLAND)

My mother was happy today. She cleaned the house from top to bottom (including the cutlery drawer and understairs cupboard). She sang the same song over and over again.

> You can't kill the spirit
> She is like a mountain
> Old and strong.
> She goes on and on and on!

It looks like her picnic did her good.

Tuesday   August 31st

My mother went to see the Bank Manager this morning. I persuaded her to put a loose dress on so that he wouldn't know she was pregnant.

But it turned out that my father had already been whining to the bank for money and while he was there he had blabbed out all our family secrets. Mr Niggard knew that the only income my mother has is Social Security and Family Allowance so he wouldn't lend her any more.

He said she was a bad risk. There is nothing for it, I will have to get a Saturday job. I need money desperately. I've got two months' library fines to pay.

Wednesday September 1st

Got a card from Bert Baxter. It was a picture of Bradford Town Hall. Bert had written,

> Dear Laddo,
> Having a good laugh with the old 'uns, we are visiting temples and going to weddings nearly every day. The grub is good but I've had to knock off the drink on account of the other old 'uns' religion.
>   Queenie is coming out next week. So be a good lad and nip round and give the bungalow a bit of a tidy up.
>   Yours affec'ly,
>   Bert

Pandora took her One-Star Canoeing test this afternoon. Her instructor, a bloke called Bill Sampson, said that Pandora has got got 'great canoeing potential'. He raved on about Pandora's powerful shoulders, limp wrists and gripping thighs. Pandora passed her test easily. Bill Sampson has offered to prepare her for her Two-Star Test.

Pandora has asked me to join her in her new hobby, but I have got a morbid dread of capsizing so I declined. I am quite happy watching from the bank thinking my intellectual thoughts and holding the towels and thermos flask.

Thursday September 2nd

There is now no disguising the fact that my mother is pregnant. She sticks right out at the front and walks in a very peculiar manner. She finds it a bit difficult to bend down, so I spend half my time picking things up for her.

Her dungarees are too tight for her, so I am hoping that she will buy a pretty flowery maternity dress. Princess Diana looked charming during her pregnancy. One of those big white collars would really suit my mother. Also it would distract attention from her wrinkly neck.

Friday   September 3rd
FULL MOON

Pandora and her parents are leaving for the River Wye tomorrow. I have offered to go in and feed Marley, their big ginger cat. They have accepted my kind offer and have entrusted me with their keys. It is a massive responsibility, their house is chock-a-block with expensive electrical items and ancient antiques.

Saturday   September 4th

Waved goodbye to my love today. She blew kisses from the rear windows of the Volvo Estate then vanished round the corner.

I waited half an hour (in case they came back for something they had forgotten) then I let myself into the house, made myself a cup of coffee and sat down to watch their big colour telly. At dinner-time I made myself a tuna sandwich (must remember to replace the tin of tuna before they come back) and ate it at Mr Braithwaite's desk.

I couldn't help noticing a letter on his desk:

> Dear Chairperson,
> Arthur, it is with the deepest regret that I offer my resignation as vice-chairperson of the Elm Ward Labour Party.
> The Committee has moved so far to the right recently that I now find my own moderate views are regarded by them as 'extremist'.
> As you know I objected to the Committee sending a telegram of congratulations to Mrs Thatcher during the Falklands Crisis, and, because of my objections, I was called a 'Stalinist' and a 'traitor'. Mrs Benson told me to get back to Russia where I belong.

I know she is a stalwart party member and is indispensable at collecting the tea money, but her constant talk about the Royal Family has no place at a Labour Party meeting, especially with unemployment as high as it is.

And finally and sadly, your own comments about Tony Benn I find absolutely repellent. Calling a member of your own party a 'goggle-eyed goon' is just not on, Arthur. Tony Benn has served this country well in the past, and he may well lead it one day.

I am going on holiday for a week. I will speak to you when I get back.

Yours,
Ivan Braithwaite

There was a stamped, addressed envelope lying next to the letter. Mr Braithwaite had obviously been too busy to post it himself so I posted the letter on my way home.

Sunday   September 5th

I have just been to see a brilliant play at our neighbourhood centre. It was called *Woza Albert*. It was all about South Africa and how cruel their government is to the black people who do all the work. I cried a bit at the end. I swear I will never eat another Cape apple as long as I live.

Monday   September 6th
LABOUR DAY (USA AND CANADA)

Spent all day watering the Braithwaite's plants. It can't be healthy living amongst so much vegetation. It's a wonder Pandora and her parents don't die of oxygen starvation. If I was them I would keep a caged canary around the place.

Tuesday   September 7th

Went to the ante-natal clinic with my mother. We waited for two hours in a room full of red-faced pregnant women. My mother had forgotten to bring a sample of urine from home, so a nurse gave her a shiny oven tray and told her to, 'Squeeze a few drops out for us, dear.'

My mother had only just been to the loo so she took ages and ended up missing her place in the weighing queue. By the time her blood pressure was taken my mother was in a state of hypertension. She said the doctor warned her about doing too much and told her to relax more.

Wednesday September 8th

Realized with horror that school starts next Monday and I have only done one day's revising for my mock exams. Took my History folder round to the Braithwaites, fed the cat and settled down in the study. I thought perhaps the studious atmosphere might help but I can't say it made much difference. I still can't remember Archduke Ferdinand's middle name, or the date of the Battle of Mons.

Thursday September 9th

Went round to Bert Baxter's bungalow to tidy up. Queenie is coming home from hospital on Saturday. I hope the Hindus bring Bert back in time.

Did revision for mocks until 3 a.m.

Friday September 10th
MOON'S LAST QUARTER

Courtney Elliot said, 'A billet-doux for the Young Master.' It was a letter from Pan.

> Adrian Precious,
> We started at Builth Wells on Sunday evening and had quite an exciting paddle downstream. Mummy and Daddy were paddling an open Canadian. I was in a single kayak.
> We camped overnight at Llanstephan. It was lovely, I left the flap of my tent open and looked up at the stars and thought of you.
> Just beyond Llanstephan there is an orgiastic rapid called Hell Hole. The local people fear it and all the canoeing guides describe it as being 'Grade Three, must be portaged', which means you mustn't canoe down it, but instead carry your canoe and equipment *around* it.

Mummy and Daddy managed to get to the side of the river OK but the water carried me ever onwards towards Hell Hole. Honestly Adrian, it was just like *Deliverance*, I half expected a Welsh halfwit to appear on the bridge and start twanging a harp.

Anyway I went rushing into Hell Hole and the canoe turned upside down, but I managed to get out after a while. My boat was smashed in half, but I regained consciousness and swam to the bank.

See you on Sunday.
All my love,
Pandora
P.S. Mummy's nerves are off again.

I felt ill after reading Pandora's letter. I had to take a junior aspirin and lie down.

Saturday September 11th

Had horrible nightmares all night. I kept seeing Pandora's body floating under the remains of Skegness Pier.

Sunday September 12th
FOURTEENTH AFTER TRINITY

Everybody returned home today apart from my father.

Ironed my school uniform: it is much too small for me, but my mother can't afford a new one.

Monday September 13th

I am now a fifth-year and have the privilege of using the side entrance of the school. I can't wait until next year when I will be able to use the *front* entrance (sixth formers and staff only).

Perhaps I have got a perverted streak, but I really enjoyed watching the first-, second-, third- and fourth-years cramming through their low status entrance at the back of the school.

I informed Mrs Claricoates, the school secretary that once again I am on free school dinners. As usual she was full of empathy for me and said, 'Never mind, pet, it'll all come out in the wash.'

Had mock English exam. I was the first to finish. It was a doddle.

Tuesday September 14th

I have got a new form teacher. His name is Mr Lambert. He is the kind of teacher who likes being friendly. He said, 'Consider me a friend, any problems to do with school or home, I want to hear them.'

He sounded more like a Samaritan than a teacher. I have made an appointment to see him after school tomorrow.

My mother is thirty-eight today. I bought her a card which said 'Happy 18th Birthday', *but*, I cunningly changed the number one into a three by the use of Tipp-Ex and dried lentils. So it read 'Happy 38th Birthday!' Unfortunately the verse on the inside didn't match my mother's lifestyle much.

> A-tremble on the edge of life,
> One day to be a mum and wife.
> But now it's discos fun and laughter:
> Why should you care what's coming after?

The picture on the front was of a teenage girl going mad to sounds coming out of a record player. On reflection, I think it was a bad choice of card. I wish I wasn't an impulse buyer. Her present was some underarm hair remover. I noticed that the stuff she usually uses had run out.

My father sent a card picturing a sad cat. He had written inside 'Yours as ever, George'. That stinking rat Lucas sent a card from Sheffield. It was in a box and had a cartoon mouse on the front eating a piece of cheese (Edam I think). Inside Lucas had written: 'Pauline, I'll never forget that night in the pinewoods, Yours with undying love, Bimbo.'

She had ten other cards, all from women and all with pictures of flowers on the front. I don't know why women are so mad about flowers. Personally they leave me cold. I prefer trees.

Wednesday September 15th

My father phoned up before I went to school this morning. He wanted to speak to my mother, but she refused to talk to him.

Brett was crying. In the background, it sounded as if Grandma and Stick Insect were quarrelling. Somebody (it could only have been Maxwell I suppose) was playing a toy xylophone. My father sounded dead miserable. He said, 'I know I did wrong, Adrian; but the punishment hardly fits the crime.'

Had a long talk with Mr Lambert after school. He took me to a café and bought me a cup of tea and a vanilla slice. As we parted he said, 'Look, Adrian, try to detach yourself from the mess your parents are in. You're *a gifted boy* and you mustn't let them drag you down to their level.'

'*A gifted boy*!' At last someone apart from Pandora has recognized my intellectual prowess.

Had mock biology exam. I was the last to finish.

Thursday   September 16th

Barry Kent has made an appointment with Mr Lambert to talk about *his* family problems!

I hope Mr Lambert has got twenty-four hours to spare. Ha! Ha! Ha!

Had mock geography exam. Just my luck – there were no questions about the Norwegian Leather Industry.

Friday   September 17th
NEW MOON

Nearly everyone in our class has made an appointment to see Mr Lambert about their family problems. Even Pandora, whose mother is a Marriage Guidance Counsellor!

Mr Lambert is going about the school biting his nails and looking worried. He has stopped taking people to the café.

Saturday   September 18th

A Tydeman letter! Alas, yet another rejection. The gods are not yet smiling on me.

> British Broadcasting Corporation
> 17th September

Dear Adrian Mole

Thank you for your latest letter (undated – you must, if you are going to be a writer – and even if you are not – DATE your letters. We file them, you know. The BBC has lots of files, some of which are kept in warehouses in Ware, Herts, others of which are at Caversham, nr Reading. Some of the files are very valuable.)

The country seems to have made you gloomy. It often makes poets gloomy, people like Wordsworth & Co. On other occasions it uplifts them – skylarks singing, lambs bounding, daffodils daffing, waterfalls crashing. It provokes odes and things in them. So forget gloom and suicide and write something cheerful.

I'm afraid that the poem is not yet up to broadcast standard but it does show a poetic advance, so keep on trying. We will naturally, respect your copyright in your work. (The BBC is usually very good about things like that.) Copyright is dealt with by a special department and we do not bother the Director General directly with such matters. However, you have not got your break (chance) – yet.

Do not kill yourself because of another rejection. If all poets killed themselves because of early rejections there would be no poetry at all.

Yours most sincerely,
John Tydeman

Sunday   September 19th
FIFTEENTH AFTER TRINITY

Took a deep breath and went to see Bert and Queenie today. They were hostile to me because I've neglected them for a week.

Bert said, 'He's not bothered about us old 'uns no more, Queenie. He's more interested in gadding about.'

How unfair can you get? I can't remember the last time I gadded about. Queenie didn't say anything because she can't speak properly because of the stroke, but she certainly *looked* antagonistic.

Bert ordered me to come back tomorrow to clean up. Their home help comes on Tuesdays and Bert likes the place to be tidy for when she comes.

Monday September 20th

Courtney Elliot didn't bring my mother's Social Security giro this morning. I went to school worrying about it and hoping it would come in the second post. I was amazed to learn that I'd only got average marks for my mocks. Surely there has been a serious error.

Tuesday September 21st

My mother and Courtney Elliot had a row over the missing giro this morning. Courtney said, 'Don't shoot the messenger because the news is bad or non-existent, Mrs Mole.'

My mother tried to ring the Social Security Office all day, but the line was permanently engaged.

Wednesday September 22nd

I skived off school and went to the Social Security offices with my mother. She couldn't face going on her own. I'm certainly glad I went because it was no place for a pregnant woman.

My mother joined the queue of complaining people at the reception desk. And I sat down on the screwed-down chairs.

The reception clerk was hiding behind a glass screen, so everyone was forced to shout out their most intimate financial secrets to her. I heard my mother shouting with the rest, then she came back holding a ticket numbered 89, and said that we would have to wait until our number was displayed on an electronic screen.

We waited for yonks amongst what my mother called 'The casualties of Society'. (My father would have described them as 'dregs'.) A group of tramps staggered about singing and arguing with each other. Toddlers ran amok. Teenage mothers shouted and smacked. A Teddy boy on crutches lurched up the stairs helped by an old skinhead in ragged Doc Marten's. Everyone ignored the 'No Smoking' notices and stubbed their cigarettes out on the lino. The respectable people stared down at their shoes. About every ten minutes a number flashed up on the screen and somebody got up and went through a door marked 'Private Interviews'.

I didn't see any of the people who'd gone through the door *come out* again. I thought this was a bit sinister. My mother said, 'They've probably got gas chambers out there'.

Our private interview was against the Trades Description Act, because it wasn't private at all. The interviewer was also behind a glass screen, so my mother had to bellow out that she hadn't received her giro and was financially destitute.

The interviewer said, 'Your giro was posted on Friday, Mrs Moulds'.

'MRS MOULDS?' said my mother, 'My name's Mole – MOLE – as in furry mammal.'

'Sorry,' said the interviewer, 'I've got the wrong records.'

We waited another fifteen minutes, then he came back and said, 'Your giro will be put in the post tonight.'

'But I need the money now,' my mother pleaded. 'There's no food in the house and my son needs school trousers.'

'There's nothing I can do,' the bloke said wearily. 'Can't you borrow some money?'

My mother looked the man straight in the eyes and said, 'OK will *you* lend me five pounds, please?'

The man said, 'It's against the rules.'

Now I know why the furniture is screwed down. I felt like flinging a chair about myself.

Thursday   September 23rd
AUTUMNAL EQUINOX

No giro. Courtney Elliot lent my mother £5.

Friday   September 24th

8.30 a.m. No giro. But a cheque from my father arrived so we are saved! My mother gave me 15p for a Mars bar, my first in days.

4.30 p.m. My mother took the cheque to the bank this morning, but they wouldn't cash it because it needed four days to clear. Mr Niggard the manager was out officiating at a liquidation, so my mother waited for him to come back then grovelled for a temporary overdraft. Mr Niggard let her have £25.

All this trouble has made my mother's ankles swell up. Somebody is going to pay for this!

Saturday September 25th
MOON'S FIRST QUARTER

No giro!

Looked Swollen Ankles up in the *Good Housekeeping Family Health Encyclopaedia*. It calls itself the 'Complete Modern Medical Reference Book for the Home', but the index didn't have 'Swollen Ankles'. I used my initiative and looked up 'Pregnancy'. I was interested to see that 'Pregnancy' was adjacent to 'Sex and Reproduction'.

I started reading a section called 'Testes and Sperm' and was astonished to discover that my personal testes make several hundred million sperm *a day*. A DAY! Where do they all go? I know some leak out in the night and some I help to leak occasionally, but what happens to the countless billions that are left swarming around, and what about chaste people like priests? During a lifetime they must collect a trillion trillion. It makes the mind boggle, not to mention the testes.

Sunday September 26th
SIXTEENTH AFTER TRINITY

Read the whole of 'Sex and Reproduction' in bed last night. Woke up to find a few hundred million sperm had leaked out. Still, it will give the remaining sperm room to wag their tails about a bit.

Monday September 27th

No giro!

By a massive stroke of luck we did the storage of semen in human biology today. I was able to give a full and frank account of the life cycle of a sperm.

Mr Southgate the biology teacher was dead impressed. After the lesson he said, 'Mole, I don't know if you've got a natural aptitude for biology or a rather obsessive interest in things sexual. If the former I suggest you change from CSE to 'O' level, if the latter perhaps a chat with the school psychology service may be of use.'

I assured Mr Southgate that my interest was purely scientific.

Tuesday   September 28th

No giro!

Pandora and I went a walk in the woods after school only to find that a building firm had started to build executive houses in the clearings. Pandora said that the woodlands of England were being sacrificed for saunas, double garages and patio doors.

Some lucky executive is going to have the best conker tree in the Midlands in his back garden. He'll also be as sick as a dog because he'll have Barry Kent's gang chucking sticks at it every autumn. Ha! Ha! Ha!

Went back to Pandora's and watched the Labour Party Conference vote for unilateral disarmament. Mr Braithwaite explained that this means if elected the Labour Party would chuck all their nuclear weapons away. Mrs Braithwaite said, 'Yes and leave us at the mercy of the Soviet threat.' Mr Braithwaite and Mrs Braithwaite started arguing about multilateral versus unilateral disarmament. The argument got a bit nasty and Mr Braithwaite went on to accuse his wife of posting a letter of resignation to the Elm Ward Labour Party. Mrs Braithwaite shouted, 'For the last time, Ivan, I did not post that sodding letter.'

Pandora walked me home and explained that since her mother had joined the SDP her parents had worked in separate studies. She said, 'They are intellectually incompatible.'

I asked Pandora about the letter of resignation. She said that her father had written a letter but decided not to post it. He was therefore hurt when his resignation had been accepted. Pandora said, 'Poor Daddy is in the political wilderness.'

Wednesday   September 29th
MICHAELMAS DAY (QUARTER DAY)

No giro!

My mother had a letter from the bank to tell her that my father's cheque had bounced. I was sent round to Grandma's on my way to school to break the news.

Stick Insect was feeding Brett so I didn't know where to put my eyes. Is it good or bad manners to ignore a suckling baby? I kept my eyes on her neck to be on the safe side.

My grandma was getting Maxwell ready for play school. The poor kid was wrapped in so many layers of clothes that he looked a bit like Scott at the South Pole. Grandma said, 'There's a nip in the air and Maxwell has got a chest.'

My father had gone to the canal bank early, so I left a message with Grandma. She pulled her lips in a straight line and said, 'Another bouncing cheque? Your father ought to take up trampolining.'

I asked Grandma if she ever got fed up with Brett, Maxwell and Stick Insect. Grandma said she thrived on hard work, and it's true, she looks better than when all she had to do was listen to Radio Four all day. She doesn't even listen to 'The World at One' now. Brett doesn't like Robin Day's voice for some reason. It makes him scream and bring his milk up.

Thursday   September 30th

No giro!

Wrote a poem today.

> *Waiting for the Giro*
> The pantry door creaks showing empty Fablon shelves.
> The freezer echoes with mournful electrical whirrings.
> The boy goes ragged trousered to school.
> The woman waits at the letterbox.
> The bills line up behind the clock.
> The dog whimpers empty-bellied in sleep.
> The building society writes letters penned in vitriol.
> The house waits, waits, waits,
> Waits for the giro.

I am reading Philip Larkin's *The Whitsun Weddings*.

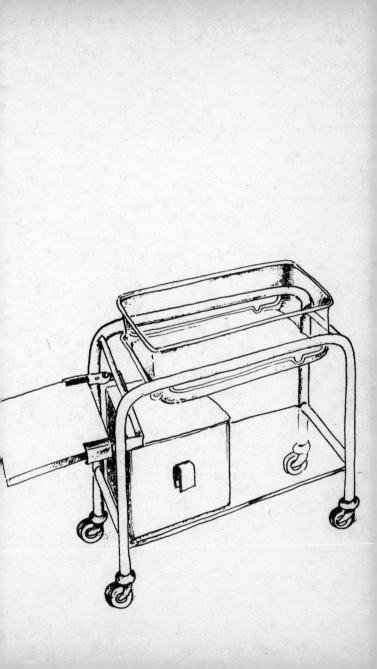

Friday   October 1st

My mother rang up the Citizens' Advice Bureau to find out who her MP is. Then she rang the MP at home, but he wasn't there. His wife said that he had gone on a fact-finding mission to the Canary Isles. She sounded very bitter.

Saturday   October 2nd

Courtney brought a letter from the Fens.

> King Edward Cottage,
> Yosserdyke,
> Norfolk.

Dear Pauline,
Your dad and me was sorry to hear about your trouble and we hopes as it is now cleared up. We never did take to George; he had a hasty temper and we think as how you're better off without him. As regards the money, Pauline, well we only got a few good days at the potato picking so we are a bit short ourselves at the moment, but we enclose a postal order for Adrian, as we know he has got a sweet tooth.

If you would put your trust in the Lord, Pauline, you wouldn't keep having such trouble in your life. God only punishes the heathens and the unbelievers. We was shocked last Christmas as to how much smoking and drinking went on under your roof. You wasn't brought up to it, Pauline. Your dad has never touched a drop in his life, nor has he been a slave to nicotine. We are decent God-fearing folk what knows our place and we only wish that you would take after us more before it's too late.

Uncle Dennis, Auntie Marcia and Cousin Maurice have moved out of the caravan and into a council house. They have got all modern facilities, Auntie Marcia jokes that it is just like Buckingham Palace. Perhaps when you have had the unwelcome baby you will come and see it for yourself.

Anyway Pauline
We are praying for you,

Yours affectionately,
Mam and Dad

P.S. Auntie Marcia asks if you ever found Maurice's grey sock that disappeared last Christmas. She's not been able to rest through wondering about it.

Sunday   October 3rd
SEVENTEENTH AFTER TRINITY. FULL MOON

My mother wrote the following reply today:

Dear Mam and Dad,
Sorry about the short delay in replying to your wonderfully comforting letter, but I have only just emerged from a drunken stupor. Adrian was ecstatic to be sent the postal order for 50 pence and rushed straight out to buy me a can of lager. He's such a thoughtful kid.

Nothing would give me greater pleasure than to come down and inspect Auntie Marcia's council house, but I fear that I will be quite unable to drag myself away from the endless round of parties that my life now revolves around. You know what us hedonists are like – living for kicks and not going to church.

I fear that a meticulous search has failed to turn up the missing grey sock. I can appreciate Auntie Marcia's anxiety on this point, so I enclose my last pound note to enable Auntie Marcia to buy a pair and therefore rest in peace.

What you say about George is quite true, but I married him because at that time he laughed a lot. There weren't a lot of laughs in our cottage in the middle of the potato field were there?

Cordial greetings,
Your Daughter Pauline
And Grandson Adrian

I begged her not to send it. She said she would think about it and put it behind the bread bin.

Monday   October 4th
NO GIRO!

Tuesday   October 5th

No giro!

My mother cracked today. She phoned up the local radio station and told them that she was going to abandon her child at the Social Security office unless she was given her giro.

My digital clock radio woke me up to the sound of my own mother's voice telling the airwaves about our financial difficulties. She was downstairs on the hall phone talking to Mitchell Malone, the halfwit DJ. My mother said she was going to abandon me at the Social Security offices unless the SS Manager contacted her by noon.

Mitchell Malone got dead excited and said, 'Listeners, we're in a High Noon situation here. Will Pauline Mole, pregnant single parent, abandon her only child in the Social Security office? Or will Mr Gudgeon, the Social Security office manager who was on this programme last week, present Pauline with her long overdue cheque? Keep tuned for regular updates on Central, your local Radio Station.'

We sat and waited for the phone to ring. At 12.30 my mother said, 'Put your coat on, Adrian, I'm taking you to be abandoned.'

At 12.35 as we were going out of the door the phone rang. It was my father pleading for his name not to be mentioned on the air.

The presence of radio reporters and journalists caused a mini-riot in the Social Security office. All the claimants wanted to tell their stories. The tramps got over-excited and started brawling amongst themselves. The staff staged a walk-out and the police were called.

Mitchell Malone was doing an outside broadcast, he played a record called 'The Lunatics are taking over the Asylum.'

I was only abandoned for forty-five minutes before Mr Gudgeon gave my mother an 'Emergency Needs Payment' of £25. He said it would see us through the weekend. He asked my mother to come in and see him on Monday morning, but a police sergeant said, 'No, Mr Gudgeon, you will go and see Mrs Mole at home.'

Mr Gudgeon sucked his ragged moustache and said, 'But I've got a meeting on Monday morning.'

The sergeant swung his truncheon about and said, 'Yes, your

meeting is with Mrs Mole.' Then he strolled off and started knocking the tramps about.

Wednesday   October 6th

A picture of my mother and me was on the front of the paper tonight. (My spots hardly showed up at all.) The headline said: 'A MOTHER'S ANGUISH.' The article underneath said:

> Attractive mother-to-be Pauline Vole (58) took the desperate action of abandoning her only child Adrian (5) in the Carey Street Social Security office yesterday.
>
> Mrs Vole claims to have waited three weeks for a giro cheque. She said, 'I was desperate. Adrian means more to me than life itself, but I was driven to take the drastic step of abandoning him to draw attention to our plight.'
>
> Mr Gudgeon (42) the manager of the Carey Street office, said today: 'Mrs Vole has been the unfortunate victim of a staff shortage. The member of staff who deals with the computer broke his toe drinking squash.'

Thursday   October 7th

The following corrections appeared in the local paper tonight:

> Mrs Pauline Vole would like to correct an inaccurate statement attributed to her in yesterday's edition of the paper.
>
> She did not say, 'Adrian means more to me than life itself.'
>
> In the same article 'drinking squash' should have read 'playing squash'.
>
> We apologize to Mrs Vole and Mr Reginald Gudgeon and thank them for pointing out these unintentional errors.

Friday   October 8th

My mother phoned the local paper to demand that they print the following statement:

> Mrs Pauline Mole is 38 and not 58, as was reported in Wednesday's edition.

My mother is fed up with the neighbours talking. Last night Mr O'Leary called out, 'Sure you're a fine-looking woman for your age Mrs Mole.'

Saturday October 9th
MOON'S LAST QUARTER

The Guiness Book of Records rang up today. A posh bloke spoke to my mother and asked if she would mind her name being included in the 'Oldest Women to Give Birth' section.

He asked my mother to send her birth certificate. My mother said she hadn't given birth yet and she was only thirty-eight.

The bloke said, 'Sorry for troubling you, Mrs Vole,' and rang off.

Read the paper from cover to cover, but nothing about my mother's age appeared tonight.

Sunday October 10th
EIGHTEENTH AFTER TRINITY

My mother spent the day reading *The Observer* with her ankles raised above her head.

I took the dog out. We went to the woods to see the half-built executive houses.

We explored a house called the 'Winchester'. The dog cocked its leg in the master bedroom and started to squat down on the Bar-B-Q patio so I dragged it away.

Monday October 11th
COLUMBUS DAY (USA). THANKSGIVING DAY (CANADA)

Courtney brought a dead exciting postcard. It said:

> Dear Adrian Mole,
> Your work interests me enormously. If you would like to see it published please write to me and I will furnish you with details.
> Sincerely yours,
> L.S. Caton

It was sent from an address in Bolton. I wonder how L.S. Caton heard about me? Perhaps Mr Tydeman mentioned me over the dinner table at a BBC banquet.

I sent Mr Caton a short but dignified reply asking for further details.

Gudgeon turned up and gave my mother the rest of her money. On his way out he asked who the men's size ten shoes under the sofa belonged to. My mother told him that they belonged to her son Adrian. She said, 'I'm not likely to start co-habiting in my condition am I?' Mr Gudgeon blushed and tripped over the dog in his haste to get out.

We had a brillo dinner tonight; chicken curry and my mother put a strand of saffron in the rice. We ate it off our knees (to be strictly accurate my mother ate it off her lump) in front of the television while we watched an old Tudor wreck called the *Mary Rose* get dragged up from the sea bottom.

My mother said, 'From what I can see of it the sea bottom is the best place for it.' I was disappointed not to see any skeletons but the commentator told us that it was an historic occasion, so I tried to feel a bit overawed.

Tuesday   October 12th

A first-year called Anne Louise Wirgfield asked me for my autograph today. She said, 'I saw your picture in the paper and told my mummy that you go to our school, but mummy said you didn't because the paper said you're only five. So I want your autograph to prove that I know you.'

I gave the kid my autograph, I will have to get used to being pestered one day, I suppose.

Practised my signature all through Maths. Came home; watched the Falklands Task Force marching through London. Looked for Clive Kent, but didn't see him.

Wednesday   October 13th

My mother has received a clothing voucher for school trousers from the Social Security. It is made out for £10.

To get the trousers though I have to take the voucher to one of three special shops approved by Social Security. All the shops named – Henry Blogetts and Sons, School Outfitters, Swingin'

Sixty's and Mick n' Dave's – are notorious for selling crap clothes at big prices.

I will not demean myself by taking the voucher in. I have put it in my wallet. When I am rich and famous I will look at it and perhaps show it to my friends to prove that I once knew the sour taste of poverty.

Thursday   October 14th

Went to see how Brett is getting on today. He seemed to know I was his brother because when I looked into his cot he gave me a daft gummy smile and held onto my finger dead tight.

His skin has cleared up now so perhaps there is hope for the kid.

Grandma is looking dead haggard, but not as haggard as Stick Insect. The two women are getting on each other's nerves. Grandma doesn't approve of Stick Insect using plain flour for Yorkshire puddings and Stick Insect doesn't like the way Grandma wraps Maxwell's chest up in Vick and brown paper at night. She says the rustling prevents her from sleeping.

When I got home my mother cross-questioned me about Stick Insect and Grandma. She wanted me to recall every expression of face and nuance of voice during my visit.

Friday   October 15th

I have put my name down for the school play. We are doing *The Importance of Being Earnest* by Oscar Wilde.

I am having my audition next Monday. I hope to get to play Earnest, although my mother says the handbag is the best part. She thinks she's such a wit.

Monday   October 18th

The weekend was far, far, far too boring to write about. Mr Golightly, the Drama teacher, stopped me halfway through my *Henry V* speech. He said, 'Look, Adrian, *The Importance of Being Earnest* is a brittle comedy of manners, not a macho war epic. I want to know if you can time a comic line.' He gave me a speech about Victoria Station to read, listened, then said: 'Yes, you'll do.'

I have decided to be an actor when I grow up. I will write my novels during breaks in rehearsal.

Tuesday   October 19th

Mrs Singh accompanied my mother to the ante-natal clinic today. The gynaecologist has told my mother she must rest more or she will be forced into hospital and made to stay in bed. Her swollen ankles are caused by high blood pressure. She is dead old to be having a baby so the doctors are giving her more attention in case she dies and they get into trouble.

Wednesday   October 20th

When I said 'Hello' to Pandora in Geography my voice wobbled out of control. I kept quiet for the rest of the lesson.

Thursday   October 21st

My mother asked why I was so quiet. She said, 'You've hardly said a word since *Blue Peter*. Is anything wrong?' I shrilled, 'No', and left the room.

Friday   October 22nd

My voice can't be trusted. One minute it's booming and loud like Ian Paisley, the next it's shrill and shrieking like Margaret Thatcher's used to be before she had voice lessons from an advertising agency.

Saturday   October 23rd

Bert Baxter rang up to tell me that my father has got the sack from Manpower Services. I kept silent. Bert said, 'Ain't you got nought to say?'

I wobbled 'No' and put the phone down. I will have to go to the doctor's about my voice. It can't be normal to suffer like this.

Sunday October 24th
TWENTIETH AFTER TRINITY
BRITISH SUMMER TIME ENDS

The dog went beserk and ripped the Sunday papers up today. It had no explanation for its bizarre behaviour.

The hall was covered with pieces of newsprint saying 'Ken Livingstone today defended' . . . 'Falklands' upkeep rockets to £700 million' . . . 'Israeli soldiers watched helpless as' . . . 'trouser zips enquiry' . . . 'Firemen will accept 7½% but mood is explosive' . . . .

I swept the pieces up and put them in the dustbin and put the lid on the outside world.

Monday October 25th
HOLIDAY (REPUBLIC OF IRELAND)
MOON'S FIRST QUARTER

After a silent day at school I took my unstable voice to Dr Gray's surgery. Dr Gray didn't look up from his horrible scribbling, he just said, 'Yes?' I wobbled and shrilled and boomed all my fears about having a defective voice box.

Dr Gray said, 'For Christ's sake it's only your voice breaking, youth! It's come a bit late but then you're physically immature generally. You should take up a physical sport and get more fresh air.'

I asked how long the uncertainty would last.

He said, 'Who knows? I'm not a bloody prophet, am I?'

I could hardly believe my ears. The first thing I do after leaving school will be to take out a subscription to BUPA.

I have resigned from *The Importance of Being Earnest*. To act you need a reliable voice and I haven't got one.

Tuesday October 26th

Barry Kent has committed educational suicide by wearing his Hells Angels clothes to school. Mr Lambert pretended not to notice (Barry Kent is four inches taller than him) but Mr Scruton spotted Kent in school dinners and ordered him to take them off, saying that the studs could cause 'somebody to lose an eye.'

Kent went into the fourth-years' cloakroom and took his jacket off. He was wearing a studded death's head shirt underneath so Scruton made him remove that as well, only to reveal a leather-studded vest.

I don't know how Kent manages to carry around so much weight. Mr Scruton has sent Kent home with a note.

Wednesday   October 27th

Some of the more impressionable fourth-years came to school with studs on the back of their blazers.

Thursday   October 28th

Mr Scruton has added another school rule to the million others. Studs are not allowed to be worn anywhere in school except on the soles of sports boots.

After school Pandora and some of her gang rushed out to buy studs to put on the hem of their underskirts.

Friday   October 29th

My mother has the baby in two weeks' time! The hospital did a test on her today. She is getting into a panic because the spare room is still a spare room and not a nursery. We are still dead short of money. The maternity grant only bought half a second-hand pram!

Saturday   October 30th

The dog went berserk again and ripped up my priceless collection of old *Beano*'s. I have been collecting them since I was seven so I was heartbroken to see them defiled.

I felt like booting the dog around my bedroom but I let it off lightly by chucking it down the stairs.

It's always respected literature in the past. It will have to go to the vet's, just in case it's got a brain malfunction.

Sunday   October 31st

TWENTY-FIRST AFTER TRINITY. HALLOWE'EN. DAY-
LIGHT SAVING TIME ENDS (USA AND CANADA)

At five o'clock I was asked by my so-called best friend Nigel to
go to his Hallowe'en party.

He said, 'Forgot to send you an invite, zit face, but come
anyway, dress as a warlock or you won't get in.'

I decided not to go as a warlock; I wanted to break away from
stereotypes, so I went as a fiend. My mother helped me to
assemble a costume. We used my father's old flippers, one of my
mother's long-legged black leotards and an orange fright wig she
bought years ago when she went to my father's fishing club
dinner and dance.

I looked a bit indecent in the leotard so I put my swimming
trunks over the top, but when I got the whole lot on I didn't look
a bit fiendish, I just looked dead stupid. My mother had the idea
of putting a nylon stocking over my fiendishly made-up face. It
looked a bit better but my costume still lacked a certain
something.

At seven o'clock I had a crisis of confidence and almost took
everything off, but my mother fetched a can of green neon spray
paint that we used to perk up last year's Christmas tree. She
sprayed me from head to toe with it. The dog whimpered and
ran under the draining board. So I knew I must have achieved
the right effect.

The short walk to Nigel's house was an ordeal. A gang of little
kids in pointed hats ran up to me screaming: 'Trick or Treat.' I
kept telling them to bugger off but they followed me to Nigel's,
trying to tread on my flippers. Nigel wouldn't let me in at first
because I wasn't in warlock costume. (He's so literal! He'll end
up working with computers if he's not careful.) But I explained
that I was a fiend and he relented. Nigel's mother and father
were upstairs watching telly, so we raided their drinks cupboard
and drank Tia Maria and Egg Flip Cocktails.

There were no girls at the party, which was a bit strange. Nigel
said that girls make him sick. The warlocks and me danced in the
pumpkin light to Duran Duran records. It was OK, I suppose,
but without girls it lacked a certain *je ne sais quoi* (French for
something or other). At ten o'clock Nigel's mother ran in with a

running buffet. The food was all gone in ten minutes. Most of it was eaten, but a lot got thrown about. Without the civilizing influence of girls, boys return to the wild.

The school are making me read *Lord of the Flies* by William Golding. I am sharing a book with three dumbos who take half an hour to read one page, so it is turning out to be a frustrating experience.

Monday   November 1st
FULL MOON

After school I went to the hairdresser's with my massive mother. She didn't want me to go but she can't be allowed out of doors on her own, can she? Women are always having babies in phone boxes, buses, lifts etc. It is a well-known fact.

Franco's is run by an Italian bloke. He shouted at my mother as soon as she got through the bamboo door. He said, 'Hey, Pauline, why you no come to see Franco once a week like before, heh?'

My mother explained that she couldn't afford to have her hair done regularly now.

Franco said, 'What foolish thing you say! Hair first, food second. You want your bambino to open his eyes and see an ugly mama?'

I was astonished to hear the way he bossed my mother about, but for once she didn't seem to mind. He wrapped a sheet around her neck and said, 'Sit down, shut up, and keep still,' then he tipped her backwards and shampooed her hair. He told her off for having a few grey hairs and moaned about split ends and the condition. Then he dried her hair in a towel and made her sit in front of a mirror.

My mother said, 'I'll just have a trim please, Franco.'

But Franco said, 'No way, Pauline. I cut it all off and we start again.' And my mother sat there and let him do it!

She also let him spray her bristle-cut hair purple and she paid him for doing it. *And* gave him a tip!

Tuesday   November 2nd

There is a new channel on television. It is called Channel Four and it is for minorities, like intellectuals and people that belong to jigsaw clubs.

At last I have found my spiritual viewing home.

I predict that Channel Four will transform British society. All the morons in the country will start watching it, and get a taste for education and culture! Yes, Britain is in for a new renaissance!

Wednesday   November 3rd

My mother has packed her little weekend case and put it in the hall.

Thursday   November 4th

My father rang today and asked me how my mother was. I said she was as well as could be expected, for an eight-and-a-half-months pregnant woman.

He asked if the baby's head was engaged yet. I answered coldly that I wasn't conversant with the technicalities of childbirth.

I asked him how his own baby was, he said, 'That's right, Adrian, turn the knife.' Then he put the phone down.

Friday   November 5th
BONFIRE NIGHT!

Locked the dog in the coal shed, as advised by the media. Then went to the Marriage Guidance Council Bonfire party.

It was crowded with couples bickering over the fireworks, so Pandora and I slipped away and shared a packet of sparklers behind the wall of the Co-op bakery. I wrote 'PANDORA' in the air with my sparkler. Pandora wrote 'ADRAIN.' I was very upset: we've been going out for over a year. She ought to know how to spell my name by now.

Went back to the community bonfire and found our dog watching the firework display and chewing a hot-dog.

I lost count of the times nosy adults said, 'That dog should be locked up out of harm's way.'

I tried to explain that our dog is an individualist and can't be treated like other dogs, but what with the exploding of fireworks and the crowds going, 'Oooh!' and, 'Aaaah!' every time a pathetic rocket was launched, it was a bit difficult.

In the end I took the stupid dog home, thus missing the 'Best Dressed Guy' competition.

Saturday   November 6th

Wrote a political poem. I am going to send it to the *New Statesman*. Mr Braithwaite told me that they print a seditious poem every week.

> *Mrs Thatcher by A. Mole*
> Do you weep, Mrs Thatcher, do you weep?
> Do you wake, Mrs Thatcher, in your sleep?
> Do you weep like a sad willow?
> On your Marks and Spencer's pillow?
> Are your tears molten steel?
> Do you weep?
> Do you wake with '*Three million*' on your brain?
> Are you sorry that they'll never work again?
> When you're dressing in your blue, do you see the waiting
>   queue?
> Do you weep, Mrs Thatcher, do you weep?

I think my poem is extremely brilliant. It is the sort of poem that could bring the government to its knees.

Sunday   November 7th

Went to see Bert and Queenie with my mother.

Everyone we met on the way asked my mother when the baby was due, or made comments like, 'I expect you'll be glad when the baby's here, won't you?'

My mother was very ungracious in her replies.

Bert opened the door, he said, 'Ain't you dropped that sprog yet?'

My mother said, 'Shut your mouth, you clapped-out geriatric.'

Honestly, sometimes I long for the bygone days, when people spoke politely to each other. You would never guess that my mother and Bert are fond of each other.

Everyone was too old, or too ill, or too pregnant to do any cooking (I developed a sudden ache in both wrists). So we ate bread and cheese for our Sunday dinner. Then, in the afternoon we took it in turns to teach Queenie to speak again.

I got her to say, 'A jar of beetroot please,' dead clearly. I might be a speech therapist when I grow up. I have got a definite flair for it. We got a taxi back home because my mother's ankles got a bit swollen. The taxi driver moaned because the distance was only half a mile.

Monday   November 8th

I was woken up at 3 a.m. by the sound of my mother crying.

She wouldn't say what was wrong, so after patting her on the shoulder I went back to bed.

I wish she'd let my dad come back. After all he *has* said he's sorry.

Tuesday   November 9th

Couldn't concentrate at school for worrying about my mother. Mr Lambert told me off for staring out of the window when I should have been writing about the future of the British Steel Industry.

He said, 'Adrian, you've only got three minutes to finish your essay.' So I wrote: 'In my opinion there *is* no future for the British Steel Industry, while the present government is in power.' I know I'll get into trouble, but I gave it in anyway.

Wednesday   November 10th

My mother has gone mad cleaning the house from top to bottom. She has taken all the curtains and nets down. Now anybody passing by in the street can look in and see our most intimate moments.

I was examining my spots in the living-room mirror tonight, when Mr O'Leary shouted from the street: 'There's a fine pimple on the back of your neck, don't miss that one out, boy.'

It's taken me fifteen years to appreciate the part that curtains have played in civilized English life.

Mr Brezhnev, the Russian Prime Minister, died today. World leaders have been sending lying telegrams to the Kremlin saying how sorry they are.

Thursday   November 11th
ARMISTICE DAY

When I got home from school my mother's little suitcase was missing from the hall. She was nowhere in the house, but I found a note on the biscuit tin. It said:

> Waters broke at 3.35. I am in the labour ward of the Royal Infirmary. Call a taxi. £5 note at bottom of spaghetti jar. Don't worry.
>   Love, Mum
> P.S. Dog at Mrs Singh's.

Her writing looked dead untidy.

The taxi ride was a nightmare. I was struggling to get my hand free of the spaghetti jar all the way. The taxi driver kept saying, 'You should have tipped the jar upside down, you stupid bleeder.'

He parked outside the entrance to the hospital, and watched the jar versus my hand struggle in a bored sort of way. He said, 'I'll have to charge you waiting time.' A hundred years passed: then he said, 'And I can't change a five-pound note either.'

I was almost in tears by the time I managed to pull my hand free. I had a mental image of my mother calling for me. So I gave the taxi driver the fiver, and ran into the hospital. Found the lift and pressed the button which said 'Labour Ward.'

I emerged into another world. It looked like the space control centre at Houston.

A technician asked, 'Who are you?'

I said, 'I'm Adrian Mole.'

'And you've got permission to visit the labour ward?'

'Yes,' I said. (Why did I say yes? Why?)

'Room 13. She's being a bit stubborn.'

'Yes, she's a stubborn kind of person,' I said, and walked down the corridor. Doors opened and shut and I caught glimpses of women hooked up to gruesome-looking equipment. Moans and groans bounced around the shiny floors. I pushed the door of Room 13 open and saw my mother lying on a high bed reading, *Memoirs of a Fox-hunting Man* by Siegfried Sassoon.

She looked pleased to see me and then asked why I'd brought the spaghetti jar into the hospital. I was halfway through telling her, when she screwed her face up and started singing 'Hard Day's Night.'

After a bit she stopped singing and looked normal. She even laughed when I got to the bit about the horrible taxi driver. After a bit a kind black nurse came in and said, 'Are you all right, honey?'

My mother said, 'Yes. This is Adrian.'

The nurse said, 'Put a mask and gown on, Adrian, and sit in a corner; it's going to be action stations soon!'

After about half an hour my mother was singing more and talking less. She kept grabbing my hand and crushing it. The nurse came back in and to my relief told me to go out. But my mother wouldn't let go of my hand. The nurse told me to make myself useful and time the contractions. When she'd gone I asked my mother what contractions were.

'Pains,' she said, between clenched teeth. I asked her why she hadn't had her back frozen to stop the pain. My mother said, 'I can't stand people fiddling around with my back.'

The pains started coming every minute, and my mother went barmy, and a lot of people ran in and started telling her to push. I sat in a far corner at the head end of my mother and tried not to look at the other end where doctors and nurses were clanging about with metal things. My mother was puffing and panting, just like she does at Christmas when she's blowing balloons up. Soon everyone was shouting, 'Push, Mrs Mole, push!' My mother pushed until her eyes nearly popped out. 'Harder,' they shouted. My mother went a bit barmy again, and the doctor said, 'I can see the baby's head!'

I tried to escape then but my mother said, 'Where's Adrian? I want Adrian.'

I didn't like to leave her alone with strangers, so I said I'd stay. I stared at the beauty spot on my mother's cheek for the next three minutes, and I didn't look up, until I heard the black nurse say, 'Pant for the head.'

At 5.19 p.m. my mother had a barmy moment; then the doctor

and nurses gave a sort of loud sigh, and I looked up and saw a skinny purple thing hanging upside down. It was covered in white stuff.

'It's a lovely little girl, Mrs Mole,' the doctor said, and he looked dead pleased, as if he were the father himself.

My mother said, 'Is she all right?'

The doctor said, 'Toes and fingers all correct.'

The baby started crying in a crotchety, bad-tempered way, and she was put on my mother's flatter belly. My mother looked at her as if she was a precious piece of jewellery or something. I congratulated my mother and she said, 'Say hello to your sister.'

The doctor stared at me in my mask and gown and said, 'Aren't you Mr Mole, the baby's father?'

I said, 'No, I'm Master Mole the baby's brother.'

'Then you've broken every rule in this hospital,' he said. 'I must ask you to leave. You could be rife with childish infectious diseases.'

So, while they stood around waiting for something called the placenta to emerge, I went into the corridor. I found a waiting-room full of worried-looking men, smoking and talking about cars.

(*To be continued after sleep.*)

At 6.15 I rang Pandora and told her the news. She did big squeals down the phone. Next I rang Grandma, who did big sobs.

Then I phoned Bert and Queenie, who threatened to come and see my mother. But I managed to put them off. Then I ran out of five pence pieces, so I called in to see my mum and sister. Then went home. I walked around the empty house, trying to imagine sharing it with a little girl.

I put all my smashable possessions on the top shelf of my unit. Then went to bed. It was only 7.30 but for some reason I was dead tired. The phone woke me up at 8.15. It was my father gibbering about having a girl. He wanted to know every detail about her. I said she took after him. Half bald and angry-looking.

Friday November 12th

The Russians chose their new leader today. He is called Andropov. I am a hero at school. The story has got round that I *delivered* the baby. The dinner lady in charge of chips gave me an extra big portion. Went to the hospital to see my female relations after school.

I am staying at Pandora's house. Over supper I gave them a blow-by-blow account of the birth. Halfway through Mr Braithwaite got up and left the table.

Saturday   November 13th

Pandora and I went to see my mother and the baby this afternoon. We had to fight our way through the crowd of visitors round her bed. For such a stubborn person she is certainly popular. The baby was passed around like an exhibit in a court room. Everyone said, 'Isn't she beautiful?'

The women said, 'Ooh it makes me feel broody!'

The men said, 'Small fingernails.'

Then Queenie and Bert arrived, so a space was cleared for Bert's wheelchair, and Queenie sat on the bed and squashed my mother's legs and it was dead chaotic. The nurses started looking efficient and bossy. A staff nurse said, 'You are only allowed two visitors to a bed.' Just then my grandma and father turned up. So everyone else was pleased to go and leave these two particular visitors at the bed.

Sunday   November 14th
REMEMBRANCE SUNDAY

My mother phoned me up to tell me that she is coming home at 10.30 tomorrow morning. She told me to make sure the heating is switched on. I asked if she wanted a taxi ordering. She said, 'No, your father has kindly offered to pick us up.'

Us! I am no longer an only child.

Watched the poppies falling onto the heads of the young kids in Westminster Abbey. My eyes started running: I think I've got a cold coming on.

Monday   November 15th

Skived off school. Mrs Singh and Mrs O'Leary came round early to tidy the house. I said I was perfectly capable, but Mrs

O'Leary said: 'Sure, you're talking nonsense, child. How would a lump like you know how to make a house nice enough to pass the eagle eyes of a woman?'

At 11.15 I saw the bizarre sight of my father carrying his daughter down the front path. Followed by my thin purple-haired mother. I haven't got enough emotions to cope with all the complexities of my life. After going mad over the baby, Mrs Singh and Mrs O'Leary melted away and left my immediate family staring at each other. To break the tension I made a cup of tea.

My mother took hers to bed and I let mine go cold. My father hung about for a bit then went home to Grandma's.

The midwife came at 2.30. She did mysterious things to my mother in the privacy of the master bedroom. At 3.15 the midwife came downstairs and said my mother was suffering from after-baby blues caused by hormone trouble. She asked me who was looking after my mother. I said I was. She said, 'I see,' in a thin-lipped manner. I said, 'I am perfectly capable of pushing a Hoover around!'

She said, 'Your mother needs more support.'

So I took the pillows off my own bed and gave them to my mother. This act of kindness made my mother cry.

Tuesday   November 16th

Phoned the school secretary Mrs Claricoates and enquired about maternity leave. Scruton came on the line. He barked, 'If I don't see you in school tomorrow, Mole, I shall be severely dis-pleased!'

The baby woke up five times in the night. I know, because I sat by her cot, checking her breathing every ten minutes.

My mother has stopped crying and started wearing mascara again.

Wednesday   November 17th

Mrs Singh and Mrs O'Leary are taking it in turns to look after my mother and sister. Pandora says I am beginning to be a bore about the baby. She says that my sister's feeding pattern isn't of great interest to her. How callous can you get?

Thursday   November 18th

My father was ironing baby clothes when I got home from school. He said, 'If you laugh, I'll kill you.' My mother was feeding the baby, with her feet on the dog's back. It was a charming domestic picture, only spoiled when my father put the ironing board away and went home to his other family.

Friday   November 19th

I asked my mother what she was going to call the baby.

She said, 'I can't think beyond the next feed – let alone decide on a name.'

I suggested we both make a list, so after the next feed we did.

My mothers'	*Mine*
Charity	Tracy
Christobel	Claire
Zoe	Toyah
Jade	Diana
Frankie	Pandora
India	Sharon
Rosie	Georgina
Caitlin	
Ruth	

I only liked 'Rosie' and 'Ruth' out of my mother's list. She didn't like any in my list. She said, 'Pandora is a pretentious name!' I think it is the most evocative girl's name in the history of the world. Whenever I say it, or hear it, I get a bursting feeling behind my ribs.

Saturday   November 20th

My sister's name is Rosie Germaine Mole.

Everybody likes 'Rosie' but only my mother likes 'Germaine.' The registrar raised his eyebrows, and said 'Germaine? As in *Female Eunuch*?'

My mother said, 'Yes, have you read it?' 'No, but my wife can't put it down,' he said, smoothing his unironed shirt.

We celebrated Rosie being on the official record sheet of Great Britain by going into a café, and having a meal. Rosie was

in a baby sling squashed against my mother's chest. She was
dead well-behaved. She only woke up when my mother dropped
a warm chip on her head. After the meal, we caught a taxi home.
My mother was too tired to walk to the bus stop.

Sunday   November 21st

My father came round with £25. He mooned over my mother
while she was defrosting a shoulder of lamb under the hot tap.
They started having an intense conversation about their future
relationship. So I took the dog for a walk into the garden for a
session of obedience training, but it was a waste of time. Our dog
would have Barbara Woodhouse in tears.

Monday   November 22nd

We had to write a description of a person in English. So I wrote
about Rosie.

Rosie

Rosie is about eighteen inches long, she has got a big head
with fuzzy black hair in a Friar Tuck style. Unlike the rest
of our family, her eyes are brown. She has got quite a good
skin. Her mouth is extremely small, except when she is
screaming. Then it resembles an underground cavern. She
has got a wrinkled-up neck like a turkey's. She dresses in
unisex clothes, and always wears disposable nappies. She
lazes about all day in a carrycot and only gets out when it is
time to be fed or changed. She has got a split personality;
calm one minute, screaming like a maniac the next.

She is only eleven days old but she rules our house.

Tuesday   November 23rd

Rat fink Lucas phoned up tonight. My mother spoke to him for
about ten minutes in a mumbling sort of way, as though she
didn't want me to hear. But I certainly heard the last thing she
said before she threw the phone across the hall. Because it was
said at a high rate of decibels.

'ALL RIGHT – HAVE A BLOOD TEST!'

Perhaps Lucas thinks he's got a deadly blood disease. I hope he has.

Wednesday   November 24th

Mr O'Leary has gone to Ireland to vote in the Irish election, which is being held tomorrow. I admire his patriotism: but I can't understand why he doesn't live in Ireland all the time. I will ask him when he comes back. Mrs O'Leary is not so patriotic. She stayed at home and threw a party for somebody called 'Ann Summers.' My mother was invited but didn't go. She said Ann Summers was responsible for getting her into her present mess.

I watched the O'Learys' front door all night but all I saw was just a load of middle-aged women giggling and clutching brown paper bags.

Thursday   November 25th

Nobody won in the Irish General Election. It was a draw.

Mr O'Leary was detained at East Midlands airport on suspicion of being a terrorist but he was let off with a warning and told not to bring Action Man accessories into the country again.

Friday   November 26th

I got a dead horrible shock when I came out of the school gate today. Stick Insect was waiting for me. She stood there rocking an old royal family pram which contained Brett and Maxwell. She looked like a refugee from a Second World War newsreel. Maxwell shouted, 'Hello brudder.' I thought he was talking to Brett, but no, the kid was talking to me! I shoved a bit of Mars bar into his mouth before he could show me up any more, and introduced Pandora to Stick Insect.

I said, 'My girl-friend, Pandora,' to Stick Insect; and, 'Mrs Doreen Slater,' to Pandora. The two women looked each other up and down in a split second, and then smiled in a false way.

'What perfect darlings,' said Pandora, looking in the pram.

'They're both little buggers,' Stick Insect whined. 'I'd never have had them if I'd known.'

'Known what?' said Pandora, pretending to be innocent.

'Known that they take your life over. Don't you have none,' she warned.

Pandora said, 'I hope I shall have six!'

'*And* be editor of *The Times*?' I said sarcastically.

'Yes,' said Pandora, 'and I shall do my own painting and decorating!'

'You wait,' said Stick Insect. 'You just wait.' It was like a gypsy's curse.

I asked S.I. why she'd waited for me, and she told me that my father was awful to live with, and that Grandma was worse.

I said, 'Well what can I do about it?'

Stick Insect said, 'I just wanted to get it off my chest!' (Flat). Then she wheeled the kids back to Grandma's.

I don't know a single sane adult. They are all barmy. If they are not fighting in the Middle East, they are dressing poodles in plastic macs or having their bodies deep frozen. Or reading *The Sun*, because they think it is a newspaper.

Saturday   November 27th

Changed my first nappy tonight.

Tomorrow I am going to try doing it with my eyes open.

Sunday   November 28th

How is it that my mother can change Rosie's yukky nappies and at the same time smile and even laugh? I nearly fainted when I tried to do it without a protective device (clothes peg). Perhaps women have got poorly developed nasal passages.

I wonder if research has been done into it? If I pass 'O' level Biology I may even do it myself.

Monday   November 29th

My mother's gone right off me since Rosie was born. She was never a particularly attentive mother – I always had to clean my own shoes. But just lately I have been feeling emotionally deprived. If I turn out to be mentally deranged in adult life, it will all be my mother's fault.

I'm spending most of the time reading in my room. I've just finished reading *To Sir with Love*. It's about a black teacher who is badly treated by white yobs. But by persevering, and being kind yet firm, he triumphs over them, and decides not to be an engineer. I give it five out of ten. Which is not bad because I am very discriminating.

Tuesday November 30th
ST ANDREW'S DAY

Made my Christmas present list out in order of preference.

> *Big present list*
> Word Processor (no chance)
> Colour Telly (portable)
> Amstrad Hi-Fi unit (for future record collections)
> Electronic typewriter (for poems)
> ¾-length sheepskin coat (for warmth and status)
>
> *Small present list*
> Pair of trousers (pegs)
> Adidas trainers (size ten)
> Adidas anorak (36″ chest)
> Anglepoise lamp (for late-night poetry)
> Gigantic tin of Quality Street
> Solid gold pen set (inscribed A. Mole)
> Pair slippers
> Electric razor
> Habitat bath robe (like Pandora's dad's)
>
> *Things I always get whether I want them or not*
> *Beano* annual
> Chocolate smoking set
> Pkt felt-tip pens
> False nose/glasses/moustache

I gave my mother the list, but she wasn't in the mood for talking about Christmas. In fact just mentioning Christmas put her in a bad mood.

Wednesday December 1st

An emotion-packed phone call from Grandma: Stick Insect has taken Brett and Maxwell to stay with Maxwell's father, who has just come back from the Middle East, loaded with tax-free money and stuffed toy camels!

Apparently my father doesn't mind being deprived of his paternal rights and Maxwell's dad doesn't care that Stick Insect has had a baby in his absence. I am shocked. Am I to be the sole guardian of the little morality left in our society?

Thursday December 2nd

Maxwell's dad, Trevor Roper, doesn't mind about Brett because he thinks Brett is the result of having faulty coitus interruptus!

Stick Insect is getting married to Mr Roper as soon as his divorce is through. It's no wonder the country is on its knees. I am seriously thinking about returning to the church. (Not to go to Stick Insect's wedding either.) I have made an appointment to see a vicar, Reverend Silver. I got him out of the Yellow Pages.

Friday December 3rd

The vicar was mending his bike when I first saw him. He looked quite normal except that he was wearing a black dress.

He got up and gave me a bone-crushing handshake. Then he took me to his study and asked me what I wanted to see him about. I said I was worried about the disintegration of morals in modern life. He lit a cigarette with trembly hands, and enquired if I had asked God for guidance. I said I had stopped believing in God. He said, 'Oh God, not another one!' He talked for ages. It all boiled down to having faith. I said I hadn't got faith and asked him how to get it.

He said, 'You must have faith!' It was like listening to a stuck record. I said, 'If God exists how come He allows wars and famines and motorway crashes to happen?'

Rev. Silver said: 'I don't know, I lie awake wondering that myself.'

Mrs Silver came in with two mugs of Nescafé, and a box of Mr Kipling's iced fancies.

She said, 'Derek, your Open University thing is starting in ten minutes.'

I asked the Rev. Silver what he was studying. He said, 'Microbiology. You know where you are with microbes.'

I said goodbye and wished him luck in his change of career. He told me not to despair, and showed me out into the mad, bad, world. It was cold and dark and some yobs were throwing chips about in the street. I went home feeling worse than ever.

Saturday   December 4th

I am having a nervous breakdown. Nobody has noticed yet.

Sunday   December 5th

Went to see Bert; he is my last hope. (Pandora failed me. She blamed my mental state on my being a meat eater.) I said, 'Bert, I am having a breakdown! Bert said that he had had a breakdown in the first World War. He said his was caused by seeing thousands of dead men and being constantly afraid for his life. He asked what mine was caused by.

I said, 'The lack of morals in society.'

Bert said, 'You daft bugger, what you need is a good stint of hard work. You can start on the washing up.'

When I'd finished Queenie made me a cup of tea, and a pile of crab paste sandwiches. While I ate I watched *Songs of Praise* on the television. The church was full of happy-looking people all singing their hearts out.

How come they've got faith and I've not? Just my luck!

Monday   December 6th

I was woken up at 1 a.m., 2.30 a.m. and 4 a.m. by Rosie screaming.

I got up at 6 a.m. and listened to a farming programme on Radio Four. Some old rustic gasbag was drivelling on about geese farming in Essex. At 8.30 I went into my mother's room, to ask for my dinner money and found Rosie fast asleep in my mother's bed. This is strictly forbidden by the baby books.

I checked that Rosie could breathe properly, then, after taking three pounds out of my mother's purse, I went to school and tried to behave normally.

Tuesday December 7th

Queenie died at 3 o'clock this morning. She had a stroke in her sleep. Bert said that it was a good way to go, and I am inclined to agree with him. It was strange to go into Bert's house and see Queenie's things all over the place. I still can't believe she is dead and that her body is in the Co-op Funeral Parlour.

I didn't cry when my mother told me the news, in fact I felt like laughing. It wasn't until I saw Queenie's pot of rouge standing on the dressing table, that tears leaked out. I didn't let Bert see me crying, and he didn't let me see him crying. But I know he has been. There are no clean hankies left in his drawer.

Bert doesn't know what to do about death certificates, and funeral arrangements etc. So Pandora's father came round to do all the death paperwork.

Wednesday December 8th

Bert has asked me to write a poem to put in the Deaths column of the local paper.

10 p.m. I am terrified. In fact I have got writer's block.

11.30 p.m. Unblocked. Finished poem.

Thursday December 9th

The following announcements appeared in the paper tonight:

> **BAXTER, Maud Lilian** (Queenie.) Passed away peacefully at home on 7th December 1982. To the best girl that ever was. Bert, Sabre and Adrian.
>
> White face, red cheeks.
> Eyes like crocus buds.
> Hands deft and sure, yet worked to gnarled roots.
> A practical comfortable body, dressed in young colours.
> Feet twisted, but planted firmly on the ground.
> A sure soft voice, with a crackly sudden laugh.

Her body is lifeless and cold,
But the memory of her is joyful and as warm as a
    rockpool in August.

Funeral service and cremation, Monday 13th December at
1.30 p.m. At Gilmore's crematorium. Floral tributes to
Co-operative funeral service.
Written with love, from Adrian, on the instructions of Mr
Bertram Baxter.

BAXTER, Queenie: Sadly missed, Pauline and Rosie
Mole.

BAXTER, Maud Lilian:
    The parting was so sudden.
    We sit and wonder why.
    The saddest thing of all,
    Is that we never said goodbye.

    From your grieving son, Nathan, and your daughter-in-
    law, Maria and Jodie and Jason, grandchildren.

BAXTER, Queenie: Adieu Queenie, Mr and Mrs
Braithwaite and Pandora.

BAXTER, Queenie:
    Always a smile and a kindly word.
    She'd never pass on the things she heard.
    She bore her troubles with never a moan.
    To every stray dog she would give a bone.

    God Bless Queenie. From your friends at the 'Ever-
    greens.'

BAXTER, Queenie: Life is a struggle in search of a
vision. You have found your vision we hope. From your
friends, the Singh Family.

BAXTER, Queenie: Words can't express how much I
will miss my old pal. Your neighbour, Doris.

BAXTER, Queenie: Deepest sympathy, from John the milkman.

BAXTER, Queenie: We have lost a dear old friend. Julian and Sandy, at the 'Jolie Madame' Hair Salon.

BAXTER, Queenie: A sad loss. May and George Mole.

BAXTER, Queenie: I'll miss you, Queenie. Betty in the sweet shop and her husband, Cyril, and children Carol and Pat.

My tribute to Queenie has caused a stir. People have said it's in bad taste, and have complained that it doesn't rhyme. Must I live amongst uneducated peasants – for the rest of my life? I long for the day when I buy my first studio flat in Hampstead. I will have a notice on my door: 'NO HAWKERS TRADERS OR PHILISTINES.'

Friday   December 10th

Mr Braithwaite is very worried about Queenie's funeral. The cheapest he can arrange will cost £350. (Plain coffin, one hearse, one mourner's car.) But Queenie's funeral insurance is only worth £30. She took it out in 1931 when £30 would buy you: a fancy coffin, two teams of black horses with plumes, a funeral tea, and a gang of top-hatted attendants. The death grant the government gives you is no help. It doesn't buy a brass coffin nail.

The only solution is for Bert to take out hire-purchase and have Queenie's funeral on the never-never.

Saturday   December 11th

The finance company have turned down Bert's request for a loan. They say he is too old at nearly ninety, so it looks like Queenie will have to be buried by Social Security, (grey van, plywood coffin, ashes put in a jam jar).

Bert is dead upset. He said, 'I wanted my girl to go out properly!' I spent all night phoning around to everyone who knew Queenie, getting them to donate money. I was called a saint several times.

Sunday   December 12th

My mother has gone out with Mrs Singh, Mrs O'Leary and her women's group to have a picnic on Greenham Common. She has taken Rosie, so the house is dead peaceful.

I played my 'Toyah' records at full volume and had a bath with the door open.

10.02 p.m. I have just seen the Greenham women on the telly! They were tying babies' bootees onto the wire surrounding the missile base. Then they held hands with each other. The newscaster said that 30,000 women were there. The dog was sulking because my mother had gone out for the day. It didn't understand that she was miles away safeguarding its future.

They got back safely. The women's group came back to our house. They talked about female solidarity, while I served them coffee and tuna sandwiches. I felt excluded from the conversation so I went to bed.

2.00 a.m. Just woken up by Mr Singh and Mr O'Leary banging on our door demanding entrance. I got up and explained to them that there were about twenty women in our living room. Mr O'Leary said, 'Tell Caitlin to hurry up; I can't find my pyjamas.' Mr Singh said, 'Ask Sita to tell me how to work our electric kettle.'

I advised them to go home for their own safety.

Monday   December 13th

Queenie's funeral.

We dropped Rosie off at Mrs Singh's and walked round to Bert's bungalow. All the curtains in the street were shut out of respect for Queenie. The neighbours were out looking at the floral tributes, which were lined up alongside the little path to the front door. Bert was sitting in his wheelchair wearing his wedding suit. Sabre was sitting by his side. My mother gave Bert a kiss.

Bert said, 'I don't like to think about her lying in an unheated coffin, she never did like the cold.'

My mother acted as hostess because none of Queenie's relations came. (Queenie quarrelled with them because they disapproved when she married Bert.)

The mourners' cars arrived so me and the Co-op men carried Bert out to the leading car, then me and my mother and Doris from next door, and Mr and Mrs Braithwaite and Pandora sat in the leading car. The second car filled up with less important mourners and we set off very slowly to Gilmore's Crematorium. As we passed the cemetery gates, an old man took his hat off and bowed his head. Bert said that the old man was a stranger. I was very touched by this gesture of respect.

My mother and father sat together in the chapel, briefly united. Me and Pandora sat either side of Bert. He said he wanted to have 'young 'uns' around him.

The service was short; we sang Queenie's favourite carol, 'Away in a Manger', and her favourite song, 'If I Ruled the World.'

Then, while the organ played sad music, the coffin started sliding towards purple curtains around the altar. When the coffin reached the curtains Pandora whispered, 'God, how perfectly barbaric.'

I watched with horror as the coffin disappeared. Bert said, 'Tara old girl' and then Queenie was burnt in the oven.

I was so shocked, I could hardly walk up the aisle. Pandora and I both looked up when we got outside. Smoke was pouring out of the chimney, and was carried away by the wind. Queenie always said she wanted to fly.

I suppose there is a sort of logic to life and death. Rosie was born and so Queenie had to make way for her. The funeral tea was held at Pandora's house; it was a very jolly affair. Bert held up well, and even cracked a few jokes. But I noticed that whenever I mentioned Queenie's name, people looked away, and pretended not to hear. So Bert is on his own again, and will need more looking after than ever!

How will I cope? I've got my 'O' levels in June.

Tuesday December 14th

It was on Radio Four that the government is spending a billion pounds on buying war equipment. Yet one of our science laboratories at school is closing down after Christmas, because our school can't afford to pay a new teacher. Poor old Mr Hill is retiring after thirty years of sweating over the Bunsen burners. He will be sadly missed. He was dead strict but dead fair with it. He was never sarcastic and seemed to listen to what you were saying. Also he gave out mini Mars bars for good work.

Wednesday   December 15th

We put the Christmas tree up tonight. It had gone a bit rusty, but I tied tinsel round the worst bits. My mother insisted on hanging up the decorations I made when I was a little kid. She said they had sentimental value for her. It looked OK when all the flashy balls and bad-taste angels were bunged on it.

I picked Rosie up and showed her the finished tree, but I can't say she was overjoyed. In fact she just yawned. The dog, on the other hand, had one of its mad fits, and had to be restrained with a rolled-up *Guardian*.

Thursday   December 16th

Bought a pack of cheap Christmas cards from Cherry's, but didn't write in them. I will wait and see who sends me one first.

Friday   December 17th

The school's internal Christmas post service is as bad as the GPO's. I posted Pandora a card before assembly but she still hadn't had it by the end of the last lesson.

I will find out which first-years were on Elf duty today, and severely rebuke them.

Saturday   December 18th

Courtney has made £150 in tips from his post round. He is spending it on a weekend in Venice. He says that Christmas in Venice is an experience that everyone should have at least once in their lives. I wish I could have that experience. Courtney said that English canals are not a patch on Venetian ones.

Sunday December 19th

Today Rosie Germaine Mole smiled for the first time. The recipient of the smile was the dog.

My father rang to ask what we are doing for Christmas. My mother said, 'The usual seasonal things, George: eating turkey, getting drunk, buying replacement bulbs for the fairy lights.'

My father said, 'Mother and me will be having *a quiet time, on our own, alone. Just the two of us. Away from our nearest and dearest.*'

My mother said, 'It sounds divine. Well I must dash. A crowd of pre-Christmas revellers have just turned up with the champagne.'

This was a complete and utter lie. It was only me coming into the room with a cup of cocoa.

Monday December 20th

We break up tomorrow. So the school has gone a bit wild. The girls are doing no work at all, they just sit around the classrooms counting how many Christmas cards they've received from each other, and writing out hundreds more. The Elf postal service is being swamped.

I haven't sent any cards at all yet. I'm still waiting to see if anybody sends me one.

Tomorrow is the day of the school concert. It will be the first year I have had nothing to do. My mother is glad because it means she won't have to go.

Tuesday December 21st

Last day of school
Thank God! I got seven Christmas cards. Three tasteful. Four in putrid taste and printed on flimsy rubbish paper that won't stand up. On receipt I quickly wrote out seven cards and gave them to a passing elf. Mr Golightly, director of the Christmas play, *The Importance Of Being Ernest Christmas Show*, was very irritable today when I wished him good luck for tonight. He said, 'Thanks to your abdication, Adrian, I have got a midget playing Ernest.' (Peter Brown, whose mother smoked throughout her pregnancy!)

I'm glad I did abdicate from my role, because the play was a complete fiasco. Lady Bracknell forgot to say, 'A handbag?' And Peter Brown stood behind a chair so that the audience only saw the top of his head. Simone Bates, as Gwendoline, was quite good but what a shame her costume didn't hide her tattoos! The other parts are just not worth writing about.

The best thing in the show was the scenery. I congratulated Mr Animba, the woodwork teacher, on his dedication. He said, 'Do you think anybody noticed that it was adapted from the *Peter Pan* scenery of three years ago?' I assured him that nobody had complained that the view from the French windows was of a palm-fringed island.

Mr Golightly was nowhere to be seen at the end of the play. Somebody told me that he had run from the wings shortly before the end, saying he had to visit his mother in hospital.

The best thing about the evening was the interval when Pandora played her viola in the refreshment room.

Wednesday   December 22nd

Drew £15 out of my Building Society today.

I know it's a lot but I've got an extra person to buy for: Rosie.

9.30 p.m. Forgot that Queenie isn't here any more. I needn't have been so extravagant. My memory!

Thursday   December 23rd

Made a list and went to Woolworth's, as they have got a good selection of festive gifts.

Dog	False bone	(£1.25)
Pandora	Solid gold chain	(£2.00)
Mother	Egg Timer	(About £1.59)
Rosie	Chocolate Santa	(79p)
Bert	20 Woodbines	(£1.09)
Nigel	He gets nothing this year	His best friend is now Clive Barnes
Father	Festive tin of anti-freeze	(£1.39)

Grandma	Gift pack of dusters	(£1.29)
Auntie Susan	Hankie Set	(99p)
Sabre	Dog Comb	(£1.29)

Woolworth's was swarming with last-minute shoppers, so I had to queue for half an hour at the checkout till. Why do people wait to do their shopping until there are only two days left before Christmas?

I couldn't get on a bus home because of the stupid lemmings. Went to the 'Off the Streets' Youth Club party with Pandora. Nigel caused a scandal by dancing with Clive Barnes who was wearing lipstick and mascara!

Everyone was saying that Nigel is gay, so I made sure that everyone knew that he is no longer my best friend. Barry Kent smuggled two cans of 'Tartan' bitter through the fire doors. His gang of six shared them, and got leglessly drunk. At the end of the party Rick Lemon put 'White Christmas' by some old crumblie on the record deck and all the couples danced romantically together. I told Pandora how much I adored her and she said, 'Aidy, my pet, how long will our happiness last?'

Trust Pandora to put a damp cloth on everything. Saw her home. Kissed her twice. Went home. Fed dog. Checked Rosie's pulse. Went to bed.

Friday December 24th
CHRISTMAS EVE

My mother is being kept a prisoner by Rosie; so I have had to do all the Christmas preparations. I was up at 7.30 queuing in the butcher's for a fresh turkey, pork joint, and sausage meat.

By 9 a.m. I was in the queue at the greengrocer's: 3lbs sprouts, 24 tangerines, 2lbs mixed nuts, 2 bunches of holly (make sure they have berries), salad (don't forget green pepper), 2 boxes of dates (get those with camel on lid), 3lbs of apples (if no Cox's get G. Smith), 6lbs potatoes (check each one for signs of sprouting).

By 11.15 I was in the launderette washing and drying the loose covers off the three-piece suite.

2 p.m. saw me at the grocer's with a long list, and Rosie's pram outside to cart everything home. £2.50's worth of Stilton (make sure good blue colour, firm texture), 2 boxes sponge fingers, red and yellow jelly . . . tin of fruit salad. . . . It went on for ever.

At 4.10 p.m. I was struggling into Woolworth's front doors, and trying to fight my way to the fairy-light counter. At 4.20 I got to the counter only to find empty shelves and other desperate people swapping rumours: 'Curry's have got some lantern style', 'Rumbelow's have got two packets of the "star type"', 'Habitat have got the High Tech styles but they're pricey!'

I went to all the above shops and more, but at 5 p.m. I admitted defeat and joined the long queue at the bus stop.

Drunken youths covered in 'crazy foam' and factory girls wearing tinsel garlands paraded around the town singing carols. Jesus would have turned in his tomb.

At 5.25 I had a panic attack and left the queue and rushed into Marks and Spencer's to buy something.

I was temporarily deranged. A voice inside my head kept saying: 'Only five minutes before the shops shut. Buy! Buy! Buy!'

The shop was full of sweating men buying women's underwear. At 5.29 I came to my senses, and went back to bus stop. Just in time to see the bus leaving. I got home at 6.15 after buying a packet of fairy lights from Cherry's shop which is just around the corner from our house.

My mother has made the lounge look especially nice (she'd even dusted the skirting board) and when the new fairy lights were switched on, and the fruit arranged, and the holly stuck up etc, it looked like a room on a Christmas card. Me and my mother had a quick drink before Bert arrived in an Age Concern car, driven by a kind volunteer.

We settled him in front of the telly with a beetroot sandwich and a bottle of brown ale, and we went into the kitchen to start the mincepies and trifles.

1 a.m. Just got back from the Midnight Service. It was very moving (even for an atheist), though I think it was a mistake to have a live donkey in the church.

2 a.m. Just remembered, forgot to buy nutcrackers.

Saturday December 25th
CHRISTMAS DAY

Got up at 7.30.

Had a wash and a shave, cleaned teeth, squeezed spots then went downstairs and put kettle on. I don't know what's happened to Christmas Day lately, but something has. It's just not the same as it used to be when I was a kid. My mother fed and cleaned Rosie, and I did the same to Bert. Then we went into the lounge and opened our presents. I was dead disappointed when I saw the shape of my present. I could tell at a glance that it didn't contain a single microchip. OK a sheepskin coat is warm but there's nothing you can *do* with it, except wear it.

In fact after only two hours of wearing it, I got bored and took it off. However, my mother was ecstatic about her egg timer; she said, 'Wow, another one for my collection.' Rosie ignored the chocolate Santa I bought her. That's 79 pence wasted! *This is what I got:*

> ¾ length sheepskin coat (out of Littlewoods catalogue)
>
> *Beano* Annual (a sad disappointment, this year's is very childish)
>
> Slippers (like Michael Caine wears, although not many people know that)
>
> Swiss army knife (my father is hoping I'll go out into the fresh air and use it)
>
> Tin of humbugs (supposedly from the dog)
>
> Knitted Balaclava helmet (from Grandma Mole. Yuk! Yuk!)
>
> *Boys' Book of Sport* (from Grandma Sugden: Stanley Matthews on cover)

I was glad when Auntie Susan and her friend Gloria turned up; at 11 o'clock. Their talk is very metropolitan and daring; and Gloria is dead glamorous and sexy. She wears frilly dresses, and lacy tights, and high heels. And she's got an itsy-bitsy voice that makes my stomach go soft. Why she's friends with Auntie Susan, who is a prison warder, smokes Panama cigars and has got hairy fingers, I'll never know.

The turkey was OK. But would have been better if the giblets and the plastic bag had been removed before cooking. Bert made chauvinist remarks during the carving. He leered at Gloria's cleavage and said, 'Give me a nice piece of breast.' Gloria wasn't a bit shocked, but I went dead red, and pretended that I'd dropped my cracker under the table.

When my mother asked me which part of the turkey I wanted, I said, 'A wing please!' I really wanted breast, leg, or thigh. But wing was the only part of the bird without sexual connotations. Rosie had a few spoons of mashed potato and gravy. Her table manners are disgusting, even worse than Bert's.

I was given a glass of Bull's Blood wine and felt dead sensual. I talked brilliantly and with consummate wit for an hour, but then my mother told me to leave the table, saying, 'One sniff of the barmaid's apron and his mouth runs away with him.'

The Queen didn't look very happy when she was giving her speech. Perhaps she got lousy Christmas presents this year, like me. Bert and Auntie Susan had a disagreement about the Royal Family. Bert said he would 'move the whole lot of 'em into council houses in Liverpool.'

Gloria said, 'Oh Bert that's a bit drastic. Milton Keynes would be more suitable. They're not used to roughing it you know.'

In the evening I went round to see Grandma and my father. Grandma forced me to eat four mincepies, and asked me why I wasn't wearing my new Balaclava helmet. My father didn't say anything; he was dead drunk in an armchair.

Sunday   December 26th
FIRST AFTER CHRISTMAS

Pandora and I exchanged presents in a candlelit ceremony in my bedroom. I put the solid gold chain round her neck, and she put a 70% wool, 10% cashmere, 20% acrylic scarf round my neck.

A cashmere scarf at fifteen!

I'll make sure the label can be seen by the public at all times.

Pandora went barmy about the solid gold chain. She kept looking at herself in the mirror, she said, 'Thank you, darling, but how on earth can you afford solid gold? It must have cost you at least a hundred pounds!'

I didn't tell her that Woolworth's were selling them cheap at two pounds a go.

Monday   December 27th
BOXING DAY, HOLIDAY (UK EXCEPT SCOTLAND). HOLI-
DAY (CANADA). BANK HOLIDAY (SCOTLAND). HOLIDAY
(REP OF IRELAND)

Just had a note handed to me from a kid riding a new BMX.

> Dear heart,
> I'm awfully sorry but I will have to cancel our trip to the
> cinema to see *ET*.
>   I woke up this morning with an ugly disfiguring rash
> around my neck.
>   Yours sincerely,
>   Pandora
> P.S. I am allergic to non-precious metal.

Tuesday   December 28th

Walked up and down the High Street in my sheepskin coat and
cashmere scarf. Saw Nigel in his new leather trousers posing at
the traffic lights. He suggested we go to his house to 'talk.' I
agreed. On the way he told me that he was trying to decide which
sort of sexuality to opt for: homo, BI or hetero. I asked him
which he felt more comfortable with. He said, 'All three, Moley.'
Nigel could never make up his mind.

He showed me his presents. He had: a multi gym, Adidas
football boots, a Mary Quant make-up hamper, and a unisex
jogging suit.

Wednesday   December 29th

Danny Thompson has turned into a Rasta. I met him when I was
walking up and down the High Street this morning. He asked me
if I could play a musical instrument. I said, 'No.'

He said, 'Too bad, man, I and I needs a bass player real
quick.'

I said I was surprised that a reggae band should need a double
bass.

He did fancy hand-clapping and laughed and said, 'Bass
guitar, what give out de rhythm.'

I said that my only contribution to the band could be as a
lyricist.

He suggested I try writing a few songs and submitting them to the brothers. Then he gave me a complicated handshake and went off down the street with a springy step and with his blonde plaits bobbing up and down.

Thursday   December 30th
FULL MOON

Me, Mum, Rosie, Auntie Susan and Gloria went to Bridgegate Park today. Bert doesn't like fresh air so he stayed at home with the dogs and leftover Christmas food. We walked four boring miles. I walked behind Gloria so that I could watch her bum and legs properly. Auntie Susan and Gloria are going back to Holloway prison tonight. They will be sadly missed, they are so gay and vital. Bert is going back to his council bungalow. He will *not* be missed. He watches ITV all day and won't let anybody else hold Rosie.

Friday   December 31st

Bert has asked if he can stay on until New Year's Day. He said he can't face seeing the New Year in with only a Voluntary Social Worker's company. My mother agreed but she took me into the kitchen and whispered, 'Look, Bert's not living here forever, Adrian. I can't look after a small baby and a geriatric at the same time!'

At eleven o'clock my father rang up to wish us all a Happy New Year. My mother's face went a bit blotchy and soft, and she invited him round for a drink.

At 11.15 rat fink Lucas rang from Sheffield, whining on about the fact that he was alone with a bottle of 'Johnnie Walker.' My mother said, 'How appalling! You should have bought a decent brand – after all it is New Year's Eve.'

She looks dead nice again now that her figure is nearly back to normal. In fact after the phone calls she looked her old cocky self. My father crossed our doorstep at one minute to twelve, with a packet of 'Zip' firelighters (the nearest he could get to coal). Then, when the Scottish people on the telly went berserk at midnight, we all stood around Bert's wheelchair, holding hands and singing 'Auld Lang Syne.' Then we talked about

Queenie and Stick Insect and said things like, 'Well I wonder what 1983 will bring us?'

Personally, nothing would surprise me any more. If my father announced that he was really a Russian agent or my mother ran away with a circus knife thrower, I wouldn't raise an eyebrow.

Pandora rang at 1 a.m. to say 'Happy New Year'. The Braithwaites' party sounded good. I wished I'd gone instead of being kind and staying at home. Went to bed rigid with fear. 1983 is my 'O' level year.

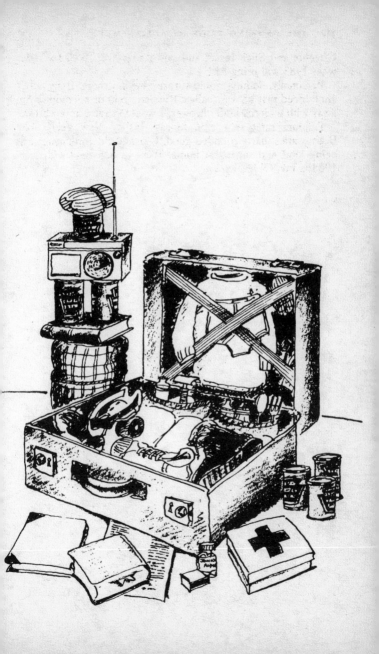

Saturday January 1st 1983

NEW YEAR'S DAY

These are my New Year resolutions:

1. I will revise for my 'O' levels at least two hours a night.
2. I will stop using my mother's Buff-Puff to clean the bath.
3. I will buy a suede brush for my coat.
4. I will stop thinking erotic thoughts during school hours.
5. I will oil my bike once a week.
6. I will try to like Bert Baxter again.
7. I will pay my library fines (88 pence) and rejoin the library.
8. I will get my mother and father together again.
9. I will cancel the *Beano*.

Sunday January 2nd

Took stock of my appearance today. I have only grown a couple of inches in the last year, so I must reconcile myself to the fact that I will be one of those people who never get a good view in the cinema.

My skin is completely disfigured, my ears stick out and my hair has got three partings and won't look fashionable whichever way I comb it.

Monday January 3rd

Negotiations are going on between my parents for a return to their married state. My mother said, 'But how can it ever work, Adrian? There is so much to forget.' I suggested hypnosis.

Tuesday January 4th

More negotiations behind closed doors. As he left, I asked my father for a report on the meeting. He said, 'No comment!' and got in his car.

Wednesday January 5th

Negotiations have broken down.

I heard the sugar bowl crashing to the kitchen floor then raised voices. Then the door slamming.

Thursday January 6th

A message was passed to an intermediary (me). That fresh negotiations would be welcomed. The message was passed on and the response was favourable, so it was left to me to arrange time, venue and baby-sitting details.

Friday January 7th

The meeting took place in a Chinese restaurant at 8 p.m. Negotiations went on throughout the evening and were only adjourned when one party returned home to feed the baby.

Saturday January 8th

Both parties have issued the following bulletin:

> It is agreed that Pauline Monica Mole and George Alfred Mole will attempt to live in mutual harmony for a trial period of one month. If during that time Pauline Monica Mole, hereafter known as P.M.M., and George Alfred Mole, hereafter known as G.A.M., break the following agreement, then the agreement shall be declared null and void, and divorce proceedings will automatically follow.

> *The Agreement*
> 1. G.A.M. SHALL CHEERFULLY AND WITHOUT NAGGING OR REMINDING DO HIS RIGHTFUL SHARE OF HOUSEHOLD TASKS.
> 2. P.M.M. SHALL KEEP HER SIDE OF THE BEDROOM IN A HYGIENIC AND PRESENTABLE CONDITION.
> 3. BOTH PARTIES TO GO TO THE PUB AT SUNDAY LUNCHTIMES.
> 4. THE CHILDREN OF THE MARRIAGE, ADRIAN AND ROSIE

MOLE, TO BE GIVEN FAIR AND EQUAL ATTENTION FROM BOTH PARENTS.

5. FINANCIAL MATTERS TO BE DISCUSSED EACH FRIDAY NIGHT AT 7 P.M.

6. A SEPARATE BANK ACCOUNT TO BE OPENED FOR P.M.M.

7. NEITHER PARTY TO INDULGE IN FLIRTATION, SEDUCTION OR ADULTERY WITH THE OPPOSITE SEX WITHOUT THE FULL KNOWLEDGE, OR CONSENT OF THE OTHER PARTY.

8. P.M.M. TO REPLACE CAP ON TOOTHPASTE AFTER USE.

9. G.A.M. TO WASH OWN HANDKERCHIEFS.

10. BOTH PARTIES TO HAVE UNLIMITED FREEDOM FOR THE PURSUIT OF HOBBIES, POLITICAL INTERESTS, DEMONSTRATIONS, AND SOCIAL INTERCOURSE OUTSIDE THE HOME.

11. G.A.M. TO THROW BOTH PAIRS OF CAVALRY TWILL TROUSERS AWAY.

12. P.M.M. WILL NOT CONSTANTLY HARP ON DOREEN SLATER EPISODE. G.M.M. WILL NOT DO THE SAME RE: LUCAS EPISODE.

> Signed on this day the 8TH JANUARY 1983
> Pauline Mole
> George Mole
> A. Mole, 1st Witness
> Rosie Mole, 2nd Witness. Her mark. X

Sunday   January 9th

My father burnt his cavalry twills in the back garden today. As he poked the gobs of burning cloth he said, 'Well, it's the straight and narrow for me from now on.' I don't know whether he meant his life or his trousers.

Monday   January 10th

Lousy stinking school started today. Everybody was flashing their new calculators around. My sheepskin caused a bit of a stir wherever it went – and it went everywhere. It is far too valuable to leave in the cloakroom. Pandora and I held hands in assembly. But were spotted by Mr Scruton. He said, 'Keep your silly adolescent courtship rituals to outside school hours.' Pandora was still upset at break, but I comforted her in the Boys' toilets, by explaining that Mr Scruton was probably impotent, and it enraged him to see young lovers who were brimming with Eastern promise.

Tuesday   January 11th

Saw Roy Hattersley on the television tonight. He is putting weight on. He ought to go on a diet in case there's a General Election. The viewers don't like fat politicians. Look what happened to Churchill after the war. He was slung out because he got too fat. I know all this because we had a film of the Second World War in History today. I might be a historian if my memory improves.

Wednesday   January 12th

Nigel has formed a Gay Club at school. He is the only member so far, but it will be interesting to see who else joins. I noticed Brain Box Henderson hovering around the poster looking worried.

Thursday   January 13th

Mr Scruton has ordered the closure of the Gay Club, saying that he and the school governors couldn't sanction the use of the school gym for 'immoral purposes'. Nigel pretended to be innocent. He said, 'But sir, the Gay Club is for pupils who want to be frisky, frolicsome, lively, playful, sportive, vivacious or gamesome during the dinner break. What is immoral about gaiety?'

Mr Scruton said, 'Nigel, the word "Gay" has changed its meaning over the past years. It now means something quite different.'

Nigel said, 'What does it mean, sir?'

Scruton started sweating and messing about with his pipe, and not answering, so Nigel let him off the hook by saying: 'Sorry, sir, I can see that I will have to get an up-to-date dictionary!'

Friday January 14th

Must go and see how Bert is getting on. God! I wish I'd never got involved with him; he is like an Ancient Mariner around my neck.

Saturday January 15th

There is a new joke craze sweeping the school. In my opinion these so-called jokes are puerile. I watch in amazement as my fellow pupils roll helplessly in the corridors with tears of laughter coursing down their cheeks after relating them to each other.

1. Q. What do you call a man with a seagull on his head?
   A. Cliff.
2. Q. What do you call a man with a shovel in his head?
   A. Doug.
3. Q. What do you call a man without a shovel in his head?
   A. Douglas.
4. Q. What do you call an Irishman, who's been buried for fifty years?
   A. Pete.
5. Q. What do you call a man with fifty rabbits up his bum?
   A. Warren.

Come back, Oscar Wilde. Your country needs you.

Sunday January 16th

6 p.m. My father put on his new straight-legged jeans today. He looks dead stupid in them. Talk about mutton dressed as lamb. He looks like stewing steak dressed as 'Flash Fry'.

I had to look after Rosie while my parents swanned down to the pub. I was also in charge of the pork and roast potatoes, and switching on the greens. I fed Rosie OK but it took ages to get her wind up. I patted her back for ages but it wasn't until I turned her upside down that she burped. I pretended not to notice that her nappy needed changing and acted surprised when my mother pointed out that there was a yukky smell in the room.

10 p.m. Now I come to a difficult entry. How exactly do I feel about my father's return home? It's been a week now and I've had plenty of time to think about it, but they've had these reconciliations before and they've ended in tragedy. So, I think I'll reserve my judgment until the slopping has stopped and they are back to normal.

12.15 a.m. Why didn't I go and see Bert? Why are you such a rat fink, Mole?

Monday   January 17th

Breakfast telly started today. I got up at 5.45 a.m. so I wouldn't miss history in the making. I made breakfast for me and the dog, and took it into the lounge. Normally cornflakes are banned from the lounge, on account of the odd one falling out of the bowl and sticking to the carpet, but I felt sure my mother wouldn't mind on this special occasion.

The dog fouled things up a bit by trampling into its bowl and scattering Pedigree Chum and Winalot into the shag pile. But I scraped the worst of the mess up with an empty fag packet, and we settled down to wait for 6.30. At 6.25 I woke my parents up by shouting loudly up the stairs that Breakfast Television was starting. My father shouted loudly down the stairs that he didn't want to see bloody Frank Bough at 6.30 a.m. in the morning, and that he'd break my neck if I didn't turn the volume down.

Rosie woke up and started crying. I got the blame for that, and what with all the rowing and screaming I missed the very beginning. This is just my luck!

I enjoyed the Horoscopes, the News, the Celebrities and Frank Bough. He looks a steady sort of bloke. I wouldn't mind having a father like him. But best of all was Selina Scott, with her ravishing looks and quicksilver brain.

Courtney Elliott joined me in front of the screen at 7.45 a.m. He pronounced it 'lacking in intellectual fibre' and said he would stick to listening to Radio Four on his headset. I was late for school because Frank wasn't allowed to open the champagne until nearly nine o'clock!

I have written to the Director General to complain.

> Dear Sir,
> I wish to convey to you my congratulations on your new programme *Breakfast Time*. I saw the first episode and I

thought it was a remarkable achievement considering. However, me and my fellow pupils were late for school, due to the late opening of the champagne.

Either this shows a flagrant disregard for your teenage audience, or a woeful ignorance on your part, of the time I and my cohorts have to arrive at school in the morning.

I suggest, Sir, that you do your research rather more thoroughly. Finally can I make a plea that in future episodes, any special items ie Ernest Hemingway chatting about his latest book, or Princess Diana having her horoscope read, will take place *before* 8.30 a.m. (except on Fridays when we don't have assembly).

Thanking you in anticipation of a reply,

Your most obedient servant,

A . Mole (aged 15 and 9 months)

Tuesday January 18th

Lord Franks has published his report on the Falklands War, but I will make no further comment until I have studied today's *Guardian* editorial on the matter.

10.30 p.m. Can't find *Guardian*: it's not in its usual place in the dog's basket.

Wednesday January 19th

Found *Guardian* in dust-bin wrapped round yesterday's supply of disposable nappies. I made strong objections to my mother. Her feeble excuse was that she'd run out of plastic pedal bin liners.

Thursday January 20th

Selina Scott is haunting my dreams: last night she was walking down our street selling cucumbers door to door. I bought half a dozen with a £50 note I had in my wallet. She smiled shyly and said, 'Prithee, how old are you, sire?' I answered, 'I be fifteen years, pretty maid.' Then the dog jumped on my face and woke me up.

I tried to tell my mother about my dream, but she refused to listen. She said, 'There is only one thing more deadly boring than listening to other people's dreams, and that is listening to other people's problems.'

Friday January 21st

Last night Selina Scott and I were rowing the Atlantic single handed. Selina fell overboard and was swallowed by a dolphin. I swam into the dolphin's belly, and joined Selina: it was quite cosy. We had a glass of champagne then swam out and got back into the boat where we found Frank Bough teaching Pandora how to read out football results.

I told my father every detail of my dream (what Selina was wearing, etc) but I could tell he wasn't really interested. Now I know why people pay to go to psychiatrists. (They are the only people who will listen.)

Saturday January 22nd

No Selina this morning, so I had to make do with going into town with Pandora, who wanted to buy a pair of neon pink legwarmers. After trekking round fifty shops while Pandora sneered at inferior pinks and rejected them all, I suggested we went for a cup of coffee. While I scraped the froth off, I confessed to Pandora how I felt about Selina. Pandora took it very calmly. She said, 'Yes, Selina Scott is to be congratulated, not many women could have borne the pain of so much plastic surgery!'

According to Pandora, Selina has had her nose, mouth, breasts, ears, and eyes remodelled by the surgeon's knife. Poor Selina has to spend three hours in the make-up chair in order to disguise the operation scars. Pandora went on to say, 'Of course she booked into the clinic under her real name, which is Edna Grubbe!'

I asked Pandora how she got her insight into the lives of the famous. Pandora stubbed her cigarette out and said, 'My family used to be on intimate terms with a high-up in the BBC.'

I asked who, a window-cleaner? But I said it quietly because Pandora had got into one of her moods. We resumed our search but none of the legwarmer shops had neon pink so Pandora is getting an 'Away Day' and going to London to buy some. She said, 'God how I hate the wretched provinces.'

Sunday   January 23rd

Rat fink Lucas rang up today. I told him that my mother was at the pub with my father. He asked me which pub, so I told him but instead of ringing off he asked me loads of questions about Rosie, and even asked me to bring her to the phone so that he could hear her gurgling. I told him that she was a late developer and was still at the screaming stage. Then Lucas said a weird thing: he said, 'That's my girl!'

My mother came home in a bad mood and my father came home in an even worse mood. It seems that my mother had left the pub's darts match at a crucial point in order to answer a telephone call.

Monday   January 24th

The water workers have gone on strike, so my father made us all have a bath tonight. The dog included. Then he went around collecting containers and filling them up. While he was doing it he was whistling and looking cheerful. My father loves a crisis.

Tuesday   January 25th

Fabulous! Amazing! Brilliant! Magic!

Showers have been banned at school!

The twice-weekly torture of displaying my inferior muscle development is over. I hope the water workers prolong the strike until I've left full-time education. They should stick out for £500 a week, in fact.

Wednesday   January 26th

Courtney Elliot has offered to give me private tuition for my 'O' levels. It seems he is a Doctor of Philosophy who left academic life after a quarrel in a university common room about the allocation of new chairs. Apparently he was promised a chair and didn't get it.

It seems a trivial thing to leave a good job for. After all, one chair is very much like another. But then I am an existentialist to whom nothing really matters.

I don't care which chair I sit in.

I am reading *On the Road* by Jack Kerouac.

Thursday January 27th

Ken Livingstone was on the telly tonight, talking about his triumph in getting the High Court to cut bus fares in London. This led to me asking my parents for the bus fare to get to school. I am tired out by the time I have walked a whole mile in the morning. My father said that he used to walk four miles to school and four miles back, through wind, rain, snow, hail, and broiling sun and fog.

I said sarcastically (though wittily), 'What strange climatic conditions prevailed in the Midlands in the nineteen-fifties!'

My father said, 'Weather was weather in those days. You wouldn't know proper weather if it came up and smashed you in the face.'

Friday January 28th

I reminded my Father that the law about seat belts comes into force on Monday. He said, 'Nobody makes George Mole wear a baby harness.'

My mother said, 'A policeman will, so belt up!'

Saturday January 29th

Bert Baxter rang to ask why I hadn't been round. I said I'd been too busy.

Bert said, 'Yes, too busy to visit an old lonely widower.'

I promised to go round tomorrow after dinner. Bert said, 'Dinner? What's that?'

I said, 'You remember, Bert, it's meat and three veg and gravy and stuff.'

Bert said that it was so long since he'd eaten properly that his vocabulary was suffering.

I asked him round for dinner tomorrow and told him that my father would give him a lift. But when I told my parents they went mad, and said that they'd arranged to visit some *properties* tomorrow and were planning to get a Chinese take-away.

Properties! Why didn't they consult me? After all, it is my 'O' level year and it is most important that I suffer no violent change, trauma or neurosis.

Sunday January 30th

Spent Sunday afternoon reading the *News of the World* out loud to Bert. I was amazed at how many vicars are leaving their flocks and running away with attractive divorcees.

I also read him a few bits from *The Sunday Times* colour supplement, but Bert stopped me, saying, 'Do you think I'm interested in bleedin' Italian furniture, or "A day in the life" of a soddin' piano player?'

I said, 'I think you ought to keep up with modern cultural patterns!'

Bert said that whenever he heard the word 'culture' he reached for his bottle opener.

At 7 p.m. Bert's Age Concern volunteer turned up to take Bert to the pub. He is a thin, nervous-looking man called Wesley. Sabre growled and bared his horrible fangs when he came into the room. Bert said, 'Don't make any sudden moves, Wesley, Sabre's bite is worse than his bark.'

I couldn't resist showing off by throwing Sabre about and tickling his belly. I even did my party trick of putting my head in Sabre's mouth. I didn't leave it in long though; Sabre's breath stank of cheap dog meat.

After Wesley and Bert left I tidied up a bit. I found Bert and Queenie's wedding photo under Bert's pillow. Funny to think that old, smelly, unattractive people can be sentimental.

Monday January 31st

On the way to school me and Nigel had a dead good time signalling to car drivers who had forgotten to put their seat belts on. Hardly any of them thanked us.

Tuesday   February 1st

The first cracks in the new marital alliance appeared today: an argument about money.

We are kept by the state in the style that the state wants to keep us, ie in poverty. My parents just can't cope with being poor. It's all right for me because I'm used to it. I've never had more than three quid a week to call my own.

Wednesday   February 2nd

Lucas turned up on our doorstep halfway through *Coronation Street* demanding to see Rosie. My father said that Rosie was busy and couldn't be disturbed, but Lucas started shouting in his loud sing-song voice, so my father let him in to stop the neighbours talking.

My mother went dead pale under her Max Factor. Lucas said, 'Pauline, I want access to my child!'

My father's knees buckled a bit and he sat down on the arm of the settee to recover. He said weakly, 'Pauline, tell me that Rosie is mine!'

My mother said, 'Of course she's yours, George!'

Lucas took out a black 1982 diary and said, 'Pauline and I resumed our affair of the heart on February 16th 1982. However we did not consummate our new relationship until Sunday March 13th 1982, when Pauline came to a protest rally in Sheffield.'

My mother shouted, 'But I was wearing my new cap, I couldn't have got pregnant.'

My father said, 'Adulteress!'

'I'm not an adulteress,' my mother sobbed.

My father yelled, 'If the cap fits, wear it!'

'But I *did* wear it,' said my mother in anguish.

Lucas tried to put his arms around her but she Karate-chopped him on the back of the neck.

Everybody had forgotten I was there until I ran from the room, saying, 'I can't stand this eternal insecurity!'

As I ran to my room I passed Rosie in her cot. She was playing with her toes, unaware that her paternity was being settled downstairs.

Thursday February 3rd

During the month of March 1982 it would seem that both my parents were carrying on clandestine relationships, which resulted in the birth of two children. Yet my diary for that period records my childish fourteen-year-old thoughts and preoccupations.

I wonder, did Jack the Ripper's wife innocently write:

> *10.30 p.m.* Jack late home. Perhaps he is kept late at the office.
>
> *12.10 a.m.* Jack home covered in blood; an offal cart knocked him down.

Pandora is standing by me at this time of crisis. She is a true pillar of salt.

Friday February 4th

I had to spend the day in matron's office due to feeling weak in the first lesson. (PE.)

She asked me if there was anything wrong at home. I started to cry and said that everything was.

She said, 'Adults have complicated lives, Adrian. It's not all staying up late and having your own door key!'

I said that *parents* ought to be moral and consistent and have principles.

She said, 'It's a lot to ask.'

I made her promise not to tell anyone that she'd seen me crying. She promised and kindly let me stay until my eyes had got back to normal.

Saturday February 5th

Lucas continues to persecute us.

A solicitor's letter arrived today. He is taking us to court unless he is allowed access to Rosie.

Courtney Elliot suggested we find a good solicitor and get him to write a letter back saying that, unless Lucas stops his campaign, we will get an injunction out.

I don't know what it means, but it sounds dead threatening.

Sunday   February 6th

I broke the silence of months and went to make my peace with Grandma. She was a bit frosty at first, but then she offered to make me some treacle toffee, so I knew I was forgiven.

She has bought a budgie called Russell. (Named after Russell Harty, her favourite person in the world after me.) She said, 'This little bird has given me more pleasure than my whole family put together, and what's more he listens and doesn't answer back.'

I didn't tell her about the Lucas affair. A further shock could kill her. She said that after the Stick Insect/Trevor Roper scandal, her hair fell out and has not grown back.

This explains why she was wearing her hat in the house.

Monday   February 7th

Michael Heseltine has chickened out of a public debate on cruise missiles with CND. I expect he is scared of being shown up.

A similar thing is happening in our house; my father is refusing to talk to Pandora's mother, who is a marriage guidance counsellor.

Rosie is teething. She is getting through six bibs a day. Dribble hangs permanently from her mouth. She looks like a rabid dog.

Tuesday   February 8th

Don't ask me how I am getting through the long school day. Just don't ask. I am walking around like a smiling robot. But my soul is weeping, weeping, weeping. If only the teachers knew that an unkind word from them brings tears to my eyes.

I am getting away with it by saying I've got conjunctivitis but it's a near thing sometimes.

The trial period is up today.

1 a.m. The two parties have agreed on an extension.

Wednesday   February 9th

The racehorse Shergar has been kidnapped by the IRA. Pandora seems more concerned about the horse's troubles than mine. I said, 'Haven't you got things out of perspective Pandora?'

She said, 'No, Shergar is highly bred and extremely sensitive. He must be suffering terribly.'

I don't know who to turn to for help. I might run away to London.

Thursday   February 10th

I've changed my mind about going to London.

According to *The Guardian* lead pollution is sending the cockneys who live there mad.

Friday   February 11th

We have got a solicitor called Cyril Hill. He has written a stern letter to rat fink Lucas, warning him to lay off our family.

The letter cost us £20.

Saturday   February 12th

The atmosphere at home is as thick as treacle, so I went to see Bert. I could hardly get in the door for Voluntary Social Workers, queuing up to be given their orders. None of them wanted to attend to Sabre's needs, however, so I mucked his kennel out and brushed his coat and then took him for his daily prowl round the recreation ground.

Barry Kent and his gang were there – tying the swings in knots, but with Sabre by my side I felt confident enough to have a go on the slide.

On the way back I passed several Alsatians and their male owners; perhaps it was a coincidence but *every* owner was practically a midget. Their Alsatians came up to their waists. I don't know what it means. But it must mean something.

Sunday   February 13th

It's Valentine's Day tomorrow. I think I'll have the day off school. I can't stand being the only kid in my class who doesn't come into the classroom with a fistful of garish cards, and a self-congratulatory smile. I'll know I'll get one from Pandora, but she doesn't count; I've been going out with her for over a year.

Monday   February 14th
ST VALENTINE'S DAY

Got four cards: one from Pandora, one from Grandma, one from my mother and one from Rosie.

Big, big deal!

I got Pandora a Cupid card and a mini pack of 'After Eights'. Lucas sent one to Rosie. My parents didn't bother this year, they are saving their money to pay for the solicitor's letter.

Tuesday   February 15th
SHROVE TUESDAY

Pandora is not speaking to me because I absent-mindedly wrote 'Best Wishes' in her Valentine's card. She said, 'It's symptomatic of our decaying relationship, Adrian.'

I think she could be right. I'm going off her. She is too clever by half. My mother was too busy with Rosie to make pancakes, so I had a go. I don't know why my father went so mad, the kitchen ceiling needed decorating anyway.

Wednesday   February 16th
ASH WEDNESDAY

Today is my parents' special day.

They are getting through thirty fags a day each. If Social Security hear about it they will get done and quite rightly!

Thursday   February 17th

I wrote a poem on the toilet wall at school today.

I thought it was a good way of getting a bit of political consciousness over to my moronic fellow pupils.

The Future
What future is there for the young?
What songs are waiting to be sung?
There are no mountains left to climb,
No poetry without a rhyme.
No jobs to go to after school.
We divide and still they rule.
They give us Job Creation Schemes.
When what we want are hopes and dreams.
     A. MOLE

Friday February 18th

I was sent to see the headmaster today. He has found out about my toilet poem. I asked him how he knew I'd written it. He said, 'You signed it, idiot boy.' I have been suspended for a week.

Saturday February 19th

Barry Kent and his gang called for me today. Kent said, 'We're going down town, you can come if you like!'

I was feeling a bit nihilistic so I went.

Sunday February 20th

Hung around the deserted shopping centre with Barry Kent and the lads. I feel a curious affinity with the criminal classes. I am beginning to understand why Lord Longford (another noted intellectual) spends his time hanging around prisons.

Barry graciously gave me permission to call him 'Baz'.

Monday February 21st
WASHINGTON'S BIRTHDAY OBSERVANCE

Baz took me home and introduced me to his family today.

Mrs Kent said, 'Ain't you the lad what's 'ad all the scandal?'

I said, 'Yeah that's me, but so what?'

Mrs Kent said, 'That's no way to talk, young man.'

Mr Kent said, 'You keep a civil tongue in your head. That's my wife you're talking to.' I immediately apologized and remembered my manners. In fact I got up and offered Mrs Kent the unbroken chair.

The Kent children were swarming about in the living room, watching a television programme about the population explosion. A lurid coloured photo of Clive Kent in his army uniform stood on top of the radiogram. I asked how he was. Mrs Kent said, 'He's in an army hospital: his nerves is shot to pieces after the Falklands.'

I had a nice tea with the family; chip sandwiches with tomato sauce, and once I'd got used to the funny smell in the house I was able to relax for the first time in weeks.

Tuesday   February 22nd

A note from Pandora:

> Adrian,
> As you seem to prefer the company of louts and anti-social drop-outs, I think it best if we finish. You have chosen to tread a different path from the one I intend to make my way on in the world.
> > Thank you for the good times,
> > Pandora Braithwaite

Wednesday   February 23rd

Today I drew some money out of my Building Society account, and bought my first pair of Doc Marten's. They are bully-boy brown and have got ten rows of lace holes.

They add an inch to my height.

Thursday   February 24th

Spent the early part of the evening standing outside the off-licence with the gang. I made witty remarks about passing girls and made the gang laugh. They have started calling me 'Brains'. Baz has hinted that I have got leadership qualities.

Friday   February 25th

Mrs Kent has decided to have some new furniture, so the gang went to the rubbish tip to see what we could find. We came back with: two almost unbroken kitchen chairs, a wicker linen basket, and a fireside rug. We are going back tomorrow with Rosie's pram to fetch a washing machine with mangle attachment.

Mrs Kent was very pleased with our haul: she said, 'It's a crying shame what folks chuck away!' Mr Kent lost his job two months ago, when the dairy closed down. He looked a bit ashamed when we brought the new furniture in. I heard him say to his wife, 'For better or worse, eh, Ida.'

Saturday   February 26th

I borrowed the pram OK but unfortunately Rosie was in it. She had to be taken out and carried for our journey back from the rubbish tip.

But she was a good kid and didn't cry once. Mrs Kent was overjoyed with her new washing machine. It looked OK when it had been wiped down. Mr Kent unscrewed the faulty motor, and started cleaning it down on the hearth rug, and Mrs Kent didn't murmur! My mother would have gone berserk. She won't let my father fill his lighter in the lounge.

Sunday   February 27th

Good news. The washing machine is working. There was a line of grey nappies on Mrs Kent's washing line today. I told her about 'Ariel' washing powder and she said, 'I'll buy some tomorrow when I get my family allowance.'

Monday   February 28th

Rosie has got her first tooth. My index finger is still bleeding.

Tuesday   March 1st

Spent the evening outside the Chinese chip shop chucking prawn crackers about with the gang. I haven't read a book for ages. Instead of reading about life I am living it.

Wednesday March 2nd
ST DAVID'S DAY

We are being persecuted by the police!

Tonight, as we were messing about in the shopping precinct, a police patrol car went by dead slowly, and the driver *looked* at us.

Talk about a police state!

Thursday March 3rd

The community policeman, PC Gordon, has been to see my parents, to warn them that I am running wild with a notorious gang. He is calling round tomorrow to give me a lecture on responsible citizenship.

Friday March 4th

PC Gordon is the sort of bloke you can't help liking. He is thin and jolly and he calls everybody 'Bucko.' But he said things like: 'You're obviously a clever lad, Adrian;' and: 'You're from a good family,' (Ha!); and: 'Kent and his gang are no-hopers, they'll do you no favours.'

He asked me why I had suddenly gone off the rails. I said that I was an existentialist nihilist.

He said, 'Lads usually say they get into trouble because they're bored.'

I smiled cynically and said, 'Yes existential nihilism is just one step further.' I could tell he was impressed by my vocabulary.

Later on my parents came in and used clichés like: 'He's a good lad at home' (my father); and: 'Barry Kent has led him astray' (my mother).

When he'd gone I polished my boots and went to bed with the dog.

Saturday March 5th

Grandma rang and said that it was all round the Evergreens that I was 'keeping bad company'. She made me go round for tea. I didn't want to go, but there is something about Grandma's voice that makes you obey orders so I went.

While Grandma toasted crumpets on the electric coal fire she told me that my father had been in trouble with the police in 1953. She said, 'He got caught scrumping apples. The shame nearly killed me and your poor dead Grandad.'

I asked if my father had continued his criminal career.

She said, 'Yes, in fact he went from bad to worse, he went on to scrump pears and plums.'

I was curious to know how my father had been persuaded from taking up a life of crime. Grandma said, 'Your Grandad gave him a good thrashing with the buckle end of his belt.' Poor Dad! It explains why he is full of inner rage.

Sunday   March 6th

Being in a gang is not as exciting as I thought it would be. All we do is hang around shopping precincts and windy recreation grounds. Sometimes I long to be in my bedroom, reading, with the dog at my side.

Monday   March 7th

Just got back after a cold boring night of shouting in quiet streets. Barry Kent tipped a rubbish bin over for a laugh, but in fact it wasn't very funny and I had to force myself to guffaw with the others in the gang. Barry Kent said, 'If it wasn't for me, my Uncle Pedro would lose his job!' His Uncle Pedro is a street cleaner.

After Barry went home I picked the broken glass up and replaced it in the bin. I wouldn't like a little kid to fall on it.

Tuesday   March 8th

There was a very unpleasant incident tonight.

Barry Kent shouted horrible names at two of the Singh kids. I said, 'Oh lay off em eh, Baz, they're all right!'

Barry sneered and said, 'I 'ate anyone who ain't English.'

I reminded him about his Uncle Pedro and he said, 'Except Spaniels.'

I can't go on leading this double life for much longer.

Wednesday   March 9th

I have decided not to take my 'O' levels. I am bound to fail them anyway so why waste all that neurosis in worrying? I'll need all the neurosis I can get when I start writing for a living.

Thursday   March 10th

The first page of my new novel:

Precint by A. Mole, aged 15 years 11 months
Jake Butcher closed his eyes against the cruel wind that whistled over the paving slabs of the deserted shopping precinct. His cigarette dropped with a curse from his lips. 'Damn,' he expectorated.

It was his last cigarette. He ground the forlorn fag under the sole of his trusty Doc Marten's boot. He dug both fists into the womb-like pockets of his anorak, and with his remaining hand he adjusted the fastening on his Adidas sports bag.

Just then a sudden shaft of bright sunlight illuminated the windows of Tesco's. 'Christ,' said Jake to himself, 'those windows are the same yellow as in Van Gogh's sunflower painting!' Thus, ruminating on art and culture, did Jake pass the time.

Quite soon a sudden clap of thunder announced itself. 'Christ,' said Jake, 'that thunder sounds like the cannons of the 1812 Symphony!'.

He bitterly drew his anorak hood over his head, as raindrops like giant's tears fell onto the concrete waste-land. 'What am I doing here?' questioned Jake to himself. 'Why did I come?' he anguished. 'Where am I going?' he agonized. Just then a sudden rainbow appeared.

'Christ,' said Jake, 'that rainbow looks like. . . . '

I had to stop there; I don't know where Jake came from, or where he's going either.

Friday   March 11th

Pandora Braithwaite is going out with Brain Box Henderson. I hope they'll both be very happy. Nigel says they spend all their time together talking about higher mathematics.

Did a bit of shouting outside the Youth Club doors tonight.

Rick Lemon pretended not to hear us, but I noticed that the vein in his temple was throbbing. Why don't my parents notice that I am turning into a yob?

Saturday   March 12th

Saw Danny Thompson, the white Rasta, outside the Chinese chip shop tonight. He asked me if I'd written any lyrics for the group yet. I said I'd go home straight away and write some. I was glad of an excuse to leave. I was tired of Barry Kent shoving his prawn balls down my trousers.

Sunday   March 13th
MOTHERING SUNDAY

Rat fink Lucas sent my mother a mother's day card signed 'Rosie'.

Grandma sent Stick Insect a card signed 'Brett'.

My mother sent Grandma Mole a card signed 'George'.

My father sent my Grandma Sugden a card signed 'Pauline'.

I didn't send the woman who gave birth to me a card this year. Interpersonal relationships in our family have gone completely to pot. This is what living with the shadow of the bomb does to you.

Monday   March 14th
COMMONWEALTH DAY

Barry Kent has been arrested for vandalizing hyacinths in the town hall square yesterday morning at 7 a.m.

He is pleading extenuating circumstances; they were to be a gift for his mother.

Tuesday   March 15th

Reasons for living	*Reasons for not living*
Things might get better	You die anyway
	Life is nothing but anguish

> There is too much cruelty
> in the world
> 'O' levels in June
> My parents hate me
> I've lost Pandora
> Nobody leaves Barry
> Kent's gang alive.

Wednesday   March 16th

Elizabeth Sally Broadway keeps snatching my school scarf from round my neck and running away with it, forcing me to chase her. This is a sure sign that she is romantically interested in me. I can feel my hormones stirring for the first time in months.

Thursday   March 17th
ST PATRICK'S DAY

Elizabeth grabbed my executive brief case and sprinted across the sports field during the afternoon break.

I caught up with her in the shrubbery where we had a very enjoyable tussle which lasted five minutes and climaxed in me removing her glasses and hair pins.

She looked different unspectacled and with her hair down her back.

I said, 'But Elizabeth, you're beautiful.'

God knows what would have happened if the bell hadn't rung for the next lesson.

2 a.m. Can't sleep for the noise of Irish bagpipes leaking out of the O'Learys' house.

4 a.m. Just woken up by the sound of breaking glass.

6 a.m. A police car has just left the O'Learys' house taking Sean O'Leary with it. Sean looked quite cheerful, in fact he was singing a song about Forty Shades of Green.

Friday   March 18th

At last! My parents have noticed that I am out of control, and have banned me from going out after school.

Spent the evening re–reading *Black Beauty* for the fifth time.

Saturday March 19th

I have written a letter to Barry Kent, resigning from the gang.

> Dear Baz,
> The crumblies have said I've got to stay in for a week. So
> I'll have to give hanging about with you and the lads a miss.
> Also Baz, they are forcing me to take my stinking exams in
> June, so I'd better resign from my place in the gang and
> leave it open for somebody who needs it. I hope your court
> case goes well. No hard feelings eh?
> Yours Fraternally,
> Brains

Sunday March 20th
BRITISH SUMMER TIME BEGINS

8 p.m. Rained solidly all day.

10.30 p.m. How can it rain 'solidly'? What a strange mistress is
the English language.

Monday March 21st

My parents have hardly spoken to me since Friday night. They
are too busy watching Rosie's manual dexterity develop.

Every time the kid grabs a plastic brick or shoves a rusk in her
mouth, she gets a round of applause.

Tuesday March 22nd

I have decided to leave home.

Nobody will care. In fact my parents probably won't notice
that I've gone. I have given the Building Society one week's
notice of my intention to withdraw £50. There is no point in
losing interest unnecessarily.

Wednesday March 23rd

I am making preparations to leave. I have already written my
goodbye letters.

Pandora,
I may be gone for some time.
    Adrian

Dear Mum and Dad,
By the time you read this I will be far away. I know I am
breaking the law in running away before my 16th birthday,
but, quite honestly, a life as a fugitive is preferable to my
present miserable existence.
    From your son,
    A. Mole

Dear Bert,
I've taken your advice and gone off to see the world. You
don't need me now that you've got all those wimpy
volunteers hanging around you. But watch out, Bert, you
are only popular because they think you are a character.
Any day now they will find out that you are bad-tempered
and foul-mouthed. I will send you a postcard from one of
the corners of the world.
    Adios Amigo,
P.S. Give my love to Sabre, and don't forget to give him his
Bob Martins.

Dear Grandma,
Sorry to worry you but I have gone away for a bit. Please
stop feuding with Mum and Dad. 'They know not what
they do.' Rosie is lovely now, she would really like to see
you.
    Lots of love,
    Adrian

Dear Mr Scruton,
By the time you read this I will be miles away from your
scabby school. So don't bother sending the truant officer
round. I intend to educate myself in the great school of life,
and will never return.
    A. Mole
P.S. Did you know that your nickname is 'Pop-Eye'?
So-called because of your horrible manic sticking-out

eyes. Everybody laughs at you behind your back, especially Mr Jones the PE teacher.

P.P.S. I think you should be ashamed of the fact that Barry Kent *still can't read* after spending five years in your school.

Dearest Elizabeth,

I'm sorry that I have to leave just as our love was bursting into bud. But a boy has to do what a boy has to do.

Don't wait for me, Elizabeth. I may be gone for some time.

Yours with regrets and fondest memories,
Aidy Mole

Baz,

I've blown town. The pigs will be looking for me. Try and put 'em off the scent will you?
Brains

Nigel,

Good luck with being gay. I, too, am different from the herd; so I understand what it is like to be always out of step.

It's the ordinary people who will have to learn to accept us.

Any road up as we say in these parts.

Rock on tommy!
Your old mate,
Aidy

Thursday   March 24th

Five days to go. I am growing a beard.

I have borrowed my dead grandad's suitcase. Luckily he had the same initials as me. His name was Arnold.

Grandma thinks I am using it for a camping trip with the Youth Club. The truth would kill her.

Friday   March 25th

I have started packing my case. A certain amount of rationalization has had to take place regarding clean socks and underwear.

I will have to lower my standards and only change them every other day. No sign of the beard yet.

Saturday   March 26th

Courtney Elliot has been instructed by my father not to deliver any letters with a Sheffield postmark. But he brought one into the kitchen this morning saying, 'The Royal Mail has to get through, Mr Mole. We're like the Pony Express in that respect!'

My father ripped the letter into tiny pieces and foot-pedalled them into the bin.

Later on I retrieved the bits and stuck them together.

> . . . ole.
> . . . structed . . . client . . . ucas, civil action unless . . .
> Ros . . . ole . . . is his daughter. He wishes the aforesaid
> child to . . . Rosie Lucas.
>> My client . . . blood test . . . under oath that . . . inter-
>> course took . . . Pauline Mole . . . to hear from you . . .
>> Yours Faithfully,
>> Coveney, Tinker, Shulman, Solicitors

Sunday   March 27th
BRITISH SUMMER TIME BEGINS

The crumblies spent three hours forcing Rosie to sit up on her own. But she kept sliding down the cushions and laughing. If she could talk I know what she would say, 'Stop interfering in my development, I'll do it when I'm ready!'

I pointed out that her back muscles are not strong enough yet, but the crumblies wouldn't listen. They said things like, 'Rosie is exceptionally forward,' and 'You were nowhere near as advanced as she is at five months!'

They will be sorry for these cutting words on Tuesday.

Monday   March 28th

An old American bloke called Ian MacGregor has been put in charge of the National Coal Board. It is a disgrace!

England has got loads of ruthless, out-of-work executives who would be delighted to be given the chance to close their own country's coalmines down. Mr Scargill is quite right to protest, he has my full support on this issue.

Packed my pyjamas and dressing gown.

It is RA day tomorrow. I have made out a list of vital equipment, clothing etc.

Roller skates
Shaving kit
3 jumpers
2 shirts
3 pairs trousers
5 pairs socks
Wellingtons
Doc Marten's
Plimsolls
Orange waterproof trousers
4 pairs underpants
4 vests
Diary
Survival handbook
Robinson Crusoe
*Down and Out in Paris and
   London*

*Penguin Medical
   Dictionary*
Junior aspirins
First aid box
Sleeping bag
Camping stove
Matches
6 tins beans
Spoon
Knife
Fork
Cruet
Serviettes
Transistor radio
The dog

Tuesday   March 29th

6 a.m.	Packed everything on list apart from the dog.
6.05	Took everything out.
6.10	Repacked.
6.15	Took everything out.
6.30	Repacked, but no good. Still can't get suitcase lid to shut. Decide not to take roller skates.
6.33	Ditto wellingtons.
6.35	Ditto camping stove.

6.37   Suitcase lid shuts.

6.39   Try to pick up suitcase. Can't.

6.40   Take out tins of beans.

6.44   Repack.

6.45   Get in a rage.

6.48   Take cruet and serviettes out.

6.55   Take Doc Marten's out of suitcase. Decide to wear them instead. Spend fifteen precious minutes in doing the sodding laces up.

7.10   Examine spots in bathroom.

7.13   Check farewell letters have got stamps on.

7.14   Pick suitcase up. Not bad. Not good.

7.15   Repack suitcase with half previous clothes.

7.19   Pick suitcase up. Better.

7.20   Remember sleeping bag. Try to pack it in suitcase.

7.21   Get in another rage.

7.22   Kick suitcase across bedroom floor.

7.22.30 secs.   Crumblies shout from their bedroom. Demanding to know what all the noise is about.

7.24   Make tea. Crumblies ask why I have got a tin opener in the breast pocket of my blazer. I lie and say that I've got Domestic Science for my first lesson.

7.31   Feed dog, make baby's breakfast slops.

7.36   Check Building Society account book.

7.37   Groom dog. Pack its personal possessions in suitcase: dog bowl, brush, vaccination certificate, worm tablets, lead, choke chain, 5 tins Chum, bag of Winalot.

7.42   Try to pick up suitcase, can't.

7.47   Decide to leave dog behind. Break the news to it.

7.49   Dog cries. Crumblies shout at it to be quiet.

7.50   Decide to take the dog after all.

8.00   Pack minimum amount of stuff in Adidas bag.

8.10   Hide Grandad's suitcase in wardrobe.

8.15   Say goodbye to Rosie.

8.20   Put dog on lead.

8.21   Wait until crumblies are distracted.

8.25   Leave house with dog.

8.30   Post farewell letters.

9.00   Draw £50 out of Building Society, and head North.

Wednesday   March 30th

3 p.m. Watford Gap Service Station. M1 *Motorway.*

My first mistake was waiting for a lift on the southern bound side of the motorway approach road.

My second mistake was bringing the dog.

7.31 Sheffield.

Got a lift in a pig delivery lorry. This is just my luck!

I had a very long conversation with the driver, which is a miracle really, because I couldn't hear a word he was saying over the noise of the engine. I am having to keep a low profile. Sheffield is rat fink Lucas's stamping ground.

Why doesn't my beard hurry up and grow?

9.30 p.m. Leeds.

Tuned into the Radio Four nine o'clock news. But no mention was made of my mysterious disappearance. I am writing this at the side of the canal. A man has just come up and asked me if I want to sell the dog. I was tempted but said no.

11.00 p.m. Rang home but the phone wasn't snatched up immediately like it is in the films about runaway children.

Another sign of their indifference.

Thursday   March 31st

1 a.m. The man who asked about the dog has just approached me and asked me if I want to sell *myself.* I said, 'No,' and told him my father was the Chief Constable of Wales.

He said, 'Why are you sleeping rough in Leeds?'

I told another lie, I said, 'My father has sent me on an initiative test. If I survive this he'll put me down for Hendon Police College.'

Why did I tell him such an elaborate lie? Why? I had to listen while he told me his many grievances against the police. I promised to pass them on to my father and copied his name and address into my diary:

> Stanley Gibbons,
> c/o Room 2,
> The Laurels Community Care Hostel,
> Paradise Cuttings,
> Leeds

He invited me to spend the night on his put-u-up, but I demurred, saying that my father was checking up on me via a long-distance telescope. He went then.

Friday April 1st
GOOD FRIDAY. ALL FOOLS' DAY

10 a.m. Leeds. (A launderette.)

Thank God for launderettes, if they hadn't been invented I'd be dead of hydrophobia by now. Nowhere else is open.

It cost a *pound* to dry my sleeping bag. But I was so wet and cold that I didn't care at the time.

I am waiting for the dog to wake up. It was on guard duty last night protecting our respective bodies from Stanley Gibbons. I am sixteen tomorrow. But still no sign of a beard. Good Friday!

Saturday April 2nd

Manchester Railway Station.
Got here by fish lorry. Pretended to be asleep in order to avoid driver's conversation.

10.31 a.m. I wonder what my mum and dad have bought me for my birthday. I hope they are not too worried. Perhaps I ought to ring them and convince them that I am well and happy.

12.15 p.m. We have been ordered out of the railway station café by a bad-tempered waitress. It's the stupid dog's fault. It kept going behind the counter and begging for bits of bacon.

Yet I bought it a bacon roll all to itself this morning.

3 p.m. Nobody has said 'Happy Birthday' to me.

3.05 I'm not well (I've got a cold) and I'm not happy. In fact I'm extremely unhappy.

5.30 p.m. Bought myself a birthday card. Inside I wrote:

> To our darling first-born child on his sixteenth birthday.
> With all the love it is possible to give,
> From your admiring and loving parents.
> PS. Come home son. Without you the house is devoid of life and laughter.

6.15 p.m. There was nothing about me on the six o'clock news.

7.30 p.m. Can't face another night in the open.

9 p.m. Park bench.

I have asked three policemen the time, but none of them have spotted me as a runaway. It's obvious that my description hasn't been circulated.

9.30 p.m. Just rang the police station, using a disguised voice. I said, 'Adrian Mole, a sixteen-year-old runaway, is in the vicinity of the Blood Transfusion Headquarters. His description is as follows: small for his age, slight build, mousey hair, disfigured skin. He is wearing a green school blazer. Orange waterproof trousers. A blue shirt. Balaclava helmet. Brown Doc Martens. With him is a mongrel dog, of the following description: medium height, hairy face, squint in left eye. Wearing a tartan collar and matching lead.'

The desk sergeant said, 'April Fool's Day was yesterday, sonny.'

10.00 p.m. Waited outside the Blood Transfusion place but there wasn't a policeman in sight. There is never one around when you need one.

11.39 p.m. I have walked past the police station twenty-four times, but none of the cretins in blue have given me a second glance.

11.45 p.m. I have just been turned away from an Indian Restaurant on the grounds that I wasn't wearing a tie, and was accompanied by a scruffy dog.

Sunday April 3rd
EASTER SUNDAY

Still in Manchester. (St Ignatius's church porch.)

1 a.m. It is traditional for the homeless to sleep in church porches so why don't vicars make sure that their porches are more comfortable? It wouldn't kill them to provide a mattress, would it?

7.30 a.m. Got up at six. Had a wash in a bird bath. Read the inscriptions on the gravestones. Then went in search of a shop. Found one; bought two Cadbury's creme eggs. Ate one myself, gave the other to the dog. The poor thing was so hungry it ate the silver paper as well. I hope it won't be ill; I can't afford to pay for veterinary attention. I've only got £15.00 left.

Monday April 4th

St Ignatius's church porch, Manchester.

6 a.m. For two days I have had the legal right to buy cigarettes, have sex, ride a moped, and live away from home. Yet, strangely, I don't want to do any of them now I'm able to.

Must stop. A woman with a kind face is coming through the gravestones.

9 a.m. I am in the vicar's wife's bed. She is a true Christian. She doesn't mind that I am an existentialist nihilist. She says I'll grow out of it. The dog is downstairs lying on top of the Aga.

10 a.m. Mrs Merryfield, the vicar's wife, has phoned my parents and asked them to come and fetch me. I asked Mrs Merryfield for my parents' reactions. She crumpled her kind face up in thought then said, 'Angry relief is the nearest I can get to it, dear!'

I haven't seen the vicar yet. He is having a lie-in because of being so busy yesterday. I hope he doesn't mind that a stranger is occupying his wife's bed.

12.30 p.m. The vicar has just gone. Thank God! What a bore! No wonder poor Mrs Merryfield sleeps apart from him. I expect that she is scared he'll talk about comparative religions in his sleep. I have just spent a week living rough. The last thing I want is a lecture on 'Monophysitism'.

2.30 p.m. The Reverend Merryfield brought my dinner in at 1.30, then gabbled on about 'Lamaism', the Tibetan religion, while my dinner got cold, and eventually congealed.

6 p.m. I notice my parents are not breaking their necks to get here. I wish they would hurry up. I've had 'Mithraism', 'Orphism' and 'Pentecostalism' up to here.

I'm all for a man having outside interests, but this is ridiculous.

Tuesday   April 5th

Bedroom. Home.

Well, there were no banners in the street, or crowds of people jostling to get a view as I got out of my father's car. Just my mother's haggard face at the lounge window, and Grandma's even haggarder one behind her.

My father doesn't talk when he's driving on motorways, so we had hardly said a word to each other, since leaving St Ignatius's vicarage. (And Reverend Merryfield saw to it that we didn't talk *at* the vicarage, what with his rabbiting on about Calvinism and Shakers. Mrs Merryfield tried to stop him: she said, 'Please be quiet, darling,' but it just set him off on Quietism.)

But my mother and Grandma said a great many things. Eventually I pleaded for mercy and went to bed and pulled the crispy white sheets over my head.

Wednesday   April 6th

Dr Grey has just left my bedside. He has diagnosed that I am suffering from a depressive illness brought on by worry. The treatment is bedrest, and no quarrelling in the family.

My parents are bowed down by guilt.

I can't rest for worrying about the letter I wrote to 'Pop-Eye' Scruton.

Thursday   April 7th

The dog is at the vet's, having the blisters on its paws treated. I got up for five minutes and looked out of my bedroom window today. But there was nothing in the urban landscape to interest me, so I got back into bed.

I haven't opened my birthday presents yet.

Friday   April 8th

Ate a Mars bar.

I can feel my physical strength returning, but my mental strength is still at rock bottom.

Saturday April 9th

10 a.m. I suffered a relapse so Dr Grey called round.
I lay back listlessly on the pillows and let him feel my pulse etc.
He muttered, 'Bloody Camille,' as he left the room.
Perhaps Camille is a drug that he's thinking of using on me.

12 noon. I asked my mother to draw the curtains against the sun.

Sunday April 10th

Lay all day with my head turned to the wall. Rosie was brought in to cheer me up, but her childish gibbering merely served to irritate so she was taken away.

Monday April 11th

Bert Baxter was carried up to my bedside, but his coarse exhortation, 'Get out of your pit, you idle bugger!' failed to stir me from my nihilistic thoughts.

Tuesday April 12th

Nigel has just left, after trying to arouse me by playing my favourite 'Toyah' tapes at a discreet volume.
I signalled that I would prefer both his and Toyah's absence.

Wednesday April 13th

A sign that my parents are now frantic with worry about me; Barry Kent was allowed into the house.
His inarticulate ramblings about the gang's activities failed to interest or stimulate me, so he was led out of the darkened room.

Thursday April 14th

A consultant psychologist has been ordered.
Dr Grey has admitted his failure.

Friday April 15th

Dr Donaldson has just left my bedside after listening to my worries with grave attention.

When I'd sunk back onto my pillows he said, 'We'll take them one by one.'

1. Nuclear war *is* a worry, but do something positive about your fear – join CND.
2. If you fail your 'O' levels you can retake them next year, or never take them – like the Queen.
3. Of course your parents love you. They didn't sleep during the time you were away.
4. You are *not* hideously ugly. You are a pleasant, average-looking boy.
5. Your sister's paternity problems are nothing to do with you, and there is nothing you can do to help.
6. I've never heard of a sixteen-year-old having their own poetry programme on Radio Four. You must set yourself realistic targets.
7. I will write to Mr Scruton ('Pop-Eye') and inform him that you were under great stress at the time you wrote the letter.
8. Pandora comes under the heading of insoluble problems.

Saturday April 16th

Grandma came to my room at 8 a.m. this morning and ordered me out of bed!

She said, 'You've been pampered enough. Now pull yourself together, and go and shave that bum-fluff off your face!'

I weakly protested that I needed more time to find myself.

Grandma said, 'I need to wash those sheets so get out of bed!'

I said, 'But I'm angst-ridden.'

'Who wouldn't be after lying in a bed like a dying swan for a week!' was her callous reply.

My Grandma is a good honest woman, but her grasp of the intellectual niceties is minimal.

Spent the day on the settee sipping Lucozade.

Sunday   April 17th

Settee.

My parents are speaking to me in tones of forced gaiety. They are making pathetic attempts to bring me back into normal life by drawing my attention to items of interest on the television. 'Watch the news!' they brightly exclaimed. I did.

It was full of stories about murder, bombing, uncovered spies and disasters of rail, road and air. The only remotely cheerful item was about a man with no legs who'd walked from John O'Groats to Land's End. This proof of the cruelty of fate versus the magnificence of the human spirit reduced me to silent sobs into the Dralon cushions.

Monday   April 18th

The school holidays started today.

It is just my luck to be too ill to appreciate the break.

Tuesday   April 19th

> *Daffodils by A. Mole*
> While on my settee I lie
> From out of the corner of my eye
> I spot a clump of Yellow Daffodils,
> Bowing and shaking as a lorry goes by.
> Brave green stalks supporting yellow bonnets.
> Like the wife of a man who writes Love Sonnets.

Wednesday   April 20th

Ate four Shredded Wheat today.

I can feel my strength slowly returning.

Thursday   April 21st

Pandora came to see me for ten minutes this afternoon.

Brain Box Henderson stood at our gate, fiddling with his calculator. Perhaps he was trying to work out how much he loves Pandora.

Well it won't be as much as me, Henderson. I can assure you of that fact!

Pandora was wearing Monochromatic rags. She told me it was the latest fashion. She is coming back tomorrow.

Friday   April 22nd

I asked my mother if she would go to town and buy me three tee-shirts. One black, one white and one grey.

When she came back I set about the tee-shirts with a pair of scissors. Grandma took this to be a symptom of my escalating madness. I tried to explain that it was how we in the teenage sub-culture are dressing now. But she couldn't take it in.

When my father saw me wearing rags he went pale and almost said something. But my mother whispered, 'Not now, George, don't set him off again!'

Pandora came round at 5 p.m. By the end of *John Craven's News Round* we were in each other's arms. Our rags entangled, our lips on fire.

Saturday   April 23rd

Pandora went round to Brain Box Henderson's house to break the news, but he was out buying floppy discs, so she left a message on his word processor. Getting Pandora back from him is a triumph of Art over Technology.

Sunday   April 24th

I am reading *Kingsley, The Life, Letters and Diaries of Kingsley Martin*, by C.H. Rolf. Strangely, it doesn't mention that he wrote *Lucky Jim*.

Monday   April 25th

Went for a walk with Pandora and Rosie.

(That is to say Pandora and I walked, but lucky Rosie was pushed in her pram.) We called in to see Bert. He was dead pleased to see us. He has been deserted by his voluntary helpers, and hadn't got any Woodbines in the house. He smelt rotten so we stripped him off and put him in the bath. (Bert insisted that Pandora put a flannel over her eyes for this part of the operation.) Then I washed his bit of remaining hair and gave him a good scrub down, while Pandora took Rosie and Sabre and went to Mr Patel's for Woodbines.

When Pandora came back we lifted Bert out of the bath. (Pandora promised to keep her eyes shut) and I dried him and put him into clean pyjamas. He looked lovely with his white hair all fluffy and sticking out at the back of his head. If I'd been a householder I would have invited him to stay there and then. Bert needs twenty-four-hour round-the-clock care, by people who love him.

The problem is that very few people, apart from Mother Theresa and a few nuns, could put up with Bert for more than a couple of days.

I asked him if there was any chance of him turning Catholic, he said, 'About as much chance as there is of Mrs Thatcher turning into a woman!'

On the way home we played a good game. We pretended we were married and that Rosie was our baby. Pandora tired of the game before I did but not before several people had been fooled.

Tuesday April 26th

The dog had an unfortunate accident on the kitchen floor this morning. Unfortunate for me, that is, because I had to clear it up. Knowing its use for such emergencies, I grabbed this week's copy of *The Sunday Times*, and made the thrilling discovery that HITLER'S DIARIES HAVE BEEN FOUND! I quote, 'After being hidden in a German hayloft for nearly forty years, *The Sunday Times* today tells the full story of this historic discovery!' I read on avidly. And to think I nearly used such a revelatory article to wipe up a piece of dog crap!

Wednesday April 27th

Is there no trust left in the world?

The Hitler Diaries are being subjected to meticulous tests by scientists. Why can't they take *The Sunday Times'* word for it that the diaries are genuine? Even a sceptic like me knows that *The*

Sunday Times wouldn't risk its reputation if there was the faintest chance that the diaries were a forgery.

Thursday   April 28th

Herr Wolf-Rudiger Hess, son of Rudolph Hess (Hitler's Deputy Maniac) has said that the Hitler Diaries are genuine. So there, Pandora! Incidentally, Rudolph Hess is eighty-nine. The same age as Bert Baxter.

Friday   April 29th

My father took me and Rosie to the bank. To help him get a bank loan. Mr Niggard, the Bank Manager, looked at my rags in a pitying way. Then said, 'Why do you require this loan, Mr Mole? A car, a house extension or clothes for the children perhaps?'

My father said, 'No. I can't afford to *buy* anything. I just want to feel some money in my hand again.'

But, after hearing that my parents were both out of work and on the Social, Mr Niggard refused the loan, saying: 'I am saving you from yourself. You will thank me one day.'

My father said, 'No I won't, I'm taking my overdraft elsewhere.'

Saturday   April 30th

My mother has decided that sugar is the cause of all the evil in the world, and has banned it from the house.

She smoked two cigarettes while she informed me of her decision.

Sunday   May 1st

I overheard my father say, 'Well it looks like the North Sea for me, Pauline.'

I ran into the kitchen and said, 'Don't do it, Dad. The economy is bound to pick up!'

My father looked puzzled. Perhaps he was surprised to hear such an emotional outburst from me.

I was surprised myself.

Monday   May 2nd
BANK HOLIDAY

Lord Dacre has vouched for the Hitler Diaries' authenticity.
So Pandora owes me £1.50 in a lost bet. Ha! Ha! Ha!

Tuesday   May 3rd
BACK TO SCHOOL

Quite a few changes have taken place since I was last at school.
Mr Jones the PE teacher has got the sack, and Mr Lambert has
married Ms Fossington-Gore; he is now called Mr Lambert-
Fossington-Gore. She is called Ms Fossington-Gore-Lambert.

Mr Scruton is on sick leave, suffering from a breakdown due
to compiling the timetable, so Podgy Pickles the Deputy head
has taken over his functions. The new regime is a bit more
relaxed, though not yet liberal enough to enable me to wear my
rags to school.

We spent the first day back being taught how to revise for the
dreaded 'O' levels.

6 p.m. Started revising English, Biology and Geography.

7 p.m. Decided to concentrate on one subject at a time. Chose
English.

8 p.m. Finished revising when Bert Baxter phoned and requested
my help. His toilet is blocked again.

Wednesday   May 4th

Got a letter from L.S. Caton – the man who recognises my
writing talent. The postmark said '*New York.*'

> Dear Adrian Mole,
> Thank you for sending me the first page of your novel,
> *Longing for Wolverhampton*. I am sure that any publishing
> house worth its salt would jump at the chance to publish
> such a promising piece of work.
> For a small consideration (shall we say, $100), I would
> be pleased to promote your book.

Make your cheque out to: L.S. Caton Ltd.
and send it to me, c/o The Dixon Motel,
                    1,599 Block 19,
                    NY State
                    USA

My father refused to give me the money after reading the
first page of *Longing for Wolverhampton*! He said, 'I've read
some rubbish in my life, but this . . . .'

Thursday   May 5th

My father has gone for an interview to be a roustabout on an oil
rig in the North Sea.

My father a roustabout!

It is nearly as good as having a cowboy for a father. I hope he
gets the job. He will be away one fortnight in two.

Friday   May 6th

Yet another disenchantment.

The Hitler Diaries are a hoax. I have paid Pandora £1.50.

I am dead disappointed, I was looking forward to reading
about what maniacs eat for breakfast, and how they behave in
private.

Saturday   May 7th

Spent all day revising with Pandora in her mother's study.

Our house is intolerable because my father is beside himself
with grief at being turned down by the oil rig firm.

I *told him* it was a bit premature to buy the check shirts and
jeans, before he'd been notified that he'd got the job, but he
wouldn't listen.

Now he owes Grandma £38.39.

Sunday   May 8th

The Sunday Times has printed a grovelling apology to its readers,
and ex-readers.

I will save today's edition and use it to clean up any future dog crap. Adrian Mole does not like being made to look a fool.

Especially in front of the future Mrs Adrian Mole, *née* Pandora Braithwaite.

Monday   May 9th

Mrs Thatcher has called a General Election for June 9th!

How selfish can you get?

Doesn't she know that the May and early June period is supposed to be kept quiet, while teenagers revise for their exams? How can we study when loudspeakers are blaring out lying promises, day and night and canvassers are continually knocking on the door, reminding floating voters that it's 'make your mind up' time? It's all right for her to announce she is going to the country, but some of us can't afford that luxury.

Tuesday   May 10th

I keep getting anxiety attacks every time I think about the exams.

I know I'm going to fail.

My overriding problem is that I'm *too* intellectual: I am constantly thinking about things, like: was God married? and: if Hell is other people, is Heaven empty?

These thoughts overload my brain, causing me to forget *facts*. Such as: the average rainfall in the average Equatorial Forest and other boring stuff.

Wednesday   May 11th

Grandma has given me some brain pills as a revision aid.

They are concocted from a disgusting part of a bull. She said, 'Your dead Grandad swore by them.' I swallowed two this morning but by the afternoon I still couldn't remember the capital of British Honduras.

I swore by them as well.

Thursday   May 12th

I thought my parents had given up the idea of moving house, but no! My mother struck terror into my heart and bowels at breakfast time by announcing that after the exams, we are going to sell our house and move to a desolate area of Wales! She said, 'I want to give us a chance of surviving a nuclear attack.'

I have written to the Council asking to be put on the waiting list.

I requested a two-bedroom flat facing south, with balcony and a working lift.

Friday   May 13th

My mother and father are having to negotiate a new Marriage Contract. I'm not surprised; my father hates Wales. He even complains when it is shown on television.

My mother has borrowed ominous books from the library: *The Treatment of Radiation Burns*; *Bee-Keeping, an Introduction*; and *Living without Men – A Practical Guide*.

Saturday   May 14th

10 a.m. A bloke in a blue-and-white pin-striped suit, blue shirt, blue tie, blue Rosette, has just knocked at the door. Thrust his hand out, said, 'Julian Pryce-Pinfold: your Conservative candidate, 'I trust I have your vote!'

I was quite pleased to be taken for eighteen. But I said, 'No, you are planning to exterminate the working class!'

Pryce-Pinfold laughed like a horse and said, 'I say, don't go over the top old chap, we're just trying to trim 'em down a bit!'

He left his poster so I drew devil's horns on his head and wrote '666' on his forehead, and put it up in the lounge window.

Sunday   May 15th

A bloke in a grey suit, white shirt, and red tie, has just disturbed my Biology revision by knocking on the door and announcing that he is the Labour Candidate. He said, 'I'm Dave Blakely and I'm going to get Britain back to work!'

My father asked him if there were any jobs going in the Labour Party headquarters. (A sign of his desperation.)

Dave Blakely said that he had never been to the headquarters so he didn't know.

He said, 'I disagree with official Labour policy.'

My mother harangued him about nuclear disarmament and criticized the Labour Party's record on housing, education and trade union co-operation.

Dave Blakely said, 'I suppose you're a Tory are you madam?'

My mother snapped: 'Certainly not, I have voted Labour all my life!'

Monday   May 16th

A blonde man in a blazer, with a regimental badge stood outside the school gates handing out election leaflets this afternoon. I read mine on the way home. The man is called Duncan McIntosh and his party is called 'The Send 'Em Back Where They Come From Party.' Its policy is the compulsory repatriation of: black people, brown people, yellow people, tinged people, Jewish, Irish, Welsh, Scottish, Celtic and all those who have Norman blood.

In fact only those who can prove to be pure-bred flaxen-haired Saxons are to be allowed to live in this country.

My mother has worked out that if he came to power the population of Great Britain would be reduced to one.

Tuesday   May 17th

Barry Kent has threatened Duncan McIntosh with grievous bodily harm unless he keeps away from our school.

He has joined 'Rock against Racism' (Barry Kent not Duncan McIntosh).

Wednesday   May 18th

The SDP candidate (green suit, orange shirt, neutral tie, nervous smile) has just left our house on the verge of tears, after my mother refused to let her kiss Rosie.

Thursday May 19th

I was shown a blurred picture of a broken-down cottage this morning, and asked if I would like to live there.

I replied in the negative.

My mother said, 'It sounds perfect. It's two miles from the nearest shop and fifty-five miles from the nearest American Air Base! Wouldn't you like to get up in the morning and feed the chickens, Adrian?'

I replied, 'I hate chickens. Their nasty beaks and cruel eyes absolutely repel me.'

Friday May 20th

Scruton has retired on the grounds of ill health (gone barmy) and Podgy Pickles has got his name screwed onto the Headmaster's door.

I have never been taught by Podgy, but by all accounts he is a nice bloke who talks about his family, and informs his class when he is thinking of buying a new car.

He took assembly this morning. He had dried egg yolk running down the length of his tie. I know because I was standing next to him. He had called me up to the stage to address the school on 'Why I think school uniform should be abolished!' I spoke from the heart, citing my parents' poverty, and bringing tears to the eyes of Ms Fossington-Gore-Lambert.

Saturday May 21st

My father ordered three politicians out of our front garden this morning. He said, 'My son is upstairs studying for a better future, and your constant clamouring for attention is distracting him!'

Actually I was measuring my thing at the time, but their noise *was* distracting. I kept losing my place on the tape-measure.

Sunday May 22nd

Rosie started crawling at 5 p.m.

My parents gave her a standing ovation.

Monday   May 23rd

My English essay 'Despair' was read out to the class.

Everyone looked dead miserable at the end. It is a story about a hamster with an incurable disease. I asked Mr Lambert-Fossington-Gore if it was of sufficient quality to send to the BBC.

He laughed and said, 'Only the Natural History Unit at Bristol.'

I have taken his advice and sent it.

Tuesday   May 24th

I have hung a notice on my door. It says: 'ATTENTION! NO ONE ALLOWED PAST THIS POINT!'

I am sick of having my privacy invaded.

Wednesday   May 25th

No one came into my room to wake me up. So I was late for school and when I got home my dirty washing was still on the floor and my curtains were drawn.

Thursday   May 26th

My racing bike has been stolen from out of the back garden.

The prime suspects are the dustmen. They have never forgiven us for having maggots in our dustbin last summer.

Friday   May 27th

Followed the dustbin men up our road and tried to overhear any suspicious conversation, but they were only talking about Len Fairclough.

One of them warned me to keep away from the mangling machinery at the back. Was this a hint of the violence to come, if I voice my suspicions to the police?

Saturday   May 28th

Nigel brought my bike back today.

He intended to run away on it to avoid his 'O' levels, but

decided not to after his father bought him a set of video cassette study aids. We are the only family in our street who haven't got a video, so there's no point in asking my parents for similar technological help. I will just have to rely on my brain.

Sunday May 29th

Stayed in bed all day revising.

Bert Baxter phoned three times but each time I told my parents to tell him that I was out of town.

The third time he rang, my mother said, 'Was it anything important, Bert?' Bert said, 'Not really, I just wanted to tell him that I think I'm ninety today.'

Felt such a rat fink that I pretended to return from out of town. I went to see him and gave him ninety gentle bumps (although I'm sure he's due at least one more).

It seemed to do him good.

Monday May 30th

Wrote some lyrics for Danny Thomson's reggae band.

> *Hear what he saying by A. Mole*
> Sisters and Brothers listen to Jah,
> Hear his words from near and far,
> Haile Selassie he sit on the throne.
> Hear what he saying, Hear what he saying. (*Repeated 10 times.*)
> JAH! JAH! JAH!
>
> Rise up and follow Selassie, the king.
> A new tomorrow to you he will bring. (*Repeat.*)
> E-the-o-pi-a,
> He'll bring new hope to ya.
> Hear what he saying, Hear what he saying. (*Repeated 20 times.*)

I gave it to Danny Thomson in Geography.

He read it, and said, 'Not bad, for a honky!'

What a cheek, he's twice as white as I am!

Pandora's mother has decided that the dynamics in our family are beyond her. She has recommended that we go to see a family therapist.

Tuesday May 31st

Got a letter from Johnny Tydeman.

I can't remember any of the references it contains. Did I really write a poem called 'Autumn Renewal'?

I must have written it while the balance of my mind was disturbed in April.

British Broadcasting Corporation
30th May

Dear Adrian Mole,
I do not think I will call you 'Aidy' and I think that it is a little premature in our correspondence for you to call me 'Johnny.' In fact I am never known as 'Johnny', only as 'John.' I do not wish to sound like a stuffy old grown-up, but when you are writing to people officially it is polite for one of your years to address them formally – though I do not mind, at this stage in our correspondence, your addressing me as 'Dear John Tydeman.' But 'Johnny', no! I do have several nicknames by which my friends know me but I am not going to reveal them to you. They relate largely to my surname rather than my Christian name.

Your last letter was altogether rather peculiar. Had you been at your parents' cocktail cabinet by any chance? Or had you drained the dregs of the previous night's vino? I do hope you had not tried glue-sniffing again. At least I am very pleased to hear that you have decided not to kill yourself this year. It would be a shocking waste. A poet can only die young when he has written a number of successful poems – *vide*: Keats, Shelley, Chatterton and Co. Most poets write drivel in their old age – *vide*: Wordsworth and quite a lot of Tennyson. I am sure your mother would miss you very much, so it is best that you remain alive.

Perhaps under the influence of something or other, your grammar seems to have gone to pot, eg: 'I have wrote some.' But your poem 'Autumn's Renewal' certainly has its moments. I like the pun about chaps. A bit rude though. 'Dandeline' (sic – not 'sick!') is actually spelt 'dandelion' so you can't make it rhyme with 'decline' nor 'vaseline' – try as you will.

Do not worry about our files. They will be shredded

before the KGB can get to them. Your secrets are safe in Ware and Caversham.

With my best wishes and continued good luck with your writing efforts.

Yours,
John Tydeman

Wednesday   June 1st

This will be my last entry; until the exams are over.

Courtney Elliot is coming round to give me last-minute coaching; must stop, his taxi has just drawn up outside.

Thursday   June 2nd

My parents went to see a family therapist last night. During their absence Pandora and I indulged in extremely heavy petting; so heavy that I felt a weight fall from me.

If I don't pass my exams it won't matter.

I have known what it is to have the love of a good woman.

True Confessions
of Adrian Albert Mole

To Lin Hardcastle
childhood friend

Adrian Mole's Christmas

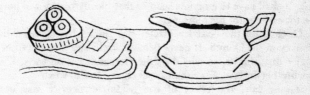

Monday   December 24th
CHRISTMAS EVE

Something dead strange has happened to Christmas. It's just not the same as it used to be when I was a kid. In fact I've never really got over the trauma of finding out that my parents had been lying to me annually about the existence of Santa Claus.

To me then, at the age of eleven, Santa Claus was a bit like God, all-seeing, all-knowing, but without the lousy things that God allows to happen: earthquakes, famines, motorway crashes. I would lie in bed under the blankets (how crude the word blankets sounds today when we are all conversant with the Tog rating of continental quilts), my heart pounding and palms sweaty in anticipation of the virgin *Beano* album. I would imagine big jolly Santa looking from his celestial sledge over our cul-de-sac and saying to his elves: 'Give Adrian Mole something decent this year. He is a good lad. He never forgets to put the lavatory seat down.' Ah . . . the folly of the child!

Alas, now at the age of maturity, (sixteen years, eight months and twenty-two days, five hours and six minutes) . . . I know that my parents walk around the town centre wild-eyed with consumer panic chanting desperately, 'What shall we get for Adrian?' Is it any wonder that Christmas Eve has lost its awe?

2.15am Just got back from the Midnight Service. As usual it dragged on far too long. My mother started getting fidgety after the first hour of the co-op young wives' carols. She kept whispering, 'I shall have to go home soon or that bloody turkey will never be thawed out for the morning.'

Once again the Nativity Playlet was ruined by having a live donkey in the church. It never behaves itself, and always causes a major disturbance, so why does the vicar inflict it on us? O K so his brother-in-law runs a donkey sanctuary, but so what?

To be fair, the effect of the Midnight Service was dead moving. Even to me who is a committed nihilistic existentialist.

Tuesday   December 25th
CHRISTMAS DAY

Not a bad collection of presents considering my Dad's redundant. I got the grey zip-up cardigan I asked for. My mother said, 'If you want to look like a sixteen-year old Frank Bough then go ahead and wear the thing!'

The Oxford Dictionary will come in useful for increasing my word power. But the best present of all was the electric shaver. I have already had three shaves. My shin is as smooth as a billiard ball. Somebody should get one for Leon Brittain. It is not good for Britain's image for a cabinet minister to go around looking like a gangster who has been in the cells of a New York Police Station all night.

The lousy Sugdens, my mother's inbred Norfolk relations, turned up at 11.30am. So I got my parents out of bed and then retired to my room to read my *Beano* annual. Perhaps I am too worldly and literate nowadays, but I was quite disappointed at its childish level of humour.

I emerged from my room in time for Christmas dinner and was forced to engage the Sugdens in conversation. They told me in minute, mind-boggling detail, about the life-cycle of King Edward potatoes, from tuber to chip pan. They were not a bit interested in my conversation about the Norwegian Leather Industry. In fact they looked bored. Just my luck to have philistines for relations. Dinner was late as usual. My mother has never learnt the secret of co-ordinating the ingredients of a meal. Her gravy is always made before the roast potatoes have turned brown. I went into the kitchen to give her some advice, but she shouted, 'Bugger off out' through the steam. When it came the meal was quite nice but there was no witty repartee over the table; not a single hilarious anecdote was told. In fact I wish I'd had my Xmas dinner with Ned Sherrin. His relations are dead lucky to have him. I bet their sides ache from laughing.

The Sugdens don't approve of drink, so every time my parents even *looked* at a bottle of spirits they tightened their lips and sipped their tea. (And yes it *is* possible to do both, I've seen it with my own eyes.) In the evening we all had a desultory game of cards. Grandad Sugden won four thousand pounds off my father. There was a lot of joking about my father giving Grandad Sugden an I O U but father said to me in the kitchen, 'No way am I putting my name to paper, that mean old git would have me in court as fast as you could say King Edward!'

The Sugdens went to bed early on our rusty camp beds. They are leaving for Norfolk at dawn because they are worried about potato poachers. I now know why my mother turned out to be wilful and prone to alcohol abuse. It is a reaction against her lousy moronic upbringing in the middle of the potato fields of Norfolk.

Wednesday December 26th
BOXING DAY

I was woken at dawn by the sound of Grandad Sugden's rusty Ford Escort refusing to start. I know I should have gone down into the street and helped to push it but Grandma Sugden seemed to be doing all right on her own. It must be all those years of flinging sacks of potatoes about. My parents were wisely pretending to be asleep, but I know they were awake because I could hear coarse laughter coming from their bedroom, and when the Sugdens' engine came alive and the Escort finally turned the corner of our cul-de-sac I distinctly heard the sound of a champagne cork popping and the chink of glasses. Not to mention the loud 'Cheers'.

Went back to sleep but the dog licked me awake at 9.30, so I took it for a walk past Pandora's house. Her dad's Volvo wasn't in the drive so they must still be staying with their rich relations. On the way I passed Barry Kent, who was kicking a football up against the wall of the old people's home. He seemed full of seasonal good will for once and I stopped to talk with him. He asked what I'd had for Christmas; I told him and I asked him what he'd had. He looked embarrassed and said, 'I ain't 'ad much this year 'cos our dad's lost his job'. I asked him what happened, he said, 'I dunno. Our dad says Mrs Thatcher took it off him.' I said 'What, personally?' Barry shrugged and said, 'Well that's what our dad reckons.'

Barry asked me back to his house for a cup of tea so I went to show that I bore him no grudge from the days when he used to demand money with menaces from me. The outside of the Kents' council house looked very grim. (Barry told me that the council have been promising to mend the fences, doors and windows for years) but the inside looked magical. Paper chains were hung everywhere, almost completely hiding the cracks in the walls and ceilings. Mr Kent had been out into the community and found a large branch, painted it with white gloss paint and stuck it into the empty paint tin. This branch effectively took the place of a Christmas tree in my opinion, but Mrs Kent said, sadly, 'But it's not the same really, not if the only reason you've got it is because you can't afford to have a real, plastic one.' I was going to say that their improvised tree was modernistic and Hi Tech but I kept my mouth shut.

I asked the Kent children what they'd had for Christmas and they said, 'Shoes.' So I had to pretend to admire them. I had no choice because they kept sticking them under my nose. Mrs Kent laughed and said, 'And Mr Kent and me gave each other a packet of fags!' As you know, dear diary, I disapprove of smoking but I could understand their need to have a bit of pleasure at Christmas so I didn't give them my anti-smoking lecture.

I didn't like to ask any more questions and politely declined the mince pies they offered . . . from where I was sitting I could see into their empty pantry.

Walking back home I wondered how my parents were able to buy decent Christmas presents for me. After all my father and

Mr Kent were both innocent victims of the robot culture where machines are preferred to people.

As I came through our back door I found out. My father was saying, 'But how the hell am I going to pay the next Access bill, Pauline?' My mother said, 'We'll have to sell something George, whatever happens we've got to hang on to at least one credit card because it's impossible to live on the dole and social security!'

So my family's Christmas prosperity is a thin veneer. We've had it on credit.

In the afternoon we went round to Grandma's for Boxing Day tea. As she slurped out the trifle she complained bitterly about her Christmas Day spent at the Evergreen Club. She said, 'I knew I shouldn't have gone; that filthy communist Bert Baxter got disgustingly drunk on a box of liqueur chocolates and sang crude words at the Carol Service!'

My father said, 'You should have come to us, mum, I did ask you!'

Grandma said, 'You only asked me *once* and anyway the Sugdens were there.' This last remark offended my mother; she is always criticising her family but she hates anybody else to do the same. The tea ended in disaster when I broke a willow pattern plate that Grandma has had for years. I know Grandma loves me but I have to record that on this occasion she looked at me with murder in her eyes. She said, 'Nobody will ever know what that plate meant to me!' I offered to pick the pieces up but she pushed me away with the end of the hand brush. I went into the bathroom to cool down. After twenty minutes my mother banged on the door and said, 'C'mon, Adrian, we're going home. Grandma's just told your dad that it's his own fault he's been made redundant.' As I passed through the living room the silence between my father and my Grandma was as solid as a double-glazed window.

As we passed Pandora's house in the car, I saw that the fairy lights on the fir tree in her garden were switched on, so I asked my parents to drop me off. Pandora was ecstatic to see me at first. She raved about the present I bought her (a solid gold bracelet from Tesco's, £2.49) but after a while she cooled a bit and started going on about the Christmas house-party she'd been to. She made a lot of references to a boy called Crispin Wartog-Lowndes. Apparently he is an expert rower and he rowed Pandora across a lake on Christmas day. Whilst doing so he quoted from the works of Percy Bysshe Shelley. According to Pandora there was a mist on the lake. I got into a silent jealous rage and imagined pushing Crispin Wartog-Lowndes's aristocratic face under the lake until he'd forgotten about Pandora, Christmas and Shelley. I got into bed at 1am, worn out with all the emotion. In fact, as I lay in the dark, tears came to my eyes; especially when I remembered the Kents' empty pantry.

The Mole/Mancini Letters

January 1st 1985

From
Hamish Mancini
196 West Houston Street
New York, N.Y.

Hi there Aidy!
How are you kid? . . . How's the zits . . . your face still
look like the surface of the moon? Hey don't worry, I
gotta cure. You rub the corpse of a dead frog into your
face at night. Do you have frogs in England? . . . Your
mum gotta blender? . . . OK, here's what you do:

1. You find a dead frog.
2. You put it in the blender. (Gory, but you don't have to
   look.)
3. You depress the button for 30 seconds. (Neither do you
   have to listen.)
4. You pour the resulting gunk into a jar.
5. You wash the blender, huh?
6. Last thing at night (clean your teeth *first*) you apply the
   gunk to your face. It works! I now gotta complexion like

a baby's ass. Hey! It was great reading your diary, even the odd unflattering remark about me. Still, old buddy, I forgive you on account of how you were of unsound mind at the time you wrote the stuff. An' I got questions . . .

1. What does RSPCA stand for?
2. Who's Malcolm Muggeridge?
3. For chrissake, what are PE shorts?
4. Is the *Morning Star* a commie newspaper?
5. Where's Skegness? . . . What's Skegness rock?
6. 'V' sign? . . . Like Churchill the war leader?
7. Toad in the Hole, is it food or what?
8. Woodbines? . . . Bert Baxter smokes flowers?
9. Family Allowance . . . is this a charity handout?
10. Kevin Keegan . . . who is he?
11. Barclaycard . . . what is it?
12. Yorkshire Puddings . . . what are they?
13. Broadcasting House?
14. How much in dollars is 25 pence?
15. Is a Mars Bar candy?
16. Is Sainsbury's a hypermarket?
17. What's the PDSA, some kinda animal hospital?
18. GCEs, what *are* they?
19. Think I can guess what *Big and Bouncy* magazine is like . . . but gimme some *details*, kid?
20. Bovril – sounds disgusting! . . . Is it?
21. Evergreens? . . . Explain please.
22. Social Services?
23. Spotted Dick . . . jeezus! . . . This some sexual disease?
24. Is a 'detention centre' jail?
25. You bought your mother 'Black Magic' – what is she, a witch or something?
26. Where's Sheffield?
27. What's Habitat?
28. Radio Four, is it some local station?
29. O' level what?
30. What is a copper's nark?
31. Noddy? That the goon in the little car?
32. Dole . . . 'Social Security' . . . is this like our Welfare?

33. Sir Edmund Hilary . . . he a relation of yours?
34. Alma Cogan . . . she a singer?
35. Lucozade . . . did you get drunk?
36. What's a conker?
37. The dog is AWOL . . . what is or was AWOL?
38. Who is or was Noel Coward?
39. What is BUPA?
40. What are 'wellingtons'?
41. Who is Tony Benn?
42. Petrol . . . you mean gas?
43. Is *The Archers* a radio serial about Robin Hood?
44. Is the Co-op a commie-run store?
45. Is VAT a kinda tax?
46. *Eating* a chapati? . . . Isn't chapati French for hat?
47. Rouge? . . . Don't you mean blusher?
48. Is an Alsatian a German Shepherd?
49. What's a Rasta?

Send info back soonest,
Yours eagerly, your old buddy
    Hamish

PS. Mum's in the Betty Ford Clinic.
She's doin' OK, they've cured everything but the
kleptomania.

Leicester
February 1st 1985

Dear Hamish,
Thanks for your long letter but please try to put postage
stamps on the envelope next time you write. You are rich
and I am poor, I cannot afford to subsidise your
scribblings. You owe me twenty-six pence. Please send it
immediately.
    I am no *so* desperate about my complexion that I have
to resort to covering my face with purée of frog. In fact,
Hamish, I was repelled and disgusted by your advice, and
anyway my mother *hasn't* got a blender. She has stopped

cooking entirely. My father and I forage for ourselves as best we can. I'm pleased that you enjoyed reading my diary even though many of the references were unfamiliar to you. I am enclosing a glossary for your edification.

1. RSPCA stands for: the Royal Society for the Prevention of Cruelty to Animals.
2. Malcolm Muggeridge: is an old intellectual who is always on TV. A bit like Gore Vidal, only more wrinkles.
3. PE shorts: running shorts as worn in Physical Education.
4. Yes, the *Morning Star* is a communist newspaper.
5. Skegness is a proletarian sea-side resort. Skegness rock is tubular candy.
6. 'V' sign: it means . . . get stuffed!
7. Toad in the hole: a batter pudding containing sausages.
8. Woodbines: small, lethally strong cigarettes.
9. Family Allowance: a small government payment made to parents of all children.
10. Kevin Keegan: a genius footballer now retired.
11. Barclaycard: plastic credit card.
12. Yorkshire Puddings: batter puddings minus sausages.
13. Broadcasting House: headquarters of the BBC.
14. Work it out for yourself.
15. Mars Bars: yes, it's candy, and very satisfying it is too.
16. Sainsbury's: is where teachers, vicars and suchlike do their food shopping.
17. PDSA: People's Dispensary for Sick Animals. A place where poor people take their ill animals.
18. GCEs are exams.
19. *Big and Bouncy:* a copy is on its way to you. Hide it from your mum.
20. Bovril: is a nourishing meat extract drink.
21. Evergreens: a club for wrinklies over 65 years.
22. Social Services: government agency to help the unfortunate, the unlucky, and the poor.
23. Spotted Dick: is a suet pudding containing sultanas. I find your sexual innuendos about my favourite pudding offensive in the extreme.

24. Detention Centre: jail for teenagers.
25. Black Magic: dark chocolates.
26. Sheffield: refer to map.
27. Habitat: store selling cheap, fashionable furniture.
28. Radio Four: BBC-run channel, bringing culture, news and art to Britain's listening masses.
29. O' level: see GCE's.
30. Copper's nark: rat fink who gives the police information about criminal activity.
31. Noddy: fictional figure from childhood. I hate his guts.
32. Dole: Social Security: yes, it's Welfare.
33. Sir Edmund Hilary: first bloke to climb Everest.
34. Alma Cogan: singer, now alas dead.
35. Lucozade: non-alcoholic drink. Invalids guzzle it.
36. Conker: round shiny brown nut. The fruit of the horse chestnut. British children thread string through them, and then engage in combat by smashing one conker against another. The kid whose conker gets smashed loses.
37. AWOL: British Army expression. It means absent without leave.
38. Noel Coward: wit, singer, playwright, actor, songwriter. Ask your mother, she probably *knew* him.
39. BUPA: private medicine, a bit like the Blue Cross.
40. Wellingtons: rubber boots. The queen wears them.
41. Tony Benn: an ex-aristocrat, now a fervent Socialist politician.
42. Petrol: OK . . . OK . . . gas.
43. The Archers: a radio serial about English countryfolk.
44. The Co-op: a grocery chain run on Socialist principles.
45. VAT: a tax. The scourge of small businesses.
46. Chapati: *not* a French hat. It's a flat Indian bread!
47. Rouge: *you* can call it blusher if you like. *I* call it *rouge*.
48. Alsatian: yes, also called German Shepherd, terrifying whatever they're called.
49. Rasta: a member of the Rastafarian religion. Members are usually black. Wear their hair in dreadlocks (plaits) and smoke illegal substances. They have complicated handshakes.

Look Hamish, I'm at the end of my patience now. If there is anything else you cannot understand please refer to the reference books. Ask your mother or any passing Anglophile. And please! . . . please! . . . send my diaries back. I would hate them to fall into unfriendly, possible commercial hands. I am afraid of blackmail; as you know my diaries are full of sex and scandal. Please for the sake of our continuing friendship . . . send my diaries back!

I remain, Hamish,

Your trusting, humble and obedient servant and friend.

A. Mole

A Letter to the BBC

Leicester
February 14th

Dear Mr Tydeman,
I am sending you, as requested, my latest poem. Please
write back by return of post if you wish to broadcast the
said poem. Our telephone has been disconnected (again).
   I remain, Sir, your most humble and obedient servant,
    A. Mole

Throbbing

Pandora,
I am but young
I am but small
(with cratered skin)
Yet! Hear my call.

Oh, rapturous girl
With skin sublime
Whose favourite programme's 'Question Time'
Look over here
To where I stand
A throbbing
Like a swollen gland.

        A Mole

Adrian Mole on
'Pirate Radio Four'

Art Culture and Politcs

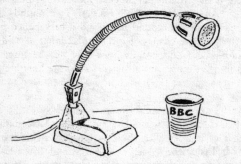

August 1985

I would like to thank the BBC for inviting me to talk to you on Radio 4. It's about time they had a bit of culture on in the morning. Before I begin properly I'd just like to take this opportunity to reassure my parents that I got here safely.

Hello, Mum. Hello, Dad. The train was OK. Second Class was full so I went into First Class and sat down and pretended to be a lunatic. Fortunately the ticket inpsector has got a lunatic in his family so he was quite sympathetic and took me to sit on a stool in the guard's van. As you know I am normally an introvert, so pretending to be a lunatic extrovert for an hour and twenty minutes wore me out, and I was glad when the train steamed into the cavernous monolith that is St Pancras station. Well to be quite honest the train didn't steam in because as you, Dad, will know, steam has been phased out and is now but an erotic memory in a train spotter's head.

Anyway I got a taxi like you told me, a black one with a high roof. I got in and said, 'Take me to the BBC'. The driver said, 'Which BBC?' in a surly sort of tone. I *nearly* said, 'I don't like your tone my man', but I bit my tongue back and explained: 'I'm speaking on Radio Four this morning'. He said, 'Good job you ain't goin' on the telly wiv your face.' He must have been referring to the bits of green toilet paper sticking to my shaving cuts. I didn't know what to say to his cruel remark, so I kept quiet and watched the money clock like you told me to do. You won't believe it, Mum, but it cost me two pounds forty-five pence! . . . I know . . . incredible isn't it? Two pounds forty-five pence! I gave him two pound notes and a fifty pence piece and told him to keep the change. I can't repeat what *he* said because this is Radio Four and not Radio Three but he flung his five pence tip into the gutter and drove off shouting horrible things. I grovelled in the gutter for ages, but you'll be pleased to hear that I found the five pence.

A bloke in a general's uniform barred my way to the hallowed portals of Broadcasting House. He said, 'And whom might you be sunshine?' I said quite coldly (because once again I didn't care for his tone), 'I am Adrian Mole, the Diarist and Juvenile Philosopher'. He turned to another general . . . in fact, thinking about it, it could have been the *Director* General because this second general looked sort of noble yet careworn. Anyway, the first general shouted, 'Look on the list under Mole will you . . .?' The second general replied (in cultivated tones, so it must have been the Director General) 'Yes I've got a Mole on the list . . . Studio B 198'. Before I knew it, a wizened-up old guide appeared at my elbow and showed me into a palatial lift. Then, once out of the lift – which was twice as big as my bedroom by the way – he took me down tortured, turning corridors. It was like George Orwell's Ministry of Truth in that book called *1984*. No wonder DJs are always late turning up for work.

Eventually, exhausted and panting, we arrived outside the door of studio B 198. I was a bit worried about the old guide. To tell you the truth I thought he'd force me to give him mouth to mouth, such was his feeble condition. I really think that the BBC ought to provide oxygen on each floor for their older employees; and a trained nurse wouldn't be a bad idea either. It would save them money in the long run; they wouldn't have to keep replacing staff all the time and collecting for wreaths and things. Anyway, just thought I'd tell you that I got here all right. Oh, you know the BBC bloke I've been writing to, that producer John Tydeman.

Well he's dead scruffy. He looks like he *writes*. You know, with a beard and heavy horn-rimmed glasses. Need I say more? I'd better stop talking to you now Mum and Dad, because he's making crude signs at me through the glass – so much for the standard of education at the BBC!

Oh, before I forget, did you send that excuse to Pop-Eye Scruton telling him that I've gone down with an 'as yet unnamed' virus? If not, can you take one to school immediately after my broadcast? . . . Thanks, only, as you know, he refused me permission to come here today. How mean can you get? Fancy denying one of the foremost intellectuals in school the opportunity to talk about art and culture on the BBC. You'll be sure to mark the envelope 'for the attention of the Headmaster' won't you Dad? Don't forget and put 'Pop-Eye Scruton' on, like you did last time.

Well I'd better start properly now . . . I've got my notes somewhere . . . (*pause . . . rustling . . .*) Oh dear . . . I've left them in the taxi. Oh well, it's quite lucky that I'm good at doing 'ad hoc' spontaneous talking isn't it? . . . So, Art and Culture. Are they important?

Well, I think Art and Culture *are* important. *Dead* important. Without Art and Culture we would descend to the level of animals who aimlessly fill their time by hanging around dustbins and getting into fights. The people who don't allow Art and Culture into their lives can always be spotted. They are pale from watching too much television, and also their conversation lacks a certain *je ne sais quoi*; unless they are French of course. Cultureless people talk about the price of turnips and why bread always falls on the buttered side, and other such inane things. You never hear them mention Van Gogh or Rembrandt or Bacon (by Bacon, I'm talking about Francis Bacon the infamous artist, I don't mean streaky bacon or Danish bacon . . . the sort you eat). No, such names mean nothing to cultureless people, they will never pilgrimage to the Louvre Museum to see Michaelangelo's Mona Lisa. Nor will they thrill to a Brahms Opera. They will fill their empty days with frivolous frivolity, and eventually die never having tasted the sweet ambrosia of culture.

I therefore feel it incumbent upon me to promote artisticness wherever I tread. If I meet a low-browed person I force them into a philosophical conversation. I ask them, 'Why are we here?' Often their answers are facetious. For instance last week I asked a humble market trader that very question. He answered, 'I dunno why you're 'ere mate but I'm 'ere to flog carrots'.

Such people are to be pitied. We of superior intellect must not judge them too harshly, but gently nudge them into the direction of the theatre rather than the betting shop. The art gallery instead of the bingo hall. The local madrigal society as opposed to the discotheque. I know that there are cynics who say 'England is governed by philistines, so what do you expect?' but to those cynics I say yes, we may be governed by philistines at the moment but I'd like to take this opportunity to talk about a political party that I've started up. It is called the Mole Movement. As yet we are small, but one day our influence will be felt throughout our land. Who knows, one day our party could be the party of government. I could end up as Prime Minister. Is it so inconceivable? Not in my opinion. Mrs Thatcher was once a humble housewife and mother. So, if she can do it, why can't I?

The 'Mole Movement' was formed on Boxing Day 1985. You know what it's like on Boxing Day. You've opened the presents, you've eaten all the white meat on the turkey, your half-witted relations are bickering about Aunt Ethel's will, and why Norman didn't deserve to get the scabby old clock: a general feeling of *ennui* (*ennui* is French for bored out of your skull by the way). Yes, *ennui* hangs around the house like stale fag smoke. Anyway it was Boxing Day and my girlfriend, Pandora Braithwaite, had come round so that we could exchange belated Christmas greetings. Her family took her to stay in a hotel for Christmas because Mrs Braithwaite said that if she had to stare up the rear of another turkey she would go berserk.

Anyway, we exchanged presents; I gave her a fish ash tray I made in pottery at school, and she gave me a Marks and Spencers voucher so that I could replace my old underpants. The elastic's gone . . . yes . . . so we thanked each other and kissed for about five minutes. I didn't want us to get carried away and end up as single parents . . . not in our A' level year. It wouldn't be fair to the kid with us both studying . . . er . . . what did I start to . . .? Yes. Well, after the kissing stopped I started to talk about my aspirations, and Pandora smoked one of her stinking French fags and listened to me with grave attention. I spoke passionately about beauty and elegance, and bringing back the old branch lines on the railways. I thundered against tower blocks and leisure centres, and ended by saying 'Pandora, my love, will you join me in my Life's Work?' Pandora moved languidly on my bed and said, 'You haven't said what your life's work is yet, *chéri*'.

I stood over her and said, 'Pandora, my life's work is the pursuit of beauty over ugliness, of truth over deceit, and of justice over rich people hogging all the money'. Pandora ran to the bathroom and was violently sick, such was the dramatic effect my speech had on her. To tell the truth I was a bit misty-eyed myself, and while she was throwing up I studied my face in the wardrobe mirror and definitely saw a change for the better. For where once was adolescent uncertainty was now mature complacency.

Pandora emerged from the bathroom and said 'My God, darling, I don't know what's going to happen to you'. I pulled her into my arms and reassured her about my future. I said, 'The way ahead may be stony but I will walk it barefoot if necessary'. Our oblique conversation was interrupted by my mother making mundane enquiries about how many spoons of sugar Pandora took in her cocoa. After my mother had stamped off down the stairs I turned in despair and cried, 'Oh save me from the *petit bourgeoisie* with their inane enquiries about beverages'. We tried to continue the conversation but it was again interrupted when my father went into the bathroom and started making disgusting grunting noises. He is so uncouth! ... He can't wash his face without sounding like two warthogs mating in a watering hole. How I managed to spring from his loins I'll never know. In fact sometimes I think that it wasn't *his* loins I sprang from; my mother was once very friendly with a poet. Not a full time poet: he was a maggot farmer during the day, but at night, after the maggots had been shut up in their sheds, he would pull a pad of Basildon Bond towards him and write poems. Quite good poems as well; one of them got into the local paper. My mother cut it out and kept it ... surely the action of a woman in love. When my mother came in with the cocoa I quizzed her about her relationship with the maggot poet. 'Oh Ernie Crabtree?' she said, pretending innocence. 'Yes', I said, then went on with heavy emphasis: 'I am like him in many ways aren't I ...? The poetry for instance'. My mother said, 'You're nothing like him. He was witty and clever and unconventional and he made me laugh. Also he was six foot tall and devastatingly handsome'.

'So why didn't you marry him?' I asked. My mother sighed and sat down on my bed next to Pandora. 'Well, I couldn't stand the maggots. In the end I gave him an ultimatum. "Ernie", I said, "It's me or the maggots. You must choose between us." And he chose the maggots.' Her lips started to tremble and so I left the room and bumped into my father on the landing. By now I was determined to sort out my paternity so I quizzed him about Ernie Crabtree. 'Yeah, Ernie's done well for himself', he said. 'They call him the Maggot King in fishing circles. He's got a chain of maggot farms now and a mansion with a pack of Dobermans running in the grounds . . . yeah, good old Ernie.' 'Does he still write poetry?' I enquired. 'Listen, son', said my father, and bent so close that I could see his thirty-year-old acne scars. 'Listen, Ernie's bank statements are pure poetry. He doesn't need to *write* the stuff.' My father got into bed, took his vest off and reached for the best-selling book he was reading. (Myself I never read best-sellers on principle. It's a good rule of thumb. If the masses like it then I'm sure that I won't.)

'Dad', I said, 'what did Ernie Crabtree look like?' My father cracked the spine of his book open, lit a disgusting fag and said 'Short fat bloke with a glass eye, wore a ginger wig . . . now clear off, I'm reading'. I went back to my room to find Pandora and my mother having one of those sickening talks that women have nowadays. It was full of words like 'unfulfilled', 'potential', and 'identity'. Pandora kept chipping in with 'environment' and 'socio-economic' and 'chauvinistic attitude'. I got my pyjamas out of my drawer, signalling that I wished their conversation to desist, but neither of them took the hint so I was forced to change in the bathroom. When I came back the air was full of French cigarette smoke, and they were gassing about the Common Market and the relevance of something called 'milk quotas'.

I hung about tidying my desk and folding my clothes, but eventually I was forced to climb into bed while the conversation continued on either side of me. When they got on to cruise missiles I was forced to intercept and plead for a bit of multilateral peace.

Fortunately the dog got into a fight with a gang of dogs outside in the street so my mother was forced to run outside and separate it from the other canines with a mop handle. I took this opportunity to speak to Pandora. I said, 'While you may have been idly chatting with my mother I have been formulating important ideas. I have decided that I am going to have a party.' Pandora said, 'A fancy dress party?' 'No', I shouted, 'I'm forming a *political* party, well more of a Movement, really. It will be called the Mole Movement and membership will be £2 a year. Pandora asked what she would get for £2 a year. I replied, 'Arresting conversation and stimulation and stuff'. She opened her mouth to ask another question so I closed my eyes and feigned sleep. I heard the squelch of Pandora's moon boots as she tip-toed to the door, opened it and went off, squelching, down the stairs. Thus was the 'Mole Movement' born.

The next morning, I woke with an epic poem thundering inside my head. Even before I had cleaned my teeth I was at my desk scribbling feverishly. I was interrupted once when a visitor called from Matlock, but I declined the encyclopaedias he was selling, and returned to my desk. The poem was finished at 11.35am Greenwich Mean Time. And this is it.

THE HOI POLLOI RECEPTION
BY A. MOLE

The food stood on the table
The drink stood on the bar
The crisps lay in the glass dish
'Twixt the gherkins in the jar.
The poets were expected
The artists had sent word
The pianists and flautists
Were bringing lemon curd.

The novelists were travelling
From dim and distant lands
The journalists were trekking
O'er deep and shifting sands.
The *hoi polloi* stood standing
Outside the party room
Which glowed with invitation

Like a twenty-year-old womb.
Yet they dared not cross the portal
To taste the waiting feast
For fear of what would happen
If they dared to cross the beast.

The *hoi polloi* grew weary
And sat upon the floor
And told each other stories
Until the clock struck four.
They drew each other pictures
One person sang a song
But was careful at the end
To say 'Of course *they* won't be long'.

The artists and the poets
And the people who write books
The musicians and the journalists
And the Nouvelle Cuisine cooks
Sent word they couldn't make it
They couldn't leave the town.
They were meeting VIP's for drinks
And couldn't make it down.

The gherkins went untasted
The crisps were never crunched
The Chablis kept its cork in
The Twiglets went unmunched
But still the people waited
For a hundred million days
And just to help to pass the time
They wrote and acted plays.

They carved a pretty pattern
On the panel of the door.
They painted lovely pictures on the
Coldly concrete floor
They sang in pretty harmony
About the epic wait.
Then hush! . . . Was that a car we heard
Was that a creaking gate?

It's the sculptors on the gravel
It's the poets wild-eyed
Quick open wide the door to
Let the journalists inside.
Oh welcome to our party!
We thought you'd never come
So sad we ate the food though
We haven't left a crumb!

For in the time of waiting
The *hoi polloi* grew brave
They went into the room
And took the things they craved.
And the poets and the sculptors
And the artists and the cooks
And the women good at music
And the men who wrote the books
And the journalists and actors
And the people trained to sing
Stood waiting ever after for the party to begin.

A Mole in Moscow

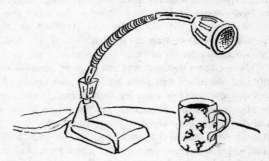

September 1985

Woke up at 6am in the morning. Got out of bed carefully because the dog was spread-eagled across my bed, flat on its back, with its legs in the air. At first I thought it was dead, but I checked its pulse and found signs of life, so I just slid out from underneath its warm fur. The dog's dead old now and needs its sleep.

After measuring my chest and shoulders I had a thorough wash in cold water. I read somewhere (I think it was one of Mr Paul Johnson's articles) that 'cold water makes a man of you'. I've been a bit worried about my maleness lately, somewhere along the line I seem to have picked up too many female hormones.

I've been to see the doctor about it, but as usual he was most unsympathetic. I asked if I could have some of my female hormones taken out. Dr Grey laughed a horrible, bitter laugh and gave his usual advice, which was to go out and have my head kicked about in a rugby scrum. As I was leaving his surgery he said 'And I don't want to see you back here for at least two months'. I asked, 'Even if I'm taken seriously ill?' He muttered,

'*Especially* if you're taken seriously ill'. I'm considering reporting him to his superiors; all this worry has affected my poetry output. I used to be able to turn out at least four poems an hour, but now I'm down to three a week. If I'm not careful I'll dry up altogether.

In my desperation I went to the Lake District on the train. I was struck down by the beauty of the place, although saddened to find that there were no daffodils flashing in my outer eye as in William Wordsworth the old Lake poet. I asked an ancient country yokel why there were no daffodils about. He said, 'It's July, lad'. I repeated loudly and clearly, (because he was obviously a halfwit) 'Yes I know that, but why are there no *daffodils* about?' 'It's July,' he roared. At that point I left the poor deranged soul. It's sad that nothing can be done for such pathetic geriatric cases. I blame the government. Since they put rat poison in the water supply most of the adult population have gone barmy.

I sat on a rock that Wordsworth once sat on and thrilled to think that where my denim was now was where his moleskin used to be. A yob had scrawled on the rock, 'What's wiv this Words-worth?' Another, more cultivated hand, had written underneath: 'You mindless vandal, how dare you bespoil this precious rock which has been here for millions of years. If you were here I'd flog you to within an inch of your life. Signed, A. Geologist'. Somebody else had written underneath, 'Flog *me* instead. Signed, A. Masochist'. After eating my tuna-fish sandwiches and drinking my low calorie orange drink, I walked around the lake trying to feel inspired, but by tea-time nothing had happened so I put my pen and exercise book back into my carrier-bag and hurried back to the station to catch the train back to the Midlands.

It was just my luck to have to share a compartment with hyperactive two-year-old twins and their worn-out mother. When the twins weren't having spectacular tantrums on the floor they were both standing six inches away from me, *staring* at me with unblinking evil eyes. It used to be my ambition to have a farmhouse full of Hovis-like children. I would imagine looking out of my study window to see them all frolicking amongst the combine harvesters. With Pandora, their mother, saying; 'Shush! . . . Daddy is working', whereupon the children would blow me kisses with their podgy fingers and run into the stone-flagged kitchen to eat the cakes that Pandora had just taken from the oven. However since my experience with the mad twins I have decided *not* to spread my seed. Indeed I may ask my parents if I can have a vasectomy for my eighteenth birthday.

When I got home I hurried round to Pandora's house to tell her about this change in my future plans. Pandora said, '*Au contraire, chéri*, should we still be having a long term relationship. I should like to have one child when I am forty-six years of age. The child will be a girl. She will be beautiful and immensely gifted. Her name will be Liberty.' I said, 'But do women's reproductive organs still reproduce at the age of forty-six?' Pandora said, '*Mais naturellement, chéri*, and anyway there is always the test tube option'.

Mr Braithwaite came into the room and said, 'Pandora, make your mind up. Are you going to Russia or are you not?' Pandora said, 'Not. I can't leave the cat.' They then had a furious row. I could hardly believe my ears. Pandora was turning down a week in Russia with her father just because her stinking old moggy was about to give birth for the fourth time! During a pause in the argument I said, 'I would give my right leg to go to the country of Dostoyevsky's birth'.

However Mr Braithwaite didn't respond with an invitation for me to accompany him. How mean can you get? The Co-op Dairy had given him two tickets to go on a fact-finding tour of milk distribution in Moscow. (Mrs Braithwaite had refused to go because she'd recently joined the SDP.) So a ticket was going spare. Yet the tight git was denying me the glorious opportunity of studying revolution in the raw. When Mr Braithwaite had gone into the garden to savagely mow the lawn Pandora said, 'You *shall* go to Russia'. She worked on her father for a whole week. She refused to eat, she played her stereo system at full decibels. She invited her 'Hell's Angels' friends for tea every day. Her punk friends came to supper and I had breakfast with the family most mornings. By the end of the week Mr Braithwaite was a broken man and Mrs Braithwaite was begging him to take me behind the Iron Curtain. Eventually, after Pandora held an open air reggae concert on the back lawn, Mr Braithwaite relented.

He came to our house at 11 o'clock one Sunday morning, so I got my parents out of bed and we had a meeting at our kitchen table. They enthusiastically agreed to me going to Russia for a week. My mother said, 'Great, George, we could have a second honeymoon while Adrian's away!' My father said, 'Yeah, mum'll look after the baby. We can rediscover ourselves, eh, Pauline?' They slopped over each other for a bit and then turned their attention back to the proceedings for, knowing that I was a virgin traveller, Mr Braithwaite had brought a passport form with him and I filled it in carefully under his supervision. I only made one mistake. Where it said 'sex' I put 'not yet', instead of putting 'male'.

We turned the house upside down looking for my birth certificate before my mother remembered that it was framed and hanging on Grandma's front room wall. My father was sent round to fetch it while Mr Braithwaite took me to have my passport photographs taken in a slot machine. On the way, in the car, I practised facial expressions. I wanted my photographs to show the *real* Adrian Mole. Warm and clever, yet enigmatic and with just a hint of sensuousness. In the event, the photographs were disappointing. I looked like a spotty youth with just a hint of derangement in my sticking-out eyes. After everyone, apart from me, had had a good laugh at the photographs my mother reluctantly wrote a cheque out for fifteen pounds and then the documents were checked and double-checked by Mr Braithwaite before being put into a large envelope. While he did this I examined him carefully, for he was to be my travelling companion and room mate for a week. Would I be able to stand the shame of being seen in the company of a man wearing flared trousers and a paisley patterned waistcoat? Too late! The die was cast! Fate had thrown us together!

As he left, clutching my documentation, he said: 'Adrian, during the week we are in Moscow do you promise, swear, give me your word, that you will not utter *one* word about the Norwegian leather industry?' Astonished I said, 'Of course. If, for some reason, you find my mini-lectures on the Norwegian leather industry *offensive*, then of course I won't mention it'. Mr Braithwaite said, 'Oh I don't find your constant monologues on the Norwegian leather industry *offensive*, just deeply, deeply boring'. Then he got into his car and went to put the documents through the door of the Passport Office.

If this was a film, then leaves would blow across the screen and pages of diaries would riffle, trains would roar and calendars would have months torn from them by unseen hands. But as this is just me speaking then all I need to tell you is that time went by, and I got my passport and my visa by second-class post. In the days before I left England for Russia I also got advice. My Grandma said, 'If the Russians offer to show you the salt mines refuse and ask to be shown a shoe factory instead'. My mother advised me *not* to mention that at the age of fourteen she had been thrown out of the Young Communist League (Norwich Branch) for fraternising with American soldiers. Pandora advised against buying her a light amber necklace saying she preferred the *dark* amber, and Mr O'Leary from over the road advised me not to go at all. He said. 'The Russians are godless heathens, Adrian'. Mrs O'Leary said, 'Yes, and so are you, Declan, you haven't been to Mass for over two years'.

The worst part of the journey to Russia was the MI motorway. Mr Braithwaite's Volvo was almost sucked under the passing lorries several times. In fact at Watford Gap Mr Braithwaite lost his nerve and the capable hands of Mrs Braithwaite took the wheel. It was the first time I had flown in a plane so I was expecting sympathy and a bit of cherishing from the air-stewardesses who stood by the plane door. I said: 'This is the first time I've flown, I may need extra attention during the flight'. The woman said in broken English, 'Well you won't get it from me, Englishman, I will be too busy flying the plane'. Mr Braithwaite went pale when I told him that the pilot was a woman. Then he remembered that he was an avowed feminist and said, 'Jolly good'. Apart from my putting my seat belt around my neck, the flight was uneventful. The passengers concentrated on hiding or eating the garlic sausage and cream crackers they were served for lunch; but they warmed up a bit when the vodka came round, and by the time we landed at the airport just outside Moscow some of them were disgustingly drunk and were not good examples of Western Capitalist Society.

The airport was ill-lit and a bit chaotic, especially when it came to collecting luggage. Nearly everybody had brought Marks and Spencers luggage so quite a few arguments ensued and suitcases had to be opened on the floor, and underwear examined before the rightful owners managed to sort out the 'Y' fronts from the silk culottes.

A big blonde woman stood in a gloomy corner of the arrival

lounge, holding a placard saying 'Intourist'. Five hundred people milled around her asking her questions.

Mr Braithwaite was bleating, 'I'm here to study milk distribution; my name is Ivan Braithwaite; am I in the right place?' The big blonde woman threw her placard down, clapped her hands and yelled 'All you foreigners are to be quiet. I am thinking I am in Moscow Zoo. Now you are to sit on your suitcases and wait.'

We waited and waited, more light bulbs went out and then in the gathering gloom four people arrived holding placards. One said, 'Siberia', one said 'Moscow'. Another one said 'Milk'. Mr Braithwaite and I stood by the 'Milk' placard and were eventually joined by two German dairy farmers, three retired English milkmen and a dyslexic American family who thought the sign said 'Minsk'. We were invited aboard a coach and our guide gave us a commentary on the Moscow suburbs we were passing through. The dyslexic American daughter peered out of the window and said, '*Gross* . . . where's the shops for chrissake?' Her mother said, 'Honey we're in the suburbs, the shops are downtown'. No shops could be seen, although one of the English ex-Milkmen spotted a dairy and applauded, which made our guide smile for the first time.

The hotel we stopped in was monolithic and swarming with every nationality on earth. Our guide screamed above the babble of languages, 'Be patient please while I am wrestling with your room keys. If I am lost forever you musk ask for Rosa. It is not my name but it will do. My name in Russian is too difficult for your clumsy tongues'. I fell asleep on the marble floor and woke hours later to the sound of a heavy metal key jangling in my ear.

Having checked the room for hidden microphones, I got into bed in my underwear because my grandma had warned me that secret television cameras were behind every mirror and I did not like the thought of my English genitals being mocked by unseen viewers. Mr Braithwaite fell instantly asleep in the bed next to me but I lay awake for hours listening to the trams outside the hotel and composing a poem in my head:

OH MOSCOW TRAMS

Are your wheels revolutionary?
Are your carriages forged from the steel
of conflict?

Are there bloodstains on the uncut moquette
of your seats?
Do your passengers keep to the tracks of
sacrifice and denial?
I, Adrian Mole will soon know
For in the morning I will be a fellow traveller.

In the morning Mr Braithwaite was nowhere to be seen. My
first thought was of abduction, but then I found a note on the
toilet seat, it said 'Enjoy your day, see you late tonight'. So, I was
alone in Moscow. I put a towel over the bathroom mirror before
attending to my toilette. Then, dressed in my best, I went down
in the lift to breakfast. The dining room was like an aircraft
hangar and was full of Communists eating black bread and
drinking coffee. I sat next to a very dark man in robes who was in
Moscow to buy gear-levers for his tractor factory in Africa. We
chatted for a while but we had little in common, so I turned to
my neighbour who turned out to be a Norwegian ... what a
stroke of luck! I spoke at great length about the Norwegian
leather industry but instead of being interested he got up and
left abruptly, leaving his breakfast half eaten. What a strange
moody race are the Scandinavians!

Rosa stomped into the dining room and ordered her party to get on
a coach. The American family, the three milkmen, the two German
farmers and me were taken to see the sights. We had ten minutes at
the Kremlin during which the American girl sold her camera, boots
and umbrella to a disaffected whining youth who complained about
his country, until Rosa hit him round the head and said, 'No other
country would let you in anyway. You are a disgraceful *pretty crook*.'
I think she must have meant *petty crook* because the youth was
very unattractive. Then we got back into the coach and went to
see the Bolshoi Theatre and the Olympic Stadium and the
residence of the British Ambassador and museums galore until it
was time for lunch.

The milkmen, Arthur, Arnold and Harry reeled across the
foyer and complained that they hadn't visited any dairies. They
had been drinking and it wasn't milk. Vodka I suspect. Rosa was
involved in a bitter argument with the American family who
wanted to know when they would be leaving for Minsk, so she
didn't listen to the milkmen's wild ramblings.

For lunch I joined a table of old aristocratic Englishwomen who were moaning that, for some inexplicable reason, they had spent the day touring Milk Distribution Centres. A deputation of them approached Rosa pleading to be taken to the Ballet.

The afternoon was free so I went for a walk in Gorky Park and looked for bodies. Loads of Russians were there walking about like English people do. Some were licking ice-creams, some were talking and laughing and some were sunbathing in their underwear with rouble notes on their noses to prevent sunburn. Indeed such was the heat that I was forced to go back to the hotel and take off my balaclava, mother's fur hat, mittens, big overcoat, four sweaters, shirt and two T-shirts.

In the evening we were coached off to the Opera where I and most of the Russians in the audience fell asleep, and the American girl sold her Sony headset. Mr Braithwaite came back very late and very drunk. Vodka doesn't smell but I *knew*. He got into bed without a word and snored very loudly. By now I was convinced he was a spy. The pattern continued throughout our three days in Moscow. I would wake up, find a note from Mr Braithwaite and so would be forced to throw myself on the mercy of 'Intourist'. By this time I was boggle-eyed with culture and longed for a bit of English apathy and gross materialism.

So, on my last afternoon in Moscow I did a brave thing. I went down into the bowels of the chandeliered metro in an attempt to find Moscow's shopping centre. I put a five kopek coin in a machine, got my ticket and descended into splendours of marble and gilt. Trains arrived every three minutes and took me and crowds of Russian people speeding along towards the shops. I attracted a few curious glances (spotty complexions are rare in Russia); but most people were reading heavy intellectual books with funny writing on them or learning piano concertos by Tchaikovsky.

I got out OK, found the shops and four hours later was returning to the hotel with a giant Russian doll which contained thirty other shrinking dolls inside it. Just like in *Tinker*, *Tailor* on TV. Pandora will get the biggest doll, and my father will get the smallest. As I entered the hotel lobby I saw Mr Braithwaite sitting on a sofa with a voluptuous Russian woman wearing a lime-green trouser suit and platform shoes. She was toying erotically with the flares of Mr Braithwaite's trousers, and I saw him catch her hand and lick the palm. God! It was a revolting sight! I felt like shouting 'Mr Braithwaite, pull yourself together, you're an Englishman'. When they saw me coming they sprang apart. She was introduced as Lara, an expert on the diseases of cow's udders.

I smiled coldly, then left them together, unable to witness the naked lust in their middle-aged eyes. Three roubles were burning a hole in my sock, so I removed my shoe, took the money out and summoned a taxi. 'Take me to Dostoyevsky's grave,' I cried. The taxi driver said: 'How much money do you have?' 'Three roubles' I replied. 'It ain't enough, sunshine' he said, 'Dostoyevsky's grave is in Leningrad'. I complimented him on his English and slunk back into the hotel, did my packing and prepared to fly back.

Lara was at the airport. She gave Mr Braithwaite a single carnation. There was a lot of palm licking and sighing and talk about their 'souls'. Mr Braithwaite gave Lara a copy of *The Dairy Farmer's Weekly*, two pairs of Marks & Spencers socks, a toilet roll and a packet of 'Bic' razors. She wept pitifully.

Mrs Braithwaite and Pandora were waiting beyond the barrier at Gatwick. As we walked towards them Mr Braithwaite sighed in a deep Russian Chekhovian way and said, 'Adrian, Mrs Braithwaite may not understand about Lara'. I said 'Mr Braithwaite, I do not understand about Lara myself. How *anyone* could have an affair with a woman wearing a lime-green trouser suit and platform shoes is beyond me'. This speech took me though the barrier and into the arms of Pandora and England. Oh, Leicester! Leicester! Leicester!

Mole on Lifestyle

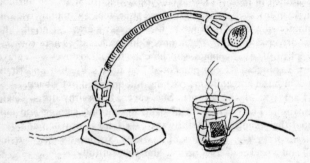

October 1985

I often look back on my callow youth, and when I do a smile flits across my now mature but pitted face. I hardly recognize the naïve boy I once was. To think that I once believed that Evelyn Waugh was a woman! Of course now, with a couple of 'O' levels under my belt, I am far more sophisticated and I know that Evelyn Waugh, should he be alive today, would be very, indeed, *dead* proud of his daughter, Auberon; because of course Evelyn is the *father* of Auberon and not as I once thought, the mother.

I occasionally glance through my early diaries and mourn for my lost innocence, for at the age of thirteen and three quarters, I thought it was sufficient to just have a *life*. I honestly didn't know then that you *can't* just have a life. You have to have a *lifestyle*. So my talk today is about 'Lifestyle', with particular reference to my own.

I will take you through a typical day. I will introduce you to my friends and family. I will refer fleetingly to my diet, toilet habits and my style of dress. My tastes in Art and Literature will be dwelt upon. At the end of my talk perhaps you will have an overview of my lifestyle. Incidentally, and by the way, 'overview' is just one of the thousands of words in my vocabulary, and with a bit of luck I will introduce other uncommon words to you, the listening masses. For I am solely aware of my duty via Radio Four to *educate* and entertain the great British public. For how else are they to rise up and take power if they don't understand the words of power? Or the power of words?

I have been told by my contemporaries that I am quite a trendsetter, although Pandora, the love of my life, maintains that *trendsetter* is a word only used by crumblies and people with one foot in the crematorium.

For instance my style of dress is idiosyncratic. Indeed it is personal to myself. Since radio is not television I will describe what I am wearing at the moment. I will start at the head and work down, to save any confusion. On my head I am wearing a balaclava helmet knitted by my ancient yet nimble-fingered Grandma. I am wearing the balaclava because my Father refuses to switch the central heating on until November 1st every year. He cares not that English summer does not exist anymore. As usual he is being selfish and thinking about paying the boring gas bill.

We move down. Around my neck is a silken cravat which was formerly owned by my dead Grandfather. It is a lucky cravat. My grandfather wore it at Epsom and won half-a-crown on a horse (whatever half-a-crown is). My shirt is proudly, indeed un-ashamedly, from a CND rummage sale. It once belonged to a Canadian lumberjack who had a sweat or, more politely, a perspiration problem, at least so my mother maintains. The smell doesn't bother me as I am used to it, although other people have complained. Under the shirt I wear an 'I love Cliff Richard' T-shirt. A reminder of when I was young and stupid. I *never* unbutton the Canadian shirt. My legs are clad in a pair of executive striped trousers bought at the closing down sale at Woolworths. On my feet are designer training shoes given to me by my best friend Nigel. Poor Nigel suffers from an obsession; he compulsively buys training shoes. The reasons are manifold:

a: He has to be the first in our small town to have the latest style.

b: Because of his inner rage Nigel is always yanking on laces too hard so that they break. He then passes the shoes on to me, claiming he can't be bothered to re-thread the new laces. My own impoverished family benefit from Nigel's impetuousness. We are all walking around in Nigel's new old shoes. Even Grandma is wearing a pair. They are too big for her but, with the wisdom of the old, she found a way of making them fit by stuffing the toes with toilet paper.

Under my training shoes I am wearing a pair of odd socks. One sock is white, one sock is black. No, think not that I am an absent-minded genius who doesn't notice what he puts on his feet. Perhaps I am a genius, but not an absent-minded one. No, my choice of hosiery is completely calculated. Indeed it is symbolic. The white socks stands for my inner purity and morality: for I am against violence and Polaris missiles and cruelty to battery hens. The black sock stands for the evil in my soul, such as wanting to go the whole hog with Pandora and fantasising about blowing up tower blocks (minus suicidal tenants of course).

Thus I am a walking dichotomy. On my feet I carry the problems of the world. Naturally the *hoi-polloi* do not recognise this salient fact. They cry out 'Eh ... yer wearin' odd socks!' To these crude rejoinders I simply reply, in my modulated tones, 'No, 'tis you who is wearing the odd socks, my friend.' Some of them walk away marvelling, although some of them, to be quite honest, don't.

As to personal adornments. I am wearing a gold-plated chain and locket. In the locket are the remains of a dried up autumn leaf. The leaf represents the frailty of the human condition. It was given to me by Pandora in a moment of autumnal ardour. Round my left wrist I wear a copper bangle which hopefully will guard against me contracting arthritis in old age. On my right wrist I wear a plastic waterproof watch which will allow me, should I feel the need, to dive to a depth of a hundred feet.

I have one other personal adornment that nobody knows about apart from me and one other person. It is a tiny tattoo secreted in a private part of my body. The tattoo says 'Mum and Dad' and dates from a time of their marital instability. I now regret my impetuosity because this tattoo will prevent me from partaking in nude sunbathing in the years to come. So, when I am a poet millionaire and I am lying on my personal Greek island I will be the only person amongst my guests to be wearing trunks.

However, the Greek Island home is for the future. My present domestic abode is a semi-detached house in a suburban cul-de-sac in the Midlands. Yes, like many of my fellow Britons, I live with a party wall between me and another family's intimate secrets. I will never understand why it is called a 'party' wall because *when* our next door neighbours throw a party every celebratory sound is heard. Tonic bottles unscrewed, cherries dropping into cocktails, women making brittle conversation, men being sick. So, if the purpose of a party wall is to prevent party noise from spilling into the house adjoining then I have this to say to the builders of Britain, 'You have failed, Sirs'. Now I will take you through one of my typical days.

The dog usually wakes me up at 7 o'clock or thereabouts. It is dead old now and has a weak bladder. I get out of bed, and in my underpants and vest I open the back door and let it out to cock its leg on our next door neighbour's lawn. I make myself a cup of coffee and take it back to bed with me while I read an edifying work of literature. At the moment I am reading *Wittgenstein Primer* written by T. Lowes MA. Trin. Dub. Sometimes for amusement I may turn to something less intellectually straining; *Wings On My Suitcase: personal adventures of an air hostess* introduced and edited by Gerard Tikell, is a good example. Then again, even reminiscences of air hostesses may prove to be too demanding at such an early hour. So for even lighter relief I will turn to my old *Beano* annuals.

I have a baby sister now and she usually climbs out of her cot at 7.30 dragging her wet nappy with her. She barges into my room and gabbles some childish gibberish to which I respond curtly, 'Go and wake Mummy and Daddy up, Rosemary'. I refuse to bastardise her name and call her 'Rosie'. She staggers out on her wobbly legs and beats her tiny fists on my parent's door. Muffled curses tell me that my parents are awake, so I quickly get out of bed and run into the bathroom before anyone else. I lie in my bath and ignore rattlings on the door and demands for entry. I insist on a period of quiet before I start my day. Anyway it's not my fault that the only lavatory is placed in the bathroom, is it? I've lost track of the times I've told my father to install a downstairs lavatory. After completing a meticulous toilette, topped off with liberal lashings of my father's after-shave mixed with my mother's Yardley water, I emerge from the bathroom, have a row with my parents, who are standing cross-legged outside the door, and go and go down to breakfast. I warm myself a frozen croissant and make a cup of Earl Grey Tea *sans* milk and sit down to study the world news. We take the *Guardian* and the *Sun* so I am quite an expert on the latest developments concerning 'whale conservation' and also the mammary development of Miss Samantha Fox. My parents are victims of Thatcherism so neither of them is working, which means they are able to hang about and linger over their breakfasts. Rosemary is a disgusting eater. I always leave the table before she starts on her porridge.

I go to my room, collect my books and study aids and go to college. I ignore most of my fellow students, who are usually thronging the corridors laughing about the previous night's drunken debauch. Instead I make my way to a classroom and quietly study before the lessons begin. For, while I am an intellectual (indeed almost a genius), at the same time I am not very clever and so need to study harder than anyone else.

I spend each break with Pandora. We usually talk about world events. Pandora only wears black clothes as she is in mourning for the world. This has led to her being called 'Barmy Braithwaite' by unthinking morons amongst the student body and also, I regret to report, some of the academic staff. We usually walk home together and on the way call in to see Bert Baxter who is now the oldest man on the electoral roll. Pandora takes Sabre the alsatian for an angry prowl around the recreation ground, while I clean Bert up and listen to his incoherent ramblings about Lenin and the 'needs of the Proletariat to rise up'. (Bert refuses to die until he sees the fall of Capitalism so it looks as though Bert will be with us for quite a while yet, unfortunately.) When Bert and Sabre have been pacified and fed and watered, Pandora and I walk home together. We part at the entrance to my cul-de-sac and she strolls off to her tree-lined avenue and her detached, book-lined house and I go to my previously described more horrible domestic living unit.

The warm scent of home baking does not greet me as I enter the kitchen. So I create my own smell by baking scones. Here is my recipe but remember before you rush for pencil and paper that the recipe is copyright and owned by me, Adrian Mole. So, should you wish to bake scones to this recipe then you will need to send money to me.

A. MOLE'S SCONES

Ingredients
4 oz flour or metric equivalent
2 oz butter or metric equivalent
2 oz sugar or metric equivalent
1 egg (eggs are still only eggs)

Method
Beat up all the ingredients. Make a tin greasy, throw it all
in. Turn oven to number 5. Wait until scones are higher
than they were. Should be 12 minutes, but keep opening
oven door every 30 seconds.

So, crunching, on my fresh-from-the-oven scones, I wind down
from my day. At this time I may give Rosemary a few moments
attention. Last night I built the GPO Tower from her lego
bricks, but while my back was turned Rosemary smashed it to
pieces, and then had the nerve to laugh amongst the rubble. This
is typical of her behaviour. I am sure she is going to grow up to
be psychotic. She is already quite unmanageable. She empties
drawers, switches the television knobs on and off, throws her soft
toys down the lavatory pan and flies into a rage if she is restrained
in any way. I have urged my parents to take her to the Child
Guidance Clinic before it is too late, but my mother defends her
saying, 'Rosie is quite normal, Adrian, all toddlers behave like
Attila the Hun. Why do you think so many mothers are on
tranquillisers?' In the early evening I make a point of watching a
soap opera or two. I think it is very important for us intellectuals
to keep in touch with popular culture. We cannot live in ivory
towers, unless of course the ivory towers have a television aerial
on the roof.

My parents are trying to save their marriage by playing badminton together on alternative Wednesdays. Otherwise, apart from
this fortnightly outing, they clutter the house up in the evenings
so I am forced to keep in my room or take to the streets. I honestly
can't understand how they can bear each other's company. Their
conversation consists of moaning about money and whining about
wages – the wages they haven't got.

I make few demands on them. All I require is a jar of multi-
vitamins once a week plus clean linen and courtesy. However I

wouldn't like you to switch off thinking that I'm not fond of my parents. In my own way I'm very close to them. It's hard not to be. We live in a small house. They do have their good points. My father is quite a wit after a couple of glasses of vodka, and my mother is known for her compassion towards other married women. In fact she is in the middle of organising a local group of them. I read somewhere that it is important for families to have bodily contact, so I make a point of patting my parents' shoulders as I pass by. It costs nothing and seems to please them. However at 8 o'clock, when the lounge is full of cigarette smoke, I make my excuses and leave for the outside world.

I sometimes meet up with Barry Kent and we chat about which of his friends is in court, and who's in borstal. Occasionally we discuss Barry's poetry; he was taught to read and write during his last period in a detention centre. It was a progressive place that had a poet in residence so instead of breaking rocks Barry was forced to split infinitives and then put them together again. Some of his stuff is quite good, primitive of course, but then Barry is practically a certified moron so it is only to be expected. Still, at least he's making a living out of his poetry. In the guise of 'Baz the Skinhead Poet' he tours pubs and rock venues, and shouts poetry at the audience. Sometimes they shout back and then there's a fight. Barry always wins.

On my way home I call in to see Pandora who is usually sitting under the anglepoise lamp bent over 'A' level homework. On the wall above her desk are two notices written in pink neon marker pen. One says, 'GET TO OXFORD OR DIE' the other says 'GO TO CAMBRIDGE AND LIVE'. There are five exclamation marks after each of them. We share a cup of cocoa, or if her parents are out, gin and tonic. Then we kiss passionately for about five minutes, longer if it's a gin night, and I make my way home racked with latent sexuality. On such occasions I am pleased to find it's raining. There's nothhing like a cold shower to ease sexual frustration.

By 11 o'clock I am in bed with the dog, reading, with a digestive biscuit and a cup of cocoa on my bedside table. It isn't the lifestyle I would choose for myself. Given the choice I would opt for a mixture of Prince Andrew and Prince Edward's social life, Ted Hughes's working life and the Wham or Mick Jagger's romantic life. But at least I've *got* a life. Some people haven't.

And I'm on the verge, the very kerb of the dual carriageway of Fate. Will I go one way towards London, celebrity and media attention? . . . Or will I go the other way, towards the provinces, and be forced to write letters to the local paper in order to see my name in print? A third possibility occurs to me. I could break down at a roundabout and remain, unsung, in limbo.

But I mustn't burden you, kind listener, with my introspective musings. And anyway I shall have to finish now – it's started raining and my jeans are on the line.

Mole's Prizewinning Essay

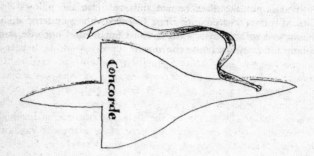

Concorde

MONDAY

Oh joy! . . . Oh rapture! . . . At last I have made my mark on the world of literature. My essay entitled 'A Day in the Life of an Air Stewardess' has won second prize in the British Airways Creative Writing Competition.

My prizes are: A Concorde-shaped bookmark inscribed in gold leaf by Melvyn Bragg, a hostess apron which has been donated by 'The Society for Distressed Air Stewardesses', and £50.

Here, for posterity, is my prizewinning essay.

A DAY IN THE LIFE OF AN AIR STEWARDESS
BY A. MOLE

Jonquil Storme opened her languorous blue eyes and looked at the clock. 'Oh drat and bother', she expectorated. The clock said seven o'clock and Jonquil was due at Heathrow Airport at seven fifteen, where she was in charge of Concorde.

Jonquil stretched out her lissome white hand and picked up the phone. Her other hand dialled the number: with her other hand she fondled an orchid that stood next to her bed in a jam jar.

'Hi, Brett!' she said into the receiver . . . 'Jonquil here, darling. I'm late, our night of passion wore me out and caused me to oversleep.' Brett's manly chuckle reverberated down the phone.

'OK Jonquil', he guffawed, 'I'll tell the passengers that there is snow on the runway. Take your time my darling!'

Jonquil put the phone down and sank into the pillows that were still impregnated with Brett's hair oil. She wondered if she would ever get to marry Brett, the Captain of Concorde, and whether the excuse about snow on the runway would be believed. After all it was *July*. Thus ruminating, Jonquil showered in the shower and dressed in the dressing room. Soon she was soignée and was climbing into her Maserati open-topped sports car to the gapes of ordinary dingy passers by.

Soon she was wriggling up the steps of Concorde in her high heeled shoes. Brett met her at the door of the plane and gave her a French kiss. The passengers didn't mind at all, in fact they applauded and cheered. A jolly American shouted 'God bless you, Captain!'

Brett flashed his manly teeth and went to the front of the plane and switched the engine on. Jonquil went round smiling at the passengers and opening jars of caviar. Soon the champagne corks were popping and the passengers were lying about in stupours. The flight was smooth and without hazards and when Concorde reached New York Brett asked Jonquil to be his bride. So, after having blood tests for diseases, Brett and Jonquil were married in the elevator of the Empire State Building. Soon it was time to turn Concorde round and go home to London. Jonquil was dead proud of her new gold ring and Brett flew the plane better than he ever had before.

As Jonquil got into bed that night she said to herself, 'What a lucky girl I am. To think I almost became a Domestic Science teacher'. She looked at Brett's matted black hair on the Laura Ashley pillow and smiled. It had been the most exciting day of her life.

THE END (Copyright World Wide owned by A. Mole)

The Sarah Ferguson Affair

Thursday July 17th

I'm sick of reading about how handome Prince Andrew is. To me he looks like the morons studying bricklaying and plastering at college, there is something about his neck that cries out for a hod of bricks. And those big white ruthless teeth! It makes me shudder to think of them nibbling at Fergie's defenceless neck. So some women like tall, well-built men who can fly helicopters and have gob-smacking bank accounts and Coutts gold cards. But personally I think Fergie is throwing herself away on him.

Miss Sarah Ferguson was born to be the wife of Adrian Mole. I have written to tell her so, and to implore her to change her mind before 23rd July. As yet I have received no reply. She must be agonising over her decision: 'Riches, glamour and publicity with Prince Andrew, or poverty, introspection and listening to poetry with Adrian Mole' – not an easy choice.

Sarah Ferguson, oh Sarah Ferguson,
Your name is on my lips constantly.
Don't marry Andy, his legs are bandy.
Come to Leicester, come to Leicester, marry me!
Leave the palace, grab a taxi,
I'll be waiting at the end of the M1.
We'll go to my house, meet my parents,
I know the dog and you will get along.

Friday July 18th

No letter from Sarah Ferguson today.

I have rung Buckingham Palace but the (no doubt powdered and bewigged) flunkey refused to let me speak to her. He said, 'Miss Ferguson is taking no calls from strangers.' I said, 'Listen, my man, I am no *stranger* to Miss Ferguson, she is my soul mate.' I'm not sure but I could have sworn the flunky muttered, 'Arsehole mate,' before he slammed the phone down. There is nothing else to do but go to Buckingham Palace and tackle her face to face.

I have sent a Telemessage to my ginger-haired love:

Sarah, I am coming to you. Meet me at the Palace gate at high noon.
Yours with unvanquished love,
Adrian Mole (18¼).
P.S. I will be wearing sunglasses, and carrying a Marks and Spencer carrier-bag.

Saturday   July 19th
BUCKINGHAM PALACE, 1.30PM.

She did not come. I asked a mounted policeman if Sarah was at home. He said, 'Yes, she's inside having waving lessons from the Queen Mother.' I asked him if he would deliver a note to her from me, but he got distracted by a coach-load of excitable Japanese tourists who were measuring his horse and taking down its specifications. No doubt they are going to copy it and flood the world with cheap police horses. Will we English never learn?

I made my way home to the dreary provinces by train. An old fat woman kept up a non-stop monologue about her plans for the royal wedding day. I wanted to cry out, 'You old fat fool, you will be watching an empty screen on the 23rd because *there will be no royal wedding*. So cancel your order for two dozen crusty cobs and a crate of assorted bottles of pop.' I *wanted* to cry these words out but, of course, I didn't; people would have thought I was a teenage lunatic obsessed with Sarah Ferguson, whereas of course I am anything but.

Sunday   July 20th

Sarah has not replied to my letter yet.
   Perhaps she has run out of stamps.

Monday   July 21st

I asked the postman if there was anything for me from Buckingham Palace. He replied, 'Ho, has Ted Hughes croaked it? H'are you the next Poet Laureate? H'if you h'are, may I h'offer my h'utmost congratulations?'
   No wonder England's going to the dogs with public servants of his calibre.

7pm. Pandora Braithwaite rang from Leningrad tonight.
   I asked her how she was getting on with her Russian lessons. She said, 'Oh, amazingly well, I joined in a most stimulating debate in the turnip queue this morning. Workers and intellectuals discussed the underlying symbolism of *The Cherry Orchard*. I ventured the opinion, in Russian of course, that the cherries represented the patriarchal balls of Mother Russia, thus proving that Chekhov was A C/D C.'
   I asked how the assembled geniuses in the turnip queue had reacted to her analysis. Pandora said, 'Oh, they failed to understand it, bloody peasants!' The line started to go faint, so Pandora shouted, 'Adrian, video-tape the royal wedding for me, darling.' Then the phone went dead, and Pandora was lost to me.

Tuesday   July 22nd

My Sarah was on the front page of the paper this morning, wearing a most indecent low-cut dress. That oaf Andrew was quite openly leering at her cleavage. When Sarah is my wife I shall insist that she wears cardigans buttoned up to the neck.

I'm with the Moslems on this one.

No letter. No hope left, the wedding is tomorrow, I shall not watch it. I shall walk the streets clutching my despair. Oh God! Oh Sarah!

Wednesday   July 23rd

MY SARAH'S WEDDING DAY

Sarah! Sarah! Sarah!

I sobbed into my pillow for so long this morning that the feathers stuck together and formed lumps like bits of dead chickens. Eventually I rose, dressed in black, and made a simple yet nutritious breakfast. My mother came down and through cigarette smoke said, 'What's up with your face?'

I replied quietly, yet with immense dignity, 'I am in the deepest despair, Mother.'

'Why, are your piles playing you up again?' She coughed.

I left the kitchen, shaking my head from side to side in a pitying fashion, whilst at the same time saying, *sotto voce*, 'Lord, have mercy on the philistines I am forced to live with, for they know not what they say.'

My father overheard and said, 'Oh, got bleedin' religion now, has he?'

I passed Grandma on her way to our house. She was carrying a tea-tray piled high with little fancy cakes, iced with the entwined initials 'FA.' Grandma was in her best clothes; her hat swayed with exotic and long extinct birds' feathers, she was wearing net gloves and a fox's claw brooch. She was ecstatically happy. She cried out, 'Hello, Adrian, my little love, have you got a kiss for your Grandma?' I kissed her rouged cheek and walked on before she saw the tears in my eyes. She croaked, 'Happy royal wedding day, Adrian.'

I passed the Co-op where the Union Jack hung upside-down, and the Sikh temple where it was hung correctly. I bought a commemorative Andy and Fergie mug and blacked Prince Andrew's big-jawed face out with a black marker pen, then I sat on the side of the canal, put some flowers in the mug and wrote a last letter to Sarah:

Dear Princess Sarah,
You will soon tire of the loon you married (he looks like the sort to hog the bedclothes to me). As soon as you grow even a little weary of him, remember I am waiting for you here in Leicester. I cannot promise you riches (although I have £139.37 in the Market Harborough Building Society) but I can offer intellectual chit-chat and my body, which is almost unsullied and is years younger than your husband's.

Well, Sarah, I won't keep you as I expect your husband is shouting oafishly for your attention.

I remain, Madam,
Your most humble and obedient servant,
Adrian Mole.

The Mole/Kent letters

To:
Barry Kent
ITK SR
Unit 2
Ridley Young Offenders Centre
Ridley-Upon-The-Dour   Leicester
LINCOLNSHIRE   April 2 1987

Dear Baz,
It was good to see you on Tuesday. The prison uniform suits
you. You should wear more blue when you get out. Also Baz,
non-smoking seems to agree with you, your breath was not as
repellent as usual, why not give up for good? I'm sorry I have
to be the bearer of bad news but somebody has to tell you that
your fiancée Cindy is living with Gary Fullbright, the body
builder, remember him? He won the 'Mr Muscle' competition in
1985. Cindy is expecting his baby in four months time. I expect
you have just reeled back with the shock, so I'll give you time
in which to recover.

　　Baz, Cindy isn't worthy of your love, don't for God's sake
grieve over her. Her fingernails were never clean, and she had

no dress sense at all. I will never forget that black rubber outfit she wore (with scuffed stilletoes and laddered fishnet tights) to your father's funeral. Also, Baz, she had the intellectual capacity of a withered rubber band. I was chatting to her once about Middle Eastern politics and it became clear to me that she thought Mr Arafat was the Arab equivalent of Mr Kipling – a type of foreign biscuit.

Onto other subjects. Nigel sends his regards, he would like to come and see you but doesn't trust himself not to burst into tears at the prison gate. Also he thinks his appearance might startle your fellow prisoners and leave you open to a certain amount of bullying in the dormitory. He is now a bald-headed Buddhist and wears orange robes and orange flip-flops (in all weathers). But, apart from these superficial changes he is still the same old Nigel, although, sadly, he got the sack from the bank: religious persecution is still alive and well in this country, I fear.

Nothing much has happened here; provincial life drags its weary way through the hours and days and months and years. I think it's time I left the library, Baz. The attitude of the general public towards the books they borrow is contemptuous. Yesterday I found a rasher of bacon inside *A Dictionary of Philosophy*. It had obviously been used as a bookmark. Further on, in the same book, I found a note addressed to a milkman:

Dear Milkman

I'd be most terribly grateful if, from now on you would be as kind as to leave one further pint of skimmed milk. That is to say dating from today (Tuesday) I would like you to deliver two pints of skimmed milk per day. I hope you will join me in my happiness at the news that my wife has returned to me. I know how much you and she enjoyed your little early morning doorstep chats. Alas, I fear I do not have my wife's common touch. However, I am fully appreciative of your achievement in delivering our milk in all weather conditions, and if, in the past, I have given the impression of being surly and uncommunicative, I'm sorry. I'm not at my best in the early morning. I am plagued with a recurring nightmare: I am lecturing to a Hall full of students

when half-way through I realise I am naked. Perhaps
you have similar disturbed nights? From what I've
seen of you from my bedroom window, you seem to
be a sensitive person. You have an intelligent mien.

Don't be offended, milkman, but I would guess
that you have had little education, so, why not let us
help you to educate yourself by browsing along our
well stocked bookshelves? You are welcome to borrow
any book – apart from the first editions which need
very careful handling – normally I would suggest that
the ill-educated use the library but our local branch is
staffed by cretins.

Do think about this proposition and communicate
either 'yea' or 'nay' at the bottom of this page.

    With warmest regards,
      Richard Blythe-Samson (No. 19)

Nay. You owe me 6 weeks money. Milkman.

Well Baz, I'll sign off now. Hope you don't take it too hard
about Cindy, but somebody had to tell you and who better than
your old mate,
    Adrian 'Brains' Mole
P.S. It's my birthday today. I am nineteen and God am I
weary of this life.

                Unit 2
                April 9th 1987
Dear 'Brains'
Cindy as wrote to me and said it is lies about her and Gary
Fullbright and she said she is not in the club she as just put on
some wait because of working in the hot spud shop she swears
on her dogs head that she stills love me and she is weighting
for me. The reeson she as not bin to see me is becars she has
had migraine you have got a nerv to critisize her you should
look in the mirrer sometime at yourself I av herd bad things
about Pandorra that she is havving it off with allsorts including
china men and yugoslavians their is a screw in hear who as got
a son at oxford university he nows pandorra an he says she is a
slagg wye did you tell me that stuff about the milkman it was

drivval I am goinng mad in hear I want to now what is goinng
on with the lads outside did spig get sentensed yet as marvin
got parrole things like that do not bothur writin if you write
drivvel and if you come to see me argain dress up smart I was
ashammd last time and I got greif from the lads after visitting.
I told them you was not all their but I still got greif my cell
mate is a fat slob is name is clifton there is not room to move
when he is standing up I am aksing for a transferr he is the
fart champion of the prison gary fullbright is lookinggg for
you

    stay cool

    Baz

April 18th 1987

Dear Baz

How dare you infer that Pandora is a slag? She mixes with
Chinese, Russians and Yugoslavians because she is taking
Russian, Serbo–Croatian and Chinese at Oxford. She no doubt
entertains them in her rooms until quite late at night, but
believe me Baz she is not engaging in sexual intercourse with
them. I know for a *fact* that Pandora is a virgin. Unlike you
and Cindy, Pandora and I have a completely honest relationship.
If she were no longer a virgin I would be the first to know. I
will make no further comment on the Cindy/Gary situation
apart from saying that I saw them *together* in *Mothercare* buying
a *baby's bath* and two maternity bras, but from now on my lips
are sealed. I'm sorry you are of the opinion that parts of my
last letter were drivel. I thought the note to the milkman would
amuse you and take your mind off your present surroundings. I
don't blame you for being bitter, though. Two years imprisonment
for criminal damage to a privet hedge does seem harsh. I'm
scared to *cough* in the street these days in case I get done under
the new Public Order Act.

    I haven't had a poem from you for ages Baz. I hope you
haven't given up scribbling. You have a rare, muscular sort of
talent which you musn't waste. You once had a lucrative career
as 'Baz, the Skinhead Poet' on the poetry club circuit. Why not
take this opportunity to write a new collection?

    Yours

    Adrian 'Brains' Mole

May 12 1986

Dear Brains
BANGED UP
Ok. I done it
I damaged a hedge
I broke a few twigs
A few leaves fell off
Hedges grow again.

They said it was privet
in court, in evidence.
Me, I didn't know
I was falling, drunk.
I grabbed this green thing
I fell in, got scratched
couldn't get out again.
The hedges owner called 999.
An old bloke he was
If he'd pulled me out I
woulda gone.
Instead the filth come.
'Hello Baz, you've broken
an hedge.
That's criminal damage, vandalism, wanton,
mindless'
Honest, it was a few twigs, a few green
leaves.
It needed cutting,
'I shan't press charges' said the old man.
But it was too late,
the law had started its machinery up.
It couldn't stop.
Not until the prison gate
opened and took me in.
'Criminal damage to an hedge'
I'm a joke in here.
Psychopaths get more respect
the old man, he was in court.
He wasn't happy. He looked at me
in the dock. His face said,

'I'm not happy.'
I gave him a salute one man to
another.
Then I went down.

BAZ KENT
(The Skinhead Poet)

June 30th 1987

Dear Baz

Its some months since I wrote to you I know but I've been
very busy with my opus, 'Tadpole', which I am hoping to get
published either in *The Literary Review* or *The Leicester
Mercury*, whichever pays the most. 'Tadpole' is the story-in-
rhyme of a tadpole's difficult journey to froghood. It is 10,000
words in length so far and the tadpole in question is still in the
canal squirming about. So, Baz, as a fellow poet, you can see
my problem. All my waking hours – apart from those in the
stinking library where I am forced to earn my living – are
spent writing. I care nothing for food or rest or taking hot
baths. I haven't changed my clothes in months (apart from
socks and underpants); what care I for the outward trappings of
petit bourgeois society?

There have been complaints at work about my appearance:
Mr Nuggett, Deputy Librarian, said yesterday, 'Mole, I am
giving you the afternoon off. Go home, bathe, wash your hair
and change into clean clothes!'

I replied (with dignity), 'Mr Nuggett, would you have spoken
to Byron, Ted Hughes, or Larkin as you've just spoken to me?'
He was dumbfounded. All he could think to say eventually was
'You used the wrong tense as far as Ted Hughes is concerned,
because, unless there has been a tragic accident or a sudden
illness, I believe Mr Hughes to be most vigorously alive.'

What a pedant!

Your poem 'Banged Up' was quite nice. Must stop now,
'The Tadpole' calls.

Hey ho.

A. Mole

P.S. Cindy has called the baby Carlsburg.

Adrian Mole Leaves Home

Monday   June 13th

I had a good, proper look at myself in the mirror tonight. I've always wanted to look clever, but at the age of twenty years and three months I have to admit that I look like a person who has never even *heard* of Jung or Updike. I went to a party last week and a girl of sixteen felt obliged to tell me who Gertrude Stein was. I tried to cut her off – inform her that I was conversant with Ms Stein, but I started to choke on a cheese and tomato pizza so the opportunity was lost.

So, the mirror showed me myself, as I am. I'm dark but not dark enough to be interesting: no Celtic broodiness. My eyes are grey. My eyelashes are medium length, nothing exciting here. My nose is high-bridged, but it's a Roman centurion's nose, rather than a senator's. My mouth is thin. Not cruel and thin, and it gets a bit sloppy towards the edges. I *have* got a chin, though. No mean achievement considering my pure English genes.

Since I was a callow youth I've spent a fortune on my skin. I've rubbed and applied hundreds of chemicals and lotions onto and into the offending pustulated layer of epidermis, but alas! to no avail. Sharon Botts, my present girl friend, once described my

complexion as being like 'one of them bubble sheets what inconti-
nent people use to protect their mattress.'

As can be seen from the above reproduction of Sharon's speech
her knowledge of correct English grammar is minimal, therefore I
have taken it upon myself to educate her. I am Henry Higgins to
her Eliza Dolittle.

She is worth it. Her measurements are 42–30–38. She's a big
girl. Unfortunately she measures thirty inches round the tops of
her thighs, and fifteen inches round her ankles. But isn't that just
like life? The most beautiful and exotic places on earth also
attract mosquitoes don't they? Nothing and nobody is perfect, are
they? Apart from Madonna, of course.

Anyway, I suggested to Sharon that she would look wonderful
in floor length skirts but she said 'Who the bleedin' hell d'you
think I am, sodding Queen Victoria?'

Summer will soon be here and I have a recurring nightmare
that Sharon decides to buy and *wear* a mini skirt. In my dream
she takes my arm and we stroll down the crowded high street.
The public stop and stare, guffawing breaks out. A three-year-old
child points at Sharon and says, 'Look at the lady's fat legs.' At
this point I wake up sweating and with a pounding heart.

You may be wondering why I, Adrian Mole, a provincial
intellectual working in a library and Sharon Botts, a provincial
dullard working in a laundry are having a relationship. The
answer is, sex. I have grown to be rather keen on it and find it
difficult to stop doing it now I've started.

Sharon and I were both virgins when we met which is a piece
of good fortune too rare to overlook. What with AIDS and
herpes rampaging round the world. But sex is where our relationship begins and ends. Sharon is as bored by my conversation
as I am by hers, so we go elsewhere for that. She goes to see her
mother and five sisters, and I go to see Pandora Braithwaite, who
is the true love of my life.

I've loved Pandora since 1980. Two years ago we went our
separate ways, Pandora to Oxford to study Russian, Chinese and
Serbo-Croat, and me to stamp books in the library in the town
where I was born. I chose library work because I wanted to
immerse myself in literature. Ha! The library I work in could
easily double as the headquarters of the local Philistines Society.

I have never had a literary conversation at work, never. Neither with the staff nor the borrowers of the books.

My days are spent taking books off shelves and putting books back on the shelves. Occasionally I am interrupted by members of the public asking mad questions: 'Is Jackie Collins here?' To this I reply, after first glancing round the library in an exaggerated fashion. 'Highly unlikely, madam. I believe she lives in Hollywood.'

Sometimes my mother visits me at work, although I have given her strict instructions not to do so. My mother cannot modulate her voice. Her laugh could pickle cabbage. Her appearance is striking and now, in her forty-third year, merging on the eccentric. She has no colour sense. She wears espadrilles. Summer and winter. She disobeys the No Smoking signs and enters doors labelled, Private Staff Only.

My father never visits the library. He claims that the sight of so many books make him ill.

Unfortunately, I am still living at home with my parents (and my five-year-old sister Rosie). This *ménage à quatre* co-exists in a sullen atmosphere. Half the time I feel like somebody in a Chekhov play. We've even got a cherry tree in the front garden.

I've tramped the streets looking for my own cheap apartment. I put an advertisement in the local paper.

> Writer requires a room, preferably garret.
> Non-smoker, respectable.
> Clean habits. References supplied.
> Rent no more than £10 a week.

I received three replies: the first from an old lady who offered me rent free accommodation in return for helping her to feed her thirty-seven cats and nine dogs. The second from an anonymous person who wished to 'thoroughly irrigate my colon'. The third from a Mr QZ Diablo.

I went to inspect the room offered by Mr Diablo. As soon as he opened the front door I knew I would not enjoy living in close proximity to him. Beards irritate me at the best of times and Mr Diablo's cascaded down from his chin and came to a straggling end somewhere near to his navel. However I allowed him to lead the way up the swaying staircase. The room was at the top of the house. It was part-furnished, with a bed and a structure resembling an altar. Purple cloaks hung from hooks in the walls. Mr QZ Diablo said, 'Of course I shall need this room on Thursday evenings for our meetings. We finish just after midnight, would that be too inconvenient?'

'I'm afraid it would,' I said. 'I'd prefer to sort of have the place to myself.'

'You *could* join us,' he suggested, helpfully. 'We're a jolly crowd, though cursed with a diabolical public image.'

I stared down at a red stain. It was on a multi-coloured carpet that only a mad man or mad woman could have designed, possibly in a workshop within the high walls of an institution.

'Only animal blood,' said QZ, reassuringly poking the stain with his bare big toe. 'We don't go in for human sacrifice,' he said comfortingly.

I said the words of the timid and cowardly: 'I'll think about it.'

'Yes you must,' said my host. He then led me down the stairs and out to freedom. I didn't want to tramp the streets on Thursday evenings and neither did I want to wear a purple cloak and mutter incantations over an animal sacrifice with a jolly crowd once a week. So I didn't go and live under Mr QZ Diablo's roof. This was last week.

Tonight my mother said, 'Look, when are you leaving home? We want to let your room'.

My mother is not an advocate of the tactful approach. It transpired that she had answered an advertisement from the University and arranged to act as a landlady to two male students. This would give her an income of seventy pounds a week. Fifty pounds more than she receives from me. No contest. The two students (of engineering) are moving into my room on Friday afternoon. A new single bed has been purchased and is leaning accusingly against the wall of my bedroom.

Tuesday   June 14th

I found it hard to concentrate on my work today. The Head Librarian, Mrs Froggatt (fat, fifty and with the colouring and features of a jaundiced badger), said at lunchtime, 'Mole you've moved all our Jane Austens from the great English Classics section to the Light Romance Section, pray explain.' I snapped, 'In my opinion they have been given their proper classification. Jane Austen's novels are merely trashy romances read only by snobbish, brainless cretins.' How was I to know that 'Jane Austen, Her Genius, Her Relevance to England in the 1950's' was the subject of Mrs Froggatt's dissertation for her degree in English Literature many years before I was born? As I've said earlier in my diary, we didn't discuss books or writers in the library.

That afternoon I was called into Mrs Froggatt's room. She informed me that the library was cutting down on staff due to Governmental financial restraints. I asked how many staff would be asked to leave. 'Just the one,' said the Jane Austen admirer, 'and, since you were the last to come, Adrian, you must also be the first to go.' Homeless and jobless!

Wednesday   June 15th

When I got home from work, where I was shunned and vilified (it turned out that all the library staff like Jane Austen), I went to my room to find that my Mother had cleared out my toy cupboard. Pinky, my pink and grey rabbit, was nowhere to be seen! I burst into the kitchen, where my mother was entertaining her neighbours to tea. Through a thick smog of cigarette smoke I looked my mother in the eye and said, 'Where's Pinky?' 'He's outside in the dustbin,' she said. She had the grace to drop her eyes. She knew she'd done me and Pinky a terrible wrong. 'How could you?' I said coldly. I flung open the door that led to the yard. Pinky's threadbare ears were visible sticking out of a black plastic bag. I pulled him out of the bag and dusted him down, then I re-crossed the kitchen and slammed the door. Huge gusts of female laughter could be heard behind me as I ran up the stairs.

Pinky is exactly the same age as me. He was purchased by my drunken father on the day of my birth. Pinky only has, only ever had, two legs; but he is still a rabbit. It is beyond my comprehension how anyone could even *think* about disposing of him. I packed my suitcase there and then. I placed Pinky carefully in a carrier bag. I went into the kitchen. I addressed my mother. 'I'm going. I shall send for my books.' I went.

Thursday   June 16th

Living here with Sharon and eight other Botts is a nightmare. I am supposed to be sleeping on the living room couch but the Botts don't go to bed. They stop up, in the living room, talking and shouting and quarrelling and watching violent videos. A few Botts, Sharon was one, went to bed at 3am but the remaining Botts had noisy discussions about babies, contraception, menstruation, death, funerals, the price of ice-cream, Clement Freud, The Queen, the man in the moon, dogs, cats, gerbils, various aches and pains they had suffered from, clothes they had tired of. Then, after an hour of malicious gossip about a woman I'd never heard of called Cynthia Bell, I closed my eyes, feigning sleep. Would they take the hint and go to bed? No.

'Funny looking bugger isn't he?' said Mrs Bott. 'What does our Sharon see in him?'

Was she referring to me?

'He's supposed to be dead brainy,' said her eldest daughter Marjorie, 'though I ain't seen no evidence of brains. He just *sits* there looking like a wet weekend.'

'He's a randy little sod,' said Farah, the youngest Bott, 'our Sharon reckons 'e can do it four times a night.'

'Do what?' screeched Mrs Bott, 'thread a needle?'

The Botts screeched and cackled for quite some time then finally, after a lot of noisy stair climbing, went to bed. Dawn was breaking as I stretched out on the couch and went to sleep.

At 6am Mr Bott, a timid and, not surprisingly, quiet man, came into the living room and switched on breakfast television.

''Ope I'm not disturbin' you,' he said politely.

'Not at all,' I said. I got up, retrieved my suitcase from the hall, and walked out into the cool morning air.

I was on the first stage of my journey to Oxford, where I intended to fall on Pandora's neck and plead for sanctuary.

Friday   June 17th

It was lunchtime when I got to Pandora's flat. Pandora wasn't in. She was having a tutorial. However, a languorous youth called Julian Twyselton-Fife *was* in. We shook hands. I've grasped firmer rubber gloves.

To make conversation I asked him what he was doing at Oxford.

'Oh I'm just farting about,' he said airily. 'I shan't sit my finals, only people who intend to *work* do that.'

He offered me Turkish coffee. I accepted, not wanting to appear provincial. When it came I regretted my inferiority complex. I asked if he shared the flat with Pandora.

'I'm married to Pandora,' he said. 'She's Mrs Twyselton-Fife. I did it as a favour to her last week. Pandora has this dinky little theory that first marriages should be gotten over with quickly, so we intend to divorce quite soon. We don't *love* each other,' he added. Then, 'In fact, I prefer my own sex.' 'Good,' I said, 'because I intend to be Pandora's second husband.'

Pinky had slid out of his carrier bag. 'I say, who *is* that divine creature?' brayed Twyselton-Fife. He grasped Pinky to his tweedy bosom. I said, 'It's Pinky.'

He crooned, 'Oh Pinky, you're a handsome one, aren't you? Now, don't deny it, sir, accept the compliment!'

Pandora came in. She looked clever and lovely.

'Hello Mrs Twyselton-Fife.' I said.

'Oh, you know then?' she said.

'Can I stay here?' I asked.

'Yes,' she said.

So that was that. I am now in a *ménage à trois*. With a bit of luck it will soon be a *ménage à deux*. For ever.

Saturday   June 18th

I phoned home this morning. One of the engineering lodgers answered. 'Hello, Martin Muffet speaking.'

'Martin *Muffett*!' I said.

'Yes,' he said, 'and spare the jokes about tuffetts and spiders will you?'

'I wish to speak to my mother, Mrs Mole', I said.

'Pauline,' he bellowed before banging the phone down on the hall table. I heard the click of my mother's lighter, then she spoke.

'Adrian, where are you?'

'I'm in Oxford.'

'At the University?'

'Not *studying* at the University, no, that honour was denied me. If I'd had a complete set of Children's Encyclopedias perhaps I'd . . .'

'Oh don't start on that again. It's not my fault you didn't get your A' levels . . .'

'I'm here with Pandora and her husband.'

'*Husband?*'

I could image the expression on my mother's face. She would be looking like a starving dog which was being offered a piece of sirloin steak.

'Who? When? Why?' asked my mother, who in the unlikely event of being asked for her recreation by the publishers of *Who's Who*, would be honour bound to reply: 'My main recreation is gossiping.'

'Do Pandora's parents know that she's married?' asked my mother, still agog.

'No,' I replied. Then I thought, 'But it won't be long before they do, will it, mother?'

In the afternoon, Pandora and I went shopping. Julian Twyselton-Fife was lying in bed reading a Rupert Bear Annual. As we were leaving, he shouted, 'Don't forget the honey, darlings.'

Once we were outside, on the street, I told Pandora that she must start divorce proceedings. 'Right now, this minute.' I offered to accompany her to a solicitor's office.

'They don't work on Saturday afternoons,' she said. 'They play golf.'

'Monday morning,' I said.

'I've got a tutorial,' she said feebly.

'Monday afternoon,' I pressed.

'I'm having tea with friends,' she said.

'Tuesday morning?' I suggested.

We went through the whole week and then the following week. Pandora's every waking moment seemed to be accounted for. Eventually I exploded, 'Look Pandora, you do *want* to marry me don't you?'

Pandora poked at a courgette (we were in a greengrocer's shop at the time), then she sighed and said, 'Well actually darling, no; I don't intend to remarry until I'm at *least* thirty-six.

'*Thirty-six!*' I screeched. 'But, by then I could be fat or bald or toothless.'

Pandora looked at me and said, 'You're not exactly an Adonis *now*, are you?' In my hurry to leave the shop I knocked a pile of Outspan oranges onto the floor. In the resulting confusion (in which several old ladies reacted to the rolling oranges as though they were hand grenades, rather than mere fruit coming towards them), I failed to see Pandora leaving.

I ran after her. Then I felt a heavy hand on my shoulder, then a growling voice: the greengrocer's.

'Runnin' off without payin' eh?' Well I'm sick of you students nickin' my stuff, this time I'm prosecutin'. You'll be in a police cell tonight, my lad.'

It was with horror that I realised I had an Outspan orange in each hand.

Sunday   June 19th

I have been charged with shoplifting. My life is ruined. I shall have a criminal record. Now I will never get a job in the Civil Service.

Pandora is standing by me. She is feeling dead guilty because when *she* ran out of the shop she forgot to pay for a pound of courgettes, a lettuce and a box of mustard and cress.

Nothing has changed. It's still the rich what gets the gravy and the poor what gets the blame.

Mole at the Department of the Environment

July 1989

Monday   July 10th

I was called into Mr Brown's office today, but first I was kept waiting in the small vestibule outside. I noticed that Brown had allowed his rubber plant to die. I was scandalised by the sight of the poor, dead thing. Taking my penknife out of my pocket, I removed the decayed leaves until a brown, shrivelled stump was left.

Brown bellowed, 'Come'. So I went, though I was annoyed at being summond in like a dog.

Brown was looking out of the window and jiggling the change in his pocket. At least I *think* that was what he was doing, the only other possible alternative doesn't bear thinking about.

He turned and glowered at me. 'I have just heard a disquieting fact about you, Mole,' he said.

'Oh,' I said.

'Oh, indeed' repeated Brown. 'Is there something you should tell me about your lavatorial habits, Mole?'

After a period of thought I said. 'No sir, if it's about the puddle on the floor last Friday, that was when I . . .'

'No, no, not at work, at home,' he snapped. I thought about the lavatory at home. Surely I used it as other men did? Or did I? Was I doing something unspeakable without knowing it? And if I was how did Brown *know*?

'Think of your lavatory *seat* Mole. You have been heard bragging about it, in the canteen.' As I was bidden I thought about the newly installed lavatory seat at home.

'*Describe* the aforementioned lavatory seat, Mole.' I fingered my penknife nervously. Brown had obviously gone mad. It was common knowledge that he wandered around on motorway embankments at night, muttering endearments to hedgehogs.

'Well sir,' I said, edging imperceptibly towards the door. 'It's sort of a reddish brown wood, and it has brass fittings . . .' Brown shouted, 'Ha, reddish brown wood! . . . Mahogany! You are a vandal, Mole, an enemy of the earth. Consider your job to be on the line! Mahogany is one of the earth's most precious and endangered woods and you have further endangered it by your vanity and lust.'

Tuesday   July 11th

Pandora and I had an in-depth discussion about the mahogany lavatory seat tonight. It ended when she slammed the lid down angrily and said, 'Well, I like it; it's warm and comfortable, and it's staying!'

I have started scanning the job pages in *The Independent*.

Wednesday   July 12th

Brown has sent a memo round to all departments ordering the expulsion of all aerosols in the building. A spot check will be carried out tomorrow. The typing pool are in an ugly mood and are threatening mutiny.

Thursday   July 13th

There were pathetic scenes throughout the day as workers tried to hang on to their underarm deodorants and canisters of hairspray. But by four o'clock Brown announced a victory. It was a perspiring and limp-haired crowd of workers who left the building. Some shook their fists at the sky and swore at the ozone layer, or the lack of it. One or the other.

Friday   July 14th

BASTILLE DAY

Now there is trouble with the cleaning ladies! Apparently Brown has left a note in each of their mop-buckets ordering them to rid themselves of their Mr Sheen and Pledge. Mrs Sprogett who cleans our office was very bitter about Brown. ''E's askin' us to go back to the dark days of lavender wax,' she said. I tried to explain to the poor woman, but she said 'What's a bleedin' ozone layer when it's at home?'

Saturday   July 15th

Made a shocking discovery this morning. Our so called mahogany seat is made entirely of chip-board! I rang the bathroom fitments showroom and informed them that they had contravened the Trade Descriptions Act. I demanded a full refund.

Monday   July 16th

Went to Brown's office to appraise him of the latest facts regarding the lavatory seat, but he wasn't there. He has been suspended on full pay pending an enquiry into his wilful neglect and cruelty to a rubber plant.

Adrian Mole
and the
Small Amphibians

Monday   July 17th 1989

My father has just telephoned the office to say that he thinks my mother is
having an affair with the lodger, Martin Muffet. I asked him what
evidence he has for his suspicions. 'I found your mother in Martin
Muffet's bed this morning,' he said. Apparently my mother claimed she
had been 'testing the tog rate' of Martin Muffet's duvet. Will I never
escape from my parents' perpetual domestic dramas? I have written to my
mother, reminding her of her parental responsibilities.

> Oxford
> Monday July 17th

Mother,

My father telephoned me at 11.00 am this morning in
some distress. He had just witnessed the unsavoury sight of
you and Martin Muffet side by side in the aforementioned's
bed. Your explanation 'testing the tog rate' etc seems a little,
on the face of it, unsatisfactory. (Especially since we are all
suffering from the highest temperatures since 1976; it was
93°F or 34°C last night. I was forced to take my pyjamas
off.)

When I lived at home I was constantly complaining about
my thin duvet, yet *not once* did you crawl into *my* bed to
investigate further. My father and I are now convinced that
your relationship with Martin Muffet is of a sexual nature.
Though how you could bring yourself to be intimate with a
man who has the complete works of Wilbur Smith by his bed
baffles me. (That reminds me, you never did acknowledge
the volume of Kafka's *Letters* I sent to you for your birthday.)
Do I have to remind you that you have a small child in the
house, namely my innocent sister, Rosie? I am confined here
in Oxford with matters domestic and intellectual but as soon
as I have fulfilled my commitments I will hasten home and
attempt to sort out the mess.

I urge you to restrain your unseemly middle-aged passion until then.

> Your son,
> Adrian

P.S. May I remind you that Muffet is a mere twenty-two years of age, whereas you are forty-five.

Friday   July 21st

A reply from my mother:

> Dear Adrian,
> Keep your nose out, you pompous git! Martin and I are in love. He doesn't give a toss that I am twenty-three years older than him. He adores me. He says that I am a 'free spirit' and that it has been a crime to shackle me to suburbia. When Martin qualifies as an engineer he is going to build bridges in the Amazon Basin, and I will be there at his side, holding his slide rule, or whatever it is that engineers use.
> Rosie is also in love with Martin; she hardly sees her father and when she does he complains that her voice gets on his nerves.
> I enclose a photocopy of something Rosie had to write at school, 'My family'. By the way, did you know that Sharon Bott is pregnant? I saw her in Tesco's and she told me she is 'three months gone'. She asked me where she could contact you. I said I'd forgotten the address, but she is bound to come back to me.
> Yours,
> Pauline

My family   by Rosie Mole.   6 yrs. 8 months
My family is my dog my mummy my martin my daddy my adrain and my grarndma who is old. I love my dog and my mummy and martin best aftar them comes daddy.

mummy and martin play at cards at night they do laughring a lot. daddy shout to be quite. adrain do not live in are house he lives in annother house. I am glad. he does moane and he has got spotts on his face.

Saturday   July 22nd

Sharon Bott *swore* to me that she was on the pill. I even saw her take one now and again. Oh God! Oh God! Oh God!

pm.   At last! Ken Dodd's ordeal at the hands of the Inland Revenue is over. He was acquitted of the charge of keeping £336,000 in cash in his attic. Dodd cried in the witness box and said his mother had told him not to trust banks. £336,000! It would buy a hell of a lot of tickling sticks.

Sunday   July 23rd

I am a little calmer today. My pulse rate is almost normal. I feared for my sanity last night. How much worry can somebody of my sensitivity *take*? There must be a point at which my frail human body cries, 'No more!'

WORRIES
Sharon Bott (pregnant)
Pandora (finding out)
Mother's adultery
Grandma (finding out)
Overdraft £129.08
Skin
Middle East
Rosie's treachery
Dog will die soon
Knocking in pipes
Third world
Ozone layer
Hole in shoes
Fridge on the blink

Monday   July 24th

The worst has happened! The fridge has broken down and two litres of ice-cream melted overnight and dripped through the cardboard wrapper onto the food below. Pandora came down to find me on my knees weeping into the salad crisper. She said, 'For Christ's *sake*, Adrian, get things into perspective,' but as I later pointed out to her, I can ill afford to throw food away, especially when I am already facing financial ruin. 'We're talking about a ten-day-old lettuce and half-a-pound of soggy tomatoes,' she said. She added, 'I hope you realise, Adrian, that you're well on your way to having a nervous breakdown.' She should know – most of her friends are having them, recovering from them or writing books about them.

No word from Sharon Bott.

Tuesday July 25th

I received the following letter from Martin Muffet this morning. I have corrected the many multifarious spelling mistakes.

> Dear Adrian,
>
> OK, so you and me don't exactly hit it off, right? I know you don't rate me because I'm an engineering student. Well I'll tell you something mate. *I* don't rate floppy-wristed so-called intellectuals who fart-arse about reading books all day, right?
>
> What's happening with me and your mother has got nothing to do with you. She is a grown woman.
>
> I have put new washers on all the taps and re-hung the doors on the kitchen cupboards. Also I have bled all the radiators and mended the lawnmower, and your mother can now use the gas oven without stooping.
>
> Your father is a lazy sod, and so are you. Do you realise that there was not even a *screwdriver* in the place when I moved in? It's a good job I have my own well-equipped tool box.
>
> One day I will be your stepfather so we will have to get on, I suppose. Your dad is looking for a flat. We all had a talk last night and thought it was for the best. We are hoping to get married next December (not me and your dad, of course, I mean me and your mother). So I hope you will by then have thrown down your gauntlet and swallowed the pill.
>
> Best wishes,
>   Martin Muffet (Lodger)
> P.S. Wilbur Smith may not be Kafka but tell me this, what did Kafka know about the Laws of the Jungle? Also, would Kafka know which rifle to use to knock out an elephant at 500 paces? Like hell he would.

I read this moronic scrawl aloud to Pandora through the bathroom door. To my amazement she took Muffet's side! She said, 'I'm with Muffet there. *I've* lost all patience with Kafka, he lacks muscularity.'

Julian Twyselton-Fife passed by and whispered, 'Our beloved Pandora's on the turn, Aidy. She's been keeping company with those thicknecks at Rocky's gym! I smell trouble ahead.'

'She's your wife,' I snapped. 'Forbid her to go to the gym.'

'My, my,' sighed Julian. 'We *are* living in post-feminist times, aren't we? You're getting quite Wilbur Smithish. You'll be marching about in a safari suit next.'

Friday   July 28th

It's ridiculous that three sets of sheets are used every week. If I shared Pandora's bed it would save on washing powder. I've pointed this out many times but the last time I did so she replied, 'You're obsessed with the bloody laundry. Look at the fuss you kicked up over losing one single handkerchief.'

Julian said, 'If you're going to go *on* about that missing blue handkerchief again I shall go simply *berserk*.'

I shut up, but quite honestly, dear diary, I am still extremely annoyed. That handkerchief was one of a set of seven: a different colour for every day of the week. Pandora says that it's time I joined the Kleenex Culture. She said nobody uses disgusting snot rags these days: she should try telling that to Mr Brown at the Department of the Environment. His wife *left him* because Brown wouldn't let her use disposable nappies.

Saturday   July 29th

Visited my father in his new flat today. It is very sparsely furnished. It has got a single bed, a stereo, a bamboo table, two plastic stacking chairs and one high armchair designed to be used by back sufferers. 'Might come in handy if I ever get a bad back,' he said.

I sat on one of the plastic chairs and tried to think of something to say to him, words of comfort, that sort of thing, but nothing came. He looked around and said, 'Not much to show for over twenty years of marriage, is it?' He offered me a can of Pils, but I declined. (After a few sips I can feel myself turning into a lager lout, no telephone box in my vicinity is safe.)

'Is there no white wine?' I asked.

'White wine?' he mocked. 'White wine? Of course there's white wine; I've got crates of the stuff; or perhaps you'd prefer champagne.' His tirade continued, 'And how about a bit of caviar to go with the champagne, and out-of-season strawberries and profiter-bloody-roles, and a good Stilton, and Carr's bleeding water biscuits?'

Later on we talked about last week's cabinet reshuffle. Mrs Thatcher has cast Sir Geoffrey Howe aside, as though he were a used tea-bag. Sir Geoff is no longer Foreign Secretary. A bloke called John Major is. Nobody in England has heard of John Major, let alone foreigners, so I predict that he won't last long. He looks like Mr Pratt, deputy manager of my building society. The one who refused me a hundred per cent mortgage.

Yeah, just wait, Pratt. When I am living in a country mansion with flamingos on my own personal lake I will invite you to take cocktails on the terrace. It will amuse me to see your jaw drop in amazement. Also, Pratt, I will take you on a tour of the house pointing out the many en-suite bathrooms, the fully equipped gym and the whirlpool baths. You will be sorry, Pratt, that you had such little faith in my poetic talent. Your claim that you 'had never heard of a rich poet' just proves your monumental ignorance. What about that best-seller, *Taking Cocoa with Wendy Cope* by Sir Kingsley Amis?

One day I will be England's best known poet. The *Restless Tadpole* opus is nearly finished; and *Lo! the Flat Hills of My Homeland*, my experimental novel, is flowing nicely. My next step is to find a literary agent. I wonder who acts for Prince Charles?

Monday   July 31st

The Writers' and Artists' Yearbook tells me that a person called Sir Gordon Giles is our Heir's agent. I have written to him offering him my work.

> Dear Sir Gordon Giles,
>   As you cannot fail to see, I have enclosed samples of two works in progress. *The Restless Tadpole*, an opus. And *Lo! the Flat Hills of My Homeland*, an experimental novel. I would like you to act on my behalf and sell the aforementioned work, I had in mind Faber and Faber for *Tadpole* and Weidenfeld for *Lo!*
>   About finance, I cannot afford to pay you the usual ten per cent. How about five per cent? My work will sell in great numbers so you won't be out of pocket. Please send the contracts to me at the following work address:
>   A.A.Mole
>   c/o Newt Dept
>   Sml Amphibians Section
>   D.O.E.

18–21 Lord David Cecil Street
OXFORD
OX1 7SD

P.S. Please do not telephone with your congratulations. My
immediate supervisor Mr Brown does not allow us incoming
private calls (unless it involves the death of a close relative). I
do not have a telephone in my domicile at present, due to
previous profligate abuse by my fellow tenants. Please excuse
the purple ink that I have used to scribe this letter; I have
run out of my usual green.

Thursday   August 3rd

I received the following letter this morning:

Adrian Mole
Newt Dept
D.O.E.
Oxford   Sir Gordon Giles Associates
                              372 Doughty Street
                              London

Dear Adrian Mole,
    Thank you for sending me your two manuscripts, the
Restless Tadpole opus and *Lo! the Flat Hills of My Homeland*.
As you cannot fail to see, I have sent them back to you.
Frankly, Mr Mole, I found it enormously difficult to read
your manuscript. Your miniscule handwriting and your use
of green ink does not make for trouble-free reading. Did you
know you had failed to put enough stamps onto your
somewhat bulky (certainly heavy) parcel?
    Whether you did or not, you owe my office one pound
seventy-five pence. I will skip over the unpleasant objects
that appeared between the pages of your manuscript as I
flicked through it. Bacon rind, bus tickets, a pristine packet
of condoms, a pressed wild flower . . . I fear that your novel
is *too* experimental to be of any interest to the general public
and the fact that it lacks all vowels makes it incomprehensible
at times.

I suggest you send *The Restless Tadpole* to the Natural
History Unit at the BBC, Whiteladies Rd, Bristol. They may
know what to make of it. I don't.
I send you my good wishes,
Sir Gordon Giles, Literary Agent

So that's where those condoms went. I note he didn't send them back!

Friday   August 4th

The Queen Mother is eighty-nine years old today! God bless her! A
certain Ms Alison Watt has unveiled her portrait of the Queen Mother.
Words fail me. The Queen Mother's head looks like a turnip. Ms Watt is
twenty-three years old. Enough said, perhaps. I too am an experimental
artist but I draw the line at experimenting with our most revered royal.

Oh Queen Mother
There will never be another
It is really true that your eyes are blue
Your charm and grace
And your lin-ed face. . . .
    (Unfinished, got bored.)

2.00am   Pandora not yet back from the gym. If she is not careful she will
have more muscles than Dublin Bay.

Saturday   August 5th

At last! The *Restless Tadpole* opus is finished! I was lying in bed thinking
about sex when the ending came to me.

So! Squiggling Squirming Sensuous one
Dweller of pond and canal
Stretch, stretch, to daylight and t'ward air!
Oh Creature of Darwin, leap, leap, onto land!
Hop Hop Hop 'tis England you inhabit!
Arise! Frog. Arise! A tadpole no more!
Your journey's done, your form is changed
Oh that I could do your trick
Transmogrified
Go! Go! Go! Croak your message to the world!

The End

I don't believe in false modesty, so I will state quietly, dearest diary, that I am certain it is a work of genius. One day schoolchildren will study it for GCSE. Perhaps I should send it to Andrew Lloyd-Webber. It would make a brilliant musical. Yes! *Tadpole!* would set the West End on fire.

TADPOLE! CAST LIST

Tadpole's Mother	Julia McKenzie
Tadpole's Father	Stephen Fry
Baby Tadpole	Madonna
Wise Frog	Bernard Levin

Query: has Bernard Levin got an Equity card?

Sunday   August 6th

Visited my mother's house today. I can no longer call it home. Muffet has transformed the place. She has got more shelves than a reference library. Everything works. There is even a chain on the plug in the bathroom washbasin. Muffet has always got a tool in his hand, looking for things to shorten, lengthen, tighten or loosen. My mother follows him around like a poodle performing obedience trials at Crufts. It is sickening to watch. They are still going ahead with their ludicrous plans to get married. Muffet asked me to be the Best Man! I gave as my answer an ironical laugh. Rosie has designed her own bridesmaid's dress. It is vulgar beyond belief. A paederast's delight: off-the-shoulder pink chiffon, held together with satin rosebuds. Nabokov, that you should be alive on this day!

I cannot bring myself to sleep under the same roof as my mother and Muffet, so I begged lodgings from my grandma. I hadn't been inside the door two minutes before I was dragged into the kitchen and forced to admire more of Muffet's handiwork, this time a set of fitted cupboards. Is there no end to the man's interference? I preferred Grandma's old, unfitted kitchen, and I told her so in no uncertain terms.

She opened Littlewoods' catalogue and showed me the outfit she has ordered for the wedding. She is paying for it over two years. I wonder if Littlewoods realise the risk they are taking? Grandma is not in the best of health, she could go at any moment.

Nipped in to see Bert Baxter before fleeing back to Oxford. Bert was having his toenails cut by a peripatetic chiropodist. When Bert saw me he said, 'Well bugger me, if it ain't Master Mole. When you gettin' rid of them bleedin' spots?'

The chiropodist – a furtive-looking dwarf with dirty fingernails – asked me if I would like a pedicure. I declined with a shudder. When the dwarf had departed I made Bert's tea; a beetroot sandwich and a can of brown ale. He ate and drank with his customary lack of manners. Then he began to reminisce about his ex-dead wife Queenie. We both got maudlin and Bert confessed that he 'couldn't wait to join his gel'. Sabre has lost his ferocity (along with his teeth). Even his bark is considerably reduced in volume. I've never seen a dog go so grey so quickly. And I was concerned to see how much weight he has lost. His collar hangs round his neck like the ring round Saturn.

Wednesday   August 9th

FAX MESSAGE FOR THE ATTENTION OF: John Tydeman Esq, Head of Radio Drama
DATE: August 9th
NO. OF PAGES: 739
SUBJECT: *Lo! the Flat Hills of My Homeland*

Here is my novel, please read it immediately and then adapt it for radio. I will charge £1,000. Please broadcast it before 8.30 pm. My grandma removes her deaf aid at 8.35 pm on the dot.

A Mole

Friday   August 11th   Broadcasting House

Dear Adrian Mole,

Have you gone off your head, boy? You clogged my fax machine up for eight solid hours. You do *not* fax 739 pages of manuscript. You parcel it up nicely and send it through the post.

Either you or my fax seems to have gobbled up the vowels of your novel, *Lo! the Flat Hills of My Homeland*. Your manuscript is awash with consonants, but vowels are very thin on the ground, thin to the point of non-existence. You expect a thousand pounds! This made me laugh quite a lot.

I do *not* adapt plays, my role at the BBC is Head of Drama. I dictate policy and encourage new writing etc. If you want your voweless novel adapting, you must do it yourself.

Yours (but only just)
John Tydeman

PS I am going to Australia. I shall be gone for some time.

Thursday   August 17th

Tadpole has been rejected by the Bristol BBC. No reason was given. They will be sorry one day, the moronic philistines. I have sent it to Craig Raine, who is the poetry editor of Faber and Faber. He is a very hirsute man, and he is sure to understand that I am trying to move English Poetry into the twenty-second century single-handedly. I was lucky; there were only just enough stamps in Brown's drawer.

Harry Corbett, the father of Sooty the glove puppet, died today.

Friday   August 18th

I was working on a projection of newt births (1995) when Brown burst into my cubicle and started ranting on about postage stamps. He virtually accused me of theft! From now on everybody in the Newt Dept has to sign in a little book, and give the destination and reason before taking a stamp. The stamps are now kept in a locked box, and only Brown has a key. I'm surprised he doesn't hire Securicor to keep a twenty-four-hour watch over his stupid box. All this is most inconvenient; Brown has a weak bladder and visits the lavatory at least ten times a day. His visits usually coincide with the times I urgently require a stamp. I will have to start *buying* stamps from the post office now. It is essential that my manuscripts are perused. It can only be a matter of time before I am discovered.

Wednesday   August 23rd

The government is selling off our water, surely this is illegal? If a cloud bursts over my house and rains over my garden does the water belong to me, God or Mrs Thatcher? An interesting legal point. Perhaps I will write to John Mortimer of Rumpole fame. It is sure to interest his legalistic brain. He may use the argument in one of his amusing TV episodes. I will have to protect my copyright of course.

I really *must* get a literary agent.

Pandora was seen getting into Rocky Armstrong's Cadillac last night. My informant was Mr Brown. He disapproves of Cadillacs because of their high fuel consumption.

Monday   August 28th

I have sent *Lo!* to Ed Victor, who is Iris Murdoch's literary agent. He will appreciate it, I am sure. After all, me and Iris are both concerned with the metaphysical world.

Thursday   August 31st

Princess Anne's marriage is over! Captain Mark Phillips has moved out of the main part of Gatcombe House and into a sort of prefab in the grounds. I expect he has taken the stereo with him.

A point of interest: 'Captain' is the name of Jack Woolley's dog in 'The Archers'.

Wednesday   September 20th

When I got home from work today I was astonished to find Rocky, the monolithic body builder, sitting at the table holding a cucumber sandwich between his massive cruise-missile-like fingers. He rose to his feet as I entered the room, but I hastily urged him to sit down. I had no wish to be dwarfed by his six-foot-four frame. Pandora said, 'Rocky and I are in love.' Rocky dipped his head bashfully and then looked at Pandora, and I swear, dear diary, there truly *was* love-light in his eyes. I somehow managed to croak out, 'I'm very happy for you,' before stumbling from the room and throwing myself onto my bed. I fantasised about Rocky choking on a piece of cucumber rind (Pandora never cuts the skin off). Or of him being allergic to cucumber and dying hideously swollen, surrounded by baffled helpless doctors.

Saturday   September 30th

Three hundred thousand Scottish people have failed to pay their Poll Tax. Mrs Thatcher will never dare to introduce it to England. It would be political suicide. Pandora is in her bedroom. I can hear Rocky pleading with her in his surprisingly high-pitched voice. 'But it's been ten days, I fort you loved me, Pan.'

I can hear her saying, 'I do, Rocky, but I prefer to keep my body to myself, now go to sleep.'

Ha Ha Ha Ha Ha!

Sunday   October 1st

Julian was furious this morning, he couldn't get into the bathroom where his creams and lotions were waiting for him. Rocky could be heard floundering in the bath like Moby Dick. Julian came into my room and sat on the end of my bed. He confessed that it was no longer amusing being married to Pandora. He said, 'I may divorce her.'

I urged him to do so.

Monday   October 2nd

A letter from Barry Kent:

> Yo!
>   I get my parole next week so Ime coming too see you ok?
> Get some beer in. Have you heard of a bloke called Blake he
> has wrote some real hard poems. Tiger Tiger is one. Nigel
> come to see me last week. He is not a buddhist monk now,
> he is joined the Socialist Worker he made me buy a
> magazine. I am writin' a poem for it.
>   Yo!
>   Baz

Barry Kent may be well known on the poetry reading circuit (Baz, the Skinhead Poet) but he is still a moron. Anyone who is remotely educated knows that Rupert Blake's poem is entitled 'Tyger! Tyger!' A 'y' not an 'i'.

I have sent a Telemessage via the phone at work ordering Kent *not* to come here next week.

> Yo! Baz.
>   Regret, have to go on newt ringing expedition next week.
> So won't be here. It is *Tyger* not Tiger.
>   Yo!
>   Aidy

Monday   October 9th

Our household now consists of Julian Twyselton-Fife, Pandora Braith-waite, Rocky (Big Boy) Livingstone, Barry Kent and me, Adrian Mole. It is prison regulations that prisoners cannot receive Telemessages or some-thing; also I had forgotten to tell British Telecom to put Barry's prison registration number on the front of the envelope, so he turned up. We are all squeezed into one living room, a kitchenette, two bedrooms, a box room and a bathroom. I am a person who needs my personal space. Sharing a box room with Kent is abhorrent to me; he takes up all my remaining floor space. There is nowhere to put my slippers. Also he reads all night.

But, dear diary (I would got *mad* without you to confide in!), what is sending me *insane* is that he has been taken up by the Oxford literary crowd! Those weak-chinned knobheads have invited him to every func-tion going. He *Barry Kent!!!* has dined *in hall* at Pandora's college! Pandora said the dons thought him an 'absolute darling'. Also he has been spouting his vile poetry to crowds of impressionable undergraduates at £75 a session. Thank God he goes back to prison tomorrow. This is what he ranted at the finest in the land last night to tumultuous applause and requests for his autograph:

> EDUCATION
> So what?
> So you know things
> So you're clever
> So what?
>
> Know how to put the boot in?
> Steal a car?
> Slop out?
> Start a riot?
>
> You know nothink!
> Nothink!
> Nothink!
> You. No. Think. No. Know. Think!

Friday   October 13th

My mother telephoned the office this morning, Brown came into my cubicle to tell me that he was allowing me to take the call because it was a 'matter of life and death' that my mother speak to me. Life or death? If *death*, who had died? If *life*, had Sharon Bott decided I was the father of her unborn child? The colour drained from my face, Brown had to help me to my feet and guide me towards the instrument of my fate, namely the telephone. As I picked it up I hesitated before speaking, savouring for a moment my innocence, my ignorance, n.y former carefree existence. Oh how sweet life was! Oh how I had wasted those so few precious moments! Brown barked, 'Well go on, Mole, speak!'

ME	(*weakly*): Hello?
MOTHER:	Who's that?
ME:	It's your son. Who's dead? Is it Grandma?
MOTHER:	Nobody's dead.
ME:	So, it's *life*. She swore she was on the pill . . . I'll pay maintenance towards the child's upkeep, but I won't marry her . . .
MOTHER:	For Christ's sake, what are you wittering on about? All I wanted you for was to ask if you want a carnation or a rose?
ME:	A carnation or a rose?
MOTHER:	Yes.

Brown jiggled the change in his pocket impatiently as I tried to understand the significance of my mother's horticultural ravings. Had she gone mad? Had I? A rose? A carnation? Was she speaking in code?

MOTHER:	Hurry up, Adrian, Martin's under the sink shouting for the mole grips.
ME:	Mole grips?
MOTHER	(*screeching*): A carnation or a rose!
ME:	How can I possibly decide? I don't know in what context . . .
MOTHER	(*berserk*): Buttonholes! Buttonholes! What do you want in your sodding buttonhole?
ME:	I haven't got a buttonhole.
MOTHER:	Don't be ridiculous, of course you've . . .
ME:	My duffle coat is fastened by *toggles*.
MOTHER:	You are not wearing that vile duffle coat to my wedding!

Brown sat down behind his desk and pretended to read a report, *The Effects of the Destruction of the Ozone Layer on the Newt Population of England, Scotland and Wales*.

ME: I have to go now . . .

MOTHER   (*going barmy*): A carnation or a rose?! . . . Answer me! One or the other?

ME: I can't possibly decide right now, aesthetics are involved . . .

MOTHER   (*screaming*): Answer me!

Brown frowned and cleared his throat. He doodled on the cover of the report. The doodle looked like a cruise missile, it was aimed at a circle. Inside the circle Brown printed: 'AM'. Did this mean 'a.m.' as in morning, or 'A.M.' as in my initials? Was the significance of the doodle that Brown wished me dead?

ME: All right, a rose!

MOTHER: Thank you!

I put the phone down and Brown pounced on me (not literally pounced, not like a jaguar or a lion would pounce) and said, 'From now on you are forbidden to touch that phone, and should your whole family end up in intensive care you will enquire of their relative conditions via a public phone booth!'

Saturday   October 14th

I couldn't face staying in my flat tonight, so I went to the cinema and watched *Annie* (a sign of my desperation). I ate two giant tubs of popcorn, three Bounty bars, one drink on a stick, one choc-ice, two Jumbo hot dogs and a quarter pound of Devon toffees. My skin will react tomorrow but I don't care. Even when my skin is relatively unblemished it doesn't seem to make any difference to my life: women do not seem to be attracted to me, and men do not seem to notice my existence. What am I doing wrong? Have I got halitosis? Should I use an underarm deodorant? Am I without dress sense? Should I stop wearing plastic shoes? I walked past a public house which was full of uncouth men laughing and backslapping, and talking in confident voices of masculine things. God, how I envied them. None of them gave a toss about the future of English poetry.

   I have never been into a pub on my own. I feel that I am trespassing somehow. Am I a normal man? Perhaps I am a bisexual? Will I be buying my underwear from the Marks and Spencer's lingerie range in future?

Sunday   October 15th

How I laughed at last night's entry regarding my sexuality! I could never wear women's underwear. It takes forever to iron; all those frills and lace bits! Rocky doesn't wear underpants, 'Y' fronts or boxer shorts. He wears thongs; there were ten of them on the bathroom towel-rail the other day, and there was still room for Pandora's 'NO POLL TAX' XXL T-shirt.

Wednesday   October 18th

Julian's sister is a qualified solicitor, her name is Davina Belling. She has informed Julian that his marriage to Pandora can be annulled on grounds of non-consumption. Pandora will have to be medically examined to prove that she is still a virgin. Davina Belling is not giving her services free: she is giving her brother a ten per cent discount. According to Julian this is because he threw Davina's Tiny Tears doll over the cliffs at Beachy Head fifteen years ago. My God! Women certainly have long memories. Mr Honecker, the East German Communist Party leader, was thrown out of office today. The East Germans are sick of him. They want the Berlin Wall to come down. Poor idealistic fools! The Wall will never come down in their lifetime or mine.

Thursday   October 26th

Sabre is dead, knocked down by a milk float. Bert telephoned the office this morning. Luckily, Brown was in the toilet at the time and I knew he'd be at least five minutes because he'd taken the *Daily Telegraph* in there with him. So I was able to give Bert my sincere condolences. I promised to go and visit him at the weekend and I said I would personally bury Sabre in Bert's little garden. He will be kept in the vet's fridge until I arrive. Pandora was distraught when she heard the news. It brought us together, briefly.

Nigel Lawson, the Chancellor of the Exchequer, has resigned. He had a row with Mrs Thatcher at breakfast. He is jealous because a certain Professor Alan Waters has been hanging about. John Major has got Lawson's job. Apparently John Major's father was a knife-thrower in the circus. I wonder if John Major stabbed Lawson in the back? Ha! Ha! Ha!

Friday   October 27th

Rocky has broken Pandora's pine bed. She is extremely angry. He is already responsible for the springs on the sofa going, and all the cupboard doors have lost their knobs. The man just doesn't know his own strength. Teaspoons crumple in his hands. Curtains and curtain tracks fall to the carpet. Doors are wrenched from their hinges.

Saturday   October 28th

Pandora and I picked up the box containing Sabre's deep chilled body from the vet's. We then drove in a taxi to Bert's bungalow where my mother and Mrs Braithwaite were waiting for us. Bert was in his wedding suit, I could tell he'd been crying because his nose and eyes were the colour of cough linctus (Halls). While the others had a cup of tea I went out to the garden to dig a grave. There was no spade, *naturellement*, so I was forced to grovel in the dirt and hack at the earth with a garden trowel. It wasn't long before I was filthy, sweating and totally exhausted. A horny-handed man of the soil I am not. My skills are intellectual and artistic.

Bert came out to the back door in his wheelchair and shouted, 'Hurry up, yer lazy bleeder. Sabre's starting to go off.'

I cursed the day I ever set eyes on Bert. He has caused me nothing but grief. It's because of him I failed my 'A' Levels. When my fellow classmates were revising under their angelpoises, I was helping Bert by cutting his corns, or taking his bottles back to the off licence. Why, God, why? Why me?

Anyway, I eventually got the hole dug. It took all three of us to carry Bert out to the garden. 'Looks like a bleedin' artillery shell's exploded,' said Bert nastily when he saw the hole. 'I wanted a proper, oblong grave.'

I choked back comment, though my eyes filled with tears of self-pity. Luckily, Pandora took my glistening eyes to be a sign of grief for Sabre, and she took my hand and squeezed it and said, 'There, there, my pet, I think it's a splendid hole, I mean grave.'

I was almost glad that Sabre had died. I love Pandora. She released my hand and we put Sabre in the hole, then everyone took it in turns to throw earth onto the corpse and Mr Braithwaite emptied a bag of John Innes Compost on top. Then my mother pressed some daffodil bulbs into the mixture and that was that. We went inside and had a drink; vodka and Slimline tonic for the women, and a can of Newcastle Brown for the men. I *hated* leaving Bert but on the other hand I also *hate* Bert, so I did.

Pandora promised that we would call round again tomorrow. Jesus! When is Bert going to die? He must surely be one of the oldest men in Great Britain by now. He was eighty-six when I first met him and that was *years* ago.

Sunday   October 29th

How could I have written the above? Bert was sad and pathetic today, I don't really hate him. It's just that he disgusts me. I have written a poem about Sabre, I hope Bert likes it.

> SABRE
> Fearless Sabre, vicious, faithful,
> furry friend of man,
> you really should have looked, and seen that
> quiet Co-op van.

I know this is a terrible poem, but Bert won't know or care.

Monday   November 6th

A letter from Ed Victor, the literary agent:

> My dear Mr Mole,
>   Are you *serious*? Is this some kind of *joke*? Your novel lacks vowels of any kind. Is this deliberate or do you have a rare form of dyslexia? You send me a handwritten manuscript in *green* ink, which is bristling with consonants, yet utterly devoid of vowels, and you expect me to *read* the goddamn thing?
>   Listen, I'm a busy man. I have houses to furnish, planes to catch. Douglas Adams is one of my authors. My hands are full, OK? Buy yourself a typewriter, kid.
>   All my good wishes,
>   Ed

Wednesday   November 8th

I have seriously burned my hand on a rogue catherine wheel at tonight's belated Bonfire Party. It is all Rocky's fault, he is very religious and said, 'It wun't be right to have it on a Sunday.'

I said, 'I doubt if God gives a toss *when* we earthlings let off our fireworks!'

Rocky shouted, 'Hey, less of the *language*, man! I mean 'e can 'ear you, you know.' He looked up to the sky as if expecting to see God frowning down because an earthling had said 'toss'.

Friday   November 10th

As I have been predicting for some time, the Berlin Wall has come down! Both types of Germans, Communist and Non-Communist, danced in the streets. Sprayed champagne (a waste, in my opinion) and stayed up late. World leaders are ecstatic, except for Mr Kohl, the German Chancellor, who is worried that the East Germans will go mad in the shops. Talking about shops; there are Christmas trees in all the shop windows. This is a bad sign. By Christmas Day I will be Martin Muffet's stepson.

Saturday   November 11th

A report was released today that England's cattle feed has been contaminated by lead. I have emptied the fridge of all cow-related products. I poured the milk down the toilet. (The sink is blocked up again.) My fellow tenants went mad because there was no milk for their tea or cornflakes. I received no thanks whatsoever for my life-saving actions. I am looking forward to alternative accommodation. Rang Rosie to wish her a happy birthday, but she was out at the cinema with Muffet.

Sunday   November 12th

It is Remembrance Sunday today. I watched some old men march past in Oxford town centre. I removed my balaclava as a sign of respect.

Saturday   November 18th

Barry Kent is out of prison. He turned up here today, trying to sell pieces of the Berlin Wall. Rocky bought four pieces. When asked why he said, 'It's 'istory, man. I'm gonna give 'em to my kids.'

Pandora looked up from her Russian language edition of *Tales of the Underground* by Dostoyevsky and said, 'Kids?' It was only one word, but it was the way she said it. It chilled us three men to the bone.

Rocky was the first to recover, he said, 'Yeah, I sorta' want kids one day, Pan.'

'Not with me you won't, dearie,' she said. 'No sex, I'm British.' Then she gave a wild laugh and went back to her book. I've got to get out of here.

Thursday   November 23rd

Barry Kent has appeared on television. The great big oaf was interviewed by a big-earringed woman about his cretinous poetry. It was only a pathetic regional arts programme but the woman carried on as though Barry was the new Messiah! Kent swore twice and the words had to be bleeped out. But we viewers could clearly see that Kent's lips had formed the letter 'F'. I have written to the TV company asking them to ban Kent from our screens.

Friday   November 24th

A picture postcard of Leningrad came back from Craig Raine. I quote the remarks on the back in full:

>   Mr Mole,
>   *The Restless Tadpole* is effete crap.

He did not send my manuscript back.

Saturday   November 25th

Woke up in a sweat. What if Craig Raine intends to keep *The Restless Tadpole* and *publish it as his own*?

Sunday   November 26th

Wyoming Homepride has flouted the Sunday Trading Laws. I am strictly against Sunday trading. However as I happened to be passing a branch of W.H., I nipped in and bought a sink plunger.

Monday   November 27th

I have been severely reprimanded by Brown. British Telecom have squealed on me regarding the Telemessage I sent to Kent ages ago. I took the reprimand like a man. But after he had dismissed me from his office I went into my cubicle and had a good cry. Janice Conlon (Ozone Dept) heard me and came in and patted my shoulder. This made me sob louder and she put her arms around me and squashed me to her (not inconsiderable) bosom. I felt my manhood stir and come up for air. About time! Who needs you, Pandora Braithwaite? Janice has asked me out for a Chinese meal. I've got one day to practice using chopsticks.

Tuesday   November 28th

Practised all morning, using two pencils and a piece of cheese covered in Branston pickle.

Wednesday   November 29th

I will never talk to Janice Conlon ever again. She has blabbed to the whole Ozone Dept that I drank the contents of the finger bowl and washed my fingers in the saki cup. I will never live this down.

Thursday   November 30th

The newt dept were in convulsions today as the news reached them about my gastronomic *faux pas*. Even Brown gave me one of his hideous half smiles when we met at the gents' urinals before lunch. He said, 'Don't forget to wash your hands after you've been to the toilet, Mole. I believe we have a cup of saki somewhere on the premises.' Ha! Ha! Ha! Brown. Ho! Ho! Ho! What a wit! Cor strike a light, guv! You ain't 'alf funny! Stand up, Brown, and accept your award for Funniest Quip of the Year! Move over, Les Dawson, your successor has arrived!

Friday   December 1st

Quite frankly, dear diary, I wouldn't give a toss if all of the newts in the world disappeared overnight. I am sick to death of them. I have asked Brown for a transfer. I have got myself in a rut lately.

> work (boring)
> sex (none)
> home life (dull)
> intellect (re-reading *Black Beauty*)

I have got nothing to look forward to in my life. Rocky suggested I become a member of his gym, but how can I possibly display my body in public? The suggestion is laughable. Would Kafka pump iron? Would A. N. Wilson jostle in a jacuzzi? Would Osbert Sitwell flick his towel in the shower? No, gyms are not for literary men like me. Sometimes I envy Rocky, he has only ever read two books in his life. (*Roar!* by Wilbur Smith, and *The Highway Code* by HMGP). He lives in a world of sights and sounds only. He does not lie awake at night worrying about the Palestinians.

Saturday   December 2nd

A letter from my mother:

> Dear Adrian,
>   Have you decided what to wear to the wedding yet? I warn you, kid, if you turn up in that mangy duffle coat I will personally tear your head from your shoulders. Why don't you use that virgin Access card of yours and buy a new suit: navy-blue, three-button jacket, no vent, trousers with pleated front and turn-ups. A pale-blue suit with discreet stripe and a silk tie (red or pink). Black slip-on shoes, black socks?
>   Have you written your speech yet? You must remember to tell the Bridesmaid and Maid of Honour how pretty they look and thank the guests for coming and read out the telegrams. *Don't* ramble on about bloody Kafka or the Norwegian leather industry. *Do* welcome Martin to the family; a hearty masculine handshake would be certain to earn you a round of applause and help to convince his parents that he is doing the right thing. (He hasn't told them I am forty-five and got kids.) I meant to invite Pandora, Julian and Rocky. Will you do this for me? And if you run into Barry Kent, ask him. It will be exciting to have a celebrity at the wedding. Did you see him on television the other night talking to Melvyn Bragg? Wasn't he brilliant? (Kent not Bragg.) I was thrilled to see that his book, *So?*, is number five in the *Sunday Times* Best-Seller List. You must be so pleased. It was you who encouraged him, wasn't it?
>   Yours,
>   Pauline (Mum)

Sunday   December 3rd

Jason Donovan, Kylie Minogue, Bros, Bananarama and Wet Wet Wet
have recorded a new version of 'Do They Know It's Christmas?' All the
money from this record is going to the starving of Ethiopia. I would pay
good money *not* to hear this record. I have sent £5 to Oxfam. I requested a
receipt.

Monday   December 11th

I am in bed suffering from the flu that is sweeping Britain like a bush fire
(Australian). Julian has been very kind. He went to Boots and bought me a
bottle of Night Nurse and a packet of Tunes (blackcurrant). I have
already used two Andrex toilet rolls in blowing my nose. Julian also rang
the office to inform Brown of my incapacity. Brown was not sympathetic.
He asked Julian to tell me that I may be 'prosecuted for stealing postage
stamps belonging to Her Majesty's Government'. A new worry.

Tuesday   December 12th

9.00am   Too ill to write. *Four* Andrex toilet rolls is the latest update.
            Query: I must have expelled at least two gallons of snot. Where
            does it all come from and where is it stored?
4.00pm   Managed a rich-tea biscuit.
5.00pm   Crumbs in bed but too weak to brush them out. I have been
            deserted. Pandora is at a tutorial, Rocky is at the gym, and
            Julian is doing his Christmas shopping.
            A playwright is in charge in Czechoslovakia! A bloke called
            Vaclav Havel was sworn in. Let's hope he doesn't make a
            drama out of a crisis.

Friday   December 15th

Ate a little Readybrek for breakfast, and now feel that I will pull through.
It has been touch and go. I have been near to death and yet have pulled
back from the brink. I am a better person for the experience. A calmness
has descended on me. I have put things into perspective. I am now above
caring about the petty things of life.
3.45pm Where is my brown comb? Who has had it? I have looked after
that comb for six years, man and boy.

Saturday   December 16th

The Wedding is next week and I have got nothing to wear. Should I buy or should I hire? Pandora has bought a new Gothic outfit from Miss Selfridge. Rocky has got nine suits already and Julian is going in his nineteen-twenties blazer, Oxford bags and cravat. I have asked him not to wear his monocle. If there is a fight at the wedding it could prove to be a hazard.

Monday   December 18th

Pandora has had her beautiful treacle-coloured hair shaved off. She hasn't got a hair on her head. She ran into the bathroom and slammed the door, but I clearly saw her bald bonce shining under the ceiling light as she passed by the kitchen door. She has been sobbing in a heartbroken manner all night, but she refused to unlock the door. I slipped a note under the door, 'Dinner is ready; do you want tinned pears after?' but I received no response. Why has she emasculated herself in such a manner? Julian, Rocky and I are baffled. Her ears will stick out more than ever now.

Went back to work today. Brown is away with the flu. I hope he is ill for a long time, develops complications etc. The police haven't been to the office to question me about the stamps so perhaps Brown has decided against prosecution. I have sent him a 'Get Well' card. The queue in the post office was snaking out of the door, so I went back to the office and took a stamp from his box, put it on his card and ran to the post box to catch the four o' clock post.

Tuesday   December 19th

Bought a suit with some difficulty. The salesman said I had 'unusually short legs'. I hadn't signed the back of my Access card, so there was a ridiculous fuss at the cash till. The manager was called. The shop was full of women buying boxer shorts, but they all stopped to watch my humiliation. After I had given my grandmother's date of birth and my mother's maiden name, the manager agreed with me that I was indeed Adrian Albert Mole, born in Leicester, and he deigned to allow me to purchase a navy-blue suit, blue shirt and red silk tie. He said, 'We have to be careful, sir.'

I said that *I* would be careful not to come into his shop again. But I said it quietly, to myself. He could easily have snatched my goods back. He looked the type.

Pandora is wearing a woolly hat with a bobble. Her ears, as I feared, look like halves of pancakes stuck to the side of her head. She refuses to give a reason for her mad action. Apart from saying, 'It's something I *had* to do.'

Wednesday   December 20th

My scalp is very itchy. Scratched all night.

Mr Patel our newsagent came round with his bill early this morning. He said he wouldn't leave until it was paid. To my horror I found it to be one hundred and forty-three pounds, nine pence! It is Julian's responsibility to pay the bill every week; he has obviously been derelict in his duty. I made Mr Patel a cup of tea and sat him in the kitchen, then I knocked on Julian's door, entered and asked him where the paper money had gone.

'Spent, dear boy, spent. On a pair of Gucci loafers. I couldn't resist them. Sorry.'

I asked Mr Patel if he would accept the Gucci loafers in lieu of payment, but he looked at me as though I was an idiot and said, 'I got enough shoes, it's money I need.'

Julian appeared in his Noël Coward dressing-gown and said, 'These are not *shoes*, Mr Patel, they are works of art. With these on your feet, you will be the king of Oxford's newsagents. You will probably end up as the Chairman of the Newsagents' Federation or something.'

Mr Patel said, 'One hundred and forty-three pounds, please. I will forget the nine pence.'

'No can do, old darling,' said Julian with a smile. 'All my spondulicks are gone, I haven't a bean, I'm flat broke. In Cary Street.'

The toilet flushed and Rocky appeared, his left trouser pocket was bulging. Was this evidence of early morning sexual excitement or did the bulge mean money? I explained the situation to Rocky in words of one syllable. Rocky said, 'So Julian's a fief, what's had our money and spent it on some Guccis? That ain't on, Jule,' chided the Neanderthal, 'I ought to give you some serious grief.'

Julian fled into the bathroom as Rocky approached him. Then Mr Patel cowered in the corner under the hanging spider plant as Rocky turned and approached *him*. 'Woss the damage, Mr Patel?' he asked; and took out a large roll of banknotes.

Mr Patel left, but not before I had cancelled the majority of our magazines and papers: the *Spectator*, the *Economist*, the *Listener*, *Body Builder*, *The Stage*, *Punch*, *Vogue*, *Elle*, *Fast Car*, the *Guardian*, the *Sun*, the *Daily Mail*, *Interiors*. They have all gone. We are left with the *Independent*, the *Mirror*, the *London Review of Books*, *Viz* and *Private Eye*. Pandora agreed to read *Marxism Today*, *Interiors* and *Vogue* in W. H. Smith. Julian had the nerve to loaf about in the Gucci loafers today. He is entirely without shame.

Saturday   December 24th
MY MOTHER'S WEDDING DAY

The first shock was that my *father* had been invited to the Registry Office and the reception. The second shock was coming eye to eye with the dead fox hanging round my grandma's neck. Rocky drove us over from Oxford in his flash car. It is so big that, had we so wished, we could have played a game of badminton in the back. We parked outside the office on double yellow lines and went inside to wait. Grandma produced a handkerchief, spat on it, and used a corner to wipe a smut off my face. She said, 'You look a proper bobby dazzler in your suit.'

Everyone took a step back as Rocky (Big Boy) Livingstone stepped into the wedding room, only to step back yet again when Julian appeared, wagging his cigarette holder about. Pandora's parents were there with Bert Baxter. Mr and Mrs Singh were talking to Mr and Mrs O'Leary about the dustbin men's latest outrage and Martin Muffet's parents stood at the back of the room looking sad. He is their only child. My mother's parents were invited but didn't turn up. They were busy slaughtering turkeys in Norfolk.

The Registrar came into the room, a nice-looking bouncy woman in a purple leaf-printed dress. She indicated towards the doorway and my mother and Muffet appeared with Rosie behind them (she looking like a petulant Lolita). I saw several faces crumple: my father's, Mr Muffet's and Mrs Muffet's.

Muffet was dressed in an appalling suit (salmon-pink), a white shirt and a red polka dot tie. Given his height (tall), and weight (thin), he looked like a stick of Skegness rock. My mother looked *old*, quite frankly, diary. She had done her best with make-up and clothes; cream suit, black accessories, floppy hat etc, but nothing could disguise the ravages of time. She looked like Martin Muffet's *mother*.

I stepped forward and joined the wedding party. I was conscious that all eyes were on my back, so I tried not to scratch the back of my scalp (which had been driving me mad with irritation for some days). The Registrar droned on and before I knew it, it was time to sign the register and give my mother and stepfather my hypocritical good wishes. Mrs Muffet wept quietly at the back of the room. Bert Baxter said loudly, 'If I don't have a pee soon, I'll wet myself.' And Rosie, whom I had picked up in order to show her the register, screamed and said, 'Look, Mummy, Adrian has got *insects* in his hair.'

People moved away from us, except for my mother, who started to examine my hair, tuft by tuft. She said quietly, but venomously, 'Your bloody head is infested with nits! And some of them have got *wings*! Keep away from Rosie.' So, while the rest of the wedding guests were roistering in the Function Room at the British Legion, I was sitting in my grandmother's house having a foul-smelling lotion – Prioderm – applied to my hair. Grandma was wearing rubber gloves and a nasty expression on her face.

I am not in any of the photographs. Julian read my speech out and was rewarded with loud laughter and applause. (He failed to give me a credit.) There was a small fight in the gents between my father and Mr Muffet senior, but it was not personal; they were fighting over the last piece of shiny toilet paper. Rocky, Julian and Pandora picked me up from Grandma's. We drove back to Oxford in silence. The car was full of foul fumes from the lotion which has to be kept on for twenty-four hours. I have decided not to carry on with my diary. Why catalogue such misery? What purpose does it serve?

2.00am   Pandora has just confessed to me that the reason she shaved her hair off was because her scalp was infested with head lice. I will never, ever, forgive her for passing them on to me. Never, ever. My love for her has gone. Kaput.

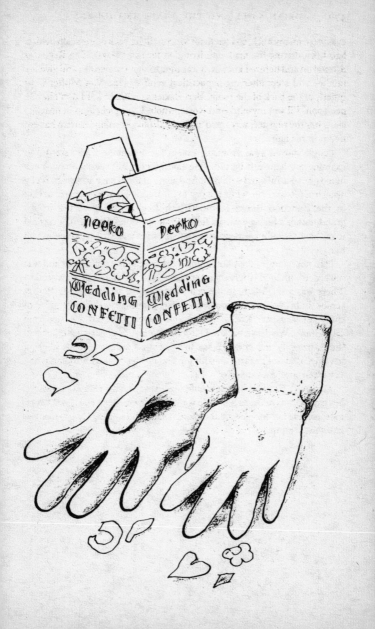

Monday   January 1st 1990

These are my New Year's Resolutions:

1. Finish *War and Peace*
2. Go to the dentist with aching molar
3. Take driving lessons
4. Change job
5. Make a diary entry every day

Tuesday   January 9th

Brown ordered me to take down the Christmas decorations in my cubicle today. He said he was 'sick of living under the dreadful spectre of Christmas'. Brown doesn't believe in Christmas. He spent Christmas Day classifying seaweed in Dungeness.

Friday   February 16th

My first driving lesson today. My instructor is a woman called Vanessa Partridge. She is no relation to my former best friend, Nigel Partridge, who is now in the army. I was expecting to spend my first lesson driving around a deserted airfield or something, but instead Ms Partridge ordered me onto the *roads*! Busy roads. I felt like an Iranian on a suicide mission. At least Iranians have their religion to comfort them, but, being an atheist, I had nothing. As I came to my first roundabout I prayed to God to protect me from all the nasty cars and lorries.

Friday   April 6th

I am getting the hang of the gears now, but I have a horrible suspicion that I am probably one of life's pedestrians. Pandora passed her test first time last week. She drives Rocky's car as though she is taking part in a *Grand Prix* race.

The inmates are still on the roof of Strangeways prison. Mrs Thatcher is having to be restrained from climbing up there and beating their brains in.

Friday   April 13th

Vanessa has got absolutely gorgeous legs. When she operates the dual controls (which is quite often), I can't take my eyes off them. I asked her when I can put in for my test. She looked shifty and said, 'Not for a while yet.' Why not? I have had *seven* driving lessons at ten pounds a time. I have very limited financial resources. I am still paying for my suit. In fact Access are hounding me for this month's payment.

Friday   April 27th

Still can't manage the clutch, and I can't stop driving too near to the kerb. I nearly wiped out a pensioner's shopping trolley today. Vanessa has had streaks put into her hair – either that or she has gone grey more or less overnight.

Friday   May 4th

Brown was waiting for me when I got back from my driving lesson today (gears better but still can't bring myself to overtake anything. I was quite happy to follow that silage spreader, but Vanessa was, I thought, rather impatient.) Anyway, Brown said that two reams of Conqueror A4 paper had gone missing from the stationery cupboard since the last audit in 1989 (March). Did I know its whereabouts? I quipped, 'Perhaps it's gone on holiday, perhaps it's sick of being stationary.' Brown was not amused.

Friday   May 11th

Received the manuscript of *The Restless Tadpole* back from Craig Raine; after many letters and telephone calls, I might add. The manuscript was in a dreadful condition and was littered with Raine's notes in the margin. 'Laughably pretentious' and 'numbingly philistine' being two of the less offensive and non-obscene terms.

My novel, *Lo! the Flat Hills of My Homeland*, is currently in the office of the chief bloke at the National Theatre, David Aukin. I have suggested to him that it could easily be adapted for the stage. The Olivier would be ideal. There would be 144 in the cast and I would need a full orchestra, a lake, and a deer park, plus half-a-dozen live deer. But I don't see why it shouldn't be done – English theatre needs spectacle. I photocopied the script using A4 Conqueror. I hope Mr Aukin is impressed.

Thank God for the warmer weather. Vanessa has discarded her black woolly tights and taken to wearing sheer stockings. I could hardly control *myself* today, let alone the lousy stinking pigging car. These driving lessons are doing my head in.

Saturday   June 2nd

Lo! came back today. Mr Aukin's note was kind.

> Dear Mr Mole,
>   Thank you for sending me your manuscript, *Lo! the Flat Hills of My Homeland*. I read it with considerable interest. However, we are operating under difficult financial constrictions, and therefore it would be impossible for us to employ a cast of 144 actors, plus six live deer.
>   I do wish you good luck,
>   David Aukin
> P.S. There seems to be something wrong with your word processor. Does it object to printing out vowels?

I am restless today. Yesterday's collision with the tar spreading lorry has upset me more than I realised. I am suffering from delayed reaction. Phoned Vanessa, she was at the chiropractor's trying to get her neck back to its original angle.

Sunday   June 3rd

Perhaps I should put the vowels back in. The world of literature is obviously not ready for another James Joyce. Barry Kent has been asked to do 'With Great Pleasure' on Radio Four. I wept when I heard this. He has asked me to join him for the evening – in the audience.

Friday   June 15th

I can now steer in a straight line. Vanessa is still wearing the surgical collar. She hates it but I quite like to see a woman with a bit of white next to her face.

Friday   June 29th

Pandora is now entitled to call herself Dr Pandora Braithwaite. And she will, dear diary, she will.

Did a three-point turn. It took fifteen goes. I asked Vanessa if she thought I was near to taking my test. She said, 'How near is Jupiter to Earth?' I had no idea she was interested in astronomy.

Sunday   July 1st

Dr Pandora Braithwaite and Rocky (Big Boy) Livingstone have gone to Barbados to meet Rocky's parents. Rocky's dad is a bank manager, and his mother is an expert on marine life. Rocky is the only one out of four children *not* to go to university. He is also the only millionaire. Rocky opened his fifth gym yesterday, in Grantham. Somebody from *Coronation Street* performed the opening ceremony. The one who serves in the shop. Not the grocery shop, the other one. I can't remember her name, anyway a thousand middle-aged women blocked Grantham's traffic trying to catch a glimpse of – Mavis? Doreen? Bet? It will come to me.

Friday   July 13th

Dual carriageway. Got up to forty-five mph!

Thursday   July 19th
OXFORD PLAYHOUSE, 7.30 PM TONIGHT

Barry Kent rambled his way through the BBC recording of 'With Great Pleasure' tonight. He had a famous actor and actress to read his favourite works of prose and poems. The actor used to be the big one in that television series to do with a Dutch policeman. The actress was the one who was always crying in the one about Victorian servants. To finish, Kent bellowed his own poem, 'Earwig'.

> EARWIG
> How to measure earwig poo?
> How to find how much they do?
> Are there scales to measure it?
> Those tiny piles of earwig shit?

The BBC have agreed to transmit the word 'shit' providing they can bleep out the more obscene words used throughout the programme. I fear this points to a lowering of standards. Kent will be on 'Desert Island Discs' next!

Friday   July 20th

Did a three-point turn in five goes. I am absolutely thrilled with myself. I have started looking at second-hand cars with a view to purchasing one. Got a postcard from my mother and Muffet today, they are in Spain.

> Dear Adrian,
>   Sun, Sand, Sex and Sangria!
> Salutations!
>   Mum and Martin

Saturday   July 21st

Went to visit my father today, he has received an identically worded postcard from his ex-wife and Muffet. He is furious because my mother has dumped Rosie on him. Rosie is even more furious because she was not invited to go to España. My father has made no attempt to amuse Rosie, apart from buying her a packet of felt-tip pens, and a dot-to-dot book. She was going 'stir crazy' so I took her to see *Bambi*. She broke down and wept in such a heartbreaking manner that an usherette shone her torch on her heaving shoulders and ordered her to be quiet. I snapped, 'My sister is a sensitive, sweet little girl, how dare you try to repress her emotions!'

I lectured the usherette on the dangers of internalising others' feelings, how it can lead to constipation, ulcers and mental illness. The usherette said, 'Yer a bleedin' loony yerself, if you ask me. An' if you don't shut yer big yap you'll find yerself in the manager's office.'

Sunday   July 22nd

Rosie clung onto my legs today and begged me to take her back to Oxford with me. My father made no attempt to restrain her outburst. He carried on watching *Songs of Praise* out of the corner of his eye. He enjoys mocking the congregation. From today onwards I am going to make a daily diary entry.

Drought conditions prevail. England looks like the parched part of Tunisia.

Thursday   August 2nd

Iraq has invaded Kuwait. I'm not sure why. Something to do with oil.

Friday   August 17th

Practised doing a hill start. Rolled down the hill as often as the Duke of York's men in the song. Vanessa has developed several nervous manner-isms, she is obviously a deeply neurotic woman. Why do *I* always get them?

Friday August 31st

I am coming to the (reluctant) conclusion that Vanessa is an incompe-tent driving instructor. I am making very little progress. I may defect and go to the British School of Motoring. I will miss her, but the facts must be faced. She is no good at her job. I'm still nowhere near to taking my test.

Saturday   September 1st

Julian has got a job as a researcher at the BBC. He is working on documentary called 'Living with Failure'. He has asked me if the producer can have a quick chat with me. Don't ask me why.

Sunday   September 2nd

Wrote to Vanessa this morning, telling her that I have decided to be a pedestrian. This is a lie but I don't want to hurt her feelings. It must be terrible to be such a failure.

Friday   September 7th

First lesson with 'Quick Pass' Driving School. My instructor is called Dave Crooks. My God! Talk about impatient! Talk about irritable! Talk about lack of self-control! He shouted at me constantly, and never took his foot off the dual controls. When I kangaroo'd to a halt outside the D.O.E. he wiped his brow and said, 'Who taught you to drive like that?' I told him and he said, 'I don't understand it. Vanessa Partridge is a brilliant instructor. Her pupils have an incredible first-time pass rate.'

Friday   September 21st

Dave Crooks and I have parted company. He said, 'I'm sorry, Adrian, but I am leaving Quick Pass: it's too dangerous. I am going to teach free-fall parachuting instead.'

Why is it that nobody has got *backbone* in England any more?

Friday   September 28th

First lesson with 'Sure Pass' Driving School. Instructor an old git called Harold Wainwright. Lesson stopped half way through. Wainwright drove off, leaving me stranded in an outer suburb. What *is* it about driving instructors? Are mad people attracted to the profession or are they sent mad by incompetent pupils? I rang 'Sure Pass' to report their employee's unprofessional behaviour, but Harold Wainwright answered the phone. It is his firm.

Friday   October 5th

'Drivepass', first lesson. 12.00am to 1.00pm. Instructor's name, Dave Singh.

Friday   October 12th

'Drivesure', instructor Mr Chan.

Friday   October 19th

'Upass', instructor Mr Abdul bin Salman.

Mr Salman has advised me against buying a second-hand car. He said, 'It would be somewhat premature, Mr Mole.'

Saturday   October 20th

Rocky has gone off with another woman! Pandora is devastated. I pointed out to her that Rocky is a red-blooded man who needs to feel that he is desirable and sexually lusted over. 'In short,' I said, 'Rocky wants sex, you won't give him any, so, not unnaturally, he has gone elsewhere; namely to Carly Pick, the receptionist at Rocky's new gym in Market Harborough.'

Pandora rang for a taxi; there was murder in her eyes. When asked for the destination she snarled, 'Market Harborough, and make it snappy, I am a doctor and this is an emergency.' She didn't tell the taxi firm she is only a doctor of philosophy.

Sunday   October 21st

My plans for a quiet time at home putting the vowels back into *Lo! the Flat Hills of My Homeland* were thrown into disarray when Carly Pick turned up at the flat with Rocky, who had come round to pick up his thongs. Pandora came out of her room looking like a harridan. She threw curses at everyone in the room (including me, unfairly I thought). Then she threw the thongs in Rocky's face and told Carly Pick that she had a face like a warthog's armpit. And that she was welcome to Rocky (Big Boy) Livingstone because he farted in bed.

Hey Ho, Hey Nonny No. Such is life. Or is it Heigh Ho? Hay Ho?

Monday   November 5th

Remembering last year's incident with the catherine wheel (I still have the scar), I decided to stay in and work on the last chapter of *Lo!* Pandora is out at a bonfire party given by Professor Cavendish, the notorious drunkard and womaniser. How he does it I don't know. (I saw him in the off-licence, he looked at least forty-five). He is scruffy and has got a battered-up face. His third wife has just left him. She has written a full account of her reasons for doing so. It appeared in the *News of the World* last Sunday under the headline CLEVER CLOGS PROF SEVEN TIMES A NIGHT 'TOO MUCH FOR ME' – WIFE.

Seven times a night! I've just reckoned it up. I've only done it five times in two years. From now on I am going to make a daily record of my doings in my diary.

Some people are predicting that Mrs Thatcher will resign. As if!

Monday   November 12th

A letter from my mother:

> Aidy,
>   Saw Sharon Bott and son today. He, Glenn, looks exactly, but exactly like you: lips, nose, ears, mad hairline – everything.
>   I know this is awkward but am I a grandmother or aren't I? I think I should be told. Are you keeping something from me? Martin sends his best and asks when you are coming to see us? Why aren't you on the phone like normal people?

Grandma is using a walking frame to get to the shops now
. . . Do you miss Mrs Thatcher? I wish John Major would do
something about his hair. It would look lovely brushed back.
Grandma has found three World War II gasmasks in the shed . . .

The rest was drivel apart from a bit at the end about the dog missing me.
Which is a lie. On my past visits the dog has completely ignored me. Two
can play at that game, dog!

From now on I will make a daily entry in my diary.

Monday   December 24th

I have just bumped into Sharon Bott in Woolworths in Leicester, where I
was purchasing Christmas presents. She had a strange-looking moon-
headed toddler with her. 'Say hello to Adrian, Glenn,' she said. I bent
over the buggy and the kid gave me a slobbery smile. Is Glenn the fruit of
my loins? Did *my* seed give him life? I must know. The kid was sucking the
head of a Ninja Turtle. He looked fed up.

Monday   December 31st

The Prime Minister, Mr John Major, is trying to negotiate with the bloke
in charge of Iraq. Some alarmists are predicting war. How absolutely
ridiculous! We live in modern times. War belongs to the Middle Ages.
There is no need to go to war. Not now we've got fax machines. Must go
now, Professor Cavendish has just come out of Pandora's bedroom. He
has promised to read *Lo!* and *Tadpole*.

Tuesday   January 1st 1991
THESE ARE MY NEW YEAR'S RESOLUTIONS

1. I will become a published writer
2. I will win the Booker Prize
3. I will marry Pandora
4. I will change my socks every day
5. I will resign from the D.O.E.
6. I will stop emptying tea leaves down the sink
7. I will work for world peace
8. I will return the videos on time
9. I will pass my driving test

10. I will change to skimmed milk
11. I will grow a beard
12. I will untie my shoelaces before removing my shoes
13. I will try to be more tolerant towards the thick and
    disadvantaged in our society, especially my parents
14. I will decide whether there is a God or not

Also available from Mandarin Paperbacks

DAVID NOBBS

Fair Do's

Since his disastrous elopement with the ravishing Liz
Rodenhirst in *A Bit of a Do*, what hope has Ted Simcock
with his new waitress friend, Sandra?

Can his ex-wife Rita find fulfilment with her Social
Liberal Democratic candidate?

And can the marriage between Liz and the immaculate
Neville Badger possibly succeed?

David Nobbs provides the answers to these and many
other questions as Rita, Ted and Liz pick their way
through social minefields of more sublimely ridiculous
'do's', including a fancy dress party, the opening of a
vegetarian restaurant and a funeral.

DAVID NOBBS

Second from Last in the Sack Race

'David Nobbs has created a most lovable character and sustained, as Henry grows up battling with religion, sex and his own conscience, a fine balance between tears and laughter.' Nina Bawden, *Daily Telegraph*

'One of the most noisily funny books I have ever read. It caused me to totally lose control of myself on a plane full of Swedish businessmen.' Michael Palin

'So entertaining I lost count of the number of times I laughed out loud.' *Lancashire Evening Post*

'Both funny and touching.' *Daily Express*

'Touching, risqué and extremely funny.' *The Lady*

'A wonderfully funny novel.'
Susan Hill, *Good Housekeeping*

A Selected List of Humour Available from Mandarin

While every effort is made to keep prices low, it is sometimes necessary to increase prices at short notice. Mandarin Paperbacks reserves the right to show new retail prices on covers which may differ from those previously advertised in the text or elsewhere.

The prices shown below were correct at the time of going to press.

☐	7493 0159 7	**The Complete Fawlty Towers**	John Cleese & Connie Booth	£5.99
☐	7493 1436 2	**Class**	Jilly Cooper	£4.99
☐	7493 0849 4	**Angels Rush In**	Jilly Cooper	£5.99
☐	7493 0178 3	**The Common Years**	Jilly Cooper	£4.99
☐	7493 0252 6	**Turn Right at the Spotted Dog**	Jilly Cooper	£3.99
☐	7493 1116 9	**How to Survive Christmas**	Jilly Cooper	£4.99
☐	7493 1164 9	**Women and Superwomen**	Jilly Cooper	£3.99
☐	7493 1163 0	**Men and Supermen**	Jilly Cooper	£3.99
☐	7493 1165 7	**Mongrel Magic**	Jilly Cooper	£8.99
☐	7493 1355 2	**When Did You Last See Your Father?**	Jeremy Hardy	£5.99
☐	7493 1147 9	**Can I Come Down Now Dad?**	John Hegley	£3.99
☐	7493 3606 4	**Second from Last in the Sack Race**	David Nobbs	£4.99
☐	7493 0020 5	**Pratt of the Argus**	David Nobbs	£4.99
☐	7493 1015 4	**A Bit of a Do**	David Nobbs	£4.99
☐	7493 0138 4	**The Secret Diary of Adrian Mole Aged 13¾**	Sue Townsend	£3.99
☐	7493 0222 4	**The Growing Pains of Adrian Mole**	Sue Townsend	£3.99
☐	7493 0229 1	**True Confessions of Adrian Albert Mole**	Sue Townsend	£3.99
☐	7493 1120 7	**Adrian Mole from Minor to Major**	Sue Townsend	£4.99
☐	7493 1503 2	**Barmy**	Victoria Wood	£5.99
☐	7493 1314 5	**Up to You, Porky**	Victoria Wood	£5.99
☐	7493 0819 2	**Lucky Bag: The Victoria Wood Songbook**	Victoria Wood	£7.99

All these books are available at your bookshop or newsagent, or can be ordered direct from the address below. Just tick the titles you want and fill in the form below.

Cash Sales Department, PO Box 5, Rushden, Northants NN10 6YX.
Fax: 0933 410321 : Phone 0933 410511.

Please send cheque, payable to 'Reed Book Services Ltd.', or postal order for purchase price quoted and allow the following for postage and packing:

£1.00 for the first book, 50p for the second; **FREE POSTAGE AND PACKING FOR THREE BOOKS OR MORE PER ORDER.**

NAME (Block letters) ....

ADDRESS ....

....

☐ I enclose my remittance for ....

☐ I wish to pay by Access/Visa Card Number

Expiry Date

Signature ....

Please quote our reference: MAND